# THE BEST TIME TRAVEL STORIES OF THE 20TH CENTURY

# THE BEST

# TIME TRAVEL

# STORIES OF THE
# 20TH CENTURY

EDITED BY HARRY TURTLEDOVE
WITH MARTIN H. GREENBERG

BALLANTINE BOOKS · NEW YORK

A Del Rey® Book
Published by The Random House Publishing Group

Introduction copyright © 2005 by Harry Turtledove
Compilation copyright © 2005 by Harry Turtledove and Martin H. Greenberg

Published in the United States by Del Rey Books, an imprint of The Random House
Publishing Group, a division of Random House, Inc., New York, and simultaneously
in Canada by Random House of Canada Limited, Toronto.

Del Rey is a registered trademark and the Del Rey colophon is a trademark of Random
House, Inc.

Owing to limitations of space, permission acknowledgments can be found on pages
427–428, which constitute an extension of this copyright page.

www.delreybooks.com

The best time travel stories of the 20th century / edited by Harry Turtledove with
    Martin H. Greenberg.— 1st ed.
        p.   cm.
    ISBN 978-0-345-46094-3 (pbk.)
    1. Time travel—Fiction.   2. Science fiction, American.   3. Science fiction,
English.   4. Fantasy fiction, American.   5. Fantasy fiction, English.   I.
Turtledove, Harry.   II. Greenberg, Martin Harry.

PS648.T55B47 2005
813'.087620834—dc22

First Edition: January 2005

147028622

# CONTENTS

# INTRODUCTION

## HARRY TURTLEDOVE

WE'RE ALL TIME TRAVELERS, whether we know it or not. We go into the future at a steady rate of one second per second, and we leave the past behind. New things come along. Old things are forgotten. My own lifetime—neither especially long nor especially short these days—has seen the rise of antibiotics, AIDS, space travel, television, CDs, videotape, DVDs, Richard Nixon (twice), civil rights, women's rights, gay rights, cell phones, the computer, and the Internet. It's seen the fall of Communism, segregation, records, smallpox (we hope!), polio, Richard Nixon (twice), the Twin Towers, and the idea that smoking is cool. It's seen hula hoops, stuffing phone booths and Volkswagen Bugs, and streaking. Some things, of course, remain constant. The Chicago Cubs haven't been in a World Series since before I was born. They haven't won one since Teddy Roosevelt was president.

Toward the end of his long life, L. Sprague de Camp would give a presentation at science-fiction conventions called "Memoirs of a Time Traveler." Sprague, who was born in 1907, had seen much more come and go than I have (he was even around the last time the Cubs won a Series). Making other people see how much that he took for granted as a child and a young man had changed since was thought-provoking, to say the least.

But what if we weren't limited to that steady one second per second progression? What if we could go against the normal flow of time from past to future instead of being trapped in it? H. G. Wells, who was—among many other things—the first great science-fiction writer to use English, published *The Time Machine* in 1895. He gave us the name for the device and the bones of one kind of time-travel story: go to the future, take a look at what's there, and come back and tell the present about it. Other writers have been exploring and expanding the concept ever since.

Traveling into the future is relatively safe. Traveling into the past starts generating paradoxes. What if you killed your own grandfather? Or, less bloodily, what if your journey into the past changed things so that your mother married somebody else? Would you disappear? (Yes, that's the one the *Back to the Future* movies look at, but you can also do it without a DeLorean.) What if you changed some important past event? Would you change its future—your own present? That particular line of time-travel stories forms one part of the spectrum of alternate history tales, some of which Del Rey recently collected in *The Best Alternate History Stories of the 20th Century*.

Dealing with the paradoxes—or not dealing with them—challenged the ingenuity of writers throughout the last century. Writing as Anson MacDonald, Robert A. Heinlein wrapped up all the problems of one man's existence in "By His Bootstraps." Close to twenty years later, Heinlein took another shot at it in "All You Zombies," which tightens his protagonist's gene pool—and the inherent paradoxes—even more. His novel *The Door into Summer* also looks at time travel in a situation where the traveler has an exactly even chance of going into the past or the future.

Isaac Asimov is better known for his Foundation stories and his tales of the Three Laws of Robotics, but he also wrote a thought-provoking novel of time travel both into the past and across varying realities in *The End of Eternity*—which, in a way, serves as the underpinning for all the other tales.

L. Sprague de Camp's *Lest Darkness Fall* is a time-travel novel not in the school of *The Time Machine*, but rather of Mark Twain's *A Connecticut Yankee in King Arthur's Court*: one that drops a modern man with all his modern knowledge into a medieval setting and challenges him to make the best of it. Unlike Twain's protagonist, de Camp's Martin Padway really is in sixth-century Rome, and establishes an alternate history by his success. De Camp's "A Gun for Dinosaur" and the other tales of Reggie Rivers collected in *Rivers of Time* exploit one of the time-travel story's favorite themes: using a time machine to go back into the past to look at and even to hunt animals extinct by the time humanity evolved. In *Genus Homo*, de Camp and P. Schuyler Miller used suspended animation as a time-travel device by which modern men could visit the future.

Poul Anderson's "The Man Who Came Early" is another variant on the theme of a modern man trying to make the best of things in the past. Unlike the Twain and de Camp stories to which it is related, though, it is marked by Anderson's strong sense of the tragic. Anderson, always a writer with a strong sense of history, used time travel in his novels *The Corridors of Time* (a sort of science-fiction companion to the fantasy *Three Hearts and Three Lions*) and *The Dancer from Atlantis.*

Perhaps the bawdiest time-travel novel ever written is Robert Silverberg's *Up the Line*. Silverberg notes that, as time travel becomes feasible for a longer and longer period, more and more travelers from the future will crowd back in time to visit such events as the Crucifixion, the opening of Hagia Sophia, or the Black Plague. Why, then, don't these historical events grow ever more crowded with observers from their futures? His answer is that they do, though just what the locals do about this is not always quite so clear.

One time-travel theme that has perhaps never quite been successfully brought off is a reversal of the time stream, so that it begins to flow from future to past rather than the other way around. Fritz Leiber's "The Man Who Never Grew Young" perhaps comes closest; several others have tried at novel length, also with results less than they might have hoped. The challenge there remains for writers yet to come.

Time travel as a vast, secret government project intended not just for exploration but also to change the past for the benefit of the government doing the sponsoring is a common theme of these stories, and has perhaps grown more common as governments have grown larger and less easily controlled by the people they rule. One of the best of these tales is Jack Finney's *Time and Again*, which seems only to have grown more relevant in the generation and a half since it appeared. It is beautifully written, beautifully researched, beautifully illustrated, and very well thought through. Its sequel, *From Time to Time*, unfortunately does not quite measure up to the high standard it set.

Another novel with a related theme, though much grittier and more cynical, is Joe Haldeman's *All My Sins Remembered*. Because of his indoctrination and training, the protagonist has a great many sins indeed to remember. The book, which dates from near the time of the Watergate scandal, is a devastating indictment of those who do things allegedly for other people's good.

Another theme often used in time-travel tales is that of the time traveler from the future who comes back to the present for his or her own nefarious purposes and has to be thwarted by moderns with technological resources small compared to those of the villain. A good recent example is S. M. Stirling's *Drakon*, which springs from his series of Draka alternate-history novels. His heroine finds herself in the late twentieth century of our timeline because of an experiment gone awry, and proceeds to do her best to remake it to her—nasty—heart's desire. If the poor hapless moderns didn't also have assistance from the future, things would turn out even worse. And, as there is room for a sequel to the novel, they may yet.

Clifford D. Simak's *The Goblin Reservation* takes time travel out of the sphere of big politics and puts it in a far less consequential arena: that of academia. He has a great deal of gentle fun with the theme. Simak's cast of characters includes a moonshining Neanderthal brought up to his future present and rechristened Alley Oop; a saber-toothed tiger; as well as elves, dwarves, a banshee, and the ghost of a prominent seventeenth-century English playwright—the only problem being, the ghost isn't sure whose ghost he is at first, so when the authentic Will Shakespeare (who turns out, in this book, *not* to be the playwright in question) is brought forward, alarming, and very funny, consequences ensue.

Simak's book is unquestionably science fiction, despite the trappings of both fantasy and popular culture that hang on its coattails. Larry Niven takes a different course in his series of time-travel stories collected in *The Flight of the Horse*. To Niven, a hard-headed rationalist, time travel is impossible. This does not keep him from writing time-travel stories, but does turn the stories he writes about it from science fiction to fantasy. His time traveler, a certain (often, much too certain for his own good) Svetz, is a bit of a bungler, and never realizes that when he travels back into the past, he's not exactly traveling back into the past with which his world is familiar. Problems with a roc, a leviathan, and too many werewolves immediately spring to mind.

Time travel through magic or other fantasy device is less commonly written of than time travel through time machine or other science-fictional device. Just why this should be so is puzzling, as time travel by either means seems equally impossible and equally implausible, but it does appear to be so.

One time-travel novel that leans more toward fantasy than sf is

*Household Gods,* by Judith Tarr and Harry Turtledove, from an idea that the late Fletcher Pratt had but did not write up before his death. Despite the fantasy trappings, the novel springs from the school of *A Connecticut Yankee* and *Lest Darkness Fall.* It drops a modern American woman dissatisfied with her life and with bumping her head against the glass ceiling into an ancestor's body in a town on the Danube frontier of the Roman Empire in the late second century A.D., just in time for a series of Germanic invasions and devastating plagues. Nicole Gunther-Perrin has the chance to see whether the glass at the end of the twentieth century is half full or half empty.

Roger Zelazny's *Roadmarks* straddles the line between fantasy and science fiction. Its protagonist is traveling down the Road of Time with a pickup truck full of automatic weapons to help the Greeks beat the Persians at Marathon. The Road, and the various characters, nasty and less so, he meets along the way are shown with Zelazny's characteristic wit and splendid writing. The Road is a concept a little reminiscent of that in Anderson's *The Corridors of Time,* but far more mutable.

These are some of the more interesting time-travel novels the field has produced over the years—not a complete list, certainly (you will want to get on to the stories themselves, after all!), but a few of the highlights. The short fiction collected here looks at similar ideas and some wildly different ones. The pieces speak for themselves; anything I say about them, I fear, would only get in the way. The only thing I can be fairly sure of is that you'll like most of them. Enjoy!

# THEODORE STURGEON

*Theodore Sturgeon's (1918–1985) fiction abounds with ordinary charac-*
*ters undone by their all-too-human shortcomings or struggling in unsym-*
*pathetic environments to find others who share their desires and feelings of*
*loneliness. Sturgeon began publishing science fiction in 1939, and made*
*his mark early in both fantasy and science fiction with stories that have*
*since become classics. "Microcosmic God" concerns a scientist who plays*
*God with unexpectedly amusing results when he repeatedly challenges a*
*microscopic race he has created with threats to their survival. "It" focuses*
*on the reactions of characters in a rural setting trying to contend with a*
*rampaging inhuman monster. "Killdozer" is a variation on the theme of*
*Frankenstein in which a construction crew is trapped on an island where*
*a bulldozer has become imbued with the electrical energy of an alien life*
*form.*

*Fiction Sturgeon wrote after World War II showed the gentle humor of*
*his earlier work shading into pathos. "Memorial" and "Thunder and*
*Roses" were cautionary tales about the abuses of use of nuclear weapons.*
*"A Saucer of Loneliness" and "Maturity" both used traditional science-*
*fiction scenarios to explore feelings of alienation and inadequacy. Stur-*
*geon's work at novel length is memorable for its portrayals of characters*
*who rise above the isolation their failure to fit into normal society imposes.*
*More Than Human tells of a group of psychologically dysfunctional in-*
*dividuals who pool their individual strengths to create a superhuman*
*gestalt consciousness. In* The Dreaming Jewels, *a young boy discovers*
*that his behavioral abnormalities are actually the symptoms of super-*
*human powers. Sturgeon is also renowned for his explorations of taboo*

*sexuality and restrictive moralities in such stories as* Some of Your Blood, "The World Well Lost," *and* "If All Men Were Brothers Would You Let One Marry Your Sister?" *His short fiction has been collected in* Without Sorcery, E Pluribus Unicorn, Caviar, *and* A Touch of Strange. *The compilations* The Ultimate Egoist, Thunder and Roses, A Saucer of Loneliness, The Perfect Host, Baby Is Three, The Microcosmic God, *and* Killdozer, *edited by Paul Williams, are the first seven volumes in a series that will eventually reprint all of Sturgeon's short fiction.*

*Traveling into the past only to discover that the past isn't there any more is a popular conceit of the genre. "Yesterday Was Monday," one of his most-often reprinted tales, is one of the early time-travel stories that were published after the pulp era, where the emphasis wasn't on science yet so much as strangeness, evoking a surreal feeling that this story embodies perfectly. Making the protagonist of the story an everyday person waking up in his own past instead of a scientist or an inventor only adds to the unusual blend of time travel and fantasy.*

# YESTERDAY WAS MONDAY

## THEODORE STURGEON

HARRY WRIGHT ROLLED over and said something spelled "Bzzzzhha-a-aw!" He chewed a bit on a mouthful of dry air and spat it out, opened one eye to see if it really would open, opened the other and closed the first, closed the second, swung his feet onto the floor, opened them again and stretched. This was a daily occurrence, and the only thing that made it remarkable at all was that he did it on a Wednesday morning, and—

Yesterday was Monday.

Oh, he knew it was Wednesday all right. It was partly that, even though he knew yesterday was Monday, there was a gap between Monday and now; and that must have been Tuesday. When you fall asleep and lie there all night without dreaming, you know, when you wake up, that time has passed. You've done nothing that you can remember; you've had no particular thoughts, no way to gauge time, and yet you know that some hours have passed. So it was with Harry Wright. Tuesday had gone wherever your eight hours went last night.

But he hadn't slept through Tuesday. Oh no. He never slept, as a matter of fact, more than six hours at a stretch, and there was no particular reason for him doing so now. Monday was the day before yesterday; he had turned in and slept his usual stretch, he had awakened, and it was Wednesday.

It *felt* like Wednesday. There was a Wednesdayish feel to the air.

Harry put on his socks and stood up. He wasn't fooled. He knew what day it was. "What happened to yesterday?" he muttered. "Oh—yesterday was Monday." That sufficed until he got his pajamas off. "Monday," he mused, reaching for his underwear, "was quite a while back, seems as though." If he had been the worrying type, he would have started then and there. But he wasn't. He was an easygoing sort, the kind of man that gets himself into a rut and stays there until he is pushed out. That was why he was an automobile mechanic at twenty-three dollars a week; that's why he had been one for eight years now, and would be from now on, if he could only find Tuesday and get back to work.

Guided by his reflexes, as usual, and with no mental effort at all, which was also usual, he finished washing, dressing, and making his bed. His alarm clock, which never alarmed because he was of such regular habits, said, as usual, six twenty-two when he paused on the way out, and gave his room the once-over. And there was a certain something about the place that made even this phlegmatic character stop and think.

It wasn't finished.

The bed was there, and the picture of Joe Louis. There were the two chairs sharing their usual seven legs, the split table, the pipe-organ bedstead, the beige wallpaper with the two swans over and over and over, the tiny corner sink, the tilted bureau. But none of them were finished. Not that there were any holes in anything. What paint there had been in the first place was still there. But there was an odor of old cut lumber, a subtle, insistent air of building, about the room and everything in it. It was indefinable, inescapable, and Harry Wright stood there caught up in it, wondering. He glanced suspiciously around but saw nothing he could really be suspicious of. He shook his head, locked the door and went out into the hall.

On the steps a little fellow, just over three feet tall, was gently stroking the third step from the top with a razor-sharp chisel, shaping up a new scar in the dirty wood. He looked up as Harry approached, and stood up quickly.

"Hi," said Harry, taking in the man's leather coat, his peaked cap, his wizened, bright-eyed little face. "Whatcha doing?"

"Touch-up," piped the little man. "The actor in the third floor front has a nail in his right heel. He came in late Tuesday night and cut the wood here. I have to get it ready for Wednesday."

"This is Wednesday," Harry pointed out.

"Of course. Always has been. Always will be."

Harry let that pass, started on down the stairs. He had achieved his amazing bovinity by making a practice of ignoring things he could not understand. But one thing bothered him—

"Did you say that feller in the third floor front was an actor?"

"Yes. They're all actors, you know."

"You're nuts, friend," said Harry bluntly. "That guy works on the docks."

"Oh yes—that's his part. That's what he acts."

"No kiddin'. An' what does he do when he isn't acting?"

"But he—Well, that's all he does do! That's all any of the actors do!"

"Gee— I thought he looked like a reg'lar guy, too," said Harry. "An actor? 'Magine!"

"Excuse me," said the little man, "but I've got to get back to work. We mustn't let anything get by us, you know. They'll be through Tuesday before long, and everything must be ready for them."

Harry thought: this guy's crazy nuts. He smiled uncertainly and went down to the landing below. When he looked back the man was cutting skillfully into the stair, making a neat little nail scratch. Harry shook his head. This was a screwy morning. He'd be glad to get back to the shop. There was a '39 sedan down there with a busted rear spring. Once he got his mind on that he could forget this nonsense. That's all that matters to a man in a rut. Work, eat, sleep, pay day. Why even try to think anything else out?

The street was a riot of activity, but then it always was. But not quite this way. There were automobiles and trucks and buses around, aplenty, but none of them were moving. And none of them were quite complete. This was Harry's own field; if there was anything he didn't know about motor vehicles, it wasn't very important. And through that medium he began to get the general idea of what was going on.

Swarms of little men who might have been twins of the one he had spoken to were crowding around the cars, the sidewalks, the stores and buildings. All were working like mad with every tool imaginable. Some were touching up the finish of the cars with fine wire brushes, laying on networks of microscopic cracks and scratches. Some, with ball peens and mallets, were denting fenders skillfully, bending bumpers in an artful crash pattern, spider-webbing safety-glass windshields. Others were aging top dressing with high-pressure, needlepoint sandblasters. Still others were pumping dust into upholstery, sandpapering the dashboard finish around light switches, throttles, chokes, to give a finger-worn appearance. Harry stood aside as a half dozen of the workers scampered down the street bearing a fender which they riveted to a 1930 coupé. It was freshly bloodstained.

Once awakened to this highly unusual activity, Harry stopped, slightly open-mouthed, to watch what else was going on. He saw the same process being industriously accomplished with the houses and stores. Dirt was being laid on plate-glass windows over a coat of clear sizing. Woodwork was being cleverly scored and the paint peeled to make it look correctly weather-beaten, and dozens of leather-clad laborers were on their hands and knees, poking dust and dirt into the cracks between the paving blocks. A line of them went down the sidewalk, busily chewing gum and spitting it out; they were followed by another crew who carefully placed the wads according to diagrams they carried, and stamped them flat.

Harry set his teeth and muscled his rocking brain into something like its normal position. "I ain't never seen a day like this or crazy people like this," he said, "but I ain't gonna let it be any of my affair. I got my job to go to." And trying vainly to ignore the hundreds of little, hard-working figures, he went grimly on down the street.

When he got to the garage he found no one there but more swarms of stereotyped little people climbing over the place, dulling the paint work, cracking the cement flooring, doing their hurried, efficient little tasks of aging. He noticed, only because he was so familiar with the garage, that they were actually *making* the marks that had been there as long as he had known the place. "Hell with it," he gritted, anxious to submerge himself into his own world of wrenches and grease guns. "I got my job; this is none o' my affair."

He looked about him, wondering if he should clean these interlopers out of the garage. Naw—not his affair, He was hired to repair cars, not to police the joint. Long as they kept away from him—and, of course, animal caution told him that he was far, far outnumbered. The absence of the boss and the other mechanics was no surprise to Harry; he always opened the place.

He climbed out of his street clothes and into coveralls, picked up a tool case and walked over to the sedan, which he had left up on the hydraulic rack yester—that is, Monday night. And that is when Harry Wright lost his temper. After all, the car was his job, and he didn't like having anyone else mess with a job he had started. So when he saw his job—his '39 sedan—resting steadily on its wheels over the rack, which was down under the floor, and when he saw that the rear spring was repaired, he began to burn. He dived under the car and ran deft fingers over the rear wheel suspensions. In spite of his anger at this unprecedented occurrence, he had to admit to himself that the job had been done well. "Might have done it myself," he muttered.

A soft clank and a gentle movement caught his attention. With a roar he reached out and grabbed the leg of one of the ubiquitous little men, wriggled out from under the car, caught his culprit by his leather collar, and dangled him at arm's length.

"What are you doing to my job?" Harry bellowed.

The little man tucked his chin into the front of his shirt to give his windpipe a chance, and said, "Why, I was just finishing up that spring job."

"Oh. So you were just finishing up on that spring job," Harry whispered, choked with rage. Then, at the top of his voice, "Who told you to touch that car?"

"Who told me? What do you— Well, it just had to be done, that's all. You'll have to let me go. I must tighten up those two bolts and lay some dust on the whole thing."

"You must *what*? You get within six feet o' that car and I'll twist your head offn your neck with a Stillson!"

"But— It has to be done!"

"You won't do it! Why, I oughta—"

"Please let me go! If I don't leave that car the way it was Tuesday night—"

"When was Tuesday night?"

"The last act, of course. Let me go, or I'll call the district supervisor!"

"Call the devil himself. I'm going to spread you on the sidewalk outside; and heaven help you if I catch you near here again!"

The little man's jaw set, his eyes narrowed, and he whipped his feet upward. They crashed into Wright's jaw; Harry dropped him and staggered back. The little man began squealing, "Supervisor! Supervisor! Emergency!"

Harry growled and started after him; but suddenly, in the air between him and the midget workman, a long white hand appeared. The empty air was swept back, showing an aperture from the garage to blank, blind nothingness. Out of it stepped a tall man in a single loose-fitting garment literally studded with pockets. The opening closed behind the man.

Harry cowered before him. Never in his life had he seen such noble, powerful features, such strength of purpose, such broad shoulders, such a deep chest. The man stood with the backs of his hands on his hips, staring at Harry as if he were something somebody forgot to sweep up.

"That's him," said the little man shrilly. "He is trying to stop me from doing the work!"

"Who are you?" asked the beautiful man, down his nose.

"I'm the m-mechanic on this j-j— Who wants to know?"

"Iridel, supervisor of the district of Futura, wants to know."

"Where in hell did you come from?"

"I did not come from hell. I came from Thursday."

Harry held his head. "What *is* all this?" he wailed. "Why is today Wednesday? Who are all these crazy little guys? What happened to Tuesday?"

Iridel made a slight motion with his finger, and the little man scurried back under the car. Harry was frenzied to hear the wrench busily tightening bolts. He half started to dive under after the little fellow, but Iridel said, "Stop!" and when Iridel said, "Stop!" Harry stopped.

"This," said Iridel calmly, "is an amazing occurrence." He regarded Harry with unemotional curiosity. "An actor on stage before the sets are finished. Extraordinary."

"What stage?" asked Harry. "What are you doing here anyhow, and what's the idea of all these little guys working around here?"

"You ask a great many questions, actor," said Iridel. "I shall answer them, and then I shall have a few to ask you. These little men are stage hands— I am surprised that you didn't realize that. They are setting the stage for Wednesday. Tuesday? That's going on now."

"Arrgh!" Harry snorted. "How can Tuesday be going on when today's Wednesday?"

"Today isn't Wednesday, actor."

"Huh?"

"Today is Tuesday."

Harry scratched his head. "Met a feller on the steps this mornin'— one of these here stage hands of yours. He said this was Wednesday."

"It *is* Wednesday. Today is Tuesday. Tuesday is today. 'Today' is simply the name for the stage set which happens to be in use. 'Yesterday' means the set that has just been used; 'Tomorrow' is the set that will be used after the actors have finished with 'today.' This is Wednesday. Yesterday was Monday; today is Tuesday. See?"

Harry said, "No."

Iridel threw up his long hands. "My, you actors are stupid. Now listen carefully. This is Act Wednesday, Scene 6:22. That means that everything you see around you here is being readied for 6:22 a.m. on Wednesday. Wednesday isn't a time; it's a place. The actors are moving along toward it now. I see you still don't get the idea. Let's see . . . ah. Look at that clock. What does it say?"

Harry Wright looked at the big electric clock on the wall over the compressor. It was corrected hourly and highly accurate, and it said 6:22. Harry looked at it amazed. "Six tw— but my gosh, man, that's what time I left the house. I walked here, an' I been here ten minutes already!"

Iridel shook his head. "You've been here no time at all, because there is no time until the actors make their entrances."

Harry sat down on a grease drum and wrinkled up his brains with the effort he was making. "You mean that this time proposition ain't something that moves along all the time? Sorta—well, like a road. A road don't go no place— You just go places along it. Is that it?"

"That's the general idea. In fact, that's a pretty good example. Suppose we say that it's a road; a highway built of paving blocks. Each block is a day; the actors move along it, and go through day after day. And our job here—mine and the little men—is to . . . well, pave that road. This is the clean-up gang here. They are fixing up the last little details, so that everything will be ready for the actors."

Harry sat still, his mind creaking with the effects of this information. He felt as if he had been hit with a lead pipe, and the shock of it was being drawn out infinitely. This was the craziest-sounding thing he had ever run into. For no reason at all he remembered a talk he had had once with a drunken aviation mechanic who had tried to explain to him how the air flowing over an airplane's wings makes the machine go up in the air. He hadn't understood a word of the man's discourse, which was all about eddies and chords and cambers and foils, dihedrals and the Bernoulli effect. That didn't make any difference; the things flew whether he understood how or not; he knew that because he had seen them. This guy Iridel's lecture was the same sort of thing. If there was nothing in all he said, how come all these little guys were working around here? Why wasn't the clock telling time? Where was Tuesday?

He thought he'd get that straight for good and all. "Just where is Tuesday?" he asked.

"Over there," said Iridel, and pointed. Harry recoiled and fell off the drum; for when the man extended his hand, it *disappeared!*

Harry got up off the floor and said tautly, "Do that again."

"What? Oh— Point toward Tuesday? Certainly." And he pointed. His hand appeared again when he withdrew it.

Harry said, "My gosh!" and sat down again on the drum, sweating and staring at the supervisor of the district of Futura. "You point, an' your hand—ain't," he breathed. "What direction is that?"

"It is a direction like any other direction," said Iridel. "You know yourself there are four directions—forward, sideward, upward, and"—he pointed again, and again his hand vanished—"*that* way!"

"They never tole me that in school," said Harry. "Course, I was just a kid then, but—"

Iridel laughed. "It is the fourth dimension—it is *duration*. The actors move through length, breadth, and height, anywhere they choose to within the set. But there is another movement—one they can't control— and that is duration."

"How soon will they come . . . eh . . . here?" asked Harry, waving an arm. Iridel dipped into one of his numberless pockets and pulled out a watch. "It is now eight thirty-seven Tuesday morning," he said. "They'll be here as soon as they finish the act, and the scenes in Wednesday that have already been prepared."

Harry thought again for a moment, while Iridel waited patiently, smiling a little. Then he looked up at the supervisor and asked, "Hey— this 'actor' business—what's that all about?"

"Oh—that. Well, it's a play, that's all. Just like any play—put on for the amusement of an audience."

"I was to a play once," said Harry. "Who's the audience?"

Iridel stopped smiling. "Certain— Ones who may be amused," he said. "And now I'm going to ask you some questions. How did you get here?"

"Walked."

"You *walked* from Monday night to Wednesday morning?"

"Naw— From the house to here."

"Ah— But how did you get to Wednesday, six twenty-two?"

"Well I— Damfino. I just woke up an' came to work as usual."

"This is an extraordinary occurrence," said Iridel, shaking his head in puzzlement. "You'll have to see the producer."

"Producer? Who's he?"

"You'll find out. In the meantime, come along with me. I can't leave you here; you're too close to the play. I have to make my rounds anyway."

Iridel walked toward the door. Harry was tempted to stay and find himself some more work to do, but when Iridel glanced back at him and motioned him out, Harry followed. It was suddenly impossible to do anything else.

Just as he caught up with the supervisor, a little worker ran up, whipping off his cap.

"Iridel, sir," he piped, "the weather makers put .006 of one percent too little moisture in the air on this set. There's three sevenths of an ounce too little gasoline in the storage tanks under here."

"How much is in the tanks?"

"Four thousand two hundred and seventy-three gallons, three pints, seven and twenty-one thirty-fourths ounces."

Iridel grunted. "Let it go this time. That was very sloppy work. Someone's going to get transferred to Limbo for this."

"Very good, sir," said the little man. "Long as you know we're not responsible." He put on his cap, spun around three times and rushed off.

"Lucky for the weather makers that the amount of gas in that tank doesn't come into Wednesday's script," said Iridel. "If anything interferes with the continuity of the play, there's the devil to pay. Actors haven't sense enough to cover up, either. They are liable to start whole series of miscues because of a little thing like that. The play might flop and then we'd all be out of work."

"Oh," Harry oh-ed. "Hey, Iridel—what's the idea of that patchy-looking place over there?"

Iridel followed his eyes. Harry was looking at a corner lot. It was tree-lined and overgrown with weeds and small saplings. The vegetation was true to form around the edges of the lot, and around the path that ran diagonally through it; but the spaces in between were a plain surface. Not a leaf nor a blade of grass grew there; it was naked-looking, blank, and absolutely without any color whatever.

"Oh, that," answered Iridel. "There are only two characters in Act Wednesday who will use that path. Therefore it is as grown-over as it should be. The rest of the lot doesn't enter into the play, so we don't have to do anything with it."

"But— Suppose someone wandered off the path on Wednesday," Harry offered.

"He'd be due for a surprise, I guess. But it could hardly happen. Special prompters are always detailed to spots like that, to keep the actors from going astray or missing any cues."

"Who are they—the prompters, I mean?"

"Prompters? G.A.'s—Guardian Angels. That's what the script writers call them."

"I heard o' them," said Harry.

"Yes, they have their work cut out for them," said the supervisor. "Actors are always forgetting their lines when they shouldn't, or remembering them when the script calls for a lapse. Well, it looks pretty good here. Let's have a look at Friday."

"Friday? You mean to tell me you're working on Friday already?"

"Of course! Why, we work years in advance! How on earth do you think we could get our trees grown otherwise? Here—step in!" Iridel put out his hand, seized empty air, drew it aside to show the kind of absolute nothingness he had first appeared from, and waved Harry on.

"Y-you want me to go in there?" asked Harry diffidently.

"Certainly. Hurry, now!"

Harry looked at the section of void with a rather weak-kneed look, but could not withstand the supervisor's strange compulsion. He stepped through.

And it wasn't so bad. There were no whirling lights, no sensations of falling, no falling unconscious. It was just like stepping into another room—which is what had happened. He found himself in a great round chamber, whose roundness was touched a bit with the indistinct. That is, it had curved walls and a domed roof, but there was something else about it. It seemed to stretch off in that direction toward which Iridel had so astonishingly pointed. The walls were lined with an amazing array of control machinery—switches and ground-glass screens, indicators and dials, knurled knobs, and levers. Moving deftly before them was a crew of men, each looking exactly like Iridel except that their garments had no pockets. Harry stood wide-eyed, hypnotized by the enormous complexity of the controls and the ease with which the men worked among them. Iridel touched his shoulder. "Come with me," he said. "The producer is in now; we'll find out what is to be done with you."

They started across the floor. Harry had not quite time to wonder how long it would take them to cross that enormous room, for when they had taken perhaps a dozen steps they found themselves at the opposite wall. The ordinary laws of space and time simply did not apply in the place.

They stopped at a door of burnished bronze, so very highly polished that they could see through it. It opened and Iridel pushed Harry through. The door swung shut. Harry, panic-stricken lest he be separated from the only thing in this weird world he could begin to get used to, flung himself against the great bronze portal. It bounced him back, head over heels, into the middle of the floor. He rolled over and got up to his hands and knees.

He was in a tiny room, one end of which was filled by a colossal teakwood desk. The man sitting there regarded him with amusement. "Where'd you blow in from?" he asked; and his voice was like the angry bee sound of an approaching hurricane.

"Are you the producer?"

"Well, I'll be darned," said the man, and smiled. It seemed to fill the whole room with light. He was a big man, Harry noticed; but in this deceptive place, there was no way of telling how big. "I'll be most verily darned. An actor. You're a persistent lot, aren't you? Building houses for me that I almost never go into. Getting together and sending requests for better parts. Listening carefully to what I have to say and then ignoring or misinterpreting my advice. Always asking for just one more chance, and when you get it, messing that up too. And now one of you crashes the gate. What's your trouble, anyway?"

There was something about the producer that bothered Harry, but he could not place what it was, unless it was the fact that the man awed him and he didn't know why. "I woke up in Wednesday," he stammered, "and yesterday was Tuesday. I mean Monday. I mean—" He cleared his throat and started over. "I went to sleep Monday night and woke up Wednesday, and I'm looking for Tuesday."

"What do you want me to do about it?"

"Well—couldn't you tell me how to get back there? I got work to do."

"Oh—I get it," said the producer. "You want a favor from me. You know, someday, some one of you fellows is going to come to me wanting to give me something, free and for nothing, and then I am going to drop quietly dead. Don't I have enough trouble running this show without taking up time and space by doing favors for the likes of you?" He drew a couple of breaths and then smiled again. "However—I have always tried to be just, even if it is a tough job sometimes. Go on out and tell Iridel to show you the way back. I think I know what happened to you; when you made your exit from the last act you played in, you somehow managed to walk out behind the wrong curtain when you reached the wings. There's going to be a prompter sent to Limbo for this. Go on now—beat it."

Harry opened his mouth to speak, thought better of it and scuttled out the door, which opened before him. He stood in the huge control chamber, breathing hard. Iridel walked up to him.

"Well?"

"He says for you to get me out of here."

"All right," said Iridel. "This way." He led the way to a curtained doorway much like the one they had used to come in. Beside it were two dials, one marked in days, and the other in hours and minutes.

"Monday night good enough for you?" asked Iridel.

"Swell," said Harry.

Iridel set the dials for 9:30 p.m. on Monday. "So long, actor. Maybe I'll see you again some time."

"So long," said Harry. He turned and stepped through the door.

He was back in the garage, and there was no curtained doorway behind him. He turned to ask Iridel if this would enable him to go to bed again and do Tuesday right from the start, but Iridel was gone.

The garage was a blaze of light. Harry glanced up at the clock— It said fifteen seconds after nine-thirty. That was funny; everyone should be home by now except Slim Jim, the night man, who hung out until four in the morning serving up gas at the pumps outside. A quick glance around sufficed. This might be Monday night, but it was a Monday night he hadn't known.

The place was filled with the little men again!

Harry sat on the fender of a convertible and groaned. "Now what have I got myself into?" he asked himself.

He could see that he was at a different place-in-time from the one in which he had met Iridel. There, they had been working to build, working with a precision and nicety that was a pleasure to watch. But here—

The little men were different, in the first place. They were tired-looking, sick, slow. There were scores of overseers about, and Harry winced with one of the little fellows when one of the men in white lashed out with a long whip. As the Wednesday crews worked, so the Monday gangs slaved. And the work they were doing was different. For here they were breaking down, breaking up, carting away. Before his eyes, Harry saw sections of paving lifted out, pulverized, toted away by the sackload by lines of trudging, browbeaten little men. He saw great beams upended to support the roof, while bricks were pried out of the walls. He heard the gang working on the roof, saw patches of roofing torn away. He saw walls and roof both melt away under that driving, driven onslaught, and before he knew what was happening he was standing alone on a section of the dead white plain he had noticed before on the corner lot.

It was too much for his overburdened mind; he ran out into the night, breaking through lines of laden slaves, through neat and growing piles of rubble, screaming for Iridel. He ran for a long time, and finally dropped down behind a stack of lumber out where the Unitarian church used to be, dropped because he could go no farther. He heard footsteps and tried to make himself smaller. They came on steadily; one of the overseers rounded the corner and stood looking at him. Harry was in deep shadow, but he knew the man in white could see in the dark.

"Come out o' there," grated the man. Harry came out.

"You the guy was yellin' for Iridel?"

Harry nodded.

"What makes you think you'll find Iridel in Limbo?" sneered his captor. "Who are you, anyway?"

Harry had learned by this time. "I'm an actor," he said in a small voice. "I got into Wednesday by mistake, and they sent me back here."

"What for?"

"Huh? Why— I guess it was a mistake, that's all."

The man stepped forward and grabbed Harry by the collar. He was about eight times as powerful as a hydraulic jack. "Don't give me no guff, pal," said the man. "Nobody gets sent to Limbo by mistake, or if he didn't do somethin' up there to make him deserve it. Come clean, now."

"I didn't do nothin'," Harry wailed. "I asked them the way back, and they showed me a door, and I went through it and came here. That's all I know. Stop it, you're choking me!"

The man dropped him suddenly. "Listen, babe, you know who I am? Hey?" Harry shook his head. "Oh—you don't. Well, I'm Gurrah!"

"Yeah?" Harry said, not being able to think of anything else at the moment.

Gurrah puffed out his chest and appeared to be waiting for something more from Harry. When nothing came, he walked up to the mechanic, breathed in his face. "Ain't scared, huh? Tough guy, huh? Never heard of Gurrah, supervisor of Limbo an' the roughest, toughest son of the devil from Incidence to Eternity, huh?"

Now Harry was a peaceable man, but if there was anything he hated, it was to have a stranger breathe his bad breath pugnaciously at him. Before he knew it had happened, Gurrah was sprawled eight feet away, and Harry was standing alone rubbing his left knuckles—quite the more surprised of the two.

Gurrah sat up, feeling his face. "Why, you . . . you hit me!" he roared. He got up and came over to Harry. "You hit me!" he said softly, his voice slightly out of focus in amazement. Harry wished he hadn't—wished he was in bed or in Futura or dead or something. Gurrah reached out with a heavy fist and—patted him on the shoulder. "Hey," he said, suddenly friendly, "you're all right. Heh! Took a poke at me, didn't you? Be damned! First time in a month o' Mondays anyone ever made a pass at me. Last was a feller named Orton. I killed 'im." Harry paled.

Gurrah leaned back against the lumber pile. "Dam'f I didn't enjoy that, feller. Yeah. This is a hell of a job they palmed off on me, but what can you do? Breakin' down—breakin' down. No sooner get through one job, workin' top speed, drivin' the boys till they bleed, than they give you the devil for not bein' halfway through another job. You'd think I'd been in the business long enough to know what it was all about, after more than eight hundred an' twenty million acts, wouldn't you? Heh. Try to tell *them* that. Ship a load of dog houses up to Wednesday, sneakin' it past backstage nice as you please. They turn right around and call me up. 'What's the matter with you, Gurrah? Them dog houses is no good. We sent you a list o' worn-out items two acts ago. One o' the items was dog houses. Snap out of it or we send someone back there who can read an' put you on a toteline.' That's what I get—act in and act out. An' does it do any good to tell 'em that my aide got the message an' dropped dead before he got it to me? No. Uh-uh. If I say anything about that, they tell me to stop workin' 'em to death. If I do that, they kick because my shipments don't come in fast enough."

He paused for breath. Harry had a hunch that if he kept Gurrah in a good mood it might benefit him. He asked, "What's your job, anyway?"

"Job?" Gurrah howled. "Call this a job? Tearin' down the sets, shippin' what's good to the act after next, junkin' the rest?" He snorted.

Harry asked, "You mean they use the same props over again?"

"That's right. They don't last, though. Six, eight acts, maybe. Then they got to build new ones and weather them and knock 'em around to make 'em look as if they was used."

There was silence for a time. Gurrah, having got his bitterness off his chest for the first. time in literally ages, was feeling pacified. Harry didn't know how to feel. He finally broke the ice. "Hey, Gurrah—How'm I goin' to get back into the play?"

"What's it to me? How'd you— Oh, that's right, you walked in from the control room, huh? That it?"

Harry nodded.

"An' how," growled Gurrah, "did you get inta the control room?"

"Iridel brought me."

"Then what?"

"Well, I went to see the producer, and—"

"Th' *producer!* Holy— You mean you walked right in and—" Gurrah mopped his brow. "What'd he say?"

"Why—he said he guessed it wasn't my fault that I woke up in Wednesday. He said to tell Iridel to ship me back."

"An' Iridel threw you back to Monday." And Gurrah threw back his shaggy head and roared.

"What's funny," asked Harry, a little peeved.

"Iridel," said Gurrah. "Do you realize that I've been trying for fifty thousand acts or more to get something on that pretty ol' heel, and he drops you right in my lap. Pal, I can't thank you enough! He was supposed to send you back into the play, and instead o' that you wind up in yesterday! Why, I'll blackmail him till the end of time!" He whirled exultantly, called to a group of bedraggled little men who were staggering under a cornerstone on their way to the junkyard. "Take it easy, boys!" he called. "I got ol' Iridel by the short hair. No more busted backs! No more snotty messages! *Haw haw haw!*"

Harry, a little amazed at all this, put in a timid word, "Hey—Gurrah. What about me?"

Gurrah turned. "You? Oh. *Tel-e-phone!*" At his shout two little workers, a trifle less bedraggled than the rest, trotted up. One hopped up and perched on Gurrah's right shoulder; the other draped himself over the left, with his head forward. Gurrah grabbed the latter by the neck, brought the man's head close and shouted into his ear. "Give me Iridel!" There was a moment's wait, then the little man on his other shoulder spoke in Iridel's voice, into Gurrah's ear, "Well?"

"Hiyah, fancy pants!"

"Fancy— I beg your— Who is this?"

"It's Gurrah, you futuristic parasite. I got a couple things to tell you."

"Gurrah! How—*dare* you talk to me like that! I'll have you—"

"You'll have me in your job if I tell all I know. You're a wart on the nose of progress, Iridel."

"What is the meaning of this?"

"The meaning of this is that you had instructions sent to you by the producer an' you muffed them. Had an actor there, didn't you? He saw the boss, didn't he? Told you he was to be sent back, didn't he? Sent him right over to me instead of to the play, didn't you? You're slippin', Iridel. Gettin' old. Well, get off the wire. I'm callin' the boss, right now."

"The boss? Oh—don't do that, old man. Look, let's talk this thing over. Ah—about that shipment of three-legged dogs I was wanting you to round up for me; I guess I can do without them. Any little favor I can do for you—"

"—you'll damn well do, after this. You better, Goldilocks." Gurrah knocked the two small heads together, breaking the connection and probably the heads, and turned grinning to Harry. "You see," he explained, "that Iridel feller is a damn good supervisor, but he's a stickler for detail. He sends people to Limbo for the silliest little mistakes. He never forgives anyone and he never forgets a slip. He's the cause of half the misery back here, with his hurry-up orders. Now things are gonna be different. The boss has wanted to give Iridel a dose of his own medicine for a long time now, but Irrie never gave him a chance."

Harry said patiently, "About me getting back now—"

"My fran'!" Gurrah bellowed. He delved into a pocket and pulled out a watch like Iridel's. "It's eleven forty on Tuesday," he said. "We'll shoot you back there now. You'll have to dope out your own reasons for disappearing. Don't spill too much, or a lot of people will suffer for it—you the most. Ready?"

Harry nodded; Gurrah swept out a hand and opened the curtain to nothingness. "You'll find yourself quite a ways from where you started," he said, "because you did a little moving around here. Go ahead."

"Thanks," said Harry.

Gurrah laughed. "Don't thank me, chum. You rate all the thanks! Hey—if, after you kick off, you don't make out so good up there, let them toss you over to me. You'll be treated good; you've my word on it. Beat it; luck!"

Holding his breath, Harry Wright stepped through the doorway.

He had to walk thirty blocks to the garage, and when he got there the boss was waiting for him.

"Where you been, Wright?"

"I—lost my way."

"Don't get wise. What do you think this is—vacation time? Get going on the spring job. Damn it, it won't be finished now till tomorra."

Harry looked him straight in the eye and said, "Listen. It'll be finished tonight. I happen to know." And, still grinning, he went back into the garage and took out his tools.

# HENRY KUTTNER

The versatile Henry Kuttner (1914–1958) began his career writing weird fiction under the influence of H. P. Lovecraft for Weird Tales. By the late 1930s, he had branched out to write prolifically for a variety of adventure, detective, and science-fiction magazines. He married science-fiction writer C. L. Moore in 1940, and the two became leading writers for Astounding Science-Fiction during the war years. Much of the fiction that appeared under Kuttner's name or the Lewis Padgett and Lawrence O'Donnell pseudonyms was collaborations between the two. His distinguished work from this period includes the wacky robot stories assembled as Robots Have No Tails, the "Baldy" stories of mutant supermen collected as Mutant, the reality-twisting short novels Tomorrow and Tomorrow and The Fairy Chessmen, and the classic time-travel story "Vintage Season." He also collaborated with Moore on several pastiches of A. Merritt, including The Dark World, The Valley of the Flame, and The Time Axis. His best fiction has been collected in A Gnome There Was, Ahead of Time, Line to Tomorrow, No Boundaries, Bypass to Otherness, and Return to Otherness.

The idea of containing a time warp in an object has probably never been written about quite so cleverly as in "Time Locker." Kuttner's story of a dishonest attorney trying to subvert the future for his own ends could be considered almost a progenitor of the hard science-fiction story, with the tipsy scientist providing the scientific background on why the mysterious locker does what it does, and to explain why the events that happen during the story are as inevitable as the passage of time itself.

# TIME LOCKER

## HENRY KUTTNER

GALLEGHER PLAYED BY EAR, which would have been all right had he been a musician — but he was a scientist. A drunken and erratic one, but good. He'd wanted to be an experimental technician, and would have been excellent at it, for he had a streak of genius at times. Unfortunately, there had been no funds for such specialized education, and now Gallegher, by profession an integrator machine supervisor, maintained his laboratory purely as a hobby. It was the damnedest-looking lab in six states. Gallegher had once spent months building what he called a liquor organ, which occupied most of the space. He could recline on a comfortably padded couch and, by manipulating buttons, siphon drinks of marvelous quantity, quality, and variety down his scarified throat. Since he had made the liquor organ during a protracted period of drunkenness, he never remembered the basic principles of its construction. In a way, that was a pity.

There was a little of everything in the lab, much of it incongruous. Rheostats had little skirts on them, like ballet dancers; and vacuously grinning faces of clay. A generator was conspicuously labeled, "Monstro," and a much smaller one rejoiced in the name of "Bubbles." Inside a glass retort was a china rabbit, and Gallegher alone knew how it had got there. Just inside the door was a hideous iron dog, originally intended for Victorian lawns or perhaps for hell, and its hollowed ears served as sockets for test tubes.

"But how do you do it?" Vanning asked.

Gallegher, his lank form reclining under the liquor organ, siphoned a shot of double martini into his mouth. "Huh?"

"You heard me. I could get you a swell job if you'd use that screwball brain of yours. Or even learn to put up a front."

"Tried it," Gallegher mumbled. "No use. I can't work when I concentrate, except at mechanical stuff. I think my subconscious must have a high I.Q."

Vanning, a chunky little man with a scarred, swarthy face, kicked his heels against Monstro. Sometimes Gallegher annoyed him. The man never realized his own potentialities, or how much they might mean to Horace Vanning, Commerce Analyst. The "commerce," of course, was extra-legal, but the complicated trade relationships of the day left loopholes a clever man could slip through. The fact of the matter was, Vanning acted in an advisory capacity to crooks. It paid well. A sound knowledge of jurisprudence was rare in these days; the statutes were in such a tangle that it took years of research before one could even enter a law school. But Vanning had a staff of trained experts, a colossal library of transcripts, decisions, and legal data, and, for a suitable fee, he could have told Dr. Crippen how to get off scot-free.

The shadier side of his business was handled in strict privacy, without assistants. The matter of the neuro-gun, for example—

Gallegher had made that remarkable weapon, quite without realizing its function. He had hashed it together one evening, piecing out the job with court plaster when his welder went on the fritz. And he'd given it to Vanning, on request. Vanning didn't keep it long. But already he had earned thousands of credits by lending the gun to potential murderers. As a result, the police department had a violent headache.

A man in the know would come to Vanning and say, "I heard you can beat a murder rap. Suppose I wanted to—"

"Hold on! I can't condone anything like that."

"Huh? But—"

"Theoretically, I suppose a perfect murder might be possible. Suppose a new sort of gun had been invented, and suppose—just for the sake of an example—it was in a locker at the Newark Stratoship Field."

"Huh?"

"I'm just theorizing. Locker Number Seventy-nine, combination thirty-blue-eight. These little details always help one to visualize a theory, don't they?"

"You mean—"

"Of course if our murderer picked up this imaginary gun and used it, he'd be smart enough to have a postal box ready, addressed to . . . say . . . Locker Forty, Brooklyn Port. He could slip the weapon into the box, seal it, and get rid of the evidence at the nearest mail conveyor. But that's all theorizing. Sorry I can't help you. The fee for an interview is three thousand credits. The receptionist will take your check."

Later, conviction would be impossible. Ruling 875-M, Illinois Precinct, case of State vs. Dupson, set the precedent. Cause of death must be determined. Element of accident must be considered. As Chief Justice Duckett had ruled during the trial of Sanderson vs. Sanderson, which involved the death of the accused's mother-in-law—

Surely the prosecuting attorney, with his staff of toxicological experts, must realize that—

And in short, your honor, I must respectfully request that the case be dismissed for lack of evidence and proof of *casus mortis*—

Gallegher never even found out that his neuro-gun was a dangerous weapon. But Vanning haunted the sloppy laboratory, avidly watching the results of his friend's scientific doodling. More than once he had acquired handy little devices in just this fashion. The trouble was, Gallegher wouldn't *work!*

He took another sip of martini, shook his head, and unfolded his lanky limbs. Blinking, he ambled over to a cluttered workbench and began toying with lengths of wire.

"Making something?"

"Dunno. Just fiddling. That's the way it goes. I put things together, and sometimes they work. Trouble is, I never know exactly what they're going to do. *Tsk!*" Gallegher dropped the wires and returned to his couch. "Hell with it."

He was, Vanning reflected, an odd duck. Gallegher was essentially amoral, thoroughly out of place in this too-complicated world. He seemed to watch, with a certain wry amusement, from a vantage point of his own, rather disinterested for the most part. And he made things—

But always and only for his own amusement. Vanning sighed and glanced around the laboratory, his orderly soul shocked by the mess. Automatically he picked up a rumpled smock from the floor, and looked for a hook. Of course there was none. Gallegher, running short of conductive metal, had long since ripped them out and used them in some gadget or other.

The so-called scientist was creating a zombie, his eyes half-closed.

Vanning went over to a metal locker in one corner and opened the door. There were no hooks, but he folded the smock neatly and laid it in the floor of the locker.

Then he went back to his perch on Monstro.

"Have a drink?" Gallegher asked.

Vanning shook his head. "Thanks, no. I've got a case coming up tomorrow."

"There's always thiamin. Filthy stuff. I work better when I've got pneumatic cushions around my brain."

"Well, I don't."

"It is purely a matter of skill," Gallegher hummed, "to which each may attain if he will. . . . What are you gaping at?"

"That—locker," Vanning said, frowning in a baffled way. "What the—" He got up. The metal door hadn't been securely latched and had swung open. Of the smock Vanning had placed within the metal compartment there was no trace.

"It's the paint," Gallegher explained sleepily. "Or the treatment. I bombarded it with gamma rays. But it isn't good for anything."

Vanning went over and swung a fluorescent into a more convenient position. The locker wasn't empty, as he had at first imagined. The smock was no longer there, but instead there was a tiny blob of—something, pale-green and roughly spherical.

"It melts things?" Vanning asked, staring.

"Uh-uh. Pull it out. You'll see."

Vanning felt hesitant about putting his hand inside the locker. Instead, he found a long pair of test tube clamps and teased the blob out. It was—

Vanning hastily looked away. His eyes hurt. The green blob was changing in color, shape and size. A crawling, nongeometrical blue of motion rippled over it. Suddenly the clamps were remarkably heavy.

No wonder. They were gripping the original smock.

"It does that, you know," Gallegher said absently. "Must be a reason, too. I put things in the locker and they get small. Take 'em out, and they get big again. I suppose I could sell it to a stage magician." His voice sounded doubtful.

Vanning sat down, fingering the smock and staring at the metal locker. It was a cube, approximately $3 \times 3 \times 5$, lined with what seemed to be grayish paint, sprayed on. Outside, it was shiny black.

"How'd you do it?"

"Huh? I dunno. Just fiddling around." Gallegher sipped his zombie. "Maybe it's a matter of dimensional extension. My treatment may have altered the spatiotemporal relationships inside the locker. I wonder what that means?" he murmured in a vague aside. "Words frighten me sometimes."

Vanning was thinking about tesseracts. "You mean it's bigger inside than it is outside?"

"A paradox, a paradox, a most delightful paradox. *You* tell *me*. I suppose the inside of the locker isn't in this space-time continuum at all. Here, shove that bench in it. You'll see." Gallegher made no move to rise; he waved toward the article of furniture in question.

"You're crazy. That bench is bigger than the locker."

"So it is. Shove it in a bit at a time. That corner first. Go ahead."

Vanning wrestled with the bench. Despite his shortness, he was stockily muscular.

"Lay the locker on its back. It'll be easier."

"I . . . *uh!* . . . O.K. Now what?"

"Edge the bench down into it."

Vanning squinted at his companion, shrugged, and tried to obey. Of course the bench wouldn't go into the locker. One corner did, that was all. Then, naturally, the bench stopped, balancing precariously at an angle.

"Well?"

"Wait."

The bench moved. It settled slowly downward. As Vanning's jaw dropped, the bench seemed to crawl into the locker, with the gentle motion of a not-too-heavy object sinking through water. It wasn't sucked down. It melted down. The portion still outside the locker was unchanged. But that, too, settled, and was gone.

Vanning craned forward. A blur of movement hurt his eyes. Inside the locker was—something. It shifted its contours, shrank, and became a spiky sort of scalene pyramid, deep purple in hue.

It seemed to be less than four inches across at its widest point.

"I don't believe it," Vanning said.

Gallegher grinned. "As the Duke of Wellington remarked to the subaltern, it was a demned small bottle, sir."

"Now wait a minute. How the devil could I put an eight-foot bench inside of a five-foot locker?"

"Because of Newton," Gallegher said. "Gravity. Go fill a test tube with water and I'll show you."

"Wait a minute . . . O.K. Now what?"

"Got it brim-full? Good. You'll find some sugar cubes in that drawer labeled FUSES. Lay a cube on top of the test tube, one corner down so it touches the water."

Vanning racked the tube and obeyed. "Well?"

"What do you see?"

"Nothing. The sugar's getting wet. And melting."

"So there you are," Gallegher said expansively. Vanning gave him a brooding look and turned back to the tube. The cube of sugar was slowly dissolving and melting down.

Presently it was gone.

"Air and water are different physical conditions. In air a sugar cube can exist as a sugar cube. In water it exists in solution. The corner of it extending into water is subject to aqueous conditions. So it alters physically, though not chemically. Gravity does the rest."

"Make it clearer."

"The analogy's clear enough, no? The water represents the particular condition existing inside that locker. The sugar cube represents the workbench. Now! The sugar soaked up the water and gradually dissolved in it, so gravity could pull the cube down into the tube as it melted. See?"

"I think so. The bench soaked up the . . . the $x$ condition inside the locker, eh? A condition that shrank the bench—"

"*In partis*, not *in toto*. A little at a time. You can shove a human body into a small container of sulphuric acid, bit by bit."

"Oh," Vanning said, regarding the cabinet askance. "Can you get the bench out again?"

"Do it yourself. Just reach in and pull it out."

"*Reach* in? I don't want my hand to melt!"

"It won't. The action isn't instantaneous. You saw that yourself. It takes a few minutes for the change to take place. You can reach into the locker without any ill effects, if you don't leave your hand exposed to the conditions for more than a minute or so. I'll show you." Gallegher languidly arose, looked around, and picked up an empty demijohn. He dropped this into the locker.

The change wasn't immediate. It occurred slowly, the demijohn altering its shape and size till it was a distorted cube the apparent size of a cube of sugar. Gallegher reached down and brought it up again, placing the cube on the floor.

It grew. It was a demijohn again.

"Now the bench. Look out."

Gallegher rescued the little pyramid. Presently it became the original workbench.

"You see? I'll bet a storage company would like this. You could probably pack all the furniture in Brooklyn in here, but there'd be trouble in getting what you wanted out again. The physical change, you know—"

"Keep a chart," Vanning suggested absently. "Draw a picture of how the thing looks inside the locker, and note down what it was."

"The legal brain," Gallegher said. "I want a drink." He returned to his couch and clutched the siphon in a grip of death.

"I'll give you six credits for the thing," Vanning offered.

"Sold. It takes up too much room anyway. Wish I could put it inside itself." The scientist chuckled immoderately. "That's very funny."

"Is it?" Vanning said. "Well, here you are." He took credit coupons from his wallet. "Where'll I put the dough?"

"Stuff it into Monstro. He's my bank. . . . Thanks."

"Yeah. Say, elucidate this sugar business a bit, will you? It isn't just gravity that affects the cube so it slips into a test tube. Doesn't the water soak up into the sugar—"

"You're right at that. Osmosis. No, I'm wrong. Osmosis has something to do with eggs. Or is that ovulation? Conduction, convection— absorption! Wish I'd studied physics; then I'd know the right words. Just a mad genius, that's me. I shall take the daughter of the Vine to spouse," Gallegher finished incoherently and sucked at the siphon.

"Absorption," Vanning scowled. "Only not water, being soaked up by the sugar. The . . . the conditions existing inside the locker, being soaked up by your workbench—in that particular case."

"Like a sponge or a blotter."

"The bench?"

"Me," Gallegher said succinctly, and relapsed into a happy silence, broken by occasional gurgles as he poured liquor down his scarified gullet. Vanning sighed and turned to the locker. He carefully closed and latched the door before lifting the metal cabinet in his muscular arms.

"Going? G'night. Fare thee well, fare thee well—"

"Night."

"*Fare*—thee—well!" Gallegher ended, in a melancholy outburst of tunefulness, as he turned over preparatory to going to sleep.

Vanning sighed again and let himself out into the coolness of the night. Stars blazed in the sky, except toward the south, where the aurora of Lower Manhattan dimmed them. The glowing white towers of sky-scrapers rose in a jagged pattern. A sky-ad announced the virtues of Vambulin *It Peps You Up.*

His speeder was at the curb. Vanning edged the locker into the trunk compartment and drove toward the Hudson Floatway, the quickest route downtown. He was thinking about Poe.

The Purloined Letter, which had been hidden in plain sight, but re-folded and readdressed, so that its superficial appearance was changed. Holy Hecate! What a perfect safe the locker would make! No thief could crack it, for the obvious reason that it wouldn't be locked. No thief would *want* to clean it out. Vanning could fill the locker with credit coupons and instantly they'd become unrecognizable. It was the ideal cache.

How the devil did it work?

There was little use in asking Gallegher. He played by ear. A prim-rose by the river's rim a simple primrose was to him—not *Primula vul-garis.* Syllogisms were unknown to him. He reached the conclusion without the aid of either major or minor premises.

Vanning pondered. Two objects cannot occupy the same space at the same time. Ergo, there was a different sort of space in the locker—

But Vanning was jumping at conclusions. There was another answer—the right one. He hadn't guessed it yet.

Instead, he tooled the speeder downtown to the office building where he maintained a floor, and brought the locker upstairs in the freight lift. He didn't put it in his private office; that would have been too obvious. He placed the metal cabinet in one of the storerooms, sliding a file cabinet in front of it for partial concealment. It wouldn't do to have the clerks using this particular locker.

Vanning stepped back and considered. Perhaps—

A bell rang softly. Preoccupied, Vanning didn't hear it at first. When he did, he went back to his own office and pressed the acknowledgment button on the Winchell. The gray, harsh, bearded face of Counsel Hat-ton appeared, filling the screen.

"Hello," Vanning said.

Hatton nodded. "I've been trying to reach you at your home. Thought I'd try the office—"

"I didn't expect you to call now. The trial's tomorrow. It's a bit late for discussion, isn't it?"

"Dugan & Sons wanted me to speak to you. I advised against it."

"Oh?"

Hatton's thick gray brows drew together. "I'm prosecuting, you know. There's plenty of evidence against MacIlson."

"So you say. But speculation's a difficult charge to prove."

"Did you get an injunction against scop?"

"Naturally," Vanning said. "You're not using truth serum on my client!"

"That'll prejudice the jury."

"Not on medical grounds. Scop affects MacIlson harmfully. I've got a covering prognosis."

"Harmfully is right!" Hatton's voice was sharp. "Your client embezzled those bonds, and I can prove it."

"Twenty-five thousand in credits, it comes to, eh? That's a lot for Dugan & Sons to lose. What about that hypothetical case I posed? Suppose twenty thousand were recovered—"

"Is this a private beam? No recordings?"

"Naturally. Here's the cut-off." Vanning held up a metal-tipped cord. "This is strictly sub rosa."

"Good," Counsel Hatton said. "Then I can call you a lousy shyster."

"*Tch!*"

"Your gag's too old. It's moth-eaten. MacIlson swiped five grand in bonds, negotiable into credits. The auditors start checking up. MacIlson comes to you. You tell him to take twenty grand more, and offer to return that twenty if Dugan & Sons refuse to prosecute. MacIlson splits with you on the five thousand, and on the plat standard, that ain't hay."

"I don't admit to anything like that."

"Naturally you don't, not even on a closed beam. But it's tacit. However, the gag's moth-eaten, and my clients won't play ball with you. They're going to prosecute."

"You called me up just to tell me that?"

"No, I want to settle the jury question. Will you agree to let 'em use scop on the panel?"

"O.K.," Vanning said. He wasn't depending on a fixed jury tomorrow. His battle would be based on legal technicalities. With scop-tested talesmen, the odds would be even. And such an arrangement would save days or weeks of argument and challenge.

"Good," Hatton grunted. "You're going to get your pants licked off."

Vanning replied with a mild obscenity and broke the connection. Reminded of the pending court fight, he forced the matter of the fourth-dimensional locker out of his mind and left the office. Later—

————

Later would be time enough to investigate the possibilities of the re-markable cabinet more thoroughly. Just now; he didn't want his brain cluttered with nonessentials. He went to his apartment, had the servant mix him a short highball, and dropped into bed.

And, the next day, Vanning won the case. He based it on compli-cated technicalities and obscure legal precedents. The crux of the mat-ter was that the bonds had not been converted into government credits. Abstruse economic charts proved that point for Vanning. Conversion of even five thousand credits would have caused a fluctuation in the graph line, and no such break existed. Vanning's experts went into monstrous detail.

In order to prove guilt, it would have been necessary to show, either actually or by inference, that the bonds had been in existence since last December 20th, the date of their most recent check-and-recording. The case of Donovan vs. Jones stood as a precedent.

Hatton jumped to his feet. "Jones later confessed to his defalcation, your honor!"

"Which does not affect the original decision," Vanning said smoothly. "Retroaction is not admissible here. The verdict was not proven."

"Counsel for the defense will continue."

Counsel for the defense continued, building up a beautifully intri-cate edifice of casuistic logic.

Hattan writhed. "Your honor! I—"

"If my learned opponent can produce one bond—just one of the bonds in question—I will concede the case."

The presiding judge looked sardonic. "Indeed! If such a piece of evi-dence could be produced, the defendant would be jailed as fast as I could pronounce sentence. You know that very well, Mr. Vanning. Pro-ceed."

"Very well. My contention, then, is that the bonds never existed. They were the result of a clerical error in notation."

"A clerical error in a Pederson Calculator?"

"Such errors have occurred as I shall prove. If I may call my next witness—"

Unchallenged, the witness, a math technician, explained how a Pederson Calculator can go haywire. He cited cases.

Hatton caught him up on one point. "I protest this proof. Rhodesia, as everyone knows, is the location of a certain important experimental industry. Witness has refrained from stating the nature of the work performed in this particular Rhodesian factory. Is it not a fact that the Henderson United Company deals largely in radioactive ores?"

"Witness will answer."

"I can't. My records don't include that information."

"A significant omission," Hatton snapped. "Radioactivity damages the intricate mechanism of a Pederson Calculator. There is no radium nor radium by-product in the offices of Dugan & Sons."

Vanning stood up. "May I ask if those offices have been fumigated lately?"

"They have. It is legally required."

"A type of chlorine gas was used?"

"Yes."

"I wish to call my next witness."

The next witness, a physicist and official in the Ultra Radium Institute, explained that gamma radiations affect chlorine strongly, causing ionization. Living organisms could assimilate by-products of radium and transmit them in turn. Certain clients of Dugan & Sons had been in contact with radioactivity—

"This is ridiculous, your honor! Pure theorization—"

Vanning looked hurt. "I cite the case of Dangerfield vs. Austro Products, California, 1963. Ruling states that the uncertainty factor is prime admissible evidence. My point is simply that the Pederson Calculator which recorded the bonds could have been in error. If this be true, there were no bonds, and my client is guiltless."

"Counsel will continue," said the judge, wishing he were Jeffreys so he could send the whole damned bunch to the scaffold. Jurisprudence should be founded on justice, and not be a three-dimensional chess game. But, of course, it was the natural development of the complicated political and economic factors of modern civilization. It was already evident that Vanning would win his case.

And he did. The jury was directed to find for the defendant. On a last, desperate hope, Hatton raised a point of order and demanded scop, but his petition was denied. Vanning winked at his opponent and closed his briefcase.

That was that.

———

Vanning returned to his office. At four-thirty that afternoon trouble started to break. The secretary announced a Mr. MacIlson, and was pushed aside by a thin, dark, middle-aged man lugging a gigantic suedette suitcase.

"Vanning! I've got to see you—"

The attorney's eyes hooded. He rose from behind his desk, dismissing the secretary with a jerk of his head. As the door closed, Vanning said brusquely, "What are you doing here? I told you to stay away from me. What's in that bag?"

"The bonds," MacIlson explained, his voice unsteady. "Something's gone wrong—"

"You crazy fool! Bringing the bonds here—" With a leap Vanning was at the door, locking it. "Don't you realize that if Hatton gets his hands on that paper, you'll be yanked back to jail? And I'll be disbarred! Get 'em out of here."

"Listen a minute, will you? I took the bonds to Finance Unity, as you told me, but . . . but there was an officer there, waiting for me. I saw him just in time. If he'd caught me—"

Vanning took a deep breath. "You were supposed to leave the bonds in that subway locker for two months."

MacIlson pulled a news sheet from his pocket. "But the government's declared a freeze on ore stocks and bonds. It'll go into effect in a week. I couldn't wait—the money would have been tied up indefinitely."

"Let's see that paper." Vanning examined it and cursed softly. "Where'd you get this?"

"Bought it from a boy outside the jail. I wanted to check the current ore quotations."

"Uh-huh. I see. Did it occur to you that this sheet might be faked?"

MacIlson's jaw dropped. "Fake?"

"Exactly. Hatton figured I might spring you, and had this paper ready. You bit. You led the police right to the evidence, and a swell spot you've put me in."

"B-but—"

Vanning grimaced. "Why do you suppose you saw that cop at Finance Unity? They could have nabbed you any time. But they wanted to scare you into heading for my office, so they could catch both of us on the same hook. Prison for you, disbarment for me. Oh, hell!"

MacIlson licked his lips. "Can't I get out a back door?"

"Through the cordon that's undoubtedly waiting? Orbs! Don't be more of a sap than you can help."

"Can't you—hide the stuff?"

"Where? They'll ransack this office with X-rays. No, I'll just—" Vanning stopped. "Oh. Hide it, you said. *Hide it—*"

He whirled to the dictograph. "Miss Horton? I'm in conference. Don't disturb me for anything. If anybody hands you a search warrant, insist on verifying it through headquarters. Got me? O.K."

Hope had returned to MacIlson's face. "Is it all right?"

"Oh, shut up!" Vanning snapped. "Wait here for me. Be back directly." He headed for a side door and vanished. In a surprisingly short time he returned, awkwardly lugging a metal cabinet.

"Help me . . . *uh!* . . . here. In this corner. Now get out."

"But—"

"Flash," Vanning ordered. "Everything's under control. Don't talk. You'll be arrested, but they can't hold you without evidence. Come back as soon as you're sprung." He urged MacIlson to the door, unlocked it, and thrust the man through. After that, he returned to the cabinet, swung open the door, and peered in. Empty. Sure.

The suedette suitcase—

Vanning worked it into the locker, breathing hard. It took a little time, since the valise was larger than the metal cabinet. But at last he relaxed, watching the brown case shrink and alter its outline till it was tiny and distorted, the shape of an elongated egg, the color of a copper cent piece.

"*Whew!*" Vanning said.

Then he leaned closer, staring. Inside the locker, something was moving. A grotesque little creature less than four inches tall was visible. It was a shocking object, all cubes and angles, a bright green in tint, and it was obviously alive.

Someone knocked on the door.

The tiny—thing—was busy with the copper-colored egg. Like an ant, it was lifting the egg and trying to pull it away. Vanning gasped and reached into the locker. The fourth-dimensional creature dodged. It wasn't quick enough. Vanning's hand descended, and he felt wriggling movement against his palm.

He squeezed.

The movement stopped. He let go of the dead thing and pulled his hand back swiftly.

The door shook under the impact of fists.

Vanning closed the locker and called, "Just a minute."

"Break it down," somebody ordered.

But that wasn't necessary. Vanning put a painful smile on his face and turned the key. Counsel Hatton came in, accompanied by bulky policemen. "We've got MacIlson," he said.

"Oh? Why?"

For answer Hatton jerked his hand. The officers began to search the room. Vanning shrugged.

"You've jumped the gun," he said. "Breaking and entering—"

"We've got a warrant."

"Charge?"

"The bonds, of course." Hatton's voice was weary. "I don't know where you've hid that suitcase, but we'll find it."

"What suitcase?" Vanning wanted to know.

"The one MacIlson had when he came in. The one he didn't have when he came out."

"The game," Vanning said sadly, "is up. You win."

"Eh?"

"If I tell you what I did with the suitcase, will you put in a good word for me?"

"Why . . . yeah. Where—"

"I ate it," Vanning said, and retired to the couch, where he settled himself for a nap. Hatton gave him a long, hating look. The officers tore in—

They passed by the locker, after a casual glance inside. The X-rays revealed nothing, in walls, floor, ceiling, or articles of furniture. The other offices were searched, too. Vanning applauded the painstaking job.

In the end, Hatton gave up. There was nothing else he could do.

"I'll clap suit on you tomorrow," Vanning promised. "Same time I get a habeas corpus on MacIlson."

"Step to hell," Hatton growled.

" 'By now."

Vanning waited till his unwanted guests had departed. Then, chuckling quietly, he went to the locker and opened it.

The copper-colored egg that represented the suedette suitcase had vanished. Vanning groped inside the locker, finding nothing.

The significance of this didn't strike Vanning at first. He swung the cabinet around so that it faced the window. He looked again, with identical results.

The locker was empty.

Twenty-five thousand credits in negotiable ore bonds had disappeared.

Vanning started to sweat. He picked up the metal box and shook it. That didn't help. He carried it across the room and set it up in another corner, returning to search the floor with painstaking accuracy. *Holy—*

Hatton?

No. Vanning hadn't let the locker out of his sight from the time the police had entered till they left. An officer had swung open the cabinet's door, looked inside, and closed it again. After that the door had remained shut, till just now.

The bonds were gone.

So was the abnormal little creature Vanning had crushed. All of which meant—what?

Vanning approached the locker and closed it, clicking the latch into position. Then he reopened it, not really expecting that the copper-colored egg would reappear.

He was right. It didn't.

Vanning staggered to the visor and called Gallegher.

"Whatzit? Huh? Oh. What do you want?" The scientist's gaunt face appeared on the screen, rather the worse for wear. "I got a hangover. Can't use thiamin, either, I'm allergic to it. How'd your case come out?"

"Listen," Gallegher said urgently, "I put something inside that damn locker of yours and now it's gone."

"The locker? That's funny."

"No! The thing I put in it. A . . . a suitcase."

Gallegher shook his head thoughtfully. "You never know, do you? I remember once I made a—"

"The hell with that. I want that suitcase back!"

"An heirloom?" Gallegher suggested.

"No, there's money in it."

"Wasn't that a little foolish of you? There hasn't been a bank failure since 1999. Never suspected you were a miser, Vanning. Like to have the stuff around, so you can run it through your birdlike fingers, eh?"

"You're drunk."

"I'm *trying*," Gallegher corrected, "But I've built up an awful resistance over a period of years. It takes time. Your call's already set me back two and a half drinks. I must put an extension on the siphon, so I can teletalk and guzzle at the same time."

Vanning almost chattered incoherently into the mike. "My suitcase! What happened to it? I want it back."

"Well, I haven't got it."

"Can't you find out where it is?"

"Dunno. Tell me the details. I'll see what I can figure out."

Vanning complied, revising his story as caution prompted.

"O.K." Gallegher said at last, rather unwillingly. "I hate working out theories, but just as a favor. . . . My diagnosis will cost you fifty credits."

"What? Now listen—"

"Fifty credits," Gallegher repeated unflinchingly. "Or no prognosis."

"How do I know you can get it back for me?"

"Chances are I can't. Still, maybe . . . I'll have to go over to Mechanistra and use some of their machines. They charge a good bit, too. But I'll need forty-brain-power calculators—"

"O.K., O.K.!" Vanning growled. "Hop to it. I want that suitcase back."

"What interests me is that little bug you squashed. In fact, that's the only reason I'm tackling your problem. Life in the fourth dimension—" Gallegher trailed off, murmuring. His face faded from the screen. After a while Vanning broke the connection.

He reexamined the locker, finding nothing new. Yet the suedette suitcase had vanished from it, into thin air. Oh, hell!

Brooding over his sorrows, Vanning shrugged into a topcoat and dined ravenously at the Manhattan Roof. He felt very sorry for himself.

The next day he felt even sorrier. A call to Gallegher had given the blank signal, so Vanning had to mark time. About noon MacIlson dropped in. His nerves were shot.

"You took your time in springing me," he started immediately. "Well, what now? Have you got a drink anywhere around?"

"You don't need a drink," Vanning grunted. "You've got a skinful already, by the look of you. Run down to Florida and wait till this blows over."

"I'm sick of waiting. I'm going to South America. I want some credits."

"Wait'll I arrange to cash the bonds."

"I'll take the bonds. A fair half, as we agreed."

Vanning's eyes narrowed. "And walk out into the hands of the police? Sure."

MacIlson looked uncomfortable. "I'll admit I made a boner. But this time—no, I'll play smart now."

"You'll wait, you mean."

"There's a friend of mine on the roof parking lot, in a helicopter. I'll go up and slip him the bonds, and then I'll just walk out. The police won't find anything on me."

"I said no," Vanning repeated. "It's too dangerous."

"It's dangerous as things are. If they locate the bonds—"

"They won't."

"Where'd you hide 'em?"

"That's my business."

MacIlson glowered nervously. "Maybe. But they're in this building. You couldn't have finagled 'em out yesterday before the cops came. No use playing your luck too far. Did they use X-rays?"

"Yeah."

"Well, I heard Counsel Hatton's got a batch of experts going over the blueprints on this building. He'll find your safe. I'm getting out of here before he does."

Vanning patted the air. "You're hysterical. I've taken care of you, haven't I? Even though you almost screwed the whole thing up."

"Sure," MacIlson said, pulling at his lip. "But I—" He chewed a finger nail. "Oh, damn! I'm sitting on the edge of a volcano with termites under me. I can't stay here and wait till they find the bonds. They can't extradite me from South America—where I'm going, anyway."

"You're going to wait," Vanning said firmly. "That's your best chance."

There was suddenly a gun in MacIlson's hand. "You're going to give me half the bonds. Right now. I don't trust you a little bit. You figure you can stall me along—hell, get those bonds!"

"No," Vanning said.

"I'm not kidding."

"I know you aren't. I can't get the bonds."

"Eh? Why not?"

"Ever heard of a time lock?" Vanning asked, his eyes watchful. "You're right; I put the suitcase in a concealed safe. But I can't open that safe till a certain number of hours have passed."

"Mm-m." MacIlson pondered. "When—"

"Tomorrow."

"All right. You'll have the bonds for me then?"

"If you want them. But you'd better change your mind. It'd be safer."

For answer MacIlson grinned over his shoulder as he went out. Vanning sat motionless for a long time. He was, frankly, scared.

The trouble was, MacIlson was a manic-depressive type. He'd kill. Right now, he was cracking under the strain, and imagining himself a desperate fugitive. Well—precautions would be advisable.

Vanning called Gallegher again, but got no answer. He left a message on the recorder and thoughtfully looked into the locker again. It was empty, depressingly so.

———

That evening Gallegher let Vanning into his laboratory. The scientist looked both tired and drunk. He waved comprehensively toward a table, covered with scraps of paper.

"What a headache you gave me! If I'd known the principles behind that gadget, I'd have been afraid to tackle it. Sit down. Have a drink. Got the fifty credits?"

Silently Vanning handed over the coupons. Gallegher shoved them into Monstro. "Fine. Now—" He settled himself on the couch. "Now we start. The fifty-credit question."

"Can I get the suitcase back?"

"No," Gallegher said flatly. "At least, I don't see how it can be worked. It's in another spatiotemporal sector."

"Just what does that mean?"

"It means the locker works something like a telescope, only the thing isn't merely visual. The locker's a window, I figure. You can reach through it as well as look through it. It's an opening into Now plus x."

Vanning scowled. "So far you haven't said anything."

"So far all I've got is theory, and that's all I'm likely to get. Look. I was wrong originally. The things that went into the locker didn't appear in another space because there would have been a spatial constant. I mean, they wouldn't have got smaller. Size is size. Moving a one-inch cube from here to Mars wouldn't make it any larger or smaller."

"What about a different density in the surrounding medium? Wouldn't that crush an object?"

"Sure, and it'd stay squashed. It wouldn't return to its former size and shape when it was taken out of the locker again. X plus y never equal xy. But x times y—"

"So?"

"That's a pun," Gallegher broke off to explain. "The things we put in the locker went into time. Their time-rate remained constant, but not the spatial relationships. Two things can't occupy the same place at the same time. Ergo, your suitcase went into a different time. Now plus x. And what x represents I don't know, though I suspect a few million years."

Vanning looked dazed. "The suitcase is a million years in the future?"

"Dunno how far, but—I'd say plenty. I haven't enough factors to finish the equation. I reasoned by induction, mostly, and the results are screwy as hell. Einstein would have loved it. My theorem shows that the universe is expanding and contracting at the same time."

"What's that got to do—"

"Motion is relative," Gallegher continued inexorably. "That's a basic principle. Well, the universe *is* expanding, spreading out like a gas, but its component parts are shrinking at the same time. The *parts* don't actually grow, you know—not the suns and atoms. They just run away from the central point. Galloping off in all directions . . . where was I? Oh. Actually, the universe, taken as a unit, is shrinking."

"So it's shrinking. Where's my suitcase?"

"I told you. In the future. Deductive reasoning showed that. It's beautifully simple and logical. And it's quite impossible of proof, too. A hundred, a thousand, a million years ago the Earth—the universe—was larger than it is now. And it continues to contract. Sometime in the future the Earth will be just half as small as it is now. Only we won't notice it because the universe will be proportionately smaller."

Gallegher went on dreamily. "We put a workbench into the locker, so it emerged sometime in the future. The locker's an open window into a different time, as I told you. Well, the bench was affected by the conditions of that period. It shrank, after we gave it a few seconds to soak up the entropy or something. Do I mean entropy? Allah knows. Oh, well."

"It turned into a pyramid."

"Maybe there's geometric distortion, too. Or it might be a visual illusion. Perhaps we can't get the exact focus. I doubt if things will really look different in the future—except that they'll be smaller—but we're using a window into the fourth dimension. We're taking a pleat in time. It must be like looking through a prism. The alteration in size is real, but the shape and color are altered to our eyes by the fourth-dimensional prism."

"The whole point, then, is that my suitcase is in the future. Eh? But why did it disappear from the locker?"

"What about that little creature you squashed? Maybe he had pals. They wouldn't be visible till they came into the very narrow focus of the whatchmacallit, but—figure it out. Sometime in the future, in a hundred or a thousand or a million years, a suitcase suddenly appears out of thin air. One of our descendants investigates. You kill him. His pals come along and carry the suitcase away, out of range of the locker. In space it may be anywhere, and the time factor's an unknown quantity. Now plus x. It's a time locker. Well?"

"Hell!" Vanning exploded. "So that's all you can tell me? I'm supposed to chalk it up to profit and loss?"

"Uh-huh. Unless you want to crawl into the locker yourself after the suitcase. God knows where you'd come out, though. The composition of the air probably would have changed in a few thousand years. There might be other alterations, too."

"I'm not that crazy."

———

So there he was. The bonds were gone, beyond hope of redemption. Vanning could resign himself to that loss, once he knew the securities wouldn't fall into the hands of the police. But MacIlson was another matter, especially after a bullet spattered against the glassolex window of Vanning's office.

An interview with MacIlson had proved unsatisfactory. The defaulter was convinced that Vanning was trying to bilk him. He was removed forcibly, yelling threats. He'd go to the police—he'd confess—

Let him. There was no proof. The hell with him. But, for safety's sake, Vanning clapped an injunction on his quondam client.

It didn't land. MacIlson clipped the official on the jaw and fled. Now, Vanning suspected, he lurked in dark corners, armed, and anxious to commit suicide. Obviously a manic-depressive type.

Vanning took a certain malicious pleasure in demanding a couple of plainclothes men to act as his guards. Legally, he was within his rights, since his life had been threatened. Until MacIlson was under sufficient restriction, Vanning would be protected. And he made sure that his guards were two of the best shots on the Manhattan force.

He also found out that they had been told to keep their eyes peeled for the missing bonds and the suedette suitcase. Vanning televised Counsel Hatton and grinned at the screen.

"Any luck yet?"

"What do you mean?"

"My watchdogs. Your spies. They won't find the bonds, Hatton. Better call 'em off. Why make the poor devils do two jobs at once?"

"One job would be enough. Finding the evidence. If MacIlson drilled you, I wouldn't be too unhappy."

"Well, I'll see you in court," Vanning said. "You're prosecuting Watson, aren't you?"

"Yes. Are you waiving scop?"

"On the jurors? Sure. I've got this case in the bag."

"That's what you think," Hatton said, and broke the beam.

Chuckling, Vanning donned his topcoat, collected the guards, and headed for court. There was no sign of MacIlson —

Vanning won the case, as he had expected. He returned to his offices, collected a few unimportant messages from the switchboard girl, and walked toward his private suite. As he opened the door, he saw the suedette suitcase on the carpet in one corner.

He stopped, hand frozen on the latch. Behind him he could hear the heavy footsteps of the guards. Over his shoulder Vanning said, "Wait a minute," and dodged into the office, slamming and locking the door behind him. He caught the tail end of a surprised question.

The suitcase. There it was, unequivocally. And, quite as unequivocally, the two plainclothes men, after a very brief conference, were hammering on the door, trying to break it down.

Vanning turned green. He took a hesitant step forward, and then saw the locker, in the corner to which he had moved it. The time locker—

That was it. If he shoved the suitcase inside the locker, it would become unrecognizable. Even if it vanished again, that wouldn't matter.

What mattered was the vital importance of getting rid—immediately!—of incriminating evidence.

The door rocked on its hinges. Vanning scuttled toward the suitcase and picked it up. From the corner of his eye he saw movement.

In the air above him, a hand had appeared. It was the hand of a giant, with an immaculate cuff fading into emptiness. Its huge fingers were reaching down—

Vanning screamed and sprang away. He was too slow. The hand descended, and Vanning wriggled impotently against the palm.

The hand contracted into a fist. When it opened, what was left of Vanning dropped squashily to the carpet, which it stained.

The hand withdrew into nothingness. The door fell in and the plain-clothes men stumbled over it as they entered.

————

It didn't take long for Hatton and his cohorts to arrive. Still, there was little for them to do except clean up the mess. The suedette bag, containing twenty-five thousand credits in negotiable bonds, was carried off to a safer place. Vanning's body was scraped up and removed to the morgue. Photographers flashed pictures, fingerprint experts insufflated their white powder, X-ray men worked busily. It was all done with swift efficiency, so that within an hour the office was empty and the door sealed.

Thus there were no spectators to witness the advent of a gigantic hand that appeared from nothingness, groped around as though searching for something, and presently vanished once more—

The only person who could have thrown light on the matter was Gallegher, and his remarks were directed to Monstro, in the solitude of his laboratory. All he said was:

"So that's why that workbench materialized for a few minutes here yesterday. Hm-m-m. Now plus x—and x equals about a week. Still, why not? It's all relative. But—I never thought the universe was shrinking *that* fast!"

He relaxed on the couch and siphoned a double martini.

"Yeah, that's it," he murmured after a while. "*Whew!* I guess Vanning must have been the only guy who ever reached into the middle of next week and—killed himself! I think I'll get tight."

And he did.

# ARTHUR C. CLARKE

A sense of the cosmic underlies much of Arthur C. Clarke's fiction and manifests in a variety of forms: the computer-accelerated working out of prophecy in "The Nine Billion Names of God"; the sentient telecommunications network given the spark of life in "Dial F for Frankenstein"; and the mysterious extraterrestrial overseers guiding human destiny in the novelization of his screenplay for 2001: A Space Odyssey. Clarke's best-known story, 2001, and its sequels, 2010: Odyssey Two and 2061: Odyssey Three, represent the culmination of ideas on man's place in the universe introduced in his 1951 story, "The Sentinel," and elaborated more fully in Childhood's End, his elegiac novel on humankind's maturation as a species and ascent to a greater purpose in the universal scheme.

Clarke grounds the cosmic mystery of these stories in hard science. Degreed in physics and mathematics, Clarke was a contributor to numerous scientific journals and first proposed the idea for the geosynchronous orbiting communications satellite in 1945. Some of his best known work centers around the solution to a scientific problem or enigma. A Fall of Moondust tells of efforts to rescue a ship trapped under unusual conditions on the lunar surface. The Fountains of Paradise concerns the engineering problems encountered building an earth elevator to supply orbiting space stations. His Hugo- and Nebula Award–winning Rendezvous with Rama extrapolated his solid scientific inquiry into provocative new territory, telling of the human discovery of an apparently abandoned alien space ship and human attempts to understand its advanced scientific principles. Clarke's other novels include Prelude to Space, The Sands of Mars, Earthlight, Imperial Earth, and The Deep Range, a futuristic ex-

*ploration of undersea life in terms similar to his speculations on space travel. He has written the novels* Islands in the Sky *and* Dolphin Island *for young readers, and his short fiction has been collected in* Expedition to Earth, Reach for Tomorrow, Tales from the White Hart, The Wind from the Sun, *and others. His numerous books of nonfiction include his award-winning* The Exploration of Space, *and the autobiographical* Astounding Days. *Clarke was knighted in 2000.*

*The plot of traveling back to prehistoric times, particularly to the time of the dinosaur, followed soon after the first time travel stories were written. Arthur C. Clarke's cunningly plotted story extrapolates one of these encounters both from the present point of view and, at the same time, millions of years in the past. His story also gives rise to the idea that perhaps prehistoric creatures wouldn't be as afraid of man as one might think.*

# TIME'S ARROW

## ARTHUR C. CLARKE

THE RIVER WAS DEAD and the lake already dying when the monster had come down the dried-up watercourse and turned onto the desolate mud-flats. There were not many places where it was safe to walk, and even where the ground was hardest the great pistons of its feet sank a foot or more beneath the weight they carried. Sometimes it had paused, surveying the landscape with quick, birdlike movements of its head. Then it had sunk even deeper into the yielding soil, so that fifty million years later men could judge with some accuracy the duration of its halts.

For the waters had never returned, and the blazing sun had baked the mud to rock. Later still the desert had poured over all this land, sealing it beneath protecting layers of sand. And later—very much later— had come Man.

———

"Do you think," shouted Barton above the din, "that Professor Fowler became a palaeontologist because he likes playing with pneumatic drills? Or did he acquire the taste afterward?"

"Can't hear you!" yelled Davis, leaning on his shovel in a most professional manner. He glanced hopefully at his watch.

"Shall I tell him it's dinnertime? He can't wear a watch while he's drilling, so he won't know any better."

"I doubt if it will work," Barton shrieked. "He's got wise to us now and always adds an extra ten minutes. But it will make a change from this infernal digging."

With noticeable enthusiasm the two geologists downed tools and started to walk toward their chief. As they approached, he shut off the drill and relative silence descended, broken only by the throbbing of the compressor in the background.

"About time we went back to camp, Professor," said Davis, wrist-watch held casually behind his back. "You know what cook says if we're late."

Professor Fowler, M.A., F.R.S., F.G.S., mopped some, but by no means all, of the ocher dust from his forehead. He would have passed anywhere as a typical navvy, and the occasional visitors to the site seldom recognized the Vice-President of the Geological Society in the brawny, half-naked workman crouching over his beloved pneumatic drill.

It had taken nearly a month to clear the sandstone down to the sur-face of the petrified mud-flats. In that time several hundred square feet had been exposed, revealing a frozen snapshot of the past that was probably the finest yet discovered by palaeontology. Some scores of birds and reptiles had come here in search of the receding water, and left their footsteps as a perpetual monument eons after their bodies had perished. Most of the prints had been identified, but one—the largest of them all—was new to science. It belonged to a beast which must have weighed twenty or thirty tons: and Professor Fowler was following the fifty-million-year-old spoor with all the emotions of a big-game hunter tracking his prey. There was even a hope that he might yet overtake it; for the ground must have been treacherous when the unknown monster went this way and its bones might still be near at hand, marking the place where it had been trapped like so many creatures of its time.

Despite the mechanical aids available, the work was very tedious. Only the upper layers could be removed by the power tools, and the final uncovering had to be done by hand with the utmost care. Professor Fowler had good reason for his insistence that he alone should do the preliminary drilling, for a single slip might cause irreparable harm.

The three men were halfway back to the main camp, jolting over the rough road in the expedition's battered jeep, when Davis raised the question that had been intriguing the younger men ever since the work had begun.

"I'm getting a distinct impression," he said, "that our neighbors down the valley don't like us, though I can't imagine why. We're not in-terfering with them, and they might at least have the decency to invite us over."

"Unless, of course, it *is* a war research plant," added Barton, voicing a generally accepted theory.

"I don't think so," said Professor Fowler mildly. "Because it so happens that I've just had an invitation myself. I'm going there tomorrow."

————

If his bombshell failed to have the expected result, it was thanks to his staff's efficient espionage system. For a moment Davis pondered over this confirmation of his suspicions; then he continued with a slight cough:

"No one else has been invited, then?"

The Professor smiled at his pointed hint. "No," he said. "It's a strictly personal invitation. I know you boys are dying of curiosity but, frankly, I don't know any more about the place than you do. If I learn anything tomorrow, I'll tell you all about it. But at least we've found out who's running the establishment."

His assistants pricked up their ears. "Who is it?" asked Barton. "My guess was the Atomic Development Authority."

"You may be right," said the Professor. "At any rate, Henderson and Barnes are in charge."

This time the bomb exploded effectively; so much so that Davis nearly drove the jeep off the road—not that that made much difference, the road being what it was.

"Henderson and Barnes? In *this* god-forsaken hole?"

"That's right," said the Professor gaily. "The invitation was actually from Barnes. He apologized for not contacting us before, made the usual excuses, and wondered if I could drop in for a chat."

"Did he say what they are doing?"

"No; not a hint."

"Barnes and Henderson?" said Barton thoughtfully. "I don't know much about them except that they're physicists. What's their particular racket?"

"They're *the* experts on low-temperature physics," answered Davis. "Henderson was Director of the Cavendish for years. He wrote a lot of letters to *Nature* not so long ago. If I remember rightly, they were all about Helium II."

Barton, who didn't like physicists and said so whenever possible, was not impressed. "I don't even know what Helium II is," he said smugly. "What's more, I'm not at all sure that I want to."

This was intended for Davis, who had once taken a physics degree in, as he explained, a moment of weakness. The "moment" had lasted for several years before he had drifted into geology by rather devious routes, and he was always harking back to his first love.

"It's a form of liquid helium that only exists at a few degrees above absolute zero. It's got the most extraordinary properties—but, as far as I can see, none of them can explain the presence of two leading physicists in this corner of the globe."

They had now arrived at the camp, and Davis brought the jeep to its normal crash-halt in the parking space. He shook his head in annoyance as he bumped into the truck ahead with slightly more violence than usual.

"These tires are nearly through. Have the new ones come yet?"

"Arrived in the 'copter this morning, with a despairing note from Andrews hoping that you'd make them last a full fortnight this time."

"Good! I'll get them fitted this evening."

The Professor had been walking a little ahead; now he dropped back to join his assistants.

"You needn't have hurried, Jim," he said glumly. "It's corned beef again."

It would be most unfair to say that Barton and Davis did less work because the Professor was away. They probably worked a good deal harder than usual, since the native laborers required twice as much supervision in the Chief's absence. But there was no doubt that they managed to find time for a considerable amount of extra talking.

Ever since they had joined Professor Fowler, the two young geologists had been intrigued by the strange establishment five miles away down the valley. It was clearly a research organization of some type, and Davis had identified the tall stacks of an atomic-power unit. That, of course, gave no clue to the work that was proceeding, but it did indicate its importance. There were still only a few thousand turbo-piles in the world, and they were all reserved for major projects.

There were dozens of reasons why two great scientists might have hidden themselves in this place: most of the more hazardous atomic research was carried out as far as possible from civilization, and some had been abandoned altogether until laboratories in space could be set up. Yet it seemed odd that this work, whatever it was, should be carried out so close to what had now become the most important center of geological research in the world. It might, of course, be no more than a coincidence; certainly the physicists had never shown any interest in their compatriots near at hand.

Davis was carefully chipping round one of the great footprints, while Barton was pouring liquid perspex into those already uncovered so that they would be preserved from harm in the transparent plastic. They were working in a somewhat absentminded manner, for each was unconsciously listening for the sound of the jeep. Professor Fowler had promised to collect them when he returned from his visit, for the other vehicles were in use elsewhere and they did not relish a two-mile walk back to camp in the broiling sun. Moreover, they wanted to have any news as soon as possible.

"How many people," said Barton suddenly, "do you think they have over there?"

Davis straightened himself up. "Judging from the buildings, not more than a dozen or so."

"Then it might be a private affair, not an ADA project at all."

"Perhaps, though it must have pretty considerable backing. Of course, Henderson and Barnes could get that on their reputations alone."

"That's where the physicists score," said Barton. "They've only got to convince some war department that they're on the track of a new weapon, and they can get a couple of million without any trouble."

He spoke with some bitterness; for, like most scientists, he had strong views on this subject. Barton's views, indeed, were even more definite than usual, for he was a Quaker and had spent the last year of the War arguing with not-unsympathetic tribunals.

The conversation was interrupted by the roar and clatter of the jeep, and the two men ran over to meet the Professor.

"Well?" they cried simultaneously.

Professor Fowler looked at them thoughtfully, his expression giving no hint of what was in his mind. "Had a good day?" he said at last.

"Come off it, Chief!" protested Davis. "Tell us what you've found out."

The Professor climbed out of the seat and dusted himself down. "I'm sorry, boys," he said with some embarrassment, "I can't tell you a thing, and that's flat."

There were two united wails of protest, but he waved them aside. "I've had a very interesting day, but I've had to promise not to say anything about it. Even now I don't know exactly what's going on, but it's something pretty revolutionary—as revolutionary, perhaps, as atomic power. But Dr. Henderson is coming over tomorrow; see what you can get out of him."

For a moment, both Barton and Davis were so overwhelmed by the sense of anticlimax that neither spoke. Barton was the first to recover. "Well, surely there's a reason for this sudden interest in our activities?"

The Professor thought this over for a moment. "Yes; it wasn't entirely a social call," he admitted. "They think I may be able to help them. Now, no more questions, unless you want to walk back to camp!"

———

Dr. Henderson arrived on the site in the middle of the afternoon. He was a stout, elderly man, dressed rather incongruously in a dazzling white laboratory smock and very little else. Though the garb was eccentric, it was eminently practical in so hot a climate.

Davis and Barton were somewhat distant when Professor Fowler introduced them; they still felt that they had been snubbed and were determined that their visitor should understand their feelings. But Henderson was so obviously interested in their work that they soon thawed, and the Professor left them to show him round the excavations while he went to supervise the natives.

The physicist was greatly impressed by the picture of the world's remote past that lay exposed before his eyes. For almost an hour the two geologists took him over the workings yard by yard, talking of the creatures who had gone this way and speculating about future discoveries. The track which Professor Fowler was following now lay in a wide trench running away from the main excavation, for he had dropped all other work to investigate it. At its end the trench was no longer continuous: to save time, the Professor had begun to sink pits along the line of the footprints. The last sounding had missed altogether, and further digging had shown that the great reptile had made a sudden change of course.

"This is the most interesting bit," said Barton to the slightly wilting physicist. "You remember those earlier places where it had stopped for a moment to have a look around? Well, here it seems to have spotted something and has gone off in a new direction at a run, as you can see from the spacing."

"I shouldn't have thought such a brute *could* run."

"Well, it was probably a pretty clumsy effort, but you can cover quite a bit of ground with a fifteen-foot stride. We're going to follow it as far as we can. We may even find what it was chasing. I think the Professor has hopes of discovering a trampled battlefield with the bones of the victim still around. That would make everyone sit up."

Dr. Henderson smiled. "Thanks to Walt Disney, I can picture the scene rather well."

Davis was not very encouraging. "It was probably only the missus banging the dinner gong," he said. "The most infuriating part of our work is the way everything can peter out when it gets most exciting. The strata have been washed away, or there's been an earthquake—or, worse still, some silly fool has smashed up the evidence because he didn't recognize its value."

Henderson nodded in agreement. "I can sympathize with you," he said. "That's where the physicist has the advantage. He knows he'll get the answer eventually, if there is one."

He paused rather diffidently, as if weighing his words with great care. "It would save you a lot of trouble, wouldn't it, if you could actually *see* what took place in the past, without having to infer it by these laborious and uncertain methods. You've been a couple of months following these footsteps for a hundred yards, and they may lead nowhere for all your trouble."

There was a long silence. Then Barton spoke in a very thoughtful voice.

"Naturally, Doctor, we're rather curious about your work," he began. "Since Professor Fowler won't tell us anything, we've done a good deal of speculating. Do you really mean to say that—"

The physicist interrupted him rather hastily. "Don't give it any more thought," he said. "I was only daydreaming. As for our work, it's a very long way from completion, but you'll hear all about it in due course. We're not secretive—but, like everyone working in a new field, we don't want to say anything until we're sure of our ground. Why, if any other palaeontologists came near this place, I bet Professor Fowler would chase them away with a pick-axe!"

"That's not quite true," smiled Davis. "He'd be much more likely to set them to work. But I see your point of view; let's hope we don't have to wait too long."

———

That night, much midnight oil was burned at the main camp. Barton was frankly skeptical, but Davis had already built up an elaborate super-structure of theory around their visitor's remarks.

"It would explain so many things," he said. "First of all, their pres-ence in this place, which otherwise doesn't make sense at all. We know the ground level here to within an inch for the last hundred million years, and we can date any event with an accuracy of better than one per cent. There's not a spot on Earth that's had its past worked out in such detail—it's the obvious place for an experiment like this!"

"But do you think it's even theoretically possible to build a machine that can see into the past?"

"I can't imagine how it could be done. But I daren't say it's impossible—especially to men like Henderson and Barnes."

"Hmmm. Not a very convincing argument. Is there any way we can hope to test it? What about those letters to *Nature*?"

"I've sent to the College Library; we should have them by the end of the week. There's always some continuity in a scientist's work, and they may give us some valuable clues."

But at first they were disappointed; indeed, Henderson's letters only increased the confusion: As Davis had remembered, most of them had been about the extraordinary properties of Helium II.

"It's really fantastic stuff," said Davis. "If a liquid behaved like this at normal temperatures, everyone would go mad. In the first place, it hasn't any viscosity at all. Sir George Darwin once said that if you had an ocean of Helium II, ships could sail in it without any engines. You'd give them a push at the beginning of their voyage and let them run into buffers on the other side. There'd be one snag, though; long before that happened the stuff would have climbed straight up the hull and the whole outfit would have sunk—gurgle, gurgle, gurgle . . . "

"Very amusing," said Barton, "but what the heck has this to do with your precious theory?"

"Not much," admitted Davis. "However, there's more to come. It's possible to have two streams of Helium II flowing in opposite directions *in the same tube*—one stream going through the other, as it were."

"That must take a bit of explaining; it's almost as bad as an object moving in two directions at once. I suppose there *is* an explanation, something to do with Relativity, I bet."

Davis was reading carefully. "The explanation," he said slowly, "is very complicated and I don't pretend to understand it fully. But it depends on the fact that liquid helium can have *negative* entropy under certain conditions."

"As I never understood what positive entropy is, I'm not much wiser."

"Entropy is a measure of the heat distribution of the Universe. At the beginning of time, when all energy was concentrated in the suns, entropy was a minimum. It will reach its maximum when everything's at a uniform temperature and the Universe is dead. There will still be plenty of heat around, but it won't be usable."

"Whyever not?"

"Well, all the water in a perfectly flat ocean won't run a hydro-electric plant—but quite a little lake up in the hills will do the trick. You must have a difference in level."

"I get the idea. Now I come to think of it, didn't someone once call entropy 'Time's Arrow'?"

"Yes—Eddington, I believe. Any kind of clock you care to mention— a pendulum, for instance—might just as easily run forward as backward. But entropy is a strictly one-way affair—it's always increasing with the passage of time. Hence the expression, 'Time's Arrow.'"

"Then *negative* entropy—my gosh!"

For a moment the two men looked at each other. Then Barton asked in a rather subdued voice: "What does Henderson say about it?"

"I'll quote from his last letter: 'The discovery of negative entropy introduces quite new and revolutionary conceptions into our picture of the physical world. Some of these will be examined in a further communication.'"

"And are they?"

"That's the snag: there's no 'further communication.' From that you can guess two alternatives. First, the Editor of *Nature* may have declined to publish the letter. I think we can rule that one out. Second, the consequences may have been *so* revolutionary that Henderson never did write a further report."

"Negative entropy—negative time," mused Barton. "It seems fantastic; yet it might be theoretically possible to build some sort of device that could see into the past. . . ."

"I know what we'll do," said Davis suddenly. "We'll tackle the Professor about it and watch his reactions. Now I'm going to bed before I get brain fever."

That night Davis did not sleep well. He dreamed that he was walking along a road that stretched in both directions as far as the eye could see. He had been walking for miles before he came to the signpost, and when he reached it he found that it was broken and the two arms were revolving idly in the wind. As they turned, he could read the words they carried. One said simply: To the Future; the other: To the Past.

————————

They learned nothing from Professor Fowler, which was not surprising; next to the Dean, he was the best poker player in the College. He regarded his slightly fretful assistants with no trace of emotion while Davis trotted out his theory.

When the young man had finished, he said quietly, "I'm going over again tomorrow, and I'll tell Henderson about your detective work. Maybe he'll take pity on you; maybe he'll tell me a bit more, for that matter. Now let's go to work."

Davis and Barton found it increasingly difficult to take a great deal of interest in their own work while their minds were filled with the enigma so near at hand. Nevertheless they continued conscientiously, though ever and again they paused to wonder if all their labor might not be in vain. If it were, they would be the first to rejoice. Supposing one could see into the past and watch history unfolding itself, back to the dawn of time! All the great secrets of the past would be revealed: one could watch the coming of life on the Earth, and the whole story of evolution from amoeba to man.

No; it was too good to be true. Having decided this, they would go back to their digging and scraping for another half-hour until the thought would come: but what if it *were* true? And then the whole cycle would begin all over again.

When Professor Fowler returned from his second visit, he was a subdued and obviously shaken man. The only satisfaction his assistants could get from him was the statement that Henderson had listened to their theory and complimented them on their powers of deduction.

That was all; but in Davis's eyes it clinched the matter, though Barton was still doubtful. In the weeks that followed, he too began to waver, until at last they were both convinced that the theory was correct. For Professor Fowler was spending more and more of his time with Henderson and Barnes; so much so that they sometimes did not see him for days. He had almost lost interest in the excavations, and had delegated all responsibility to Barton, who was now able to use the big pneumatic drill to his heart's content.

They were uncovering several yards of footprints a day, and the spacing showed that the monster had now reached its utmost speed and was advancing in great leaps as if nearing its victim. In a few days they might reveal the evidence of some eon-old tragedy, preserved by a miracle and brought down the ages for the observation of man. Yet all this seemed very unimportant now, for it was clear from the Professor's hints and his general air of abstraction that the secret research was nearing its climax. He had told them as much, promising that in a very few days, if all went well, their wait would be ended. But beyond that he would say nothing.

Once or twice Henderson had paid them a visit, and they could see that he was now laboring under a considerable strain. He obviously wanted to talk about his work, but was not going to do so until the final tests had been completed. They could only admire his self-control and wish that it would break down. Davis had a distant impression that the elusive Barnes was mainly responsible for his secrecy; he had something of a reputation for not publishing work until it had been checked and double-checked. If these experiments were as important as they believed, his caution was understandable, however infuriating.

Henderson had come over early that morning to collect the Professor, and as luck would have it, his car had broken down on the primitive road. This was unfortunate for Davis and Barton, who would have to walk to camp for lunch, since Professor Fowler was driving Henderson back in the jeep. They were quite prepared to put up with this if their wait was indeed coming to an end, as the others had more than half-hinted.

They had stood talking by the side of the jeep for some time before the two older scientists had driven away. It was a rather strained parting, for each side knew what the other was thinking. Finally Barton, as usual the most outspoken, remarked:

"Well, Doc, if this *is* Der Tag, I hope everything works properly. I'd like a photograph of a brontosaurus as a souvenir."

This sort of banter had been thrown at Henderson so often that he now took it for granted. He smiled without much mirth and replied, "I don't promise anything. It may be the biggest flop ever."

Davis moodily checked the tire pressure with the toe of his boot. It was a new set, he noticed, with an odd zigzag pattern he hadn't seen before.

"Whatever happens, we hope you'll tell us. Otherwise, we're going to break in one night and find out just what you're up to."

Henderson laughed. "You'll be a pair of geniuses if you can learn anything from our present lash-up. But, if all goes well, we may be having a little celebration by nightfall."

"What time do you expect to be back, Chief?"

"Somewhere around four. I don't want you to have to walk back for tea."

"O.K.—here's hoping!"

The machine disappeared in a cloud of dust, leaving two very thoughtful geologists standing by the roadside. Then Barton shrugged his shoulders.

"The harder we work," he said, "the quicker the time will go. Come along!"

———

The end of the trench, where Barton was working with the power drill, was now more than a hundred yards from the main excavation. Davis was putting the final touches to the last prints to be uncovered. They were now very deep and widely spaced, and looking along them, one could see quite clearly where the great reptile had changed its course and started, first to run, and then to hop like an enormous kangaroo. Barton wondered what it must have felt like to see such a creature bearing down upon one with the speed of an express; then he realized that if their guess was true this was exactly what they might soon be seeing.

By mid-afternoon they had uncovered a record length of track. The ground had become softer, and Barton was roaring ahead so rapidly that he had almost forgotten his other preoccupations. He had left Davis yards behind, and both men were so busy that only the pangs of hunger reminded them when it was time to finish. Davis was the first to notice that it was later than they had expected, and he walked over to speak to his friend.

"It's nearly half-past four!" he said when the noise of the drill had died away. "The Chief's late—I'll be mad if he's had tea before collecting us."

"Give him another half-hour," said Barton. "I can guess what's happened. They've blown a fuse or something and it's upset their schedule."

Davis refused to be placated. "I'll be darned annoyed if we've got to walk back to camp again. Anyway, I'm going up the hill to see if there's any sign of him."

He left Barton blasting his way through the soft rock, and climbed the low hill at the side of the old riverbed. From here one could see far down the valley, and the twin stacks of the Henderson-Barnes laboratory were clearly visible against the drab landscape. But there was no sign of the moving dust-cloud that would be following the jeep: the Professor had not yet started for home.

Davis gave a snort of disgust. There was a two-mile walk ahead of them, after a particularly tiring day, and to make matters worse they'd now be late for tea. He decided not to wait any longer, and was already walking down the hill to rejoin Barton when something caught his eye and he stopped to look down the valley.

Around the two stacks, which were all he could see of the laboratory, a curious haze not unlike a heat tremor was playing. They must be hot, he knew, but surely not *that* hot. He looked more carefully, and saw to his amazement that the haze covered a hemisphere that must be almost a quarter of a mile across.

And, quite suddenly, it exploded. There was no light, no blinding flash; only a ripple that spread abruptly across the sky and then was gone. The haze had vanished—and so had the two great stacks of the power-house.

Feeling as though his legs had turned suddenly to water, Davis slumped down upon the hilltop and stared open-mouthed along the valley. A sense of overwhelming disaster swept into his mind; as in a dream, he waited for the explosion to reach his ears.

It was not impressive when it came; only a dull, long-drawn-out whooooooosh! that died away swiftly in the still air. Half unconsciously, Davis noticed that the chatter of the drill had also stopped; the explosion must have been louder than he thought for Barton to have heard it too.

The silence was complete. Nothing moved anywhere as far as his eye could see in the whole of that empty, barren landscape. He waited until his strength returned; then, half running, he went unsteadily down the hill to rejoin his friend.

Barton was half sitting in the trench with his head buried in his hands. He looked up as Davis approached; and although his features were obscured by dust and sand, the other was shocked at the expression in his eyes.

"So you heard it too!" Davis said. "I think the whole lab's blown up. Come along, for heaven's sake!"

"Heard what?" said Barton dully.

Davis stared at him in amazement. Then he realized that Barton could not possibly have heard any sound while he was working with the drill. The sense of disaster deepened with a rush; he felt like a character in some Greek tragedy, helpless before an implacable doom.

Barton rose to his feet. His face was working strangely, and Davis saw that he was on the verge of breakdown. Yet, when he spoke, his words were surprisingly calm.

"What fools we were!" he said. "How Henderson must have laughed at us when we told him that he was trying to *see* into the past!"

Mechanically, Davis moved to the trench and stared at the rock that was seeing the light of day for the first time in fifty million years. Without much emotion, now, he traced again the zigzag pattern he had first noticed a few hours before. It had sunk only a little way into the mud, as if when it was formed the jeep had been traveling at its utmost speed.

No doubt it had been; for in one place the shallow tire marks had been completely obliterated by the monster's footprints. They were now very deep indeed, as if the great reptile was about to make the final leap upon its desperately fleeing prey.

# JACK FINNEY

Jack Finney (1911–1995) was fascinated with the idea of time travel, and used it in many of his stories. Born in Milwaukee, Wisconsin with the given name John Finney, he was renamed Walter Braden Finney in honor of his father, although the nickname Jack remained with him throughout his life. Well after he graduated from Knox College, his first short story, "The Widow's Walk," won a contest sponsored by Ellery Queen's Mystery Magazine in 1946. In addition to publishing novels and short stories, he also contributed articles to a number of popular periodicals like Cosmopolitan, Good Housekeeping, and The Saturday Evening Post. He moved to Marin County, California, in the early 1950s with his wife, Marguerite Guest, and their two children. Several of Finney's novels were adapted for the big screen, including the science-fiction cult classic Invasion of the Body Snatchers, the comedy novel Good Neighbor Sam, and his classic time-travel romance Time and Again. Finney died of pneumonia and emphysema in 1995 at age 84 not long after finishing the long-awaited sequel, From Time to Time.

"I'm Scared" is a Finney classic, a tale of an ordinary man (as the subjects of his stories often were) stumbling upon a terrifying bit of spatial horror, which leads him to the only inescapable conclusion. As with much speculative fiction during the 1950s, the emphasis wasn't so much on technical explanations or scientific theories, more on Finney's evocation of mood and setting, and that perhaps is why its quiet sense of terror is so completely intertwined with the theme of the story—that there is no explanation for why the events in this story are happening.

# I'M SCARED

## JACK FINNEY

I'M VERY BADLY SCARED, not so much for myself—I'm a gray-haired man of sixty-six, after all—but for you and everyone else who has not yet lived out his life. For I believe that certain dangerous things have recently begun to happen in the world. They are noticed here and there, idly discussed, then dismissed and forgotten. Yet I am convinced that unless these occurrences are recognized for what they are, the world will be plunged into a nightmare. Judge for yourself.

One evening last winter I came home from a chess club to which I belong. I'm a widower; I live alone in a small but comfortable three-room apartment overlooking Fifth Avenue. It was still fairly early, and I switched on a lamp beside my leather easy chair, picked up a murder mystery I'd been reading and turned on the radio; I did not, I'm sorry to say, notice which station it was tuned to.

The tubes warmed, and the music of an accordion—faint at first, then louder—came from the loudspeaker. Since it was good music for reading, I adjusted the volume control and began to read.

Now I want to be absolutely factual and accurate about this, and I do not claim that I paid close attention to the radio. But I do know that presently the music stopped and an audience applauded. Then a man's voice, chuckling and pleased with the applause, said, "All right, all right," but the applause continued for several more seconds. During that time the voice once more chuckled appreciatively, then firmly repeated, "All right," and the applause died down. "That was Alec Somebody-or-other," the radio voice said, and I went back to my book.

But I soon became aware of this middle-aged voice again, perhaps a change of tone as he turned to a new subject caught my attention. "And now, Miss Ruth Greeley," he was saying, "of Trenton, New Jersey. Miss Greeley is a pianist; that right?" A girl's voice, timid and barely audible, said, "That's right, Major Bowes." The man's voice—and now I recognized his familiar singsong delivery—said, "And what are you going to play?"

The girl replied, " 'La Paloma.' " The man repeated it after her, as an announcement: " 'La Paloma.' " There was a pause, than an introductory chord sounded from a piano, and I resumed my reading.

As the girl played, I was half aware that her style was mechanical, her rhythm defective, perhaps she was nervous. Then my attention was fully aroused once more by a gong which sounded suddenly. For a few notes more the girl continued to play falteringly, not sure what to do. The gong sounded jarringly again, the playing abruptly stopped and there was a restless murmur from the audience. "All right, all right," said the familiar voice, and I realized I'd been expecting this, knowing it would say just that. The audience quieted, and the voice began, "Now . . . "

The radio went dead. For the smallest fraction of a second no sound issued from it but its own mechanical hum. Then a completely different program came from the loudspeaker; the recorded voices of Bing Crosby and his son were singing the concluding bars of "Sam's Song," a favorite of mine. So I returned once more to my reading, wondering vaguely what had happened to the other program, but not actually thinking about it until I finished my book and began to get ready for bed.

Then, undressing in my bedroom, I remembered that Major Bowes was dead. Years had passed, half a decade, since that dry chuckle and familiar, "All right, all right," had been heard in the nation's living rooms.

————

Well, what does one do when the apparently impossible occurs? It simply made a good story to tell friends, and more than once I was asked if I'd recently heard Moran and Mack, a pair of radio comedians popular some twenty-five years ago, or Floyd Gibbons, an old-time news broadcaster. And there were other joking references to my crystal radio set.

But one man—this was at a lodge meeting the following Thursday— listened to my story with utter seriousness, and when I had finished he told me a queer little story of his own. He is a thoughtful, intelligent man, and as I listened I was not frightened, but puzzled at what seemed to be a connecting link, a common denominator, between this story and the odd behavior of my radio. Since I am retired and have plenty of time, I took the trouble, the following day, of making a two-hour train trip to Connecticut in order to verify the story firsthand. I took detailed notes, and the story appears in my files now as follows:

*Case 2. Louis Trachnor, coal and wood dealer, R.F.D. 1, Danbury, Connecticut, age fifty-four.*

On July 20, 1950, Mr. Trachnor told me, he walked out on the front porch of his house about six o'clock in the morning. Running from the eaves of his house to the floor of the porch was a streak of gray paint, still damp. "It was about the width of an eight-inch brush," Mr. Trachnor told me, "and it looked like hell because the house was white. I figured some kids did it in the night for a joke, but if they did, they had to get a ladder up to the eaves and you wouldn't figure they'd go to that much trouble. It wasn't smeared, either; it was a careful job, a nice even stripe straight down the front of the house."

Mr. Trachnor got a ladder and cleaned off the gray paint with turpentine.

In October of that same year Mr. Trachnor painted his house. "The white hadn't held up so good, so I painted it gray. I got to the front last and finished about five one Saturday afternoon. Next morning when I came out I saw a streak of white right down the front of the house. I figured it was the damn kids again because it was the same place as before. But when I looked close, I saw it wasn't new paint; it was the old white I'd painted over. Somebody had done a nice careful job of cleaning off the new paint in a long stripe about eight inches wide right down from the eaves! Now who the hell would go to that trouble? I just can't figure it out."

Do you see the link between this story and mine? Suppose for a moment that something had happened, on each occasion, to disturb briefly the orderly progress of time. That seemed to have happened in my case; for a matter of some seconds I apparently heard a radio broadcast that had been made years before. Suppose, then, that no one had touched Mr. Trachnor's house but himself; that he had painted his house in October, but that through some fantastic mix-up in time, a portion of that paint appeared on his house the previous summer. Since he had cleaned the paint off, at that time, a broad stripe of new gray paint was missing *after* he painted his house in the fall.

I would be lying, however, if I said I really believed this. It was merely an intriguing speculation, and I told both these little stories to friends, simply as curious anecdotes. I am a sociable person, see a good many people, and occasionally I heard other odd stories in response to mine.

Someone would nod and say, "Reminds me of something I heard recently . . . " and I would have one more to add to my collection. A man on Long Island received a telephone call from his sister in New York one Friday evening. She insists that she did not make this call until the following Monday, three days later. At the Forty-fifth Street branch of the Chase National Bank, I was shown a check deposited the day before it was written. A letter was delivered on East Sixty-eighth Street in New York City, just seventeen minutes after it was dropped into a mailbox on the main street of Green River, Wyoming.

And so on, and so on; my stories were now in demand at parties, and I told myself that collecting and verifying them was a hobby. But the day I heard Julia Eisenberg's story, I knew it was no longer that.

*Case 17. Julia Eisenberg, office worker, New York City, age thirty-one.*

Miss Eisenberg lives in a small walk-up apartment in Greenwich Village. I talked to her there after a chess-club friend who lives in her neighborhood had repeated to me a somewhat garbled version of her story, which was told to him by the doorman of the building he lives in.

In October 1947, about eleven at night, Miss Eisenberg left her apartment to walk to the drugstore for toothpaste. On her way back, not far from her apartment, a large black and white dog ran up to her and put his front paws on her chest.

"I made the mistake of petting him," Miss Eisenberg told me, "and from then on he simply wouldn't leave. When I went into the lobby of my building, I actually had to push him away to get the door closed. I felt sorry for him, poor hound, and a little guilty because he was still sitting at the door an hour later when I looked out my front window."

This dog remained in the neighborhood for three days, discovering and greeting Miss Eisenberg with wild affection each time she appeared on the street. "When I'd get on the bus in the morning to go to work, he'd sit on the curb looking after me in the most mournful way, poor thing. I wanted to take him in, but I knew he'd never go home then, and I was afraid whoever owned him would be sorry to lose him. No one in the neighborhood knew whom he belonged to, and finally he disappeared."

Two years later a friend gave Miss Eisenberg a three-week-old puppy. "My apartment is really too small for a dog, but he was such a darling I couldn't resist. Well, he grew up into a nice big dog who ate more than I did."

Since the neighborhood was quiet and the dog well behaved, Miss Eisenberg usually unleashed him when she walked him at night, for he never strayed far. "One night—I'd last seen him sniffing around in the dark a few doors down—I called to him and he didn't come back. And he never did; I never saw him again.

"Now our street is a solid wall of brownstone buildings on both sides with locked doors and no areaways. He *couldn't* have disappeared like that, he just *couldn't*. But he did."

Miss Eisenberg hunted for her dog for many days afterward, inquired of neighbors, put ads in the papers, but she never found him. "Then one night I was getting ready for bed, I happened to glance out the front window down at the street, and suddenly I remembered something I'd forgotten all about. I remembered the dog I'd chased away over two years before." Miss Eisenberg looked at me for a moment, then she said flatly, "It was the same dog. If you own a dog you know him, you can't be mistaken, and I tell you it was the same dog. Whether it makes sense or not, my dog was lost—I chased him away—two years before he was born."

She began to cry silently, the tears running down her face. "Maybe you think I'm crazy, or a little lonely and overly sentimental about a dog. But you're wrong." She brushed at her tears with a handkerchief. "I'm a well-balanced person, as much as anyone is these days, at least, and I tell you I *know* what happened."

It was at that moment, sitting in Miss Eisenberg's neat, shabby living room, that I realized fully that the consequences of these odd little incidents could be something more than merely intriguing; that they might, quite possibly, be tragic. It was in that moment that I began to be afraid.

I have spent the last eleven months discovering and tracking down these strange occurrences, and I am astonished and frightened at how many there are. I am astonished and frightened at how much more frequently they are happening now, and—I hardly know how to express this—at their increasing power to tear human lives tragically apart. This is an example, selected almost at random, of the increasing strength of— whatever it is that is happening in the world.

*Case 34. Paul V. Kerch, accountant, the Bronx, age thirty-one.*

On a bright clear Sunday afternoon, I met an unsmiling family of three at their Bronx apartment: Mr. Kerch, a chunky, darkly good-looking young man; his wife, a pleasant-faced dark-haired woman in her late twenties, whose attractiveness was marred by circles under her eyes; and their son, a nice-looking boy of six or seven. After introductions, the boy was sent to his room at the back of the house to play.

"All right," Mr. Kerch said wearily then and walked toward a bookcase, "let's get at it. You said on the phone that you know the story in general." It was half a question, half a statement.

"Yes," I said.

He took a book from the top shelf and removed some photographs from it. "There are the pictures." He sat down on the davenport beside me with the photographs in his hand. "I own a pretty good camera. I'm a fair amateur photographer, and I have a darkroom setup in the kitchen; do my own developing. Two weeks ago we went down to Central Park." His voice was a tired monotone, as though this was a story he'd repeated many times, aloud and in his own mind. "It was nice, like today, and the kid's grandmothers have been pestering us for pictures, so I took a whole roll of films, pictures of all of us. My camera can be set up and focused and it will snap the picture automatically a few seconds later, giving me time to get around in front of it and get in the picture myself."

There was a tired, hopeless look in his eyes as he handed me all but one of the photographs. "These are the first ones I took," he said. The photographs were all fairly large, perhaps seven by three and a half inches, and I examined them closely.

They were ordinary enough, very sharp and detailed, and each showed the family of three in various smiling poses. Mr. Kerch wore a light business suit, his wife had on a dark dress and a cloth coat and the boy wore a dark suit with knee-length pants. In the background stood a tree with bare branches. I glanced up at Mr. Kerch, signifying that I had finished my study of the photographs.

"The last picture," he said, holding it in his hand ready to give to me, "I took exactly like the others. We agreed on the pose, I set the camera, walked around in front, and joined my family. Monday night I developed the whole roll. This is what came out on the last negative." He handed me the photograph.

For an instant it seemed to me like merely one more photograph in the group; then I saw the difference. Mr. Kerch looked much the same, bareheaded and grinning broadly, but he wore an entirely different suit. The boy, standing beside him, wore long pants, was a good three inches taller, obviously older, but equally obviously the same boy. The woman was an entirely different person. Dressed smartly, her light hair catching the sun, she was very pretty and attractive. She was smiling into the camera and holding Mr. Kerch's hand.

I looked up at him. "Who is this?"

Wearily, Mr. Kerch shook his head. "I don't know," he said suddenly, then exploded: "I don't *know!* I've never seen her in my life!" He turned to look at his wife, but she would not return his glance, and he turned back to me, shrugging. "Well, there you have it," he said. "The whole story." And he stood up, thrusting both hands into his trouser pockets and began to pace about the room, glancing often at his wife, talking to *her* actually, though he addressed his words to me. "So who is she? How could the camera have snapped that picture? I've never seen that woman in my life!"

I glanced at the photograph again, then bent closer. "The trees here are in full bloom," I said. Behind the solemn-faced boy, the grinning man and smiling woman, the trees of Central Park were in full summer leaf.

Mr. Kerch nodded. "I know," he said bitterly. "And you know what *she* says?" he burst out, glaring at his wife. "She says that *is* my wife in the photograph, my *new* wife a couple of years from now! God!" He snapped both hands down on his head. "The ideas a woman can get!"

"What do you mean?" I glanced at Mrs. Kerch, but she ignored me, remaining silent, her lips tight.

Kerch shrugged hopelessly. "She says that photograph shows how things will be a couple of years from now. She'll be dead or"—he hesitated, then said the word bitterly—"divorced, and I'll have our son and be married to the woman in the picture."

We both looked at Mrs. Kerch, waiting until she was obliged to speak.

"Well, if it isn't so," she said, shrugging a shoulder, "then tell me what that picture does mean."

Neither of us could answer that, and a few minutes later I left. There was nothing much I could say to the Kerches; certainly I couldn't mention my conviction that, whatever the explanation of the last photograph their married life was over? . . .

*Case 72. Lieutenant Alfred Eichler, New York Police Department, age thirty-three.*

In the late evening of January 9, 1951, two policemen found a revolver lying just off a gravel path near an East Side entrance to Central Park. The gun was examined for fingerprints at the police laboratory and several were found. One bullet had been fired from the revolver and the police fired another which was studied and classified by a ballistics expert. The fingerprints were checked and found in police files; they were those of a minor hoodlum with a record of assault.

A routine order to pick him up was sent out. A detective called at the rooming house where he was known to live, but he was out, and since no unsolved shootings had occurred recently, no intensive search for him was made that night.

The following evening a man was shot and killed in Central Park with the same gun. This was proved ballistically past all question of error. It was soon learned that the murdered man had been quarreling with a friend in a nearby tavern. The two men, both drunk, had left the tavern together. And the second man was the hoodlum whose gun had been found the previous night and which was still locked in a police safe.

As Lieutenant Eichler said to me, "It's impossible that the dead man was killed with that same gun, but he was. Don't ask me how, though, and if anybody thinks we'd go into court with a case like that, they're crazy."

*Case 111. Captain Hubert V. Rihm, New York Police Department, retired, aged sixty-six.*

I met Captain Rihm by appointment one morning in Stuyvesant Park, a patch of greenery, wood benches and asphalt surrounded by the city on lower Second Avenue. "You want to hear about the Fentz case, do you?" he said, after we had introduced ourselves and found an empty bench. "All right, I'll tell you. I don't like to talk about it—it bothers me—but I'd like to see what you think." He was a big, rather heavy man with a red, tough face, and he wore an old police jacket and uniform cap with the insignia removed.

"I was up at City Mortuary," he began as I took out my notebook and pencil, "at Bellevue about twelve one night, drinking coffee with one of the interns. This was in June of 1950, just before I retired, and I was in Missing Persons. They brought this guy in and he was a funny-looking character. Had a beard. A young guy, maybe thirty, but he wore regular muttonchop whiskers, and his clothes were funny-looking. Now I was thirty years on the force and I've seen a lot of queer guys killed on the streets. We found an Arab once in full regalia, and it took us a week to find out who he was. So it wasn't just the way the guy looked that bothered me; it was the stuff we found in his pockets."

Captain Rihm turned on the bench to see if he'd caught my interest, then continued. "There was about a dollar in change in the dead guy's pocket, and one of the boys picked up a nickel and showed it to me. Now you've seen plenty of nickels, the new ones with Jefferson's picture, the buffalo nickels they made before that, and once in a while you still even see the old Liberty-head nickels; they quit making them before the first world war. But this one was even older than that. It had a shield on the front, a United States shield, and a big five on the back; I used to see that kind when I was a boy. And the funny thing was, that old nickel looked new; what coin dealers call 'mint condition,' like it was made the day before yesterday. The date on that nickel was 1876, and there wasn't a coin in his pocket dated any later."

Captain Rihm looked at me questioningly. "Well," I said, glancing up from my notebook, "that could happen."

"Sure it could," he answered in a satisfied tone, "but all the pennies he had were Indian-head pennies. Now when did you see one of them last? There was even a silver three-cent piece; looked like an old-style dime, only smaller. And the bills in his wallet, every one of them, were old-time bills, the big kind."

Captain Rihm leaned forward and spat on the patch, a needle jet of tobacco juice and an expression of a policeman's annoyed contempt for anything deviating from an orderly norm.

"Over seventy bucks in cash, and not a federal reserve note in the lot. There were two yellow-back tens. Remember them? They were payable in gold. The rest were old national-bank notes; you remember them too. Issued direct by local banks, personally signed by the bank president; that kind used to be counterfeited a lot.

"Well," Captain Rihm continued, leaning back on the bench and crossing his knees, "there was a bill in his pocket from a livery stable on Lexington Avenue; three dollars for feeding and stabling his horse and washing a carriage. There was a brass slug in his pocket good for a five-cent beer at some saloon. There was a letter postmarked Philadelphia, June 1876, with an old-style two-cent stamp and a bunch of cards in his wallet. The cards had his name and address on them, and so did the letter."

"Oh," I said, a little surprised, "you identified him right away, then?"

"Sure. Rudolph Fentz, some address on Fifth Avenue—I forget the exact number—in New York City. No problem at all." Captain Rihm leaned forward and spat again. "Only that address wasn't a residence. It's a store, and it had been for years, and nobody there ever heard of any Rudolph Fentz, and there's no such name in the phone book either. Nobody ever called or made any inquiries about the guy, and Washington didn't have his prints. There was a tailor's name in his coat, a lower Broadway address, but nobody there ever heard of this tailor."

"What was so strange about his clothes?"

The captain said, "Well, did you ever know anyone who wore a pair of pants with big black-and-white checks, cut very narrow, no cuffs, and pressed without a crease?"

I had to think for a moment. "Yes," I said then, "my father, when he was a very young man, before he was married; I've seen old photographs."

"Sure," said Captain Rihm, "and he probably wore a short sort of cutaway coat with two cloth-covered buttons at the back, a vest with lapels, a tall silk hat, a big, black oversized bow tie on a turned-up stiff collar and button shoes."

"That's how this man was dressed?"

"Like seventy-five years ago! And him no more than thirty years old. There was a label in his hat, a Twenty-third Street hat store that went out of business around the turn of the century. Now what do you make out of a thing like that?"

"Well," I said carefully, "there's nothing much you can make of it. Apparently someone went to a lot of trouble to dress up in an antique style—the coins and bills I assume he could buy at a coin dealer's—and then he got himself killed in a traffic accident."

"Got himself killed is right. Eleven-fifteen at night in Times Square—the theaters letting out, busiest time and place in the world—and this guy shows up in the middle of the street, gawking and looking around at the cars and up at the signs like he'd never seen them before. The cop on duty noticed him, so you can see how he must have been acting. The lights change, the traffic starts up, with him in the middle of the street, and instead of waiting, the damn fool, he turns and tries to make it back to the sidewalk. A cab got him and he was dead when he hit."

For a moment Captain Rihm sat chewing his tobacco and staring angrily at a young woman pushing a baby carriage, though I'm sure he didn't see her. The young mother looked at him in surprise as she passed, and the captain continued:

"Nothing you can make out of a thing like that. We found out nothing. I started checking through our file of old phone books, just as routine, but without much hope because they only go back so far. But in the 1939 summer edition I found a Rudolph Fentz, Jr., somewhere on East Fifty-second Street. He'd moved away in 'forty-two, though, the building super told me, and was a man in his sixties besides, retired from business; used to work in a bank a few blocks away, the super thought. I found the bank where he'd worked and they told me he'd retired in 'forty, and had been dead for five years; his widow was living in Florida with a sister.

"I wrote to the widow, but there was only one thing she could tell us, and that was no good. I never even reported it, not officially, anyway. Her husband's father had disappeared when her husband was a boy maybe two years old. He went out for a walk around ten one night—his wife thought cigar smoke smelled up the curtains, so he used to take a little stroll before he went to bed and smoke a cigar—and he didn't come back and was never seen or heard of again. The family spent a good deal of money trying to locate him, but they never did. This was in the middle 1870s some time; the old lady wasn't sure of the exact date. Her husband hadn't ever said too much about it.

"And that's all," said Captain Rihm. "Once I put in one of my afternoons of hunting through a bunch of old police records. And I finally found the missing persons file for 1876, and Rudolph Fentz was listed, all right. There wasn't much of a description, and no fingerprints, of course. I'd give a year of my life, even now, and maybe sleep better nights, if they'd had his fingerprints. He was listed as twenty-nine years old, wearing full muttonchop whiskers, a tall silk hat, dark coat and checked pants. That's about all it said. Didn't say what kind of tie or vest or if his shoes were the button kind. His name was Rudolph Fentz and he lived at this address on Fifth Avenue; it must have been a residence then. Final disposition of case: not located.

"Now, I hate that case," Captain Rihm said quietly. "I hate it and I wish I'd never heard of it. What do you think?" he demanded suddenly, angrily. "You think this guy walked off into thin air in 1876 and showed up again in 1950?"

I shrugged noncommittally, and the captain took it to mean no.

"No, of course not," he said. "Of *course* not—but give me some other explanation."

I could go on. I could give you several hundred such cases. A sixteen-year-old girl walked out of her bedroom one morning, carrying her clothes in her hand because they were too big for her and she was quite obviously eleven years old again. And there are other occurrences too horrible for print. All of them have happened in the New York City area alone, all within the last few years; and I suspect thousands more have occurred and are occurring, all over the world. I could go on, but the point is this: What is happening, and *why?* I believe that I know.

Haven't you noticed, too, on the part of nearly everyone you know, a growing rebellion against the *present?* And an increasing longing for the past? I have. Never before in all my long life have I heard so many people wish that they lived "at the turn of the century" or "when life was simpler" or "worth living" or "when you could bring children into the world and count on the future" or simply "in the good old days." People didn't talk that way when I was young! The present was a glorious time! But they talk that way now.

For the first time in man's history, man is desperate to escape the present. Our newsstands are jammed with escape literature, the very name of which is significant. Entire magazines are devoted to fantastic stories of escape—to other times, past and future, to other worlds and planets—escape to anywhere but here and now. Even our larger magazines, book publishers and Hollywood are beginning to meet the rising demand for this kind of escape. Yes, there is a craving in the world like a thirst, a terrible mass pressure that you can almost feel, of millions of minds struggling against the barriers of time. I am utterly convinced that this terrible mass pressure of millions of minds is already, slightly but definitely, affecting time itself. In the moments when this happens— when the almost universal longing is greatest—my incidents occur. Man is disturbing the clock of time, and I am afraid it will break. When it does, I leave to your imagination the last few hours of madness that will be left to us; all the countless moments that now make up our lives suddenly ripped apart and chaotically tangled in time.

Well, I have lived most of my life; I can be robbed of only a few more years. But it seems too bad—this universal craving to escape what could be a rich, productive, happy world. We live on a planet well able to provide a decent life for every soul on it, which is all ninety-nine of a hundred human beings ask. Why in the world can't we have it?

# RAY BRADBURY

---

*Although not the first author to write fiction set on Mars, Ray Bradbury staked a major claim to one of the most fertile landscapes in all science fiction with a series of stories published in pulp magazines of the 1940s and '50s in which he envisioned the Red Planet as a new frontier where humanity might leave its imprint, for better or for worse. His collection* The Martian Chronicles *(1950), for which these stories served as a foundation, was a breakthrough success that alerted a mainstream audience to the value of science fiction as a modern mythology that embodies timeless human dreams and fears. Frail and fallible human beings are the foremost concern of Bradbury's fiction, whether in the persona of the fireman in the future dystopia* Fahrenheit 451 *who comes to doubt the merits of his job to destroy ideas by burning books, or the ordinary middle-class Americans in the dark fantasy* Something Wicked This Way Comes, *who allow fear of their own mortality to coerce them into Faustian pacts with a Mephistophelean owner of a traveling carnival. Bradbury's lyrical stories have been collected in* The Illustrated Man, The Golden Apples of the Sun, A Medicine for Melancholy, The Machineries of Joy, *and numerous other volumes including the definitive* Stories of Ray Bradbury. *The modern Gothic stories in his collections* Dark Carnival *and* The October Country *were a major influence on contemporary horror and dark fantasy fiction.* Dandelion Wine, *his novel of a mid-century Midwestern childhood, and the loose trilogy of* Death Is a Lonely Business, A Graveyard for Lunatics, *and* Green Shadows, White Whale, *drawn from his experiences as a young writer, are quintessentially Bradburyesque explorations of the magic possibilities of everyday life. He has written the children's books*

Switch on the Night, The Halloween Tree, *and* Ahmed and the Oblivion Machine, *hundreds of poems collected in* The Complete Poems of Ray Bradbury, *a score of plays, including* The Wonderful Ice Cream Suit, *and the essay collection* Yestermorrow. *Many of his stories have been adapted for stage, screen, television, musical theatre, and the comics. His own screenwriting credits include* It Came from Outer Space *and the screenplay for John Huston's adaptation of* Moby Dick. *His many awards include the Grand Master Award of the Science Fiction and Fantasy Writers of America and the Bram Stoker Award for Life Achievement from the Horror Writers Association.*

*A legend in the field for more than five decades, Bradbury's "A Sound of Thunder" was one of the first stories to extrapolate an event from the past changing the future in unimaginable ways. His use of the infamous butterfly has a corollary in the Hurricane Butterfly Theory first postulated in 1963 and refined in 1972, though his insect's wings had a far more permanent effect on the world of his story.*

# A SOUND OF THUNDER

## RAY BRADBURY

THE SIGN ON the wall seemed to quaver under a film of sliding warm water. Eckels felt his eyelids blink over his stare, and the sign burned in this momentary darkness:

TIME SAFARI, INC.

SAFARIS TO ANY YEAR IN THE PAST.

YOU NAME THE ANIMAL.

WE TAKE YOU THERE.

YOU SHOOT IT.

A warm phlegm gathered in Eckels' throat; he swallowed and pushed it down. The muscles around his mouth formed a smile as he put his hand slowly out upon the air, and in that hand waved a check for ten thousand dollars to the man behind the desk.

"Does this safari guarantee I come back alive?"

"We guarantee nothing," said the official, "except the dinosaurs." He turned. "This is Mr. Travis, your Safari Guide in the Past. He'll tell you what and where to shoot. If he says no shooting, no shooting. If you disobey instructions, there's a stiff penalty of another ten thousand dollars, plus possible government action, on your return."

Eckels glanced across the vast office at a mass and tangle, a snaking and humming of wires and steel boxes, at an aurora that flickered now orange, now silver, now blue. There was a sound like a gigantic bonfire burning all of Time, all the years and all the parchment calendars, all the hours piled high and set aflame.

A touch of the hand and this burning would, on the instant, beauti-fully reverse itself. Eckels remembered the wording in the advertise-ments to the letter. Out of chars and ashes, out of dust and coals, like golden salamanders, the old years, the green years, might leap; roses sweeten the air, white hair turn Irish-black, wrinkles vanish; all, every-thing fly back to seed, flee death, rush down to their beginnings, suns rise in western skies and set in glorious easts, moons eat themselves op-posite to the custom, all and everything cupping one in another like Chinese boxes, rabbits into hats, all and everything returning to the fresh death, the seed death, the green death, to the time before the beginning. A touch of a hand might do it, the merest touch of a hand.

"Unbelievable." Eckels breathed, the light of the Machine on his thin face. "A real Time Machine." He shook his head. "Makes you think. If the election had gone badly yesterday, I might be here now run-ning away from the results. Thank God Keith won. He'll make a fine President of the United States."

"Yes," said the man behind the desk. "We're lucky. If Deutscher had gotten in, we'd have the worst kind of dictatorship. There's an anti-everything man for you, a militarist, anti-Christ, anti-human, anti-intellectual. People called us up, you know, joking but not joking. Said if Deutscher became President they wanted to go live in 1492. Of course it's not our business to conduct Escapes, but to form Safaris. Anyway, Keith's President now. All you got to worry about is—"

"Shooting my dinosaur," Eckels finished it for him.

"A *Tyrannosaurus rex*. The Tyrant Lizard, the most incredible mon-ster in history. Sign this release. Anything happens to you, we're not re-sponsible. Those dinosaurs are hungry."

Eckels flushed angrily. "Trying to scare me!"

"Frankly, yes. We don't want anyone going who'll panic at the first shot. Six Safari leaders were killed last year, and a dozen hunters. We're here to give you the severest thrill a real hunter ever asked for. Traveling you back sixty million years to bag the biggest game in all of Time. Your personal check's still there. Tear it up."

Mr. Eckels looked at the check. His fingers twitched.

"Good luck," said the man behind the desk. "Mr. Travis, he's all yours."

They moved silently across the room, taking their guns with them, toward the Machine, toward the silver metal and the roaring light.

First a day and then a night and then a day and then a night, then it was day-night-day-night-day. A week, a month, a year, a decade! A.D. 2055. A.D. 2019. 1999! 1957! Gone! The Machine roared.

They put on their oxygen helmets and tested the intercoms.

Eckels swayed on the padded seat, his face pale, his jaw stiff. He felt the trembling in his arms and he looked down and found his hands tight on the new rifle. There were four other men in the Machine. Travis, the Safari Leader, his assistant, Lesperance, and two other hunters, Billings and Kramer. They sat looking at each other, and the years blazed around them.

"Can these guns get a dinosaur cold?" Eckels felt his mouth saying.

"If you hit them right," said Travis on the helmet radio. "Some dinosaurs have two brains, one in the head, another far down the spinal column. We stay away from those. That's stretching luck. Put your first two shots into the eyes, if you can, blind them, and go back into the brain."

The Machine howled. Time was a film run backward. Suns fled and ten million moons fled after them. "Think," said Eckels. "Every hunter that ever lived would envy us today. This makes Africa seem like Illinois."

The Machine slowed; its scream fell to a murmur. The Machine stopped.

The sun stopped in the sky.

The fog that had enveloped the Machine blew away and they were in an old time, a very old time indeed, three hunters and two Safari Heads with their blue metal guns across their knees.

"Christ isn't born yet," said Travis. "Moses has not gone to the mountain to talk with God. The Pyramids are still in the earth, waiting to be cut out and put up. *Remember* that. Alexander, Caesar, Napoleon, Hitler—none of them exists."

The man nodded.

"That"—Mr. Travis pointed—"is the jungle of sixty million two thousand and fifty-five years before President Keith."

He indicated a metal path that struck off into green wilderness, over streaming swamp, among giant ferns and palms.

"And that," he said, "is the Path, laid by Time Safari for your use. It floats six inches above the earth. Doesn't touch so much as one grass blade, flower, or tree. It's an antigravity metal. Its purpose is to keep you from touching this world of the past in any way. Stay on the Path. Don't go off it. I repeat. *Don't go off.* For *any* reason! If you fall off, there's a penalty. And don't shoot any animal we don't okay."

"Why?" asked Eckels.

They sat in the ancient wilderness. Far birds' cries blew on a wind, and the smell of tar and an old salt sea, moist grasses, and flowers the color of blood.

"We don't want to change the Future. We don't belong here in the Past. The government doesn't *like* us here. We have to pay big graft to keep our franchise. A Time Machine is finicky business. Not knowing it, we might kill an important animal, a small bird, a roach, a flower even, thus destroying an important link in a growing species."

"That's not clear," said Eckels.

"All right," Travis continued, "say we accidentally kill one mouse here. That means all the future families of this one particular mouse are destroyed, right?"

"Right."

"And all the families of the families of the families of that one mouse! With a stamp of your foot, you annihilate first one, then a dozen, then a thousand, a million, a *billion* possible mice!"

"So they're dead," said Eckels. "So what?"

"So what?" Travis snorted quietly. "Well, what about the foxes that'll need those mice to survive? For want of ten mice, a fox dies. For want of ten foxes, a lion starves. For want of a lion, all manner of insects, vultures, infinite billions of life forms are thrown into chaos and destruction. Eventually it all boils down to this: fifty-nine million years later, a caveman, one of a dozen on the entire *world*, goes hunting wild boar or saber-toothed tiger for food. But you, friend, have *stepped* on all the tigers in that region. By stepping on *one* single mouse. So the caveman starves. And the caveman, please note, is not just *any* expendable man, no! He is an *entire future nation.* From his loins would have sprung ten sons. From *their* loins one hundred sons, and thus onward to a civilization. Destroy this one man, and you destroy a race, a people, an entire history of life. It is comparable to slaying some of Adam's grandchildren. The stomp of your foot, on one mouse, could start an earthquake, the effects of which could shake our earth and destinies down through Time, to their very foundations. With the death of that one caveman, a billion others yet unborn are throttled in the womb. Perhaps Rome never rises on its seven hills. Perhaps Europe is forever a dark forest, and only Asia waxes healthy and teeming. Step on a mouse and you crush the Pyramids. Step on a mouse and you leave your print, like a Grand Canyon, across Eternity. Queen Elizabeth might never be born, Washington might not cross the Delaware, there might never be a United States at all. So be careful. Stay on the Path. *Never* step off!"

"I see," said Eckels. "Then it wouldn't pay for us even to touch the *grass?*"

"Correct. Crushing certain plants could add up infinitesimally. A little error here would multiply in sixty million years, all out of proportion. Of course maybe our theory is wrong. Maybe Time can't be changed by us. Or maybe it can be changed only in little subtle ways. A dead mouse here makes an insect imbalance there, a population disproportion later, a bad harvest further on, a depression, mass starvation, and, finally, a change in *social* temperament in far-flung countries. Something much more subtle, like that. Perhaps only a soft breath, a whisper, a hair, pollen on the air, such a slight, slight change that unless you looked close you wouldn't see it. Who knows? Who really can say he knows? We don't know. We're guessing. But until we do know for certain whether our messing around in Time can make a big roar or a little rustle in history, we're being careful. This Machine, this Path, your clothing and bodies, were sterilized, as you know, before the journey. We wear these oxygen helmets so we can't introduce our bacteria into an ancient atmosphere."

"How do we know which animals to shoot?"

"They're marked with red paint," said Travis. "Today, before our journey, we sent Lesperance here back with the Machine. He came to this particular era and followed certain animals."

"Studying them?"

"Right," said Lesperance. "I track them through their entire existence, noting which of them lives longest. Very few. How many times they mate. Not often. Life's short. When I find one that's going to die when a tree falls on him, or one that drowns in a tar pit, I note the exact hour, minute, and second. I shoot a paint bomb. It leaves a red patch on his side. We can't miss it. Then I correlate our arrival in the Past so that we meet the Monster not more than two minutes before he would have died anyway. This way, we kill only animals with no future, that are never going to mate again. You see how *careful* we are?"

"But if you came back this morning in Time," said Eckels eagerly, "you must've bumped into us, our Safari! How did it turn out? Was it successful? Did all of us get through—alive?"

Travis and Lesperance gave each other a look.

"That'd be a paradox," said the latter. "Time doesn't permit that sort of mess—a man meeting himself. When such occasions threaten, Time steps aside. Like an airplane hitting an air pocket. You felt the Machine jump just before we stopped? That was us passing ourselves on the way back to the Future. We saw nothing. There's no way of telling *if* this expedition was a success, *if* we got our monster, or whether all of us— meaning *you*, Mr. Eckels—got out alive."

Eckels smiled palely.

"Cut that," said Travis sharply. "Everyone on his feet!"

They were ready to leave the Machine.

The jungle was high and the jungle was broad and the jungle was the entire world forever and forever. Sounds like music and sounds like flying tents filled the sky, and those were pterodactyls soaring with cavernous gray wings, gigantic bats of delirium and night fever. Eckels, balanced on the narrow Path, aimed his rifle playfully.

"Stop that!" said Travis. "Don't even aim for fun, blast you! If your gun should go off—"

Eckels flushed. "Where's our *Tyrannosaurus?*"

Lesperance checked his wristwatch. "Up ahead. We'll bisect his trail in sixty seconds. Look for the red paint! Don't shoot till we give the word. Stay on the Path. *Stay on the Path!*"

They moved forward in the wind of morning.

"Strange," murmured Eckels. "Up ahead, sixty million years, Election Day over. Keith made President. Everyone celebrating. And here we are, a million years lost, and they don't exist. The things we worried about for months, a lifetime, not even born or thought of yet."

"Safety catches off, everyone!" ordered Travis. "You, first shot, Eckels. Second, Billings, Third, Kramer."

"I've hunted tiger, wild boar, buffalo, elephant, but now, this is *it*," said Eckels. "I'm shaking like a kid."

"Ah," said Travis.

Everyone stopped.

Travis raised his hand. "Ahead," he whispered. "In the mist. There he is. There's His Royal Majesty now."

The jungle was wide and full of twitterings, rustlings, murmurs, and sighs.

Suddenly it all ceased, as if someone had shut a door.

Silence.

A sound of thunder.

Out of the mist, one hundred yards away, came *Tyrannosaurus rex*.

"It," whispered Eckels. "It . . . "

"Sh!"

It came on great oiled, resilient, striding legs. It towered thirty feet above half of the trees, a great evil god, folding its delicate watchmaker's claws close to its oily reptilian chest. Each lower leg was a piston, a thousand pounds of white bone, sunk in thick ropes of muscle, sheathed over in a gleam of pebbled skin like the mail of a terrible warrior. Each thigh was a ton of meat, ivory, and steel mesh. And from the great breathing cage of the upper body those two delicate arms dangled out front, arms with hands which might pick up and examine men like toys, while the snake neck coiled. And the head itself, a ton of sculptured stone, lifted easily upon the sky. Its mouth gaped, exposing a fence of teeth like daggers. Its eyes rolled, ostrich eggs, empty of all expression save hunger. It closed its mouth in a death grin. It ran, its pelvic bones crushing aside trees and bushes, its taloned feet clawing damp earth, leaving prints six inches deep wherever it settled its weight. It ran with a gliding ballet step, far too poised and balanced for its ten tons. It moved into a sunlit arena warily, its beautifully reptilian hands feeling the air.

"Why, why," Eckels twitched his mouth. "It could reach up and grab the moon."

"Sh!" Travis jerked angrily. "He hasn't seen us yet."

"It can't be killed." Eckels pronounced this verdict quietly, as if there could be no argument. He had weighed the evidence and this was his considered opinion. The rifle in his hands seemed a cap gun. "We were fools to come. This is impossible."

"Shut up!" hissed Travis.

"Nightmare."

"Turn around," commanded Travis. "Walk quietly to the Machine. We'll remit one half your fee."

"I didn't realize it would be this *big*," said Eckels. "I miscalculated, that's all. And now I want out."

"It *sees* us!"

"There's the red paint on its chest!"

The Tyrant Lizard raised itself. Its armored flesh glittered like a thousand green coins. The coins, crusted with slime, steamed. In the slime, tiny insects wriggled, so that the entire body seemed to twitch and undulate, even while the monster itself did not move. It exhaled. The stink of raw flesh blew down the wilderness.

"Get me out of here," said Eckels. "It was never like this before. I was always sure I'd come through alive. I had good guides, good safaris, and safety. This time, I figured wrong. I've met my match and admit it. This is too much for me to get hold of."

"Don't run," said Lesperance. "Turn around. Hide in the Machine."

"Yes." Eckels seemed to be numb. He looked at his feet as if trying to make them move. He gave a grunt of helplessness.

"Eckels!"

He took a few steps, blinking, shuffling.

"Not *that* way!"

The Monster, at the first motion, lunged forward with a terrible scream. It covered one hundred yards in six seconds. The rifles jerked up and blazed fire. A windstorm from the beast's mouth engulfed them in the stench of slime and old blood. The Monster roared, teeth glittering with sun.

Eckels, not looking back, walked blindly to the edge of the Path, his gun limp in his arms, stepped off the Path, and walked, not knowing it, in the jungle. His feet sank into green moss. His legs moved him, and he felt alone and remote from the events behind.

The rifles cracked again. Their sound was lost in shriek and lizard thunder. The great lever of the reptile's tail swung up, lashed sideways. Trees exploded in clouds of leaf and branch. The monster twitched its jeweler's hands down to fondle at the men, to twist them in half, to crush them like berries, to cram them into its teeth and its screaming throat. Its boulder-stone eyes leveled with the men. They saw themselves mirrored. They fired at the metallic eyelids and the blazing black iris.

Like a stone idol, like a mountain avalanche, *Tyrannosaurus* fell. Thundering, it clutched trees, pulled them with it. It wrenched and tore the metal Path. The men flung themselves back and away. The body hit, ten tons of cold flesh and stone. The guns fired. The Monster lashed its armored tail, twitched its snake jaws, and lay still. A fount of blood spurted from its throat. Somewhere inside, a sac of fluids burst. Sickening gushes drenched the hunters. They stood, red and glistening.

The thunder faded.

The jungle was silent. After the avalanche, a green peace. After the nightmare, morning.

Billings and Kramer sat on the pathway and threw up. Travis and Lesperance stood with smoking rifles, cursing steadily.

In the Time Machine, on his face, Eckels lay shivering. He had found his way back to the Path, climbed into the Machine.

Travis came walking, glanced at Eckels, took cotton gauze from a metal box, and returned to the others, who were sitting on the Path.

"Clean up."

They wiped the blood from their helmets. They began to curse too. The Monster lay, a hill of solid flesh. Within, you could hear the sighs and murmurs as the furthest chambers of it died, the organs malfunctioning, liquids running a final instant from pocket to sac to spleen, everything shutting off, closing up forever. It was like standing by a wrecked locomotive or a steam shovel at quitting time, all valves being released or levered tight. Bones cracked; the tonnage of its own flesh, off balance, dead weight, snapped the delicate forearms, caught underneath. The meat settled, quivering.

Another cracking sound. Overhead, a gigantic tree branch broke from its heavy mooring, fell. It crashed upon the dead beast with finality.

"There." Lesperance checked his watch. "Right on time. That's the giant tree that was scheduled to fall and kill this animal originally." He glanced at the two hunters. "You want the trophy picture?"

"What?"

"We can't take a trophy back to the Future. The body has to stay right here where it would have died originally, so the insects, birds, and bacteria can get at it, as they were intended to. Everything in balance. The body stays. But we *can* take a picture of you standing near it."

The two men tried to think, but gave up, shaking their heads.

They let themselves be led along the metal Path. They sank wearily into the Machine cushions. They gazed back at the ruined Monster, the stagnating mound, where already strange reptilian birds and golden insects were busy at the steaming armor.

A sound on the floor of the Time Machine stiffened them. Eckels sat there, shivering.

"I'm sorry," he said at last.

"Get up!" cried Travis.

Eckels got up.

"Go out on that Path alone," said Travis. He had his rifle pointed. "You're not coming back in the Machine. We're leaving you here!"

Lesperance seized Travis's arm. "Wait—"

"Stay out of this!" Travis shook his hand away. "This fool nearly killed us. But it isn't *that* so much, no. It's his *shoes*! Look at them! He ran off the Path. That *ruins* us! We'll forfeit! Thousands of dollars of insurance! We guarantee no one leaves the Path. He left it. Oh, the fool! I'll have to report to the government. They might revoke our license to travel. Who knows *what* he's done to Time, to History!"

"Take it easy, all he did was kick up some dirt."

"How do we *know?*" cried Travis. "We don't know anything! It's all a mystery! Get out there, Eckels!"

Eckels fumbled his shirt. "I'll pay anything. A hundred thousand dollars!"

Travis glared at Eckels' checkbook and spat. "Go out there. The Monster's next to the Path. Stick your arms up to your elbows in his mouth. Then you can come back with us."

"That's unreasonable!"

"The Monster's dead, you idiot. The bullets! The bullets can't be left behind. They don't belong in the Past; they might change something. Here's my knife. Dig them out!"

The jungle was alive again, full of the old tremorings and bird cries. Eckels turned slowly to regard the primeval garbage dump, that hill of nightmares and terror. After a long time, like a sleepwalker he shuffled out along the Path.

He returned, shuddering, five minutes later, his arms soaked and red to the elbows. He held out his hands. Each held a number of steel bullets. Then he fell. He lay where he fell, not moving.

"You didn't have to make him do that," said Lesperance.

"Didn't I? It's too early to tell." Travis nudged the still body. "He'll live. Next time he won't go hunting game like this. Okay." He jerked his thumb wearily at Lesperance. "Switch on. Let's go home."

————

1492. 1776. 1812.

They cleaned their hands and faces. They changed their caking shirts and pants. Eckels was up and around again, not speaking. Travis glared at him for a full ten minutes.

"Don't look at me," cried Eckels. "I haven't done anything."

"Who can tell?"

"Just ran off the Path, that's all, a little mud on my shoes—what do you want me to do—get down and pray?"

"We might need it. I'm warning you, Eckels, I might kill you yet. I've got my gun ready."

"I'm innocent. I've done nothing!"

1999. 2000. 2055.

The Machine stopped.

"Get out," said Travis.

The room was there as they had left it. But not the same as they had left it. The same man sat behind the same desk. But the same man did not quite sit behind the same desk.

Travis looked around swiftly. "Everything okay here?" he snapped.

"Fine. Welcome home!"

Travis did not relax. He seemed to be looking at the very atoms of the air itself, at the way the sun poured through the one high window.

"Okay, Eckels, get out. Don't ever come back."

Eckels could not move.

"You heard me," said Travis. "What're you *staring* at?"

Eckels stood smelling the air, and there was a thing to the air, a chemical taint so subtle, so slight, that only a faint cry of his subliminal senses warned him it was there. The colors, white, gray, blue, orange, in the wall, in the furniture, in the sky beyond the window, were . . . were . . . And there was a *feel*. His flesh twitched. His hands twitched. He stood drinking the oddness with the pores of his body. Somewhere, someone must have been screaming one of those whistles that only a dog can hear. His body screamed silence in return. Beyond this room, beyond this wall, beyond this man who was not quite the same man seated at this desk that was not quite the same desk . . . lay an entire world of streets and people. What sort of world it was now, there was no telling. He could feel them moving there, beyond the walls, almost, like so many chess pieces blown in a dry wind. . . .

But the immediate thing was the sign painted on the office wall, the same sign he had read earlier today on first entering.

Somehow, the sign had changed:

TYME SEFARI INC.

SEFARIS TU ANY YEER EN THE PAST.

YU NAIM THE ANIMALL.

WEE TAEK YU THAIR.

YU SHOOT ITT.

Eckels felt himself fall into a chair. He fumbled crazily at the thick slime on his boots. He held up a clod of dirt, trembling. "No, it *can't* be. Not a *little* thing like that. No!"

Embedded in the mud, glistening green and gold and black, was a butterfly, very beautiful and very dead.

"Not a little thing like *that*! Not a butterfly!" cried Eckels.

It fell to the floor, an exquisite thing, a small thing that could upset balances and knock down a line of small dominoes and then big dominoes and then gigantic dominoes, all down the years across Time. Eckels' mind whirled. It *couldn't* change things. Killing one butterfly couldn't be *that* important! Could it?

His face was cold. His mouth trembled, asking: "Who—who won the presidential election yesterday?"

The man behind the desk laughed. "You joking? You know very well. Deutscher, of course! Who else? Not that fool weakling Keith. We got an iron man now, a man with guts!" The official stopped. "What's wrong?"

Eckels moaned. He dropped to his knees. He scrabbled at the golden butterfly with shaking fingers. "Can't we," he pleaded to the world, to himself, to the officials, to the machine, "can't we take it *back*, can't we *make* it alive again? Can't we start over? Can't we—"

He did not move. Eyes shut, he waited, shivering. He heard Travis breathe loud in the room; he heard Travis shift his rifle, click the safety catch, and raise the weapon.

There was a sound of thunder.

# RICHARD MATHESON

*Richard Matheson was recognized as a powerful new talent in postwar fantasy with the publication of his first story, "Born of Man and Woman,"* in 1950. *His early novels* I Am Legend *and* The Shrinking Man *broke new ground through their blending of fantasy, horror, and science-fiction elements and elaborations of the theme that dominates all his writing: the individual alone in a hostile universe struggling to survive. Matheson's special interest in the paranormal has served as the foundation for his novels* A Stir of Echoes, Hell House, *and* What Dreams May Come. *His time-travel romance,* Bid Time Return, *won the World Fantasy Award. His short stories are among the most reprinted in the fields of fantasy, horror, and science fiction. Most were collected in the definitive retrospective volume* The Stories of Richard Matheson. *He is also author of the suspense novels* Ride the Nightmare *and* Seven Steps to Midnight, *and the award-winning westerns* Journal of the Gun Years *and* The Gunfight. *He has scripted many movies and television shows, and his own work has been adapted for film and television series, including* The Twilight Zone *and* Night Gallery.

*A popular exploration of the time-travel story is that of the protagonist meeting him- or herself from the future or the past. Matheson's "Death Ship" takes the idea one step further, having the space-exploring heroes of the tale encounter themselves in a very dangerous future tense. This story was filmed as an episode of the original* Twilight Zone *television series in 1963, and starred Jack Klugman and Ross Martin as two of the astronauts.*

# DEATH SHIP

## RICHARD MATHESON

MASON SAW IT FIRST.

He was sitting in front of the lateral viewer taking notes as the ship cruised over the new planet. His pen moved quickly over the graph-spaced chart he held before him. In a little while they'd land and take specimens. Mineral, vegetable, animal—if there were any. Put them in the storage lockers and take them back to Earth. There the technicians would evaluate, appraise, judge. And, if everything was acceptable, stamp the big, black INHABITABLE on their brief and open another planet for colonization from overcrowded Earth.

Mason was jotting down items about general topography when the glitter caught his eye.

"I saw something," he said.

He flicked the viewer to reverse lensing position.

"Saw what?" Ross asked from the control board.

"Didn't you see a flash?"

Ross looked into his own screen.

"We went over a lake, you know," he said.

"No, it wasn't that," Mason said. "This was in that clearing beside the lake."

"I'll look," said Ross, "but it probably was the lake."

His fingers typed out a command on the board and the big ship wheeled around in a smooth arc and headed back.

"Keep your eyes open now," Ross said. "Make sure. We haven't got any time to waste."

"Yes sir."

Mason kept his unblinking gaze on the viewer, watching the earth below move past like a slowly rolled tapestry of woods and fields and rivers. He was thinking, in spite of himself, that maybe the moment had arrived at last. The moment in which Earthmen would come upon life beyond Earth, a race evolved from other cells and other muds. It was an exciting thought. 1997 might be the year. And he and Ross and Carter might now be riding a new *Santa Maria* of discovery, a silvery, bulleted galleon of space.

"There!" he said. "There it is!"

He looked over at Ross. The captain was gazing into his viewer plate. His face bore the expression Mason knew well. A look of smug analysis, of impending decision.

"What do you think it is?" Mason asked, playing the strings of vanity in his captain.

"Might be a ship, might not be," pronounced Ross.

Well, for God's sake, let's go down and see, Mason wanted to say, but knew he couldn't. It would have to be Ross's decision. Otherwise they might not even stop.

"I guess it's nothing," he prodded.

He watched Ross impatiently, watched the stubby fingers flick buttons for the viewer. "We might stop," Ross said. "We have to take samples anyway. Only thing I'm afraid of is . . . "

He shook his head. Land, man! The words bubbled up in Mason's throat. For God's sake, let's go down!

Ross evaluated. His thickish lips pressed together appraisingly. Mason held his breath.

Then Ross's head bobbed once in that curt movement which indicated consummated decision. Mason breathed again. He watched the captain spin, push and twist dials. Felt the ship begin its tilt to upright position. Felt the cabin shuddering slightly as the gyroscope kept it on an even keel. The sky did a ninety-degree turn, clouds appeared through the thick ports. Then the ship was pointed at the planet's sun and Ross switched off the cruising engines. The ship hesitated, suspended a split second, then began dropping toward the earth.

"Hey, we settin' down already?"

Mickey Carter looked at them questioningly from the port door that led to the storage lockers. He was rubbing greasy hands over his green jumper legs.

"We saw something down there," Mason said.

"No kiddin'," Mickey said, coming over to Mason's viewer. "Let's see."

Mason flicked on the rear lens. The two of them watched the planet billowing up at them.

"I don't know whether you can . . . oh, yes, there it is," Mason said. He looked over at Ross.

"Two degrees east," he said.

Ross twisted a dial and the ship then changed its downward movement slightly.

"What do you think it is?" Mickey asked.

"Hey!"

Mickey looked into the viewer with even greater interest. His wide eyes examined the shiny speck enlarging on the screen.

"Could be a ship," he said. "Could be."

Then he stood there silently, behind Mason, watching the earth rushing up.

"Reactors," said Mason.

Ross jabbed efficiently at the button and the ship's engines spouted out their flaming gases. Speed decreased. The rocket eased down on its roaring fire jets. Ross guided.

"What do *you* think it is?" Mickey asked Mason.

"I don't know," Mason answered. "But if it's a ship," he added, half wishfully thinking, "I don't see how it could possibly be from Earth. We've got this run all to ourselves."

"Maybe they got off course," Mickey dampened without knowing.

Mason shrugged. "I doubt it," he said.

"What if it is a ship?" Mickey said. "And it's not ours?"

Mason looked at him and Carter licked his lips.

"Man," he said, "that'd be somethin'."

"Air spring," Ross ordered.

Mason threw the switch that set the air spring into operation. The unit which made possible a landing without then having to stretch out on thick-cushioned couches. They could stand on deck and hardly feel the impact. It was an innovation on the newer government ships.

The ship hit on its rear braces.

There was a sensation of jarring, a sense of slight bouncing. Then the ship was still, its pointed nose straight up, glittering brilliantly in the bright sunlight.

"I want us to stay together," Ross was saying. "No one takes any risks. That's an order."

He got up from his seat and pointed at the wall switch that let atmosphere into the small chamber in the corner of the cabin.

"Three to one we need our helmets," Mickey said to Mason.

"You're on," Mason said, setting into play their standing bet about the air or lack of it in every new planet they found. Mickey always bet on the need for apparatus. Mason for unaided lung use. So far, they'd come out about even.

Mason threw the switch, and there was a muffled sound of hissing in the chamber. Mickey got the helmet from his locker and dropped it over his head. Then he went through the double doors. Mason listened to him clamping the doors behind him. He kept wanting to switch on the side viewers and see if he could locate what they'd spotted. But he didn't. He let himself enjoy the delicate nibbling of suspense.

Through the intercom they heard Mickey's voice.

"Removing helmet," he said.

Silence. They waited. Finally, a sound of disgust.

"I lose again," Mickey said.

The others followed him out.

"God, did they hit!"

Mickey's face had an expression of dismayed shock on it. The three of them stood there on the greenish-blue grass and looked.

It *was* a ship. Or what was left of a ship for, apparently, it had struck the earth at terrible velocity, nose first. The main structure had driven itself about fifteen feet into the hard ground. Jagged pieces of superstructure had been ripped off by the crash and were lying strewn over the field. The heavy engines had been torn loose and nearly crushed the cabin. Everything was deathly silent, and the wreckage was so complete they could hardly make out what type of ship it was. It was as if some enormous child had lost fancy with the toy model and had dashed it to earth, stamped on it, banged on it insanely with a rock.

Mason shuddered. It had been a long time since he'd seen a rocket crash. He'd almost forgotten the everpresent menace of lost control, of whistling fall through space, of violent impact. Most talk had been about being lost in an orbit. This reminded him of the other threat in his calling. His throat moved unconsciously as he watched.

Ross was scuffing at a chunk of metal at his feet.

"Can't tell much," he said. "But I'd say it's our own."

Mason was about to speak, then changed his mind.

"From what I can see of that engine up there, I'd say it was ours," Mickey said.

"Rocket structure might be standard," Mason heard himself say, "everywhere."

"Not a chance," Ross said. "Things don't work out like that. It's ours all right. Some poor devils from Earth. Well, at least their death was quick."

"Was it?" Mason asked the air, visualizing the crew in their cabin, rooted with fear as their ship spun toward earth, maybe straight down like a fired cannon shell, maybe end-over-end like a crazy, fluttering top, the gyroscope trying in vain to keep the cabin always level.

The screaming, the shouted commands, the exhortations to a heaven they had never seen before, to a God who might be in another universe. And then the planet rushing up and blasting its hard face against their ship, crushing them, ripping the breath from their lungs. He shuddered again, thinking of it.

"Let's take a look," Mickey said.

"Not sure we'd better," Ross said. "We say it's ours. It might not be."

"Jeez, you don't think anything is still alive in there, do you?" Mickey asked the captain.

"Can't say," Ross said.

But they all knew he could see that mangled hulk before him as well as they. Nothing could have survived that.

The look. The pursed lips. As they circled the ship. The head movement, unseen by them.

"Let's try that opening there," Ross ordered. "And stay together. We still have work to do. Only doing this so we can let the base know which ship this is." He had already decided it was an Earth ship.

They walked up to a spot in the ship's side where the skin had been laid open along the welded seam. A long, thick plate was bent over as easily as a man might bend paper.

"Don't like this," Ross said. "But I suppose . . . "

He gestured with his head and Mickey pulled himself up to the opening. He tested each handhold gingerly, then slid on his work gloves as he found some sharp edge. He told the other two and they reached into their jumper pockets. Then Mickey took a long step into the dark maw of the ship.

"Hold *on*, now!" Ross called up. "Wait until I get there."

He pulled himself up, his heavy boot toes scraping up the rocket skin. He went into the hole too. Mason followed.

It was dark inside the ship. Mason closed his eyes for a moment to adjust to the change. When he opened them, he saw two bright beams searching up through the twisted tangle of beams and plates. He pulled out his own flash and flicked it on.

"God, is this thing wrecked," Mickey said, awed by the sight of metal and machinery in violent death. His voice echoed slightly through the shell. Then, when the sound ended, an utter stillness descended on them. They stood in the murky light and Mason could smell the acrid fumes of broken engines.

"Watch the smell, now," Ross said to Mickey who was reaching up for support. "We don't want to get ourselves gassed."

"I will," Mickey said. He was climbing up, using one hand to pull his thick, powerful body up along the twisted ladder. He played the beam straight up.

"Cabin is all out of shape," he said, shaking his head.

Ross followed him up. Mason was last, his flash moving around endlessly over the snapped joints, the wild jigsaw of destruction that had once been a powerful new ship. He kept hissing in disbelief to himself as his beam came across one violent distortion of metal after another.

"Door's sealed," Mickey said, standing on a pretzel-twisted catwalk, bracing himself against the inside rocket wall. He grabbed the handle again and tried to pull it open.

"Give me your light," Ross said. He directed both beams at the door and Mickey tried to drag it open. His face grew red as he struggled. He puffed.

"No," he said, shaking his head. "It's stuck."

Mason came up beside them. "Maybe the cabin is still pressurized," he said softly. He didn't like the echoing of his own voice.

"Doubt it," Ross said, trying to think. "More than likely the jamb is twisted." He gestured with his head again. "Help Carter."

Mason grabbed one handle and Mickey the other. Then they braced their feet against the wall and pulled with all their strength. The door held fast. They shifted their grip, pulled harder.

"Hey, it slipped!" Mickey said. "I think we got it."

They resumed footing on the tangled catwalk and pulled the door open. The frame was twisted, the door held in one corner. They could only open it enough to wedge themselves in sideways.

The cabin was dark as Mason edged in first. He played his light beam toward the pilot's seat. It was empty. He heard Mickey squeeze in as he moved the light to the navigator's seat.

There was no navigator's seat. The bulkhead had been stove in there, the viewer, the table and the chair all crushed beneath the bent plates. There was a clicking in Mason's throat as he thought of himself sitting at a table like that, in a chair like that, before a bulkhead like that.

Ross was in now. The three beams of light searched. They all had to stand, legs spraddled, because the deck slanted.

And the way it slanted made Mason think of something. Of shifting weights, of *things* sliding down. . . .

Into the corner where he suddenly played his shaking beam.

And felt his heart jolt, felt the skin on him crawling, felt his unblinking eyes staring at the sight. Then felt his boots thud him down the incline as if he were driven.

"Here," he said, his voice hoarse with shock.

He stood before the bodies. His foot had bumped into one of them as he held himself from going down any further, as he shifted his weight on the incline.

Now he heard Mickey's footsteps, his voice. A whisper. A bated, horrified whisper.

"*Mother of God.*"

Nothing from Ross. Nothing from any of them then but stares and shuddering breaths.

Because the twisted bodies on the floor were theirs, all three of them. And all three . . . dead.

———

Mason didn't know how long they stood there, wordlessly, looking down at the still, crumpled figures on the deck.

How does a man react when he is standing over his own corpse? The question plied unconsciously at his mind. What does a man say? What are his first words to be? A poser, he seemed to sense, a loaded question.

But it was happening. Here he stood—and there he lay dead at his own feet. He felt his hands grow numb and he rocked unsteadily on the tilted deck.

"God."

Mickey again. He had his flash pointed down at his own face. His mouth twitched as he looked. All three of them had their flash beams directed at their own faces, and the bright ribbons of light connected their dual bodies.

Finally Ross took a shaking breath of the stale cabin air.

"Carter," he said, "find the auxiliary light switch, see if it works." His voice was husky and tightly restrained.

"Sir?"

"The light switch—the light switch!" Ross snapped.

Mason and the captain stood there, motionless, as Mickey shuffled up the deck. They heard his boots kick metallic debris over the deck surface. Mason closed his eyes, but was unable to take his foot away from where it pressed against the body that was his. He felt bound.

"I don't understand," he said to himself.

"Hang on," Ross said.

Mason couldn't tell whether it was said to encourage him or the captain himself.

Then they heard the emergency generator begin its initial whining spin. The light flickered, went out. The generator coughed and began humming and the lights flashed on brightly.

They looked down now. Mickey slipped down the slight deck hill and stood beside them. He stared down at his own body. Its head was crushed in. Mickey drew back, his mouth a box of unbelieving terror.

"I don't get it," he said. "I don't get it. What is this?"

"Carter," Ross said.

"That's *me!*" Mickey said. "God, it's *me!*"

"Hold on!" Ross ordered.

"The three of us," Mason said quietly, "and we're all dead."

There seemed nothing to be said. It was a speechless nightmare. The tilted cabin all bashed in and tangled. The three corpses all doubled over and tumbled into one corner, arms and legs flopped over each other. All they could do was stare.

Then Ross said, "Go get a tarp. Both of you."

Mason turned. Quickly. Glad to fill his mind with simple command. Glad to crowd out tense horror with activity. He took long steps up the deck. Mickey backed up, unable to take his unblinking gaze off the heavy-set corpse with the green jumper and the caved-in, bloody head.

Mason dragged a heavy, folded tarp from the storage locker and carried it back into the cabin, legs and arms moving in robotlike sequence. He tried to numb his brain, not think at all until the first shock had dwindled.

Mickey and he opened up the heavy canvas sheet with wooden motions. They tossed it out and the thick, shiny material fluttered down over the bodies. It settled, outlining the heads, the torsos, the one arm that stood up stiffly like a spear, bent over wrist and hand like a grisly pennant.

Mason turned away with a shudder. He stumbled up to the pilot's seat and slumped down. He stared at his outstretched legs, the heavy boots. He reached out and grabbed his leg and pinched it, feeling almost relief at the flaring pain.

"Come away," he heard Ross saying to Mickey, "I said, *come away!*"

He looked down and saw Ross half dragging Mickey up from a crouching position over the bodies. He held Mickey's arm and led him up the incline.

"We're dead," Mickey said hollowly. "That's us on the deck. We're *dead.*"

Ross pushed Mickey up to the cracked port and made him look out.

"There," he said. "There's our ship over there. Just as we left it. This ship isn't ours. And those bodies. They . . . can't be ours."

He finished weakly. To a man of his sturdy opinionation, the words sounded flimsy and extravagant. His throat moved, his lower lip pushed out in defiance of this enigma. Ross didn't like enigmas. He stood for decision and action. He wanted action now.

"You saw yourself down there," Mason said to him. "Are you going to say it isn't you?"

"That's exactly what I'm saying," Ross bristled. "This may seem crazy, but there's an explanation for it. There's an explanation for everything."

His face twitched as he punched his bulky arm.

"This is me," he claimed. "I'm solid." He glared at them as if daring opposition. "I'm alive," he said.

They stared blankly at him.

"I don't get it," Mickey said weakly. He shook his head and his lips drew back over his teeth.

Mason sat limply in the pilot's seat. He almost hoped that Ross's dogmatism would pull them through this. That his staunch bias against the inexplicable would save the day. He wanted for it to save the day. He tried to think for himself, but it was so much easier to let the captain decide.

"We're all dead," Mickey said.

"Don't be a fool!" Ross exclaimed. "Feel yourself!"

Mason wondered how long it would go on. Actually, he began to expect a sudden awakening, him jolting to a sitting position on his bunk to see the two of them at their tasks as usual, the crazy dream over and done with.

But the dream went on. He leaned back in the seat and it was a solid seat. From where he sat he could run his fingers over solid dials and buttons and switches. All real. It was no dream. Pinching wasn't even necessary.

"Maybe it's a vision," he tried, vainly attempting thought, as an animal mired tries hesitant steps to solid earth.

"That's enough," Ross said.

Then his eyes narrowed. He looked at them sharply. His face mirrored decision. Mason almost felt anticipation. He tried to figure out what Ross was working on. Vision? No, it couldn't be that. Ross would hold no truck with visions. He noticed Mickey staring open-mouthed at Ross. Mickey wanted the consoling of simple explanation too.

"Time warp," said Ross.

They still stared at him.

"What?" Mason asked.

"Listen," Ross punched out his theory. More than his theory, for Ross never bothered with that link in the chain of calculation. His certainty.

"Space bends," Ross said. "Time and space form a continuum. Right?"

No answer. He didn't need one.

"Remember they told us once in training of the possibility of circumnavigating time. They told us we could leave Earth at a certain time. And when we came back we'd be back a year earlier than we'd calculated. Or a year later.

"Those were just theories to the teachers. Well, I say it's happened to us. It's logical, it could happen. We could have passed right through a time warp. We're in another galaxy, maybe different space lines, maybe different time lines."

He paused for effect.

"I say we're in the future," he said.

Mason looked at him.

"How does that help us?" he asked. "If you're right."

"We're not dead!" Ross seemed surprised that they didn't get it.

"If it's in the future," Mason said quietly, "then we're going to die."

Ross gaped at him. He hadn't thought of that. Hadn't thought that his idea made things even worse. Because there was only one thing worse than dying. And that was knowing you were going to die. And where. And how.

Mickey shook his head. His hands fumbled at his sides. He raised one to his lips and chewed nervously on a blackened nail.

"No," he said weakly, "I don't get it."

Ross stood looking at Mason with jaded eyes. He bit his lips, feeling nervous with the unknown crowding him in, holding off the comfort of solid, rational thinking. He pushed, he shoved it away. He persevered.

"Listen," he said, "we're agreed that those bodies aren't ours."

No answer.

"Use your heads!" Ross commanded. "Feel yourself!"

Mason ran numbed fingers over his jumper, his helmet, the pen in his pocket. He clasped solid hands of flesh and bone. He looked at the veins in his arms. He pressed an anxious finger to his pulse. It's true, he thought. And the thought drove lines of strength back into him. Despite all, despite Ross's desperate advocacy, he was alive. Flesh and blood were his evidence.

His mind swung open then. His brow furrowed in thought as he straightened up. He saw a look almost of relief on the face of a weakening Ross.

"All right then," he said, "we're in the future."

Mickey stood tensely by the port. "Where does that leave us?" he asked.

The words threw Mason back. It was true, where did it leave them?

"How do we know how distant a future?" he said, adding weight to the depression of Mickey's words. "How do we know it isn't in the next twenty minutes?"

Ross tightened. He punched his palm with a resounding smack.

"How do we know?" he said strongly. "We don't go up, we can't crash. That's how we know."

Mason looked at him.

"Maybe if we went up," he said, "we might bypass our death altogether and leave it in this space-time system. We could get back to the space-time system of our own galaxy and . . . "

His words trailed off. His brain became absorbed with twisting thought.

Ross frowned. He stirred restlessly, licked his lips. What had been simple was now something else again. He resented the uninvited intrusion of complexity.

"We're alive now," he said, getting it set in his mind, consolidating assurance with reasonable words, "and there's only one way we can stay alive."

He looked at them, decision reached. "We have to stay here," he said.

They just looked at him. He wished that one of them, at least, would agree with him, show some sign of definition in their minds.

"But . . . what about our orders?" Mason said vaguely.

"Our orders don't tell us to kill ourselves!" Ross said. "No, it's the only answer. If we never go up again, we never crash. We . . . we avoid it, we prevent it!"

His head jarred once in a curt nod. To Ross, the thing was settled.

Mason shook his head.

"I don't know," he said. "I don't . . . "

"I do," Ross stated. "Now let's get out of here. This ship is getting on our nerves."

Mason stood up as the captain gestured toward the door. Mickey started to move, then hesitated. He looked down at the bodies.

"Shouldn't we . . . ?" he started to inquire.

"What, what?" Ross asked, impatient to leave.

Mickey stared at the bodies. He felt caught up in a great, bewildering insanity.

"Shouldn't we . . . bury ourselves?" he said.

Ross swallowed. He would hear no more. He herded them out of the cabin. Then, as they started down through the wreckage, he looked in at the door. He looked at the tarpaulin with the jumbled mound of bodies beneath it. He pressed his lips together until they were white.

"I'm alive," he muttered angrily.

Then he turned out the cabin light with tight, vengeful fingers and left.

———

They all sat in the cabin of their own ship. Ross had ordered food brought out from the lockers, but he was the only one eating. He ate with a belligerent rotation of his jaw as though he would grind away all mystery with his teeth.

Mickey stared at the food.

"How long do we have to stay?" he asked, as if he didn't clearly realize that they were to remain permanently.

Mason took it up. He leaned forward in his seat and looked at Ross.

"How long will our food last?" he said.

"There's edible food outside, I've no doubt," Ross said, chewing.

"How will we know which is edible and which is poisonous?"

"We'll watch the animals," Ross persisted.

"They're a different type of life," Mason said. "What they can eat might be poisonous to us. Besides, we don't even know if there are any animals here."

The words made his lips raise in a brief, bitter smile. And he'd actually been hoping to contact another people. It was practically humorous.

Ross bristled. "We'll . . . cross each river as we come to it," he blurted out as if he hoped to smother all complaint with this ancient homily.

Mason shook his head. "I don't know," he said.

Ross stood up.

"Listen," he said. "It's easy to ask questions. We've all made a decision to stay here. Now let's do some concrete thinking about it. Don't tell me what we can't do. I know that as well as you. Tell me what we can do."

Then he turned on his heel and stalked over to the control board. He stood there glaring at blank-faced gauges and dials. He sat down and began scribbling rapidly in his log as if something of great note had just occurred to him. Later Mason looked at what Ross had written and saw that it was a long paragraph which explained in faulty but unyielding logic why they were all alive.

Mickey got up and sat down on his bunk. He pressed his large hands against his temples. He looked very much like a little boy who had eaten too many green apples against his mother's injunction and who feared retribution on both counts. Mason knew what Mickey was thinking. Of that still body with the skull forced in. The image of himself brutally killed in collision. He, Mason, was thinking of the same thing. And, behavior to the contrary, Ross probably was too.

Mason stood by the port looking out at the silent hulk across the meadow. Darkness was falling. The last rays of the planet's sun glinted off the skin of the crashed rocket ship. Mason turned away. He looked at the outside temperature gauge. Already it was seven degrees and it was still light. Mason moved the thermostat needle with his right forefinger.

Heat being used up, he thought. The energy of our grounded ship being used up faster and faster. The ship drinking its own blood with no possibility of transfusion. Only operation would recharge the ship's energy system. And they were without motion, trapped and stationary.

"How long can we last?" he asked Ross again, refusing to keep silence in the face of the question. "We can't live in this ship indefinitely. The food will run out in a couple of months. And a long time before that the charging system will go. The heat will stop. We'll freeze to death."

"How do we know the outside temperature will freeze us?" Ross asked, falsely patient.

"It's only sundown," Mason said, "and already it's . . . minus thirteen degrees."

Ross looked at him sullenly. Then he pushed up from his chair and began pacing.

"If we go up," he said, "we risk . . . *duplicating* that ship over there."

"But would we?" Mason wondered. "We can only die once. It seems we already have. In this galaxy. Maybe a person can die once in every galaxy. Maybe that's afterlife. Maybe . . . "

"Are you through?" asked Ross coldly.

Mickey looked up.

"Let's go," he said. "I don't want to hang around here."

He looked at Ross.

Ross said, "Let's not stick out our necks before we know what we're doing. Let's think this out."

"I have a wife!" Mickey said angrily. "Just because you're not married—"

"Shut up!" Ross thundered.

Mickey threw himself on the bunk and turned to face the cold bulkhead. Breath shuddered through his heavy frame. He didn't say anything. His fingers opened and closed on the blanket, twisting it, pulling it out from under his body.

Ross paced the deck, abstractedly punching at his palm with a hard fist. His teeth clicked together, his head shook as one argument after another fell before his bullheaded determination. He stopped, looked at Mason, then started pacing again. Once he turned on the outside spotlight and looked to make sure it was not imagination.

The light illumined the broken ship. It glowed strangely, like a huge, broken tombstone. Ross snapped off the spotlight with a soundless snarl. He turned to face them. His broad chest rose and fell heavily as he breathed.

"All right," he said. "It's *your* lives too. I can't decide for all of us. We'll hand vote on it. That thing out there may be something entirely different from what we think. If you two think it's worth the risk of our lives to go up, we'll . . . go up."

He shrugged. "Vote," he said. "I say we stay here."

"I say we go," Mason said.

They looked at Mickey.

"Carter," said Ross, "what's your vote?"

Mickey looked over his shoulder with bleak eyes.

"Vote," Ross said.

"Up," Mickey said. "Take us up. I'd rather die than stay here."

Ross's throat moved. Then he took a deep breath and squared his shoulders.

"All right," he said quietly. "We'll go up."

"God have mercy on us," Mickey muttered as Ross went quickly to the control board.

The captain hesitated a moment. Then he threw switches. The great ship began shuddering as gases ignited and began to pour like channeled lightning from the rear vents. The sound was almost soothing to Mason. He didn't care any more; he was willing, like Mickey, to take a chance. It had only been a few hours. It had seemed like a year. Minutes had dragged, each one weighted with oppressive recollections. Of the bodies they'd seen, of the shattered rocket—even more of the Earth they would never see, of parents and wives and sweethearts and children. Lost to their sight forever. No, it was far better to try to get back. Sitting and waiting was always the hardest thing for a man to do. He was no longer conditioned for it.

Mason sat down at his board. He waited tensely. He heard Mickey jump up and move over to the engine control board.

"I'm going to take us up easy," Ross said to them. "There's no reason why we should . . . have any trouble."

He paused. They snapped their heads over and looked at him with muscle-tight impatience.

"Are you both ready?" Ross asked.

*"Take us up,"* Mickey said.

Ross jammed his lips together and shoved over the switch that read: *Vertical Rise.*

They felt the ship tremble, hesitate. Then it moved off the ground, headed up with increasing velocity. Mason flicked on the rear viewer. He watched the dark earth recede, tried not to look at the white patch in the corner of the screen, the patch that shone metallically under the moonlight.

"Five hundred," he read. "Seven-fifty . . . one thousand . . . fifteen hundred. . . ."

He kept waiting. For explosion. For an engine to give out. For their rise to stop.

They kept moving up.

"Three thousand," Mason said, his voice beginning to betray the rising sense of elation he felt. The planet was getting farther and farther away. The other ship was only a memory now. He looked across at Mickey. Mickey was staring, open-mouthed, as if he were about ready to shout out *"Hurry!"* but was afraid to tempt the fates.

"Six thousand . . . *seven thousand!"* Mason's voice was jubilant. "We're *out* of it!"

Mickey's face broke into a great, relieved grin. He ran a hand over his brow and flicked great drops of sweat on the deck.

"God," he said, gasping, "my God."

Mason moved over to Ross's seat. He clapped the captain on the shoulder.

"We made it," he said. "Nice flying."

Ross looked irritated.

"We shouldn't have left," he said. "It was nothing all the time. Now we have to start looking for another planet." He shook his head. "It wasn't a good idea to leave," he said.

Mason stared at him. He turned away shaking his head, thinking . . . you can't win.

"If I ever see another glitter," he thought aloud, "I'll keep my big mouth shut. To hell with alien races anyway."

Silence. He went back to his seat and picked up his graph chart. He let out a long shaking breath. Let Ross complain, he thought, I can take anything now. Things are normal again. He began to figure casually what might have occurred down there on that planet.

Then he happened to glance at Ross.

Ross was thinking. His lips pressed together. He said something to himself. Mason found the captain looking at him.

"Mason," he said.

"What?"

"Alien race, you said."

Mason felt a chill flood through his body. He saw the big head nod once in decision. Unknown decision. His hands started to shake. A crazy idea came. No, Ross wouldn't do that, not just to assuage vanity. Would he?

"I don't . . ." he started. Out of the corner of his eye he saw Mickey watching the captain too.

"*Listen*," Ross said. "I'll tell you what happened down there. I'll *show* you what happened!"

They stared at him in paralyzing horror as he threw the ship around and headed back.

"What are you doing!" Mickey cried.

"Listen," Ross said. "Didn't you understand me? Don't you see how we've been tricked?"

They looked at him without comprehension. Mickey took a step toward him.

"Alien race," Ross said. "That's the short of it. That time-space idea is all wet. But I'll tell you what idea isn't all wet. So we leave the place. What's our first instinct as far as reporting it? Saying it's uninhabitable? We'd do more than that. We wouldn't report it at all."

"Ross, you're not taking us back!" Mason said, standing up suddenly as the full terror of returning struck him.

"You bet I am!" Ross said, fiercely elated.

"You're crazy!" Mickey shouted at him, his body twitching, his hands clenched at his sides menacingly.

"Listen to me!" Ross roared at them. "Who would be benefited by us not reporting the existence of that planet?"

They didn't answer. Mickey moved closer.

"Fools!" he said. "Isn't it obvious? There *is* life down there. But life that isn't strong enough to kill us or chase us away with force. So what can they do? They don't want us there. So what can they do?"

He asked them like a teacher who cannot get the right answers from the dolts in his class.

Mickey looked suspicious. But he was curious now, too, and a little timorous as he had always been with his captain, except in moments of greatest physical danger. Ross had always led them, and it was hard to rebel against it even when it seemed he was trying to kill them all. His eyes moved to the viewer screen where the planet began to loom beneath them like a huge dark ball.

"We're alive," Ross said, "and I say there never *was* a ship down there. We saw it, sure. We *touched* it. But you can see anything if you believe it's there! All your senses can tell you there's something when there's nothing. All you have to do is *believe* it!"

"What are you getting at?" Mason asked hurriedly, too frightened to realize. His eyes fled to the altitude gauge. Seventeen thousand . . . sixteen thousand . . . fifteen . . .

"Telepathy," Ross said, triumphantly decisive. "I say those men, or whatever they are, saw us coming. And they didn't want us there. So they read our minds and saw the death fear, and they decided that the best way to scare us away was to show us our ship crashed and ourselves dead in it. And it worked . . . until now."

"So it worked!" Mason exploded. "Are you going to take a chance on killing us just to prove your damn theory?"

"It's *more* than a theory!" Ross stormed, as the ship fell, then Ross added with the distorted argument of injured vanity, "My orders say to pick up specimens from every planet. I've always followed orders before and, by God, I still will!"

"You saw how cold it was!" Mason said. "No one can live there anyway! Use your head, Ross!"

"Damn it, *I'm* captain of this ship!" Ross yelled, "and I give the orders!"

"Not when our lives are in your hands!" Mickey started for the captain.

"Get back!" Ross ordered.

That was when one of the ship's engines stopped and the ship yawed wildly.

"You fool!" Mickey exploded, thrown off balance. "You *did* it, you *did* it!"

Outside the black night hurtled past.

The ship wobbled violently. *Prediction true* was the only phrase

Mason could think of. His own vision of the screaming, the numbing horror, the exhortations to a deaf heaven—all coming true. That hulk would be this ship in a matter of minutes. Those three bodies would be . . .

"Oh . . . *damn!*" He screamed it at the top of his lungs, furious at the enraging stubbornness of Ross in taking them back, of causing the future to be as they saw—all because of insane pride.

"No, they're not going to fool us!" Ross shouted, still holding fast to his last idea like a dying bulldog holding its enemy fast in its teeth.

He threw switches and tried to turn the ship. But it wouldn't turn. It kept plunging down like a fluttering leaf. The gyroscope couldn't keep up with the abrupt variations in cabin equilibrium and the three of them found themselves being thrown off balance on the tilting deck.

"Auxiliary engines!" Ross yelled.

"It's no use!" Mickey cried.

"*Damn it!*" Ross clawed his way up the angled deck, then crashed heavily against the engine board as the cabin inclined the other way. He threw switches over with shaking fingers.

Suddenly Mason saw an even spout of flame through the rear viewer again. The ship stopped shuddering and headed straight down. The cabin righted itself.

Ross threw himself into his chair and shot out furious hands to turn the ship about. From the floor Mickey looked at him with a blank, white face. Mason looked at him, too, afraid to speak.

"Now shut up!" Ross said disgustedly, not even looking at them, talking like a disgruntled father to his sons. "When we get down there you're going to see that it's true. That ship'll be gone. And we're going to go looking for those bastards who put the idea in our minds!"

They both stared at their captain humbly as the ship headed down backwards. They watched Ross's hands move efficiently over the controls. Mason felt a sense of confidence in his captain. He stood on the deck quietly, waiting for the landing without fear. Mickey got up from the floor and stood beside him, waiting.

The ship hit the ground. It stopped. They had landed again. They were still the same. And . . .

"Turn on the spotlight," Ross told them.

Mason threw the switch. They all crowded to the port. Mason wondered for a second how Ross could possibly have landed in the same spot. He hadn't even appeared to be following the calculations made on the last landing.

They looked out.

Mickey stopped breathing. And Ross's mouth fell open.

*The wreckage was still there.*

They had landed in the same place and they had found the wrecked ship still there. Mason turned away from the port and stumbled over the deck. He felt lost, a victim of some terrible universal prank, a man accursed.

"You said . . ." Mickey said to the captain.

Ross just looked out of the port with unbelieving eyes.

"Now we'll go up again," Mickey said, grinding his teeth. "And we'll *really* crash this time. And we'll be killed. Just like those . . . those . . . "

Ross didn't speak. He stared out of the port at the refutation of his last clinging hope. He felt hollow, void of all faith in belief in sensible things.

Then Mason spoke.

"We're not going to crash—" he said somberly—"ever."

"What?"

Mickey was looking at him. Ross turned and looked too.

"Why don't we stop kidding ourselves?" Mason said. "We all know what it is, don't we?"

He was thinking of what Ross had said just a moment before. About the senses giving evidence of what was believed. Even if there was nothing there at all . . .

Then, in a split second, with the knowledge, he saw Ross and he saw Carter. As they *were*. And he took a short shuddering breath, a last breath until illusion would bring breath and flesh again.

"Progress," he said bitterly, and his voice was an aching whisper in the phantom ship. "The Flying Dutchman takes to the universe."

# L. SPRAGUE DE CAMP

*L. Sprague de Camp (1907–2000) began writing in the 1930s, and pub-lished more than one hundred science-fiction and fantasy novels, dozens of short stories, and many acclaimed nonfiction works during his career. Known early on for his space opera novels, he was first critically and popu-larly recognized for his novel* Lest Darkness Fall, *the story of one man's at-tempt to change history during the Roman Empire. Adept in every genre he turned his hand to, he has written everything from fantasy (The In-complete Enchanter series) to Conan pastiches, revising and publishing Robert E. Howard's unfinished works in the collection* Tales of Conan, *to books on writing science fiction (Science-Fiction Handbook). He also wrote many excellent nonfiction books on topics that varied from author biographies, including books on H. P. Lovecraft and Robert E. Howard, to texts on aspects of science and even the Scopes monkey trial. He was loved, respected, and lauded in the science-fiction and fantasy field, receiving the Gandalf (the Grand Master Award for Lifetime Achievement in Fantasy) Award, and the Science Fiction and Fantasy Writers of America's Grand Master Award. In 1997, his autobiography,* Time and Chance, *received the Hugo Award for best nonfiction work. He married Catherine A. Crook in 1939, and they remained together for more than sixty years, traveling the world and writing, until her death in 2000.*

*De Camp was able to take virtually any topic and make a smooth, be-lievable story out of it by the time he was done, and "A Gun for Dinosaur" is a perfect example. In contrast to Bradbury's emphasis on the bells and whistles, he sidesteps the idea of a time paradox in about five paragraphs, and it's on to the meat (slight pun intended) of the story, hunting what would arguably be the most challenging game of all—a late Mesozoic dinosaur. The idea of time travel actually takes a backseat to the rest of the story—except, of course, for one character's admittedly gruesome end, also described in a few paragraphs where de Camp shows his mastery of answering a logical question by showing the results, and wrapping up his plot as neat as can be.*

# A GUN FOR DINOSAUR

## L. SPRAGUE DE CAMP

NO, I'M SORRY, Mr. Seligman, but I can't take you hunting Late Meso-zoic dinosaur.

Yes, I know what the advertisement says.

Why not? How much d'you weigh? A hundred and thirty? Let's see; that's under ten stone, which is my lower limit.

I could take you to other periods, you know. I'll take you to any pe-riod in the Cenozoic. I'll get you a shot at an entelodont or a uintathere. They've got fine heads.

I'll even stretch a point and take you to the Pleistocene, where you can try for one of the mammoths or the mastodon.

I'll take you back to the Triassic where you can shoot one of the smaller ancestral dinosaurs. But I will jolly well not take you to the Juras-sic or Cretaceous. You're just too small.

What's your size got to do with it? Look here, old boy, what did you think you were going to shoot your dinosaur with?

Oh, you hadn't thought, eh?

Well, sit there a minute. . . . Here you are: my own private gun for that work, a Continental .600. Does look like a shotgun, doesn't it? But it's rifled, as you can see by looking through the barrels. Shoots a pair of .600 Nitro Express cartridges the size of bananas; weighs fourteen and a half pounds and has a muzzle energy of over seven thousand foot-pounds. Costs fourteen hundred and fifty dollars. Lot of money for a gun, what?

I have some spares I rent to the sahibs. Designed for knocking down elephant. Not just wounding them, knocking them base-over-apex.

That's why they don't make guns like this in America, though I suppose they will if hunting parties keep going back in time.

Now, I've been guiding hunting parties for twenty years. Guided 'em in Africa until the game gave out there except on the preserves. And all that time I've never known a man your size who could handle the six-nought-nought. It knocks 'em over, and even when they stay on their feet they get so scared of the bloody cannon after a few shots that they flinch. And they find the gun too heavy to drag around rough Mesozoic country. Wears 'em out.

It's true that lots of people have killed elephant with lighter guns: the .500, .475, and .465 doubles, for instance, or even .375 magnum re-peaters. The difference is, with a .375 you have to hit something vital, preferably the heart, and can't depend on simple shock power.

An elephant weighs—let's see—four to six tons. You're proposing to shoot reptiles weighing two or three times as much as an elephant and with much greater tenacity of life. That's why the syndicate decided to take no more people dinosaur hunting unless they could handle the .600. We learned the hard way, as you Americans say. There were some unfortunate incidents. . . .

I'll tell you, Mr. Seligman. It's after seventeen-hundred. Time I closed the office. Why don't we stop at the bar on our way out while I tell you the story?

———

. . . It was about the Raja's and my fifth safari into time. The Raja? Oh, he's the Aiyar half of Rivers and Aiyar. I call him the Raja because he's the hereditary monarch of Janpur. Means nothing nowadays, of course. Knew him in India and ran into him in New York running the Indian tourist agency. That dark chap in the photograph on my office wall, the one with his foot on the dead sabertooth.

Well, the Raja was fed up with handing out brochures about the Taj Mahal and wanted to do a bit of hunting again. I was at loose ends when we heard of Professor Prochaska's time machine at Washington University.

Where's the Raja now? Out on safari in the Early Oligocene after ti-tanothere while I run the office. We take turn about, but the first few times we went out together.

Anyhow, we caught the next plane to St. Louis. To our mortification, we found we weren't the first. Lord, no! There were other hunting guides and no end of scientists, each with his own idea of the right way to use the machine.

We scraped off the historians and archaeologists right at the start. Seems the ruddy machine won't work for periods more recent than 100,000 years ago. It works from there up to about a billion years.

Why? Oh, I'm no four-dimensional thinker; but, as I understand it, if people could go back to a more recent time, their actions would affect our own history, which would be a paradox or contradiction of facts. Can't have that in a well-run universe, you know.

But, before 100,000 B.C., more or less, the actions of the expeditions are lost in the stream of time before human history begins. At that, once a stretch of past time has been used, say the month of January, one million B.C., you can't use that stretch over again by sending another party into it. Paradoxes again.

The professor isn't worried, though. With a billion years to exploit, he won't soon run out of eras.

Another limitation of the machine is the matter of size. For technical reasons, Prochaska had to build the transition chamber just big enough to hold four men with their personal gear, and the chamber wallah. Larger parties have to be sent through in relays. That means, you see, it's not practical to take jeeps, launches, aircraft, and other powered vehicles.

On the other hand, since you're going to periods without human beings, there's no whistling up a hundred native bearers to trot along with your gear on their heads. So we usually take a train of asses—burros, they call them here. Most periods have enough natural forage so you can get where you want to go.

As I say, everybody had his own idea for using the machine. The scientists looked down their noses at us hunters and said it would be a crime to waste the machine's time pandering to our sadistic amusements.

We brought up another angle. The machine cost a cool thirty million. I understand this came from the Rockefeller Board and such people, but that accounted for the original cost only, not the cost of operation. And the thing uses fantastic amounts of power. Most of the scientists' projects, while worthy enough, were run on a shoestring, financially speaking.

Now, we guides catered to people with money, a species with which America seems well stocked. No offense, old boy. Most of these could afford a substantial fee for passing through the machine into the past. Thus we could help finance the operation of the machine for scientific purposes, provided we got a fair share of its time. In the end, the guides formed a syndicate of eight members, one member being the partnership of Rivers and Aiyar, to apportion the machine's time.

We had rush business from the start. Our wives—the Raja's and mine—raised hell with us for a while. They'd hoped that, when the big game gave out in our own era, they'd never have to share us with lions and things again, but you know how women are. Hunting's not really dangerous if you keep your head and take precautions.

———

On the fifth expedition, we had two sahibs to wet-nurse; both Americans in their thirties, both physically sound, and both solvent. Otherwise they were as different as different can be.

Courtney James was what you chaps call a playboy: a rich young man from New York who'd always had his own way and didn't see why that agreeable condition shouldn't continue. A big bloke, almost as big as I am; handsome in a florid way, but beginning to run to fat. He was on his fourth wife and, when he showed up at the office with a blond twist with "model" written all over her, I assumed that this was the fourth Mrs. James.

"Miss Bartram," she corrected me, with an embarrassed giggle.

"She's not my wife," James explained. "My wife is in Mexico, I think, getting a divorce. But Bunny here would like to go along—"

"Sorry," I said, "we don't take ladies. At least, not to the Late Mesozoic."

This wasn't strictly true, but I felt we were running enough risks, going after a little-known fauna, without dragging in people's domestic entanglements. Nothing against sex, you understand. Marvelous institution and all that, but not where it interferes with my living.

"Oh, nonsense!" said James. "If she wants to go, she'll go. She skis and flies my airplane, so why shouldn't she—"

"Against the firm's policy," I said.

"She can keep out of the way when we run up against the dangerous ones," he said.

"No, sorry."

"Damn it!" said he, getting red. "After all, I'm paying you a goodly sum, and I'm entitled to take whoever I please."

"You can't hire me to do anything against my best judgment," I said. "If that's how you feel, get another guide."

"All right, I will," he said. "And I'll tell all my friends you're a God-damned—" Well, he said a lot of things I won't repeat, until I told him to get out of the office or I'd throw him out.

I was sitting in the office and thinking sadly of all that lovely money James would have paid me if I hadn't been so stiff-necked, when in came my other lamb, one August Holtzinger. This was a little slim pale chap with glasses, polite and formal. Holtzinger sat on the edge of his chair and said:

"Uh—Mr. Rivers, I don't want you to think I'm here under false pretenses. I'm really not much of an outdoorsman, and I'll probably be scared to death when I see a real dinosaur. But I'm determined to hang a dinosaur head over my fireplace or die in the attempt."

"Most of us are frightened at first," I soothed him, "though it doesn't do to show it." And little by little I got the story out of him.

While James had always been wallowing in the stuff, Holtzinger was a local product who'd only lately come into the real thing. He'd had a little business here in St. Louis and just about made ends meet when an uncle cashed in his chips somewhere and left little Augie the pile.

Now Holtzinger had acquired a fiancée and was building a big house. When it was finished, they'd be married and move into it. And one furnishing he demanded was a ceratopsian head over the fireplace. Those are the ones with the big horned heads with a parrot beak and a frill over the neck, you know. You have to think twice about collecting them, because if you put a seven-foot *Triceratops* head into a small living room, there's apt to be no room left for anything else.

We were talking about this when in came a girl: a small girl in her twenties, quite ordinary-looking, and crying.

"Augie!" she cried. "You can't! You mustn't! You'll be killed!" She grabbed him round the knees and said to me:

"Mr. Rivers, you mustn't take him! He's all I've got! He'll never stand the hardships!"

"My dear young lady," I said, "I should hate to cause you distress, but it's up to Mr. Holtzinger to decide whether he wishes to retain my services."

"It's no use, Claire," said Holtzinger. "I'm going, though I'll probably hate every minute of it."

"What's that, old boy?" I said. "If you hate it, why go? Did you lose a bet, or something?"

"No," said Holtzinger. "It's this way. Uh—I'm a completely undistinguished kind of guy. I'm not brilliant or big or strong or handsome. I'm just an ordinary Midwestern small businessman. You never even notice me at Rotary luncheons, I fit in so perfectly.

"But that doesn't say I'm satisfied. I've always hankered to go to far places and do big things. I'd like to be a glamorous, adventurous sort of guy. Like you, Mr. Rivers."

"Oh, come," I said. "Professional hunting may seem glamorous to you, but to me it's just a living."

He shook his head. "Nope. You know what I mean. Well, now I've got this legacy, I could settle down to play bridge and golf the rest of my life, and try to act like I wasn't bored. But I'm determined to do something with some color in it, once at least. Since there's no more real big-game hunting in the present, I'm gonna shoot a dinosaur and hang his head over my mantel if it's the last thing I do. I'll never be happy otherwise."

Well, Holtzinger and his girl argued, but he wouldn't give in. She made me swear to take the best care of her Augie and departed, sniffling.

When Holtzinger had left, who should come in but my vile-tempered friend Courtney James? He apologized for insulting me, though you could hardly say he groveled.

"I don't really have a bad temper," he said, "except when people won't cooperate with me. Then I sometimes get mad. But so long as they're cooperative I'm not hard to get along with."

I knew that by "cooperate" he meant to do whatever Courtney James wanted, but I didn't press the point. "How about Miss Bartram?" I asked.

"We had a row," he said. "I'm through with women. So, if there's no hard feelings, let's go from where we left off."

"Very well," I said, business being business.

The Raja and I decided to make it a joint safari to eighty-five million years ago: the Early Upper Cretaceous, or the Middle Cretaceous as some American geologists call it. It's about the best period for dinosaur in Missouri. You'll find some individual species a little larger in the Late Upper Cretaceous, but the period we were going to gives a wider variety.

Now, as to our equipment: The Raja and I each had a Continental .600, like the one I showed you, and a few smaller guns. At this time we hadn't worked up much capital and had no spare .600s to rent.

August Holtzinger said he would rent a gun, as he expected this to be his only safari, and there's no point in spending over a thousand dollars for a gun you'll shoot only a few times. But, since we had no spare

.600s, his choice lay between buying one of those and renting one of our smaller pieces.

We drove into the country and set up a target to let him try the .600. Holtzinger heaved up the gun and let fly. He missed completely, and the kick knocked him flat on his back.

He got up, looking paler than ever, and handed me back the gun, saying: "Uh—I think I'd better try something smaller."

When his shoulder stopped hurting, I tried him out on the smaller rifles. He took a fancy to my Winchester 70, chambered for the .375 magnum cartridge. This is an excellent all-round gun—perfect for the big cats and bears, but a little light for elephant and definitely light for dinosaur. I should never have given in, but I was in a hurry, and it might have taken months to have a new .600 made to order for him. James already had a gun, a Holland & Holland .500 double express, which is almost in a class with the .600.

Both sahibs had done a bit of shooting, so I didn't worry about their accuracy. Shooting dinosaur is not a matter of extreme accuracy, but of sound judgment and smooth coordination so you shan't catch twigs in the mechanism of your gun, or fall into holes, or climb a small tree that the dinosaur can pluck you out of, or blow your guide's head off.

People used to hunting mammals sometimes try to shoot a dinosaur in the brain. That's the silliest thing you can do, because dinosaur haven't got any. To be exact, they have a little lump of tissue the size of a tennis ball on the front end of their spines, and how are you going to hit that when it's imbedded in a six-foot skull?

The only safe rule with dinosaur is: always try for a heart shot. They have big hearts, over a hundred pounds in the largest species, and a couple of .600 slugs through the heart will slow them up, at least. The problem is to get the slugs through that mountain of meat around it.

————————

Well, we appeared at Prochaska's laboratory one rainy morning: James and Holtzinger, the Raja and I, our herder Beauregard Black, three helpers, a cook, and twelve jacks.

The transition chamber is a little cubbyhole the size of a small lift. My routine is for the men with the guns to go first in case a hungry theropod is standing near the machine when it arrives. So the two sahibs, the Raja, and I crowded into the chamber with our guns and packs. The operator squeezed in after us, closed the door, and fiddled with his dials. He set the thing for April twenty-fourth, eighty-five million B.C., and pressed the red button. The lights went out, leaving the chamber lit by a little battery-operated lamp. James and Holtzinger looked pretty green, but that may have been the lighting. The Raja and I had been through all this before, so the vibration and vertigo didn't bother us.

The little spinning black hands of the dials slowed down and stopped. The operator looked at his ground-level gauge and turned the handwheel that raised the chamber so it shouldn't materialize underground. Then he pressed another button, and the door slid open.

No matter how often I do it, I get a frightful thrill out of stepping into a bygone era. The operator had raised the chamber a foot above the ground level, so I jumped down, my gun ready. The others came after.

"Right-ho," I said to the chamber wallah, and he closed the door. The chamber disappeared, and we looked around. There weren't any dinosaur in sight, nothing but lizards.

In this period, the chamber materializes on top of a rocky rise, from which you can see in all directions as far as the haze will let you. To the west, you see the arm of the Kansas Sea that reaches across Missouri and the big swamp around the bayhead where the sauropods live.

To the north is a low range that the Raja named the Janpur Hills, after the Indian kingdom his forebears once ruled. To the east, the land slopes up to a plateau, good for ceratopsians, while to the south is flat country with more sauropod swamps and lots of ornithopod: duckbill and iguanodont.

The finest thing about the Cretaceous is the climate: balmy like the South Sea Islands, but not so muggy as most Jurassic climates. It was spring, with dwarf magnolias in bloom all over.

A thing about this landscape is that it combines a fairly high rainfall with an open type of vegetation cover. That is, the grasses hadn't yet evolved to the point of forming solid carpets over all the open ground. So the ground is thick with laurel, sassafras, and other shrubs, with bare earth between. There are big thickets of palmettos and ferns. The trees round the hill are mostly cycads, standing singly and in copses. You'd call 'em palms. Down towards the Kansas Sea are more cycads and willows, while the uplands are covered with screw pine and ginkgoes.

Now, I'm no bloody poet—the Raja writes the stuff, not me—but I can appreciate a beautiful scene. One of the helpers had come through the machine with two of the jacks and was pegging them out, and I was looking through the haze and sniffing the air, when a gun went off behind me—*bang! bang!*

I whirled round, and there was Courtney James with his .500, and an ornithomime legging it for cover fifty yards away. The ornithomimes are medium-sized running dinosaurs, slender things with long necks and legs, like a cross between a lizard and an ostrich. This kind is about seven feet tall and weighs as much as a man. The beggar had wandered out of the nearest copse, and James gave him both barrels. Missed.

I was upset, as trigger-happy sahibs are as much a menace to their party as theropods. I yelled: "Damn it, you idiot! I thought you weren't to shoot without a word from me?"

"And who the hell are you to tell me when I'll shoot my own gun?" he said.

We had a rare old row until Holtzinger and the Raja got us calmed down. I explained:

"Look here, Mr. James, I've got reasons. If you shoot off all your ammunition before the trip's over, your gun won't be available in a pinch, as it's the only one of its caliber. If you empty both barrels at an unimportant target, what would happen if a big theropod charged before you could reload? Finally, it's not sporting to shoot everything in sight, just to hear the gun go off. Do you understand?"

"Yeah, I guess so," he said.

The rest of the party came through the machine and we pitched our camp a safe distance from the materializing place. Our first task was to get fresh meat. For a twenty-one-day safari like this, we calculate our food requirements closely, so we can make out on tinned stuff and concentrates if we must, but we count on killing at least one piece of meat. When that's butchered, we go off on a short tour, stopping at four or five camping places to hunt and arriving back at base a few days before the chamber is due to appear.

Holtzinger, as I said, wanted a ceratopsian head, any kind. James insisted on just one head: a tyrannosaur. Then everybody'd think he'd shot the most dangerous game of all time.

Fact is, the tyrannosaur's overrated. He's more a carrion eater than an active predator, though he'll snap you up if he gets the chance. He's less dangerous than some of the other therapods—the flesh eaters, you know—such as the smaller *Gorgosaurus* from the period we were in. But everybody's read about the tyrant lizard, and he does have the biggest head of the theropods.

The one in our period isn't the *rex*, which is later and a bit bigger and more specialized. It's the *trionyches*, with the forelimbs not quite so reduced, though they're still too small for anything but picking the brute's teeth after a meal.

———

When camp was pitched, we still had the afternoon. So the Raja and I took our sahibs on their first hunt. We had a map of the local terrain from previous trips.

The Raja and I have worked out a system for dinosaur hunting. We split into two groups of two men each and walk parallel from twenty to forty yards apart. Each group has a sahib in front and a guide following, telling him where to go. We tell the sahibs we put them in front so they shall have the first shot. Well, that's true, but another reason is they're always tripping and falling with their guns cocked, and if the guide were in front he'd get shot.

The reason for two groups is that if a dinosaur starts for one, the other gets a good heart shot from the side.

As we walked, there was the usual rustle of lizards scuttling out of the way: little fellows, quick as a flash and colored like all the jewels in Tiffany's, and big gray ones that hiss at you as they plod off. There were tortoises and a few little snakes. Birds with beaks full of teeth flapped off squawking. And always there was that marvelous mild Cretaceous air. Makes a chap want to take his clothes off and dance with vine leaves in his hair, if you know what I mean.

Our sahibs soon found that Mesozoic country is cut up into millions of nullahs—gullies, you'd say. Walking is one long scramble, up and down, up and down.

We'd been scrambling for an hour, and the sahibs were soaked with sweat and had their tongues hanging out, when the Raja whistled. He'd spotted a group of bonehead feeding on cycad shoots.

These are the troödonts, small ornithopods about the size of men with a bulge on top of their heads that makes them look almost intelligent. Means nothing, because the bulge is solid bone. The males butt each other with these heads in fighting over the females.

These chaps would drop down on all fours, munch up a shoot, then stand up and look around. They're warier than most dinosaur, because they're the favorite food of the big theropods.

People sometimes assume that because dinosaur are so stupid, their senses must be dim, too. But it's not so. Some, like the sauropods, are pretty dim-sensed, but most have good smell and eyesight and fair hearing. Their weakness is that having no minds, they have no memories. Hence, out of sight, out of mind. When a big theropod comes slavering after you, your best defense is to hide in a nullah or behind a bush, and if he can neither see you nor smell you he'll just wander off.

We skulked up behind a patch of palmetto downwind from the bonehead. I whispered to James:

"You've had a shot already today. Hold your fire until Holtzinger shoots, and then shoot only if he misses or if the beast is getting away wounded."

"Uh-huh," said James.

We separated, he with the Raja and Holtzinger with me. This got to be our regular arrangement. James and I got on each other's nerves, but the Raja's a friendly, sentimental sort of bloke nobody can help liking.

We crawled round the palmetto patch on opposite sides, and Holtzinger got up to shoot. You daren't shoot a heavy-caliber rifle prone. There's not enough give, and the kick can break your shoulder.

Holtzinger sighted round the last few fronds of palmetto. I saw his barrel wobbling and waving. Then he lowered his gun and tucked it under his arm to wipe his glasses.

Off went James's gun, both barrels again.

The biggest bonehead went down, rolling and thrashing. The others ran away on their hind-legs in great leaps, their heads jerking and their tails sticking up behind.

"Put your gun on safety," I said to Holtzinger, who'd started forward. By the time we got to the bonehead, James was standing over it, breaking open his gun and blowing out the barrels. He looked as smug as if he'd come into another million and was asking the Raja to take his picture with his foot on the game.

I said: "I thought you were to give Holtzinger the first shot?"

"Hell, I waited," he said, "and he took so long I thought he must have gotten buck fever. If we stood around long enough, they'd see us or smell us."

There was something in what he said, but his way of saying it put my monkey up. I said: "If that sort of thing happens once more, we'll leave you in camp the next time we go out."

"Now, gentlemen," said the Raja. "After all, Reggie, these aren't experienced hunters."

"What now?" said Holtzinger. "Haul him back ourselves or send out the men?"

"We'll sling him under the pole," I said. "He weighs under two hundred."

The pole was a telescoping aluminum carrying pole I had in my pack, with padded yokes on the ends. I brought it because, in such eras, you can't count on finding saplings strong enough for proper poles on the spot.

The Raja and I cleaned our bonehead to lighten him and tied him to the pole. The flies began to light on the offal by thousands. Scientists say they're not true flies in the modern sense, but they look and act like flies. There's one huge four-winged carrion fly that flies with a distinctive deep thrumming note.

The rest of the afternoon we sweated under that pole, taking turn about. The lizards scuttled out of the way, and the flies buzzed round the carcass.

We got to camp just before sunset, feeling as if we could eat the whole bonehead at one meal. The boys had the camp running smoothly, so we sat down for our tot of whiskey, feeling like lords of creation, while the cook broiled bonehead steaks.

Holtzinger said: "Uh—if I kill a ceratopsian, how do we get his head back?"

I explained: "If the ground permits, we lash it to the patent aluminum roller frame and sled it in."

"How much does a head like that weigh?" he asked.

"Depends on the age and the species," I told him. "The biggest weigh over a ton, but most run between five hundred and a thousand pounds."

"And all the ground's rough like it was today?"

"Most of it," I said. "You see, it's the combination of the open vegetation cover and the moderately high rainfall. Erosion is frightfully rapid."

"And who hauls the head on its little sled?"

"Everybody with a hand," I said. "A big head would need every ounce of muscle in this party. On such a job there's no place for side."

"Oh," said Holtzinger. I could see he was wondering whether a cera-topsian head would be worth the effort.

The next couple of days we trekked round the neighborhood. Noth-ing worth shooting; only a herd of ornithomimes, which went bounding off like a lot of ballet dancers. Otherwise there were only the usual lizards and pterosaurs and birds and insects. There's a big lace-winged fly that bites dinosaurs, so, as you can imagine, its beak makes nothing of a human skin. One made Holtzinger leap and dance like a Red In-dian when it bit him through his shirt. James joshed him about it, say-ing:

"What's all the fuss over one little bug?"

The second night, during the Raja's watch, James gave a yell that brought us all out of our tents with rifles. All that had happened was that a dinosaur tick had crawled in with him and started drilling under his armpit. Since it's as big as your thumb even when it hasn't fed, he was understandably startled. Luckily he got it before it had taken its pint of blood. He'd pulled Holtzinger's leg pretty hard about the fly bite, so now Holtzinger repeated the words:

"What's all the fuss over one little bug, buddy?"

James squashed the tick underfoot with a grunt, not much liking to be hoist by his own what-d'you-call-it.

———

We packed up and started on our circuit. We meant to take the sahibs first to the sauropod swamp, more to see the wildlife than to collect any-thing.

From where the transition chamber materializes, the sauropod swamp looks like a couple of hours' walk, but it's really an all-day scram-ble. The first part is easy, as it's downhill and the brush isn't heavy. Then, as you get near the swamp, the cycads and willows grow so thickly that you have to worm your way among them.

I led the party to a sandy ridge on the border of the swamp, as it was pretty bare of vegetation and afforded a fine view. When we got to the ridge, the sun was about to go down. A couple of crocs slipped off into the water. The sahibs were so tired that they flopped down in the sand as if dead.

The haze is thick round the swamp, so the sun was deep red and weirdly distorted by the atmospheric layers. There was a high layer of clouds reflecting the red and gold of the sun, too, so altogether it was something for the Raja to write one of his poems about. A few little pterosaur were wheeling overhead like bats.

Beauregard Black got a fire going. We'd started on our steaks, and that pagoda-shaped sun was just slipping below the horizon, and something back in the trees was making a noise like a rusty hinge, when a sauropod breathed out in the water. They're the really big ones, you know. If Mother Earth were to sigh over the misdeeds of her children, it would sound like that.

The sahibs jumped up, shouting: "Where is he? Where is he?"

I said: "That black spot in the water, just to the left of that point."

They yammered while the sauropod filled its lungs and disappeared. "Is that all?" said James. "Won't we see any more of him?"

Holtzinger said: "I read that they never come out of the water because they're too heavy to walk."

"No," I explained. "They can walk perfectly well and often do, for egg-laying and moving from one swamp to another. But most of the time they spend in the water, like hippopotamus. They eat eight hundred pounds of soft swamp plants a day, all through those little heads. So they wander about the bottoms of lakes and swamps, chomping away, and stick their heads up to breathe every quarter-hour or so. It's getting dark, so this fellow will soon come out and lie down in the shallows to sleep."

"Can we shoot one?" demanded James.

"I wouldn't," said I.

"Why not?"

I said: "There's no point in it, and it's not sporting. First, they're almost invulnerable. They're even harder to hit in the brain than other dinosaurs because of the way they sway their heads about on those long necks. Their hearts are too deeply buried to reach unless you're awfully lucky. Then, if you kill one in the water, he sinks and can't be recovered. If you kill one on land, the only trophy is that little head. You can't bring the whole beast back because he weighs thirty tons or more, and we've got no use for thirty tons of meat."

Holtzinger said: "That museum in New York got one."

"Yes," said I. "The American Museum of Natural History sent a party of forty-eight to the Early Cretaceous with a fifty-caliber machine gun. They killed a sauropod and spent two solid months skinning it and hacking the carcass apart and dragging it to the time machine. I know the chap in charge of that project, and he still has nightmares in which he smells decomposing dinosaur. They had to kill a dozen big theropods attracted by the stench, so they had them lying around and rotting, too. And the theropods ate three men of the party despite the big gun."

Next morning, we were finishing breakfast when one of the helpers said: "Look, Mr. Rivers, up there!"

He pointed along the shoreline. There were six big crested duckbill, feeding in the shallows. They were the kind called *Parasaurolophus*, with a long spike sticking out the back of their heads and a web of skin connecting this with the back of their necks.

"Keep your voices down!" I said. The duckbill, like the other or-nithopods are wary beasts because they have neither armor nor weapons. They feed on the margins of lakes and swamps, and when a gorgosaur rushes out of the trees they plunge into deep water and swim off. Then when *Phobosuchus*, the supercrocodile, goes for them in the water, they flee to the land. A hectic sort of life, what?

Holtzinger said: "Uh—Reggie! I've been thinking over what you said about ceratopsian heads. If I could get one of those yonder, I'd be satisfied. It would look big enough in my house, wouldn't it?"

"I'm sure of it, old boy," I said. "Now look here. We could detour to come out on the shore near here, but we should have to plow through half a mile of muck and brush, and they'd hear us coming. Or we can creep up to the north end of this sandpit, from which it's three or four hundred yards—a long shot but not impossible. Think you could do it?"

"Hm," said Holtzinger. "With my scope sight and a sitting position— okay, I'll try it."

"You stay here, Court," I said to James. "This is Augie's head, and I don't want any argument over your having fired first."

James grunted while Holtzinger clamped his scope to his rifle. We crouched our way up the spit, keeping the sand ridge between us and the duckbill. When we got to the end where there was no more cover, we crept along on hands and knees, moving slowly. If you move slowly enough, directly toward or away from a dinosaur, it probably won't notice you.

The duckbill continued to grub about on all fours, every few sec-onds rising to look round. Holtzinger eased himself into the sitting posi-tion, cocked his piece, and aimed through his scope. And then—

*Bang! bang!* went a big rifle back at the camp.

Holtzinger jumped. The duckbills jerked their heads up and leaped for the deep water, splashing like mad. Holtzinger fired once and missed. I took one shot at the last duckbill before it vanished too, but missed. The .600 isn't built for long ranges.

Holtzinger and I started back toward the camp, for it had struck us that our party might be in theropod trouble.

What had happened was that a big sauropod had wandered down past the camp underwater, feeding as it went. Now, the water shoaled about a hundred yards offshore from our spit, halfway over to the swamp on the other side. The sauropod had ambled up the slope until its body was almost all out of water, weaving its head from side to side and looking for anything green to gobble. This is a species of *Alamosaurus*, which looks much like the well-known *Brontosaurus* except that it's bigger.

When I came in sight of the camp, the sauropod was turning round to go back the way it had come, making horrid groans. By the time we reached the camp, it had disappeared into deep water, all but its head and twenty feet of neck, which wove about for some time before they vanished into the haze.

When we came up to the camp, James was arguing with the Raja. Holtzinger burst out:

"You crummy bastard! That's the second time you've spoiled my shots."

"Don't be a fool," said James. "I couldn't let him wander into the camp and stamp everything flat."

"There was no danger of that," said the Raja. "You can see the water is deep offshore. It's just that our trigger-happee Mr. James cannot see any animal without shooting."

I added: "If it did get close, all you needed to do was throw a stick of firewood at it. They're perfectly harmless."

This wasn't strictly true. When the Comte de Lautrec ran after one for a close shot, the sauropod looked back at him, gave a flick of its tail, and took off the Comte's head as neatly as if he'd been axed in the tower. But, as a rule, they're inoffensive enough.

"How was I to know?" yelled James, turning purple. "You're all against me. What the hell are we on this miserable trip for, except to shoot things? Call yourselves hunters, but I'm the only one who hits anything!"

I got pretty wrothy and said he was just an excitable young skite with more money than brains, whom I should never have brought along.

"If that's how you feel," he said, "give me a burro and some food, and

I'll go back to the base by myself. I won't pollute your pure air with my presence!"

"Don't be a bigger ass than you can help," I said. "What you propose is quite impossible."

"Then I'll go alone!" He grabbed his knapsack, thrust a couple of tins of beans and an opener into it, and started off with his rifle.

Beauregard Black spoke up: "Mr. Rivers, we cain't let him go off like that. He'll git lost and starve, or be et by a theropod."

"I'll fetch him back," said the Raja, and started after the runaway.

He caught up with James as the latter was disappearing into the cycads. We could see them arguing and waving their hands in the distance. After a while, they started back with arms around each other's necks like old school pals.

This shows the trouble we get into if we make mistakes in planning such a do. Having once got back in time, we had to make the best of our bargain.

I don't want to give the impression, however, that Courtney James was nothing but a pain in the rump. He had good points. He got over these rows quickly and next day would be as cheerful as ever. He was helpful with the general work of the camp, at least when he felt like it. He sang well and had an endless fund of dirty stories to keep us amused.

We stayed two more days at that camp. We saw crocodile, the small kind, and plenty of sauropod—as many as five at once—but no more duckbill. Nor any of those fifty-foot supercrocodiles.

————

So, on the first of May, we broke camp and headed north toward the Janpur Hills. My sahibs were beginning to harden up and were getting impatient. We'd been in the Cretaceous a week, and no trophies.

We saw nothing to speak of on the next leg, save a glimpse of a gorgosaur out of range and some tracks indicating a whopping big iguanodont, twenty-five or thirty feet high. We pitched camp at the base of the hills.

We'd finished off the bonehead, so the first thing was to shoot fresh meat. With an eye to trophies, too, of course. We got ready the morning of the third, and I told James:

"See here, old boy, no more of your tricks. The Raja will tell you when to shoot."

"Uh-huh, I get you," he said, meek as Moses.

We marched off, the four of us, into the foothills. There was a good chance of getting Holtzinger his ceratopsian. We'd seen a couple on the way up, but mere calves without decent horns.

As it was hot and sticky, we were soon panting and sweating. We'd hiked and scrambled all morning without seeing a thing except lizards, when I picked up the smell of carrion. I stopped the party and sniffed. We were in an open glade cut up by those little dry nullahs. The nullahs ran together into a couple of deeper gorges that cut through a slight depression choked with denser growth, cycad, and screw pine. When I listened, I heard the thrum of carrion flies.

"This way," I said. "Something ought to be dead—ah, here it is!"

And there it was: the remains of a huge ceratopsian lying in a little hollow on the edge of a copse. Must have weighed six or eight ton alive; a three-horned variety, perhaps the penultimate species of *Triceratops*. It was hard to tell, because most of the hide on the upper surface had been ripped off, and many bones had been pulled loose and lay scattered about.

Holtzinger said: "Oh, shucks! Why couldn't I have gotten to him before he died? That would have been a darned fine head."

I said: "On your toes, chaps. A theropod's been at this carcass and is probably nearby."

"How d'you know?" said James, with sweat running off his round red face. He spoke in what was for him a low voice, because a nearby theropod is a sobering thought to the flightiest.

I sniffed again and thought I could detect the distinctive rank odor of theropod. I couldn't be sure, though, because the carcass stank so strongly. My sahibs were turning green at the sight and smell of the cadaver. I told James:

"It's seldom that even the biggest theropod will attack a full-grown ceratopsian. Those horns are too much for them. But they love a dead or dying one. They'll hang round a dead ceratopsian for weeks, gorging and then sleeping off their meals for days at a time. They usually take cover in the heat of the day anyhow, because they can't stand much direct hot sunlight. You'll find them lying in copses like this or in hollows, wherever there's shade."

"What'll we do?" asked Holtzinger.

"We'll make our first cast through this copse, in two pairs as usual. Whatever you do, don't get impulsive or panicky."

I looked at Courtney James, but he looked right back and merely checked his gun.

"Should I still carry this broken?" he asked.

"No, close it, but keep the safety on till you're ready to shoot," I said. "We'll keep closer than usual, so we shall be in sight of each other. Start off at that angle, Raja; go slowly, and stop to listen between steps."

We pushed through the edge of the copse, leaving the carcass but not its stench behind us. For a few feet, you couldn't see a thing.

It opened out as we got in under the trees, which shaded out some of the brush. The sun slanted down through the trees. I could hear nothing but the hum of insects and the scuttle of lizards and the squawks of toothed birds in the treetops. I thought I could be sure of the theropod smell, but told myself that might be imagination. The theropod might be any of several species large or small, and the beast itself might be anywhere within a half-mile's radius.

"Go on," I whispered to Holtzinger. I could hear James and the Raja pushing ahead on my right and see the palm fronds and ferns lashing about as they disturbed them. I suppose they were trying to move quietly, but to me they sounded like an earthquake in a crockery shop.

"A little closer!" I called.

Presently, they appeared slanting in toward me. We dropped into a gully filled with ferns and scrambled up the other side. Then we found our way blocked by a big clump of palmetto.

"You go round that side; we'll go round this," I said. We started off, stopping to listen and smell. Our positions were the same as on that first day, when James killed the bonehead.

We'd gone two-thirds of the way round our half of the palmetto when I heard a noise ahead on our left. Holtzinger heard it too, and pushed off his safety. I put my thumb on mine and stepped to one side to have a clear field of fire.

The clatter grew louder. I raised my gun to aim at about the height of a big theropod's heart. There was a movement in the foliage—and a six-foot-high bonehead stepped into view, walking solemnly across our front and jerking its head with each step like a giant pigeon.

I heard Holtzinger let out a breath and had to keep myself from laughing. Holtzinger said: "Uh—"

Then that damned gun of James's went off, *bang! bang!* I had a glimpse of the bonehead knocked arsy-varsy with its tail and hindlegs flying.

"Got him!" yelled James. "I drilled him clean!" I heard him run forward.

"Good God, if he hasn't done it again!" I said.

Then there was a great swishing of foliage and a wild yell from James. Something heaved up out of the shrubbery, and I saw the head of the biggest of the local flesh eaters, *Tyrannosaurus trionyches* himself.

The scientists can insist that *rex* is the bigger species, but I'll swear this blighter was bigger than any *rex* ever hatched. It must have stood twenty feet high and been fifty feet long. I could see its big bright eye and six-inch teeth and the big dewlap that hangs down from its chin to its chest.

The second of the nullahs that cut through the copse ran athwart our path on the far side of the palmetto clump. Perhaps it was six feet deep. The tyrannosaur had been lying in this, sleeping off its last meal. Where its back stuck up above the ground level, the ferns on the edge of the nullah masked it. James had fired both barrels over the theropod's head and woke it up. Then the silly ass ran forward without reloading. Another twenty feet and he'd have stepped on the tyrannosaur.

James, naturally, stopped when this thing popped up in front of him. He remembered that he'd fired both barrels and that he'd left the Raja too far behind for a clear shot.

At first, James kept his nerve. He broke open his gun, took two rounds from his belt, and plugged them into the barrels. But, in his haste to snap the gun shut, he caught his hand between the barrels and the action. The painful pinch so startled James that he dropped his gun. Then he went to pieces and bolted.

The Raja was running up with his gun at high port, ready to snap it to his shoulder the instant he got a clear view. When he saw James running headlong toward him, he hesitated, not wishing to shoot James by accident. The latter plunged ahead, blundered into the Raja, and sent them both sprawling among the ferns. The tyrannosaur collected what little wits it had and stepped forward to snap them up.

And how about Holtzinger and me on the other side of the palmettos? Well, the instant James yelled and the tyrannosaur's head appeared, Holtzinger darted forward like a rabbit. I'd brought my gun up for a shot at the tyrannosaur's head, in hope of getting at least an eye; but, before I could find it in my sights, the head was out of sight behind the palmettos. Perhaps I should have fired at hazard, but all my experience is against wild shots.

When I looked back in front of me, Holtzinger had already disappeared round the curve of the palmetto clump. I'd started after him when I heard his rifle and the click of the bolt between shots: *bang*— click-click—*bang*—click-click, like that.

He'd come up on the tyrannosaur's quarter as the brute started to stoop for James and the Raja. With his muzzle twenty feet from the tyrannosaur's hide, Holtzinger began pumping .375s into the beast's body. He got off three shots when the tyrannosaur gave a tremendous booming grunt and wheeled round to see what was stinging it. The jaws came open, and the head swung round and down again.

Holtzinger got off one more shot and tried to leap to one side. As he was standing on a narrow place between the palmetto clump and the nullah, he fell into the nullah. The tyrannosaur continued its lunge and caught him. The jaws went *chomp*, and up came the head with poor Holtzinger in them, screaming like a damned soul.

I came up just then and aimed at the brute's face, but then realized that its jaws were full of my sahib and I should be shooting him, too. As the head went on up like the business end of a big power shovel, I fired a shot at the heart. The tyrannosaur was already turning away, and I suspect the ball just glanced along the ribs. The beast took a couple of steps when I gave it the other barrel in the back. It staggered on its next step but kept on. Another step, and it was nearly out of sight among the trees, when the Raja fired twice. The stout fellow had untangled himself from James, got up, picked up his gun, and let the tyrannosaur have it.

The double wallop knocked the brute over with a tremendous crash. It fell into a dwarf magnolia, and I saw one of its huge birdlike hindlegs waving in the midst of a shower of pink-and-white petals. But the tyrannosaur got up again and blundered off without even dropping its victim. The last I saw of it was Holtzinger's legs dangling out one side of its jaws (he'd stopped screaming) and its big tail banging against the tree trunks as it swung from side to side.

The Raja and I reloaded and ran after the brute for all we were worth. I tripped and fell once, but jumped up again and didn't notice my skinned elbow till later. When we burst out of the copse, the tyrannosaur was already at the far end of the glade. We each took a quick shot but probably missed, and it was out of sight before we could fire again.

We ran on, following the tracks and spatters of blood, until we had to stop from exhaustion. Never again did we see that tyrannosaur. Their movements look slow and ponderous, but with those tremendous legs they don't have to step very fast to work up considerable speed.

When we'd got our breath, we got up and tried to track the tyrannosaur, on the theory that it might be dying and we should come up to it. But, though we found more spoor, it faded out and left us at a loss. We circled round, hoping to pick it up, but no luck.

Hours later, we gave up and went back to the glade.

Courtney James was sitting with his back against a tree, holding his rifle and Holtzinger's. His right hand was swollen and blue where he'd pinched it, but still usable. His first words were:

"Where the hell have you two been?"

I said: "We've been occupied. The late Mr. Holtzinger. Remember?"

"You shouldn't have gone off and left me; another of those things might have come along. Isn't it bad enough to lose one hunter through your stupidity without risking another one?"

I'd been preparing a warm wigging for James, but his attack so astonished me that I could only bleat: "What? We lost . . . ?"

"Sure," he said. "You put us in front of you, so if anybody gets eaten it's us. You send a guy up against these animals undergunned. You—"

"You Goddamn' stinking little swine!" I said. "If you hadn't been a blithering idiot and blown those two barrels, and then run like the yellow coward you are, this never would have happened. Holtzinger died trying to save your worthless life. By God, I wish he'd failed! He was worth six of a stupid, spoiled, muttonheaded bastard like you—"

I went on from there. The Raja tried to keep up with me, but ran out of English and was reduced to cursing James in Hindustani.

I could see by the purple color on James's face that I was getting home. He said: "Why, you—" and stepped forward and sloshed me one in the face with his left fist.

It rocked me a bit, but I said: "Now then, my lad, I'm glad you did that! It gives me a chance I've been waiting for. . . ."

So I waded into him. He was a good-sized bod, but between my sixteen stone and his sore right hand he had no chance. I got a few good ones home, and down he went.

"Now get up!" I said. "And I'll be glad to finish off!"

James raised himself to his elbows. I got set for more fisticuffs, though my knuckles were skinned and bleeding already. James rolled over, snatched his gun, and scrambled up, swinging the muzzle from one to the other of us.

"You won't finish anybody off!" he panted through swollen lips. "All right, put your hands up! Both of you!"

"Do not be an idiot," said the Raja. "Put that gun away!"

"Nobody treats me like that and gets away with it!"

"There's no use murdering us," I said. "You'd never get away with it."

"Why not? There won't be much left of you after one of these hits you. I'll just say the tyrannosaur ate you, too. Nobody could prove anything. They can't hold you for a murder eighty-five million years old. The statute of limitations, you know."

"You fool, you'd never make it back to the camp alive!" I shouted.

"I'll take a chance—" began James, setting the butt of his .500 against his shoulder, with the barrels pointed at my face. Looked like a pair of bleeding vehicular tunnels.

He was watching me so closely that he lost track of the Raja for a second. My partner had been resting on one knee, and now his right arm came up in a quick bowling motion with a three-pound rock. The rock bounced off James's head. The .500 went off. The ball must have parted my hair, and the explosion jolly well near broke my eardrums. Down went James again.

"Good work, old chap!" I said, gathering up James's gun.

"Yes," said the Raja thoughtfully, as he picked up the rock he'd thrown and tossed it. "Doesn't quite have the balance of a cricket ball, but it is just as hard."

"What shall we do now?" I said. "I'm inclined to leave the beggar here unarmed and let him fend for himself."

The Raja gave a little sigh. "It's a tempting thought, Reggie, but we really cannot, you know. Not done."

"I suppose you're right," I said. "Well, let's tie him up and take him back to camp."

We agreed there was no safety for us unless we kept James under guard every minute until we got home. Once a man has tried to kill you, you're a fool if you give him another chance.

We marched James back to camp and told the crew what we were up against. James cursed everybody.

We spent three dismal days combing the country for that tyrannosaur, but no luck. We felt it wouldn't have been cricket not to make a good try at recovering Holtzinger's remains. Back at our main camp, when it wasn't raining, we collected small reptiles and things for our scientific friends. The Raja and I discussed the question of legal proceedings against Courtney James, but decided there was nothing we could do in that direction.

When the transition chamber materialized, we fell over one another getting into it. We dumped James, still tied, in a corner, and told the chamber operator to throw the switches.

While we were in transition, James said: "You two should have killed me back there."

"Why?" I said. "You don't have a particularly good head."

The Raja added: "Wouldn't look at all well over a mantel."

"You can laugh," said James, "but I'll get you some day. I'll find a way and get off scot-free."

"My dear chap!" I said. "If there were some way to do it, I'd have you charged with Holtzinger's death. Look, you'd best leave well enough alone."

When we came out in the present, we handed him his empty gun and his other gear, and off he went without a word. As he left, Holtzinger's girl, that Claire, rushed up crying:

"Where is he? Where's August?"

There was a bloody heartrending scene, despite the Raja's skill at handling such situations.

We took our men and beasts down to the old laboratory building that the university has fitted up as a serai for such expeditions. We paid everybody off and found we were broke. The advance payments from Holtzinger and James didn't cover our expenses, and we should have precious little chance of collecting the rest of our fees either from James or from Holtzinger's estate.

And speaking of James, d'you know what that blighter was doing? He went home, got more ammunition, and came back to the university. He hunted up Professor Prochaska and asked him:

"Professor, I'd like you to send me back to the Cretaceous for a quick trip. If you can work me into your schedule right now, you can just about name your own price. I'll offer five thousand to begin with. I want to go to April twenty-third, eighty-five million B.C."

Prochaska answered: "Why do you wish to go back again so soon?"

"I lost my wallet in the Cretaceous," said James. "I figure if I go back to the day before I arrived in that era on my last trip, I'll watch myself when I arrived on that trip and follow myself around till I see myself lose the wallet."

"Five thousand is a lot for a wallet," said the professor.

"It's got some things in it I can't replace," said James.

"Well," said Prochaska, thinking. "The party that was supposed to go out this morning has telephoned that they would be late, so perhaps I can work you in. I have always wondered what would happen when the same man occupied the same stretch of time twice."

So James wrote out a check, and Prochaska took him to the chamber and saw him off. James's idea, it seems, was to sit behind a bush a few yards from where the transition chamber would appear and pot the Raja and me as we emerged.

Hours later, we'd changed into our street clothes and phoned our wives to come and get us. We were standing on Forsythe Boulevard waiting for them when there was a loud crack, like an explosion, and a flash of light not fifty feet from us. The shock wave staggered us and broke windows.

We ran toward the place and got there just as bobby and several citizens came up. On the boulevard, just off the kerb, lay a human body. At least, it had been that, but it looked as if every bone in it had been pulverized and every blood vessel burst, so it was hardly more than a slimy mass of pink protoplasm. The clothes it had been wearing were shredded, but I recognized an H. & H. .500 double-barreled express rifle. The wood was scorched and the metal pitted, but it was Courtney James's gun. No doubt whatever.

Skipping the investigations and the milling about that ensued, what had happened was this: nobody had shot at us as we emerged on the twenty-fourth, and that couldn't be changed. For that matter, the instant James started to do anything that would make a visible change in the world of eighty-five million B.C., such as making a footprint in the earth, the space-time forces snapped him forward to the present to prevent a paradox. And the violence of the passage practically tore him to bits.

Now that this is better understood, the professor won't send anybody to a period less than five thousand years prior to the time that some time traveler has already explored, because it would be too easy to do some act, like chopping down a tree or losing some durable artifact, that would affect the later world. Over longer periods, he tells me, such changes average out and are lost in the stream of time.

We had a rough time after that, with the bad publicity and all, though we did collect a fee from James's estate. Luckily for us, a steel manufacturer turned up who wanted a mastodon's head for his den.

I understand these things better now, too. The disaster hadn't been wholly James's fault. I shouldn't have taken him when I knew what a spoiled, unstable sort of bloke he was. And if Holtzinger could have used a really heavy gun, he'd probably have knocked the tyrannosaur down, even if he didn't kill it, and so have given the rest of us a chance to finish it.

———

So, Mr. Seligman, that's why I won't take you to that period to hunt. There are plenty of other eras, and if you look them over I'm sure you'll find something to suit you. But not the Jurassic or the Cretaceous. You're just not big enough to handle a gun for dinosaur.

# POUL ANDERSON

A *winner of multiple Hugo and Nebula Awards, Poul Anderson (1926–2001) wrote more than fifty novels and hundreds of short stories since his science-fiction debut in 1947. His first novel,* Brain Wave, *is a classic example of the techniques of traditional science fiction, extrapolating the impact that an abrupt universal rise in intelligence would have on the totality of human civilization in the twentieth century. Anderson is highly regarded for the detail of his stories. His vast Technic History saga, a multibook chronicle of interstellar exploration and empire building, covers fifty centuries of future history spread out over the rise and fall of three empires of a galactic federation. The vast scope of the series gave Anderson the opportunity to develop colorful, well-developed characters and to explore the long-term impact of certain ideas and attitudes—free enterprise, militarism, imperialism, individual styles of governing—on the society and political structure of a created world. Two characters, distinct products of their different times and civilizations, dominate the series' most notable episodes: Falstaffian rogue merchant Nicholas van Rijn, hero of* The Man Who Counts, Satan's World, *and* Mirkheim; *and Ensign Dominic Flandry, whose adventures include* We Claim These Stars, Earthman, Go Home! *and* A Knight of Ghosts and Shadows. *Anderson has tackled many of science fiction's classic themes, including near–light-speed travel in* Tau Zero, *time travel in the series of Time Patrol stories collected as* Guardians of Time, *and acclerated evolution in* Fire Time. *He is known for his interweaving of science fiction and history, notably in his novel* The High Crusade, *a superior first-contact tale in which a medieval army captures an alien spaceship. Much of Anderson's fantasy is rich with under-*

*currents of mythology, notably his heroic fantasy* Three Hearts and Three Lions, *and* A Midsummer Tempest, *an alternate history drawn from the background of* A Midsummer Night's Dream. *Anderson received the Tolkien Memorial Award in 1978. With his wife, Karen, he wrote the* King of Ys *Celtic fantasy quartet, and with Gordon Dickson the amusing Hoka series. His short fiction has been collected in numerous volumes, including* The Queen of Air and Darkness and Other Stories, All One Universe, Strangers from Earth, *and* Seven Conquests.

*The idea of a man going back in time to change the past has been well mined over the decades (L. Sprague de Camp's* Lest Darkness Fall *and de Camp's short story "Aristotle and the Gun" are two classic examples). Anderson's "The Man Who Came Early" is a paradigm of the idea. When all is said and done, a man sent back in time with nothing save what he is carrying on himself is just a man, no matter how grand the ideas he knows or the technology he's used in the his own time. The attention to tenth-century Nordic life makes the contrast between the erstwhile time traveler and his new surroundings all the more real.*

# THE MAN WHO CAME EARLY

## POUL ANDERSON

YES, WHEN A MAN grows old he has heard so much that is strange there's little more can surprise him. They say the king in Miklagard has a beast of gold before his high seat which stands up and roars. I have it from Eilif Eiriksson, who served in the guard down yonder, and he is a steady fellow when not drunk. He has also seen the Greek fire used, it burns on water.

So, priest, I am not unwilling to believe what you say about the White Christ. I have been in England and France myself, and seen how the folk prosper. He must be a very powerful god, to ward so many realms . . . and did you say that everyone who is baptized will be given a white robe? I would like to have one. They mildew, of course, in this cursed wet Iceland weather, but a small sacrifice to the house-elves should—No sacrifices? Come now! I'll give up horseflesh if I must, my teeth not being what they were, but every sensible man knows how much trouble the elves make if they're not fed.

Well, let's have another cup and talk about it. How do you like the beer? It's my own brew, you know. The cups I got in England, many years back. I was a young man then . . . time goes, time goes. Afterward I came back and inherited this, my father's farm, and have not left it since. Well enough to go in viking as a youth, but grown older you see where the real wealth lies: here, in the land and the cattle.

Stoke up the fires, Hjalti. It's getting cold. Sometimes I think the winters are colder than when I was a boy. Thorbrand of the Salmondale says so, but he believes the gods are angry because so many are turning from them. You'll have trouble winning Thorbrand over, priest. A stubborn man. Myself, I am open-minded, and willing to listen at least.

Now, then. There is one point on which I must set you right. The end of the world is not coming in two years. This I know.

And if you ask me how I know, that's a very long tale, and in some ways a terrible one. Glad I am to be old, and safe in the earth before that great tomorrow comes. It will be an eldritch time before the frost giants fare loose . . . oh, very well, before the angel blows his battle horn. One reason I hearken to your preaching is that I know the White Christ will conquer Thor. I know Iceland is going to be Christian erelong, and it seems best to range myself on the winning side.

No, I've had no visions. This is a happening of five years ago, which my own household and neighbors can swear to. They mostly did not believe what the stranger told; I do, more or less, if only because I don't think a liar could wreak so much harm. I loved my daughter, priest, and after the trouble was over I made a good marriage for her. She did not naysay it, but now she sits out on the ness-farm with her husband and never a word to me; and I hear he is ill pleased with her silence and moodiness, and spends his nights with an Irish leman. For this I cannot blame him, but it grieves me.

Well, I've drunk enough to tell the whole truth now, and whether you believe it or not makes no odds to me. Here . . . you, girls! . . . fill these cups again, for I'll have a dry throat before I finish the telling.

———

It begins, then, on a day in early summer, five years ago. At that time, my wife Ragnhild and I had only two unwed children still living with us: our youngest son Helgi, of seventeen winters, and our daughter Thorgunna, of eighteen. The girl, being fair, had already had suitors. But she refused them, and I am not one who would compel his daughter. As for Helgi, he was ever a lively one, good with his hands but a breakneck youth. He is now serving in the guard of King Olaf of Norway. Besides these, of course, we had about ten housefolk—two thralls, two girls to help with the women's work, and half a dozen hired carles. This is not a small stead.

You have seen how my land lies. About two miles to the west is the bay; the thorps at Reykjavik are some five miles south. The land rises toward the Long Jökull, so that my acres are hilly; but it's good hay land,

and we often find driftwood on the beach. I've built a shed down there for it, as well as a boathouse.

We had had a storm the night before—a wild huge storm with lightning flashes across heaven, such as you seldom get in Iceland—so Helgi and I were going down to look for drift. You, coming from Norway, do not know how precious wood is to us here, who have only a few scrubby trees and must get our timber from abroad. Back there men have often been burned in their houses by their foes, but we count that the worst of deeds, though it's not unheard of.

As I was on good terms with my neighbors, we took only hand weapons. I bore my ax, Helgi a sword, and the two carles we had with us bore spears. It was a day washed clean by the night's fury, and the sun fell bright on long, wet grass. I saw my stead lying rich around its courtyard, sleek cows and sheep, smoke rising from the roofhole of the hall, and knew I'd not done so ill in my lifetime. My son Helgi's hair fluttered in the low west wind as we left the buildings behind a ridge and neared the water. Strange how well I remember all which happened that day; somehow it was a sharper day than most.

When we came down to the strand, the sea was beating heavy, white and gray out to the world's edge, smelling of salt and kelp. A few gulls mewed above us, frightened off a cod washed onto the shore. I saw a litter of no few sticks, even a baulk of timber . . . from some ship carrying it that broke up during the night, I suppose. That was a useful find, though as a careful man I would later sacrifice to be sure the owner's ghost wouldn't plague me.

We had fallen to and were dragging the baulk toward the shed when Helgi cried out. I ran for my ax as I looked the way he pointed. We had no feuds then, but there are always outlaws.

This newcomer seemed harmless, though. Indeed, as he stumbled nearer across the black sand I thought him quite unarmed and wondered what had happened. He was a big man and strangely clad—he wore coat and breeches and shoes like anyone else, but they were of odd cut, and he bound his trousers with leggings rather than straps. Nor had I ever seen a helmet like his: it was almost square, and came down toward his neck, but it had no nose guard. And this you may not believe, but it was not metal, yet had been cast in one piece!

He broke into a staggering run as he drew close, flapped his arms and croaked something. The tongue was none I had heard, and I have heard many; it was like dogs barking. I saw that he was clean-shaven and his black hair cropped short, and thought he might be French. Otherwise he was a young man, and good-looking, with blue eyes and regular features. From his skin I judged that he spent much time indoors. However, he had a fine manly build.

"Could he have been shipwrecked?" asked Helgi.

"His clothes are dry and unstained," I said; "nor has he been wandering long, for no stubble is on his chin. Yet I've heard of no strangers guesting hereabouts."

We lowered our weapons, and he came up to us and stood gasping. I saw that his coat and the shirt underneath were fastened with bonelike buttons rather than laces, and were of heavy weave. About his neck he had fastened a strip of cloth tucked into his coat. These garments were all in brownish hues. His shoes were of a sort new to me, very well stitched. Here and there on his coat were bits of brass, and he had three broken stripes on each sleeve; also a black band with white letters, the same letters on his helmet. Those were not runes, but Roman—thus: MP. He wore a broad belt, with a small clublike thing of metal in a sheath at the hip and also a real club.

"I think he must be a warlock," muttered my carle Sigurd. "Why else so many tokens?"

"They may only be ornament, or to ward against witchcraft," I soothed him. Then, to the stranger: "I hight Ospak Ulfsson of Hillstead. What is your errand?"

He stood with his chest heaving and a wildness in his eyes. He must have run a long way. At last he moaned and sat down and covered his face.

"If he's sick, best we get him to the house," said Helgi. I heard eagerness; we see few faces here.

"No . . . no . . ." The stranger looked up. "Let me rest a moment—"

He spoke the Norse tongue readily enough, though with a thick accent not easy to follow and with many foreign words I did not understand.

The other carle, Grim, hefted his spear. "Have vikings landed?" he asked.

"When did vikings ever come to Iceland?" I snorted. "It's the other way around."

The newcomer shook his head as if it had been struck. He got shakily to his feet. "What happened?" he said. "What became of the town?"

"What town?" I asked reasonably.

"Reykjavik!" he cried. "Where is it?"

"Five miles south, the way you came—unless you mean the bay it-self," I said.

"No! There was only a beach, and a few wretched huts, and—"

"Best not let Hialmar Broadnose hear you call his thorp that," I counseled.

"But there was a town!" he gasped. "I was crossing the street in a storm, and heard a crash, and then I stood on the beach and the town was gone!"

"He's mad," said Sigurd, backing away. "Be careful. If he starts to foam at the mouth, it means he's going berserk."

"Who are you?" babbled the stranger. "What are you doing in those clothes? Why the spears?"

"Somehow," said Helgi, "he does not sound crazed, only frightened and bewildered. Something evil has beset him."

"I'm not staying near a man under a curse!" yelped Sigurd, and started to run away.

"Come back!" I bawled. "Stand where you are or I'll cleave your louse-bitten head."

That stopped him, for he had no kin who would avenge him; but he would not come closer. Meanwhile the stranger had calmed down to the point where he could talk somewhat evenly.

"Was it the *aitsjbom*?" he asked. "Has the war started?"

He used that word often, *aitsjbom*, so I know it now, though I am un-sure of what it means. It seems to be a kind of Greek fire. As for the war, I knew not which war he meant, and told him so.

"We had a great thunderstorm last night," I added. "And you say you were out in one too. Maybe Thor's hammer knocked you from your place to here."

"But where is here?" he answered. His voice was more dulled than otherwise, now that the first terror had lifted.

"I told you. This is Hillstead, which is on Iceland."

"But that's where I was!" he said. "Reykjavik . . . what happened? Did the *aitsjbom* destroy everything while I lay witless?"

"Nothing has been destroyed," I said.

"Does he mean the fire at Olafsvik last month?" wondered Helgi.

"No, no, no!" Again he buried his face in his hands. After a while he looked up and said: "See here. I am *Sardjant* Gerald Robbins of the United States army base on Iceland. I was in Reykjavik and got struck by lightning or something. Suddenly I was standing on the beach, and lost my head and ran. That's all. Now, can you tell me how to get back to the base?"

Those were more or less his words, priest. Of course, we did not grasp half of them, and made him repeat several times and explain. Even then we did not understand, save that he was from some country called the United States of America, which he said lies beyond Greenland to the west, and that he and some others were on Iceland to help our folk against their foes. This I did not consider a lie—more a mistake or imagining. Grim would have cut him down for thinking us stupid enough to swallow that tale, but I could see that he meant it.

Talking cooled him further. "Look here," he said, in too calm a tone for a feverish man, "maybe we can get at the truth from your side. Has there been no war you know of? Nothing which—Well, look here. My country's men first came to Iceland to guard it against the Germans. Now it is the Russians, but then it was the Germans. When was that?"

Helgi shook his head. "That never happened that I know of," he said. "Who are these Russians?" We found out later that the Gardariki folk were meant. "Unless," Helgi said, "the old warlocks—"

"He means the Irish monks," I explained. "A few dwelt here when the Norsemen came, but they were driven out. That was, hm, somewhat over a hundred years ago. Did your kingdom once help the monks?"

"I never heard of them!" he said. The breath sobbed in his throat. "You . . . didn't you Icelanders come from Norway?"

"Yes, about a hundred years ago," I answered patiently. "After King Harald Fairhair laid the Norse lands under him and—"

"A *hundred years ago!*" he whispered. I saw whiteness creep up beneath his skin. "What year is this?"

We gaped at him. "Well, it's the second year after the great salmon catch," I tried.

"What year after Christ, I mean," he prayed hoarsely.

"Oh, so you are a Christian? Hm, let me think . . . I talked with a bishop in England once, we were holding him for ransom, and he said . . . let me see . . . I think he said this Christ man lived a thousand years ago, or maybe a little less."

"A thousand—" Something went out of him. He stood with glassy eyes—yes, I have seen glass, I told you I am a traveled man—he stood thus, and when we led him toward the garth he went like a small child.

You can see for yourself, priest, that my wife Ragnhild is still good to look upon even in eld, and Thorgunna took after her. She was—is—tall and slim, with a dragon's hoard of golden hair. She being a maiden then, the locks flowed loose over her shoulders. She had great blue eyes and a heart-shaped face and very red lips. Withal she was a merry one, and kindhearted, so that she was widely loved. Sverri Snorrason went in viking when she refused him, and was slain, but no one had the wit to see that she was unlucky.

We led this Gerald Samsson—when I asked, he said his father was named Sam—we led him home, leaving Sigurd and Grim to finish gathering the driftwood. Some folks would not have a Christian in their house, for fear of witchcraft, but I am a broad-minded man, and Helgi, at his age, was wild for anything new. Our guest stumbled over the fields as if blind, but seemed to rouse when we entered the yard. His gaze went around the buildings that enclose it, from the stables and sheds to the smokehouse, the brewery, the kitchen, the bathhouse, the god shrine, and thence to the hall. And Thorgunna was standing in the doorway.

Their gazes locked for a little, and I saw her color but thought nothing of it then. Our shoes rang on the flagging as we crossed the yard and kicked the dogs aside. My two thralls halted in cleaning the stables to gawp, until I got them back to work with the remark that a man good for naught else was always a pleasing sacrifice. That's one useful practice you Christians lack; I've never made a human offering myself, but you know not how helpful is the fact that I could do so.

We entered the hall, and I told the folk Gerald's name and how we had found him. Ragnhild set her maids hopping, to stoke up the fire in the middle trench and fetch beer, while I led Gerald to the high seat and sat down by him. Thorgunna brought us the filled horns. His standing was not like yours, for whom we use our outland cups.

Gerald tasted the brew and made a face. I felt somewhat offended, for my beer is reckoned good, and asked him if aught was wrong. He laughed with a harsh note and said no, but he was used to beer that foamed and was not sour.

"And where might they make such?" I wondered testily.

"Everywhere," he said. "Iceland, too—no. . . ." He stared before him in an empty wise. "Let's say . . . in Vinland."

"Where is Vinland?" I asked.

"The country to the west whence I came. I thought you knew. . . . Wait a bit." He frowned. "Maybe I can find out something. Have you heard of Leif Eiriksson?"

"No," I said. Since then it has struck me that this was one proof of his tale, for Leif Eiriksson is now a well-known chief; and I also take more seriously those yarns of land seen by Bjarni Herjulfsson.

"His father, Erik the Red?" went on Gerald.

"Oh yes," I said. "If you mean the Norseman who came hither because of a manslaughter, and left Iceland in turn for the same reason, and has now settled with his friends in Greenland."

"Then this is . . . a little before Leif's voyage," he muttered. "The late tenth century."

"See here," broke in Helgi, "we've been forbearing with you, but now is no time for riddles. We save those for feasts and drinking bouts. Can you not say plainly whence you come and how you got here?"

Gerald looked down at the floor, shaking.

"Let the man alone, Helgi," said Thorgunna. "Can you not see he's troubled?"

He raised his head and gave her the look of a hurt dog that someone has patted. The hall was dim; enough light seeped in the loft windows that no candles were lit, but not enough to see well by. Nevertheless, I marked a reddening in both their faces.

Gerald drew a long breath and fumbled about. His clothes were made with pockets. He brought out a small parchment box and from it took a little white stick that he put in his mouth. Then he took out another box, and a wooden stick there from which burst into flame when he scratched. With the fire he kindled the stick in his mouth, and sucked in the smoke.

We stared. "Is that a Christian rite?" asked Helgi.

"No . . . not just so." A wry, disappointed smile twisted his lips. "I thought you'd be more surprised, even terrified."

"It's something new," I admitted, "but we're a sober folk on Iceland. Those fire sticks could be useful. Did you come to trade in them?"

"Hardly." He sighed. The smoke he breathed in seemed to steady him, which was odd, because the smoke in the hall had made him cough and water at the eyes. "The truth is, well, something you will not believe. I can hardly believe it myself."

We waited. Thorgunna stood leaning forward, her lips parted.

"That lightning bolt—" Gerald nodded wearily. "I was out in the storm, and somehow the lightning must have smitten me in just the right way, a way that happens only once in many thousands of times. It threw me back into the past."

Those were his words, priest. I did not understand, and told him so.

"It's hard to grasp," he agreed. "God give that I'm merely dreaming. But if this is a dream I must endure till I awaken. . . . Well, look. I was born one thousand, nine hundred, and thirty-three years after Christ, in a land to the west which you have not yet found. In the twenty-fourth year of my life, I was in Iceland with my country's war host. The lightning struck me, and now, now it is less than one thousand years after Christ, and yet I am here—almost a thousand years before I was born, I am here!"

We sat very still. I signed myself with the Hammer and took a long pull from my horn. One of the maids whimpered, and Ragnhild whispered so fiercely I could hear: "Be still. The poor fellow's out of his head. There's no harm in him."

I thought she was right, unless maybe in the last part. The gods can speak through a madman, and the gods are not always to be trusted. Or he could turn berserker, or he could be under a heavy curse that would also touch us.

He slumped, gazing before him. I caught a few fleas and cracked them while I pondered. Gerald noticed and asked with some horror if we had many fleas here.

"Why, of course," said Thorgunna. "Have you none?"

"No." He smiled crookedly. "Not yet."

"Ah," she sighed, "then you *must* be sick."

She was a level-headed girl. I saw her thought, and so did Ragnhild and Helgi. Clearly, a man so sick that he had no fleas could be expected to rave. We might still fret about whether we could catch the illness, but I deemed this unlikely; his woe was in the head, maybe from a blow he had taken. In any case, the matter was come down to earth now, something we could deal with.

I being a godi, a chief who holds sacrifices, it behooved me not to turn a stranger out. Moreover, if he could fetch in many of those fire-kindling sticks, a profitable trade might be built up. So I said Gerald should go to rest. He protested, but we manhandled him into the shut-bed, and there he lay tired and was soon asleep. Thorgunna said she would take care of him.

The next eventide I meant to sacrifice a horse, both because of the timber we had found and to take away any curse that might be on Gerald. Furthermore, the beast I picked was old and useless, and we were short of fresh meat. Gerald had spent the morning lounging moodily around the garth, but when I came in at noon to eat I found him and my daughter laughing.

"You seem to be on the road to health," I said.

"Oh yes. It . . . could be worse for me." He sat down at my side as the carles set up the trestle table and the maids brought in the food. "I was ever much taken with the age of the vikings, and I have some skills."

"Well," I said, "if you have no home, we can keep you here for a while."

"I can work," he said eagerly. "I'll be worth my pay."

Now I knew he was from afar, because what chief would work on any land but his own, and for hire at that? Yet he had the easy manner of the high-born, and had clearly eaten well throughout his life. I overlooked that he had made me no gifts; after all, he was shipwrecked.

"Maybe you can get passage back to your United States," said Helgi. "We could hire a ship. I'm fain to see that realm."

"No," said Gerald bleakly. "There is no such place. Not yet."

"So you still hold to that idea you came from tomorrow?" grunted Sigurd. "Crazy notion. Pass the pork."

"I do," said Gerald. Calm had come upon him. "And I can prove it."

"I don't see how you speak our tongue, if you hail from so far away," I said. I would not call a man a liar to his face, unless we were swapping friendly brags, but—

"They speak otherwise in my land and time," he said, "but it happens that in Iceland the tongue changed little since the old days, and because my work had me often talking with the folk, I learned it when I came here."

"If you are a Christian," I said, "you must bear with us while we sacrifice tonight."

"I've naught against that," he said. "I fear I never was a very good Christian. I'd like to watch. How is it done?"

I told him how I would smite the horse with a hammer before the god, and cut its throat, and sprinkle the blood about with willow twigs; thereafter we would butcher the carcass and feast. He said hastily:

"Here's my chance to prove what I am. I have a weapon that will kill the horse with, with a flash of lightning."

"What is it?" I wondered. We crowded around while he took the metal club out of its sheath and showed it to us. I had my doubts; it looked well enough for hitting a man, I reckoned, but had no edge, though a wondrously skillful smith had forged it. "Well, we can try," I said. You have seen how on Iceland we are less concerned to follow the rites exactly than they are in the older countries.

Gerald showed us what else he had in his pockets. There were some coins of remarkable roundness and sharpness, though neither gold nor true silver; a tiny key; a stick with lead in it for writing; a flat purse holding many bits of marked paper. When he told us gravely that some of this paper was money, Thorgunna herself had to laugh. Best was a knife whose blade folded into the handle. When he saw me admiring that, he gave it to me, which was well done for a shipwrecked man. I said I would give him clothes and a good ax, as well as lodging for as long as needful.

No, I don't have the knife now. You shall hear why. It's a pity, for that was a good knife, though rather small.

"What were you ere the war arrow went out in your land?" asked Helgi. "A merchant?"

"No," said Gerald. "I was an . . . *endjinur* . . . that is, I was learning how to be one. A man who builds things, bridges and roads and tools . . . more than just an artisan. So I think my knowledge could be of great value here." I saw a fever in his eyes. "Yes, give me time and I'll be a king."

"We have no king on Iceland," I grunted. "Our forefathers came hither to get away from kings. Now we meet at the Things to try suits and pass new laws, but each man must get his own redress as best he can."

"But suppose the one in the wrong won't yield?" he asked.

"Then there can be a fine feud," said Helgi, and went on to relate some of the killings in past years. Gerald looked unhappy and fingered his *gun*. That is what he called his fire-spitting club. He tried to rally himself with a joke about now, at last, being free to call it a gun instead of something else. That disquieted me, smacked of witchcraft, so to change the talk I told Helgi to stop his chattering of manslaughter as if it were sport. With law shall the land be built.

"Your clothing is rich," said Thorgunna softly. "Your folk must own broad acres at home."

"No," he said, "our . . . our king gives each man in the host clothes like these. As for my family, we owned no farm, we rented our home in a building where many other families also dwelt."

I am not purse-proud, but it seemed to me he had not been honest, a landless man sharing my high seat like a chief. Thorgunna covered my huffiness by saying, "You will gain a farm later."

After sunset we went out to the shrine. The carles had built a fire before it, and as I opened the door the wooden Odin appeared to leap forth. My house has long invoked him above the others. Gerald muttered to my daughter that it was a clumsy bit of carving, and since my father had made it I was still more angry with him. Some folks have no understanding of the fine arts.

Nevertheless, I let him help me lead the horse forth to the altar stone. I took the blood bowl in my hands and said he could now slay the beast if he would. He drew his gun, put the end behind the horse's ear, and squeezed. We heard a crack, and the beast jerked and dropped with a hole blown through its skull, wasting the brains. A clumsy weapon. I caught a whiff, sharp and bitter like that around a volcano. We all jumped, one of the women screamed, and Gerald looked happy. I gathered my wits and finished the rest of the sacrifice as was right. Gerald did not like having blood sprinkled over him, but then he was a Christian. Nor would he take more than a little of the soup and flesh.

Afterward Helgi questioned him about the gun, and he said it could kill a man at bowshot distance but had no witchcraft in it, only use of some tricks we did not know. Having heard of the Greek fire, I believed him. A gun could be useful in a fight, as indeed I was to learn, but it did not seem very practical—iron costing what it does, and months of forging needed for each one.

I fretted more about the man himself.

And the next morning I found him telling Thorgunna a great deal of foolishness about his home—buildings as tall as mountains, and wagons that flew, or went without horses. He said there were eight or nine thousand thousands of folk in his town, a burgh called New Jorvik or the like. I enjoy a good brag as well as the next man, but this was too much, and I told him gruffly to come along and help me get in some strayed cattle.

———

After a day scrambling around the hills I saw that Gerald could hardly tell a cow's bow from her stern. We almost had the strays once, but he ran stupidly across their path and turned them, so the whole work was to do again. I asked him with strained courtesy if he could milk, shear, wield scythe or flail, and he said no, he had never lived on a farm.

"That's a shame," I remarked, "for everyone on Iceland does, unless he be outlawed."

He flushed at my tone. "I can do enough else," he answered. "Give me some tools and I'll show you good metalwork."

That brightened me, for truth to tell, none of our household was a gifted smith. "That's an honorable trade," I said, "and you can be of great help. I have a broken sword and several bent spearheads to be mended, and it were no bad idea to shoe the horses." His admission that he did not know how to put on a shoe was not very dampening to me then.

We had returned home as we talked, and Thorgunna came angrily forward. "That's no way to treat a guest, Father," she said. "Making him work like a carle, indeed!"

Gerald smiled. "I'll be glad to work," he said. "I need a . . . a stake . . . something to start me afresh. Also, I want to repay a little of your kindness."

Those words made me mild toward him, and I said it was not his fault they had different ways in the United States. On the morrow he could begin in the smithy, and I would pay him, yet he would be treated as an equal since craftsmen are valued. This earned him black looks from the housefolk.

That evening he entertained us well with stories of his home; true or not, they made good listening. However, he had no real polish, being unable to compose a line of verse. They must be a raw and backward lot in the United States. He said his task in the war host had been to keep order among the troops. Helgi said this was unheard of, and he must be bold who durst offend so many men, but Gerald said folk obeyed him out of fear of the king. When he added that the term of a levy in the United States was two years, and that men could be called to war even in harvest time, I said he was well out of a country with so ruthless and powerful a lord.

"No," he answered wistfully, "we are a free folk, who say what we please."

"But it seems you may not do as you please," said Helgi.

"Well," Gerald said, "we may not murder a man just because he aggrieves us."

"Not even if he has slain your own kin?" asked Helgi.

"No. It is for the . . . the king to take vengeance, on behalf of the whole folk whose peace has been broken."

I chuckled. "Your yarns are cunningly wrought," I said, "but there you've hit a snag. How could the king so much as keep count of the slaughters, let alone avenge them? Why, he'd not have time to beget an heir!"

Gerald could say no more for the laughter that followed.

————

The next day he went to the smithy, with a thrall to pump the bellows for him. I was gone that day and night, down to Reykjavik to dicker with Hjalmar Broadnose about some sheep. I invited him back for an overnight stay, and we rode into my steading with his son Ketill, a red-haired sulky youth of twenty winters who had been refused by Thorgunna.

I found Gerald sitting gloomily on a bench in the hall. He wore the clothes I had given him, his own having been spoilt by ash and sparks; what had he awaited, the fool? He talked in a low voice with my daughter.

"Well," I said as I trod in, "how went the tasks?"

My man Grim snickered. "He ruined two spearheads, but we put out the fire he started ere the whole smithy burned."

"How's this?" I cried. "You said you were a smith."

Gerald stood up, defiant. "I worked with different tools, and better ones, at home," he replied. "You do it otherwise here."

They told me he had built up the fire too hot; his hammer had struck everywhere but the place it should; he had wrecked the temper of the steel through not knowing when to quench it. Smithcraft takes years to learn, of course, but he might have owned to being not so much as an apprentice.

"Well," I snapped, "what can you do, then, to earn your bread?" It irked me to be made a ninny of before Hjalmar and Ketill, whom I had told about the stranger.

"Odin alone knows," said Grim. "I took him with me to ride after your goats, and never have I seen a worse horseman. I asked him if maybe he could spin or weave, and he said no."

"That was no question to ask a man!" flared Thorgunna. "He should have slain you for it."

"He should indeed," laughed Grim. "But let me carry on the tale. I thought we would also repair your bridge over the foss. Well, he *can* barely handle a saw, but he nigh took his own foot off with the adze."

"We don't use those tools, I tell you!" Gerald doubled his fists and looked close to tears.

I motioned my guests to sit down. "I don't suppose you can butcher or smoke a hog, either," I said, "or salt a fish or turf a roof."

"No." I could hardly hear him.

"Well, then, man, whatever can you do?"

"I—" He could get no words out.

"You were a warrior," said Thorgunna.

"Yes, that I was!" he said, his face kindling.

"Small use on Iceland when you have no other skills," I grumbled, "but maybe, if you can get passage to the eastlands, some king will take you in his guard." Myself I doubted it, for a guardsman needs manners that will do credit to his lord; but I had not the heart to say so.

Ketill Hjalmarsson had plainly not liked the way Thorgunna stood close to Gerald and spoke for him. Now he leered and said: "I might also doubt your skill in fighting."

"That I have been trained for," said Gerald grimly.

"Will you wrestle with me?" asked Ketill.

"Gladly!" spat Gerald.

Priest, what is a man to think? As I grow older, I find life to be less and less the good-and-evil, black-and-white thing you call it; we are each of us some hue of gray. This useless fellow, this spiritless lout who could be asked if he did women's work and not lift ax, went out into the yard with Ketill Hjalmarsson and threw him three times running. He had a trick of grabbing the clothes as Ketill rushed him . . . I cried a stop when the youth was nearing murderous rage, praised them both, and filled the beer horns. But Ketill brooded sullen on the bench the whole evening.

Gerald said something about making a gun like his own, but bigger, a *cannon* he called it, which would sink ships and scatter hosts. He would need the help of smiths, and also various stuffs. Charcoal was easy, and sulfur could be found by the volcanoes, I suppose, but what is this saltpeter?

Too, being wary by now, I questioned him closely as to how he would make such a thing. Did he know just how to mix the powder? No, he admitted. What size must the gun be? When he told me—at least as long as a man—I laughed and asked him how a piece that size could be cast or bored, supposing we could scrape together so much iron. This he did not know either.

"You haven't the tools to make the tools to make the tools," he said.

I don't understand what he meant by that. "God help me, I can't run through a thousand years of history by myself."

He took out the last of his little smoke sticks and lit it. Helgi had tried a puff earlier and gotten sick, though he remained a friend of Gerald's. Now my son proposed to take a boat in the morning and go with him and me to Ice Fjord, where I had some money outstanding I wanted to collect. Hjalmar and Ketill said they would come along for the trip, and Thorgunna pleaded so hard that I let her come too.

"An ill thing," mumbled Sigurd. "The land trolls like not a woman aboard a vessel. It's unlucky."

"How did your fathers bring women to this island?" I grinned.

Now I wish I had listened to him. He was not a clever man, but he often knew whereof he spoke.

———

At this time I owned a half-share in a ship that went to Norway, bartering wadmal for timber. It was a profitable business until she ran afoul of vikings during the uproar while Olaf Tryggvason was overthrowing Jarl Haakon there. Some men will do anything to make a living—thieves, cutthroats, they ought to be hanged, the worthless robbers pouncing on honest merchantmen. Had they any courage or honor they would go to Ireland, which is full of plunder.

Well, anyhow, the ship was abroad, but we had three boats and took one of these. Grim went with us others: myself, Helgi, Hjalmar, Ketill, Gerald, and Thorgunna. I saw how the castaway winced at the cold water as we launched her, yet afterward took off his shoes and stockings to let his feet dry. He had been surprised to learn we had a bathhouse— did he think us savages?—but still, he was dainty as a girl and soon moved upwind of our feet.

We had a favoring breeze, so raised mast and sail. Gerald tried to help, but of course did not know one line from another and got them fouled. Grim snarled at him and Ketill laughed nastily. But erelong we were under weigh, and he came and sat by me where I had the steering oar.

He must have lain long awake thinking, for now he ventured shyly: "In my land they have . . . will have . . . a rig and rudder which are better than these. With them, you can sail so close to the wind that you can crisscross against it."

"Ah, our wise sailor offers us redes," sneered Ketill.

"Be still," said Thorgunna sharply. "Let Gerald speak."

Gerald gave her a look of humble thanks, and I was not unwilling to listen. "This is something which could easily be made," he said. "While not a seaman, I've been on such boats myself and know them well. First, then, the sail should not be square and hung from a yardarm, but three-cornered, with the two bottom corners lashed to a yard swiveling fore and aft from the mast; and there should be one or two smaller headsails of the same shape. Next, your steering oar is in the wrong place. You should have a rudder in the stern, guided by a bar." He grew eager and traced the plan with his fingernail on Thorgunna's cloak. "With these two things, and a deep keel, going down about three feet for a boat this size, a ship can move across the wind . . . thus."

Well, priest, I must say the idea has merits, and were it not for the fear of bad luck—for everything of his was unlucky—I might yet play with it. But the drawbacks were clear, and I pointed them out in a reasonable way.

"First and worst," I said, "this rudder and deep keel would make it impossible to beach the ship or go up a shallow river. Maybe they have many harbors where you hail from, but here a craft must take what landings she can find, and must be speedily launched if there should be an attack."

"The keel can be built to draw up into the hull," he said, "with a box around so that water can't follow."

"How would you keep dry rot out of the box?" I answered. "No, your keel must be fixed, and must be heavy if the ship is not to capsize under so much sail as you have drawn. This means iron or lead, ruinously costly."

"Besides," I said, "this mast of yours would be hard to unstep when the wind dropped and oars came out. Furthermore, the sails are the wrong shape to stretch as an awning when one must sleep at sea."

"The ship could lie out, and you go to land in a small boat," he said. "Also, you could build cabins aboard for shelter."

"The cabins would get in the way of the oars," I said, "unless the ship were hopelessly broad-beamed or else the oarsmen sat below a deck; and while I hear that galley slaves do this in the southlands, free men would never row in such foulness."

"Must you have oars?" he asked like a very child.

Laughter barked along the hull. The gulls themselves, hovering to starboard where the shore rose dark, cried their scorn.

"Do they have tame winds in the place whence you came?" snorted Hjalmar. "What happens if you're becalmed—for days, maybe, with provisions running out—"

"You could build a ship big enough to carry many weeks' provisions," said Gerald.

"If you had the wealth of a king, you might," said Helgi. "And such a king's ship, lying helpless on a flat sea, would be swarmed by every viking from here to Jomsborg. As for leaving her out on the water while you make camp, what would you have for shelter, or for defense if you should be trapped ashore?"

Gerald slumped. Thorgunna said to him gently: "Some folk have no heart to try anything new. I think it's a grand idea."

He smiled at her, a weary smile, and plucked up the will to say something about a means for finding north in cloudy weather; he said a kind of stone always pointed north when hung from a string. I told him mildly that I would be most interested if he could find me some of this stone; or if he knew where it was to be had, I could ask a trader to fetch me a piece. But this he did not know, and fell silent. Ketill opened his mouth, but got such an edged look from Thorgunna that he shut it again. His face declared what a liar he thought Gerald to be.

The wind turned crank after a while, so we lowered the mast and took to the oars. Gerald was strong and willing, though awkward; however, his hands were so soft that erelong they bled. I offered to let him rest, but he kept doggedly at the work.

Watching him sway back and forth, under the dreary creak of the holes, the shaft red and wet where he gripped it, I thought much about him. He had done everything wrong which a man could do—thus I imagined then, not knowing the future—and I did not like the way Thorgunna's eyes strayed to him and rested. He was no man for my daughter, landless and penniless and helpless. Yet I could not keep from liking him. Whether his tale was true or only madness, I felt he was honest about it; and surely whatever way by which he came hither was a strange one. I noticed the cuts on his chin from my razor; he had said he was not used to our kind of shaving and would grow a beard. He had tried hard. I wondered how well I would have done, landing alone in this witch country of his dreams, with a gap of forever between me and my home.

Maybe that same wretchedness was what had turned Thorgunna's heart. Women are a kittle breed, priest, and you who have forsworn them belike understand them as well as I who have slept with half a hundred in six different lands. I do not think they even understand themselves. Birth and life and death, those are the great mysteries, which none will ever fathom, and a woman is closer to them than a man.

The ill wind stiffened, the sea grew gray and choppy under low, leaden clouds, and our headway was poor. At sunset we could row no more, but must pull in to a small, unpeopled bay, and make camp as well as could be on the strand.

We had brought firewood and timber along. Gerald, though staggering with weariness, made himself useful, his sulfury sticks kindling the blaze more easily than flint and steel. Thorgunna set herself to cook our supper. We were not much warded by the boat from a lean, whining wind; her cloak fluttered like wings and her hair blew wild above the streaming flames. It was the time of light nights, the sky a dim, dusky blue, the sea a wrinkled metal sheet, and the land like something risen out of dream mists. We men huddled in our own cloaks, holding numbed hands to the fire and saying little.

I felt some cheer was needed, and ordered a cask of my best and strongest ale broached. An evil Norn made me do that, but no man escapes his weird. Our bellies seemed the more empty now when our noses drank in the sputter of a spitted joint, and the ale went swiftly to our heads. I remember declaiming the death-song of Ragnar Hairybreeks for no other reason than that I felt like declaiming it.

Thorgunna came to stand over Gerald where he sat. I saw how her fingers brushed his hair, ever so lightly, and Ketill Hjalmarsson did too. "Have they no verses in your land?" she asked.

"Not like yours," he said, glancing up. Neither of them looked away again. "We sing rather than chant. I wish I had my *gittar* here—that's a kind of harp."

"Ah, an Irish bard," said Hjalmar Broadnose.

I remember strangely well how Gerald smiled, and what he said in his own tongue, though I know not the meaning: *"Only on me mither's side, begorra."* I suppose it was magic.

"Well, sing for us," laughed Thorgunna.

"Let me think," he said. "I shall have to put it in Norse words for you." After a little while, still staring at her through the windy gloaming, he began a song. It had a tune I liked, thus:

*From this valley they tell me you're leaving.*
*I will miss your bright eyes and sweet smile.*
*You will carry the sunshine with you*
*That has brightened my life all the while. . . .*

I don't remember the rest, save that it was not quite seemly.

When he had finished, Hjalmar and Grim went over to see if the meat was done. I spied a glimmer of tears in my daughter's eyes. "That was a lovely thing," she said.

Ketill sat straight. The flames splashed his face with wild, running red. A rawness was in his tone: "Yes, we've found what this fellow can do. Sit about and make pretty songs for the girls. Keep him for that, Ospak."

Thorgunna whitened, and Helgi clapped hand to sword. Gerald's face darkened and his voice grew thick: "That was no way to talk. Take it back."

Ketill rose. "No," he said. "I'll ask no pardon of an idler living off honest yeomen."

He was raging, but had kept sense enough to shift the insult from my family to Gerald alone. Otherwise he and his father would have had the four of us to deal with. As it was, Gerald stood too, fists knotted at his sides, and said: "Will you step away from here and settle this?"

"Gladly!" Ketill turned and walked a few yards down the beach, taking his shield from the boat. Gerald followed. Thorgunna stood stricken, then snatched his ax and ran after him.

"Are you going weaponless?" she shrieked.

Gerald stopped, looking dazed. "I don't want anything like that," he said. "Fists—"

Ketill puffed himself up and drew sword. "No doubt you're used to fighting like thralls in your land," he said. "So if you'll crave my pardon, I'll let this matter rest."

Gerald stood with drooped shoulders. He stared at Thorgunna as if he were blind, as if asking her what to do. She handed him the ax.

"So you want me to kill him?" he whispered.

"Yes," she answered.

Then I knew she loved him, for otherwise why should she have cared if he disgraced himself?

Helgi brought him his helmet. He put it on, took the ax, and went forward.

"Ill is this," said Hjalmar to me. "Do you stand by the stranger, Ospak?"

"No," I said. "He's no kin or oath-brother of mine. This is not my quarrel."

"That's good," said Hjalmar. "I'd not like to fight with you. You were ever a good neighbor."

We stepped forth together and staked out the ground. Thorgunna told me to lend Gerald my sword, so he could use a shield too, but the man looked oddly at me and said he would rather have the ax. They squared off before each other, he and Ketill, and began fighting.

This was no holmgang, with rules and a fixed order of blows and first blood meaning victory. There was death between those two. Drunk though the lot of us were, we saw that and so had not tried to make peace. Ketill stormed in with the sword whistling in his hand. Gerald sprang back, wielding the ax awkwardly. It bounced off Ketill's shield. The youth grinned and cut at Gerald's legs. Blood welled forth to stain the ripped breeches.

What followed was butchery. Gerald had never used a battle-ax before. So it turned in his grasp and he struck with the flat of the head. He would have been hewn down at once had Ketill's sword not been blunted on his helmet and had he not been quick on his feet. Even so, he was erelong lurching with a dozen wounds.

"Stop the fight!" Thorgunna cried, and sped toward them. Helgi caught her arms and forced her back, where she struggled and kicked till Grim must help. I saw grief on my son's face, but a wolfish glee on the carle's.

Ketill's blade came down and slashed Gerald's left hand. He dropped the ax. Ketill snarled and readied to finish him. Gerald drew his gun. It made a flash and a barking noise. Ketill fell. Blood gushed from him. His lower jaw was blown off and the back of his skull was gone.

A stillness came, where only the wind and the sea had voice.

Then Hjalmar trod forth, his mouth working but otherwise a cold steadiness over him. He knelt and closed his son's eyes, as a token that the right of vengeance was his. Rising, he said: "That was an evil deed. For that you shall be outlawed."

"It wasn't witchcraft," said Gerald in a stunned tone. "It was like a . . . a bow. I had no choice. I didn't want to fight with more than my fists."

I got between them and said the Thing must decide this matter, but that I hoped Hjalmar would take weregild for Ketill.

"But I killed him to save my own life!" protested Gerald.

"Nevertheless, weregild must be paid, if Ketill's kin will take it," I explained. "Because of the weapon, I think it will be doubled, but that is for the Thing to judge."

Hjalmar had many other sons, and it was not as if Gerald belonged to a family at odds with his own, so I felt he would agree. However, he laughed coldly and asked where a man lacking wealth would find the silver.

Thorgunna stepped up with a wintry calm and said we would pay. I opened my mouth, but when I saw her eyes I nodded. "Yes, we will," I said, "in order to keep the peace."

"So you make this quarrel your own?" asked Hjalmar.

"No," I answered. "This man is no blood of mine. But if I choose to make him a gift of money to use as he wishes, what of it?"

Hjalmar smiled. Sorrow stood in his gaze, but he looked on me with old comradeship.

"One day he may be your son-in-law," he said. "I know the signs, Ospak. Then indeed he will be of your folk. Even helping him now in his need will range you on his side."

"And so?" asked Helgi, most softly.

"And so, while I value your friendship, I have sons who will take the death of their brother ill. They'll want revenge on Gerald Samsson, if only for the sake of their good names, and thus our two houses will be sundered and one manslaying will lead to another. It has happened often enough ere now." Hjalmar sighed. "I myself wish peace with you, Ospak, but if you take this killer's side it must be otherwise."

I thought for a moment, thought of Helgi lying with his head cloven, of my other sons on their steads drawn to battle because of a man they had never seen, I thought of having to wear byrnies each time we went down for driftwood and never knowing when we went to bed if we would wake to find the house ringed in by spearmen.

"Yes," I said, "You are right, Hjalmar. I withdraw my offer. Let this be a matter between you and him alone."

We gripped hands on it.

Thorgunna uttered a small cry and flew into Gerald's arms. He held her close. "What does this mean?" he asked slowly.

"I cannot keep you any longer," I said, "but maybe some crofter will give you a roof. Hjalmar is a law-abiding man and will not harm you until the Thing has outlawed you. That will not be before they meet in fall. You can try to get passage out of Iceland ere then."

"A useless one like me?" he replied in bitterness.

Thorgunna whirled free and blazed that I was a coward and a perjurer and all else evil. I let her have it out before I laid my hands on her shoulders.

"I do this for the house," I said. "The house and the blood, which are holy. Men die and women weep, but while the kindred live our names are remembered. Can you ask a score of men to die for your hankerings?"

Long did she stand, and to this day I know not what her answer would have been. But Gerald spoke.

"No," he said. "I suppose you have right, Ospak . . . the right of your time, which is not mine." He took my hand, and Helgi's. His lips brushed Thorgunna's cheek. Then he turned and walked out into the darkness.

———————

I heard, later, that he went to earth with Thorvald Hallsson, the crofter of Humpback Fell, and did not tell his host what had happened. He must have hoped to go unnoticed until he could somehow get berth on an eastbound ship. But of course word spread. I remember his brag that in the United States folk had ways to talk from one end of the land to another. So he must have scoffed at us, sitting in our lonely steads, and not known how fast news would get around. Thorvald's son Hrolf went to Brand Sealskin-Boots to talk about some matter, and mentioned the guest, and soon the whole western island had the tale.

Now, if Gerald had known he must give notice of a manslaying at the first garth he found, he would have been safe at least till the Thing met, for Hjalmar and his sons are sober men who would not needlessly kill a man still under the wing of the law. But as it was, his keeping the matter secret made him a murderer and therefore at once an outlaw. Hjalmar and his kin rode straight to Humpback Fell and haled him forth. He shot his way past them with the gun and fled into the hills. They followed him, having several hurts and one more death to avenge. I wonder if Gerald thought the strangeness of his weapon would unnerve us. He may not have understood that every man dies when his time comes, neither sooner nor later, so that fear of death is useless.

At the end, when they had him trapped, his weapon gave out on him. Then he took a dead man's sword and defended himself so valiantly that Ulf Hjalmarsson has limped ever since. That was well done, as even his foes admitted. They are an eldritch breed in the United States, but they do not lack manhood.

When he was slain, his body was brought back. For fear of the ghost, he having maybe been a warlock, it was burned, and everything he had owned was laid in the fire with him. Thus I lost the knife he gave me. The barrow stands out on the moor, north of here, and folk shun it, though the ghost has not walked. Today, with so much else happening, he is slowly being forgotten.

And that is the tale, priest, as I saw it and heard it. Most men think Gerald Samsson was crazy, but I myself now believe he did come from out of time, and that his doom was that no man may ripen a field before harvest season. Yet I look into the future, a thousand years hence, when they fly through the air and ride in horseless wagons and smash whole towns with one blow. I think of this Iceland then, and of the young United States men come to help defend us in a year when the end of the world hovers close. Maybe some of them, walking about on the heaths, will see that barrow and wonder what ancient warrior lies buried there, and they may well wish they had lived long ago in this time, when men were free.

# R. A. LAFFERTY

*Eccentric, outrageous, and packed with bizarre characters and incidents, R. A. Lafferty's (1914–2002) stylistically unconventional short stories are as much a part of the oral tall tale tradition as they are fantasy and science fiction. Lafferty began publishing fiction in the 1960s and was a prominent figure in science fiction's iconoclastic New Wave, where his gnomic, challenging variations on standard science-fiction and fantasy themes bridged the gap between speculative and mainstream fiction. A stylistic maverick, Lafferty fills his stories with puns and wordplay that create incongruous associations. The style of his narratives is similarly adventurous and includes mixtures of sermons, riddles, doggerel, epigrams, imagined reference works, and textbook treatises. He has written on subjects ranging from supernatural conspiracy to evil adolescents, celestial revolutionaries, Native American lore, utopia, demons, and carnal love.*

*In his novels he is fond of creating modern corrollaries for classic myths and legends.* Space Chanty *works the basic story of Homer's* Odyssey *into a wild space opera. In the Argos cycle, which includes* Archipelago, The Devil Is Dead, *and* Episodes of the Argo, *Jason and the Argonauts are reincarnated as members of a former World War II battle unit. In* Past Master, *Sir Thomas More is transported in time and space to the planet Astrobe, where he falls afoul of political intrigue and suffers his seemingly inescapable martyr's death. Lafferty's preoccupation with religious archetypes and the battle (and sometimes collusion) between good and evil gives much of his writing a mythic character.*

*His short fiction has been collected in* Nine Hundred Grandmothers, Strange Doings, Does Anyone Else Have Something Further to Add?, *and numerous other collections. His novels include* The Reefs of Earth, Fourth Mansions, Annals of Klepsis, *and* Arrive at Easterwine. *He has also written a volume of essays on fantastic literature,* It's Down the Slippery Cellar Stairs. *Interviews with him have been collected in* Cranky Old Man from Tulsa.

*"Rainbird" is one of R. A. Lafferty's early stories, but it shows the wide-ranging influences that would shape his future fiction. The notion of going back in time to "correct" mistakes that would be made by oneself has rarely been explored with as much verve and imagination as with Rainbird and his "retrogressor." Naturally, Lafferty also makes a wry comment on what can happen if one decides to tinker with the past too much.*

# RAINBIRD

## R. A. LAFFERTY

WERE SCIENTIFIC FIRSTS truly tabulated the name of the Yankee inventor, Higgston Rainbird, would surely be without peer. Yet today he is known (and only to a few specialists, at that) for an improved blacksmith's bellows in the year 1785, for a certain modification (not fundamental) in the moldboard plow about 1805, for a better (but not good) method of reefing the lateen sail, for a chestnut roaster, for the Devil's Claw Wedge for splitting logs, and for a nutmeg grater embodying a new safety feature; this last was either in the year 1816 or 1817. He is known for such, and for no more.

Were this all that he achieved his name would still be secure. And it *is* secure, in a limited way, to those who hobby in technological history.

But the glory of which history has cheated him, or of which he cheated himself, is otherwise. In a different sense it is without parallel, absolutely unique.

For he pioneered the dynamo, the steam automobile, the steel industry, ferro-concrete construction, the internal combustion engine, electric illumination and power, the wireless, the televox, the petroleum and petro-chemical industries, monorail transportation, air travel, worldwide monitoring, fissionable power, space travel, group telepathy, political and economic balance; he built a retrogressor; and he made great advances towards corporal immortality and the apotheosis of mankind. It would seem unfair that all this is unknown of him.

Even the once solid facts—that he wired Philadelphia for light and power in 1799, Boston the following year, and New York two years later—are no longer solid. In a sense they are no longer facts.

For all this there must be an explanation; and, if not that, then an account at least; and if not that, well—something anyhow.

Higgston Rainbird made a certain decision on a June afternoon in 1779 when he was quite a young man, and by this decision he confirmed his inventive bent.

He was hawking from the top of Devil's Head Mountain. He flew his falcon (actually a tercel hawk) down through the white clouds, and to him it was the highest sport in the world. The bird came back, climbing the blue air, and brought a passenger pigeon from below the clouds. And Higgston was almost perfectly happy as he hooded the hawk.

He could stay there all day and hawk from above the clouds. Or he could go down the mountain and work on his sparker in his shed. He sighed as he made the decision, for no man can have everything. There was a fascination about hawking. But there was also a fascination about the copper-strip sparker. And he went down the mountain to work on it.

Thereafter he hawked less. After several years he was forced to give it up altogether. He had chosen his life, the dedicated career of an inventor, and he stayed with it for sixty-five years.

His sparker was not a success. It would be expensive, its spark was uncertain and it had almost no advantage over flint. People could always start a fire. If not, they could borrow a brand from a neighbor. There was no market for the sparker. But it was a nice machine, hammered copper strips wrapped around iron teased with lodestone, and the thing turned with a hand crank. He never gave it up entirely. He based other things upon it; and the retrogressor of his last years could not have been built without it.

But the main thing was steam, iron, and tools. He made the finest lathes. He revolutionized smelting and mining. He brought new things to power, and started the smoke to rolling. He made mistakes, he ran into dead ends, he wasted whole decades. But one man can only do so much.

He married a shrew, Audrey, knowing that a man cannot achieve without a goad as well as a goal. But he was without issue or disciple, and this worried him.

He built a steamboat and a steamtrain. His was the first steam thresher. He cleared the forests with wood-burning giants, and designed towns. He destroyed southern slavery with a steampowered cotton picker, and power and wealth followed him.

For better or worse he brought the country up a long road, so there was hardly a custom of his boyhood that still continued. Probably no one man had ever changed a country so much in his lifetime.

He fathered a true machine-tool industry, and brought rubber from the tropics and plastic from the laboratory. He pumped petroleum, and used natural gas for illumination and steam power. He was honored and enriched; and, looking back, he had no reason to regard his life as wasted.

"Yes, I've missed so much. I wasted a lot of time. If only I could have avoided the blind alleys, I could have done many times as much. I brought machine tooling to its apex. But I neglected the finest tool of all, the mind. I used it as it is, but I had not time to study it, much less modify it. Others after me will do it all. But I rather wanted to do it all myself. Now it is too late."

He went back and worked on his old sparker and its descendents, now that he was old. He built toys along the line of it that need not always have remained toys. He made a televox, but the only practical application was that now Audrey could rail at him over a greater distance. He fired up a little steam dynamo in his house, ran wires and made it burn lights in his barn.

And he built a retrogressor.

"I would do much more along this line had I the time. But I'm pepper-bellied pretty near the end of the road. It is like finally coming to a gate and seeing a whole greater world beyond it, and being too old and feeble to enter."

He kicked a chair and broke it.

"I never even made a better chair. Never got around to it. There are so clod-hopping many things I meant to do. I have maybe pushed the country ahead a couple of decades faster than it would otherwise have gone. But what couldn't I have done if it weren't for the blind alleys! Ten years lost in one of them, twelve in another. If only there had been a way to tell the true from the false, and to leave to others what they could do, and to do myself only what nobody else could do. To see a link (however unlikely) and to go out and get it and set it in its place. Oh, the waste, the wilderness that a talent can wander in! If I had only had a mentor! If I had had a map, a clue, a hatful of clues. I was born shrewd, and I shrewdly cut a path and went a grand ways. But always there was a clearer path and a faster way that I did not see till later. As my name is Rainbird, if I had it to do over, I'd do it infinitely better."

He began to write a list of the things that he'd have done better. Then he stopped and threw away his pen in disgust.

"Never did even invent a decent ink pen. Never got around to it. Dog-eared damnation, there's so much I didn't do!"

He poured himself a jolt, but he made a face as he drank it.

"Never got around to distilling a really better whiskey. Had some good ideas along that line, too. So many things I never did do. Well, I can't improve things by talking to myself here about it."

Then he sat and thought.

"But I burr-tailed *can* improve things by talking to myself *there* about it."

He turned on his retrogressor, and went back sixty-five years and up two thousand feet.

————

Higgston Rainbird was hawking from the top of Devil's Head Mountain one June afternoon in 1779. He flew his bird down through the white fleece clouds, and to him it was sport indeed. Then it came back, climbing the shimmering air, and brought a pigeon to him.

"It's fun," said the old man, "but the bird is tough, and you have a lot to do. Sit down and listen, Higgston."

"How do you know the bird is tough? Who are you, and how did an old man like you climb up here without my seeing you? And how in hellpepper did you know that my name was Higgston?"

"I ate the bird and I remember that it was tough. I am just an old man who would tell you a few things to avoid in your life, and I came up here by means of an invention of my own. And I know your name is Higgston, as it is also my name; you being named after me, or I after you, I forget which. Which one of us is the older, anyhow?"

"I had thought that you were, old man. I am a little interested in inventions myself. How does the one that carried you up here work?"

"It begins, well it begins with something like your sparker, Higgston. And as the years go by you adapt and add. But it is all tinkering with a force field till you are able to warp it a little. Now then, you are an ewer-eared galoot and not as handsome as I remembered you; but I happen to know that you have the makings of a fine man. Listen now as hard as ever you listened in your life. I doubt that I will be able to repeat. I will save you years and decades; I will tell you the best road to take over a journey which it was once said that a man could travel but once. Man, I'll pave a path for you over the hard places and strew palms before your feet."

"Talk, you addlepated old gaff. No man ever listened so hard before."

The old man talked to the young one for five hours. Not a word was wasted; they were neither of them given to wasting words. He told him that steam wasn't everything, this before he knew that it was anything. It was a giant power, but it was limited. Other powers, perhaps, were not. He instructed him to explore the possibilities of amplification and feedback, and to use always the lightest medium of transmission of power: wire rather than mule-drawn coal cart, air rather than wire, ether rather than air. He warned against time wasted in shoring up the obsolete, and of the bottomless quicksand of cliché, both of word and of thought.

He admonished him not to waste precious months in trying to devise the perfect apple corer; there will never be a perfect apple corer. He begged him not to build a battery bobsled. There would be things far swifter than a bobsled.

Let others make the new hide scrapers and tanning salts. Let others aid the carter and the candle molder and the cooper in their arts. There was need for a better hame, a better horse block, a better stile, a better whetstone. Well, let others fill those needs. If our buttonhooks, our firedogs, our whiffletrees, our bootjacks, our cheese presses are all badly designed and a disgrace, then let someone else remove that disgrace. Let others aid the cordwainer and the cobbler. Let Higgston do only the high work that nobody else would be able to do.

There would come a time when the farrier himself would disappear, as the fletcher had all but disappeared. But new trades would open for a man with an open mind.

Then the old man got specific. He showed young Higgston a design for a lathe dog that would save time. He told him how to draw, rather than hammer wire; and advised him of the virtues of mica as insulator before other material should come to hand.

"And here there are some things that you will have to take on faith," said the old man, "things of which we learn the 'what' before we fathom the 'why.'"

He explained to him the shuttle armature and the self-exciting field, and commutation; and the possibilities that alternation carried to its ultimate might open up. He told him a bejammed lot of things about a confounded huge variety of subjects.

"And a little mathematics never hurt a practical man," said the old gaffer. "I was self-taught, and it slowed me down."

They hunkered down there, and the old man cyphered it all out in the dust on the top of Devil's Head Mountain. He showed him natural logarithms and rotating vectors and the calculi and such; but he didn't push it too far, as even a smart boy can learn only so much in a few minutes. He then gave him a little advice on the treatment of Audrey, knowing it would be useless, for the art of living with a shrew is a thing that cannot be explained to another.

"Now hood your hawk and go down the mountain and go to work," the old man said. And that is what young Higgston Rainbird did.

———

The career of the Yankee inventor, Higgston Rainbird, was meteoric. The wise men of Greece were little boys to him, the Renaissance giants had only knocked at the door but had not tried the knob. And it was unlocked all the time.

The milestones that Higgston left are breathtaking. He built a short high dam on the flank of Devil's Head Mountain, and had hydroelectric power for his own shop in that same year (1779). He had an arc light burning in Horse-Head Lighthouse in 1781. He read by true incandescent light in 1783, and lighted his native village, Knobknocker, three years later. He drove a charcoal fueled automobile in 1787, switched to a distillate of whale oil in 1789, and used true rock oil in 1790. His gasoline powered combination reaper-thresher was in commercial production in 1793, the same year that he wired Centerville for light and power. His first diesel locomotive made its trial run in 1796, in which year he also converted one of his earlier coal burning steamships to liquid fuel.

In 1799 he had wired Philadelphia for light and power, a major breakthrough, for the big cities had manfully resisted the innovations. On the night of the turn of the century he unhooded a whole clutch of new things, wireless telegraphy, the televox, radio transmission and reception, motile and audible theatrical reproductions, a machine to transmit the human voice into print, and a method of sterilizing and wrapping meat to permit its indefinite preservation at any temperature.

And in the spring of that new year he first flew a heavier-than-air vehicle.

"He has made all the basic inventions," said the many-tongued people. "Now there remains only their refinement and proper utilization."

"Horse hokey," said Higgston Rainbird. He made a rocket that could carry freight to England in thirteen minutes at seven cents a hundred-weight. This was in 1805. He had fissionable power in 1813, and within four years had the price down where it could be used for desalting sea-water to the eventual irrigation of five million square miles of remark-ably dry land.

He built a Think Machine to work out the problems that he was too busy to solve, and a Prediction Machine to pose him with new problems and new areas of breakthrough.

In 1821, on his birthday, he hit the moon with a marker. He bet a crony that he would be able to go up personally one year later and re-trieve it. And he won the bet.

In 1830 he first put on the market his Red Ball Pipe Tobacco, an aro-matic and expensive crimp cut made of Martian lichen.

In 1836 he founded the Institute for the Atmospheric Rehabilitation of Venus, for he found that place to be worse than a smokehouse. It was there that he developed that hacking cough that stayed with him till the end of his days.

He synthesized a man of his own age and disrepute who would sit drinking with him in the after-midnight hours and say, "You're so right, Higgston, so incontestably right."

His plan for the Simplification and Eventual Elimination of Gov-ernment was adopted (in modified form) in 1840, a fruit of his Political and Economic Balance Institute.

Yet, for all his seemingly successful penetration of the field, he real-ized that man was the only truly cantankerous animal, and that Human Engineering would remain one of the never completely resolved fields.

He made a partial breakthrough in telepathy, starting with the per-sonal knowledge that shrews are always able to read the minds of their spouses. He knew that the secret was not in sympathetic reception, but in arrogant break-in. With the polite it is forever impossible, but he dis-guised this discovery as politely as he could.

And he worked toward corporal immortality and the apotheosis of mankind, that cantankerous animal.

He designed a fabric that would embulk itself on a temperature drop, and thin to an airy sheen in summery weather. The weather itself he disdained to modify, but he did evolve infallible prediction of exact daily rainfall and temperature for decades in advance.

And he built a retrogressor.

———

One day he looked in the mirror and frowned.

"I never did get around to making a better mirror. This one is hideous. However (to consider every possibility) let us weigh the thesis that it is the image and not the mirror that is hideous."

He called up an acquaintance.

"Say, Ulois, what year is this anyhow?"

"1844."

"Are you sure?"

"Reasonably sure."

"How old am I?"

"Eighty-five, I think, Higgston."

"How long have I been an old man?"

"Quite a while, Higgston, quite a while."

Higgston Rainbird hung up rudely.

"I wonder how I ever let a thing like that slip up on me?" he said to himself. "I should have gone to work on corporal immortality a little earlier. I've bungled the whole business now."

He fiddled with his Prediction Machine and saw that he was to die that very year. He did not seek a finer reading.

"What a saddle-galled splay-footed situation to find myself in! I never got around to a tenth of the things I really wanted to do. Oh, I was smart enough; I just ran up too many blind alleys. Never found the answers to half the old riddles. Should have built the Prediction Machine at the beginning instead of the end. But I didn't know how to build it at the beginning. There ought to be a way to get more done. Never got any advice in my life worth taking except from that nutty old man on the mountain when I was a young man. There's a lot of things I've only started on. Well, every man doesn't hang, but every man does come to the end of his rope. I never did get around to making that rope extensible. And I can't improve things by talking to myself here about it."

He filled his pipe with Red Ball crimp cut and thought a while.

"But I hill-hopping *can* improve things by talking to myself *there* about it."

Then he turned on his retrogressor and went back and up.

———

Young Higgston Rainbird was hawking from the top of Devil's Head Mountain on a June afternoon in 1779. He flew his hawk down through the white clouds, and decided that he was the finest fellow in the world and master of the finest sport. If there was earth below the clouds it was far away and unimportant.

The hunting bird came back, climbing the tall air, with a pigeon from the lower regions.

"Forget the bird," said the old man, "and give a listen with those out-sized ears of yours. I have a lot to tell you in a very little while, and then you must devote yourself to a concentrated life of work. Hood the bird and clip him to the stake. Is that bridle clip of your own invention? Ah yes, I remember now that it is."

"I'll just fly him down once more, old man, and then I'll have a look at what you're selling."

"No. No. Hood him at once. This is your moment of decision. That is a boyishness that you must give up. Listen to me, Higgston, and I will orient your life for you."

"I rather intended to orient it myself. How did you get up here, old man, without my seeing you? How, in fact, did you get up here at all? It's a hard climb."

"Yes, I remember that it is. I came up here on the wings of an invention of my own. Now pay attention for a few hours. It will take all your considerable wit."

"A few hours and a perfect hawking afternoon will be gone. This may be the finest day ever made."

"I also once felt that it was, but I manfully gave it up. So must you."

"Let me fly the hawk down again and I will listen to you while it is gone."

"But you will only be listening with half a mind, and the rest will be with the hawk."

But young Higgston Rainbird flew the bird down through the shining white clouds, and the old man began his rigmarole sadly. Yet it was a rang-dang-do of a spiel, a mummy-whammy of admonition and exposition, and young Higgston listened entranced and almost forgot his hawk. The old man told him that he must stride half a dozen roads at once, and yet never take a wrong one; that he must do some things earlier that on the alternative had been done quite late; that he must point his technique at the Think Machine and the Prediction Machine, and at the unsolved problem of corporal immortality.

"In no other way can you really acquire elbow room, ample working time. Time runs out and life is too short if you let it take its natural course. Are you listening to me, Higgston?"

But the hawk came back, climbing the steep air, and it had a gray dove. The old man sighed at the interruption, and he knew that his project was in peril.

"Hood the hawk. It's a sport for boys. Now listen to me, you spraddling jack. I am telling you things that nobody else would ever be able to tell you! I will show you how to fly falcons to the stars, not just down to the meadows and birch groves at the foot of this mountain."

"There is no prey up there," said young Higgston.

"There *is*. Gamier prey than you ever dreamed of. Hood the bird and snaffle him."

"I'll just fly him down one more time and listen to you till he comes back."

The hawk went down through the clouds like a golden bolt of summer lightning.

Then the old man, taking the cosmos, peeled it open layer by layer like an onion, and told young Higgston how it worked. Afterwards he returned to the technological beginning and he lined out the workings of steam and petro- and electromagnetism, and explained that these simple powers must be used for a short interval in the invention of greater power. He told him of waves and resonance and airy transmission, and fission and flight and over-flight. And that none of the doors required keys, only a resolute man to turn the knob and push them open. Young Higgston was impressed.

Then the hawk came back, climbing the towering air, and it had a rainbird.

The old man had lively eyes, but now they took on a new light.

"Nobody ever gives up pleasure willingly," he said, "and there is always the sneaking feeling that the bargain may not have been perfect. This is one of the things I have missed. I haven't hawked for sixty-five years. Let me fly him this time, Higgston."

"You know how?"

"I am adept. And I once intended to make a better gauntlet for hawkers. This hasn't been improved since Nimrod's time."

"I have an idea for a better gauntlet myself, old man."

"Yes. I know what your idea is. Go ahead with it. It's practical."

"Fly him if you want to, old man."

And old Higgston flew the tercel hawk down through the gleaming clouds, and he and young Higgston watched from the top of the world. And then young Higgston Rainbird was standing alone on the top of Devil's Head Mountain, and the old man was gone.

"I wonder where he went? And where in appleknocker's heaven did he come from? Or was he ever here at all? That's a danged funny machine he came in, if he did come in it. All the wheels are on the inside. But I can use the gears from it, and the clock, and the copper wire. It must have taken weeks to hammer that much wire out that fine. I wish I'd paid more attention to what he was saying, but he poured it on a little thick. I'd have gone along with him on it if only he'd have found a good stopping place a little sooner, and hadn't been so insistent on giving up hawking. Well, I'll just hawk here till dark, and if it dawns clear I'll be up again in the morning. And Sunday, if I have a little time, I may work on my sparker or my chestnut roaster."

————

Higgston Rainbird lived a long and successful life. Locally he was known best as a hawker and horse racer. But as an inventor he was recognized as far as Boston.

He is still known, in a limited way, to specialists in the field and period; known as contributor to the development of the moldboard plow, as the designer of the Nonpareil Nutmeg Grater with the safety feature, for a bellows, for a sparker for starting fires (little used), and for the Devil's Claw Wedge for splitting logs.

He is known for such, and for no more.

# LARRY NIVEN

Larry Niven established his credentials as a master of the hard-science-fiction story with his Nebula Award–winning novel Ringworld, about a ribbonlike planetary body with a million-mile radius and six-hundred-million-mile circumference that rings a remote star and poses unique technical problems in navigation and escape for its human inhabitants. The novel and its sequels, Ringworld Engineers and Ringworld Throne, are part of Niven's vast Tales of Known Space saga, an acclaimed future history of humankind's populating of interstellar space that has accommodated exploration of a wide variety of themes including alien cultures, immortality, time travel, terraforming, genetic engineering, and teleportation. The novels World of Ptavvs, A Gift from Earth, Protector, The Patchwork Girl, The Integral Trees, and The Smoke Ring, as well as the story collections Neutron Star, The Shape of Space, Crashlander, and Flatlander, elaborate an epic billion-and-a-half-year history that integrates innovative technologies with colorful developments of alien races and human and extraterrestrial interactions. The allure of Niven's invention can be measured by the seven volumes in the Man-Kzin Wars anthology series, which have attracted his colleagues in hard science fiction to contribute stories, bolstering the plausibility of the series through a shared-world sensibility. Niven has also written the novel A World Out of Time, a far-future projection in which human evolution leads to immortality, and the series of science fiction mystery stories collected in The Long ARM of Gil Hamilton.

Much of his work at novel length has been written in collaboration. The Mote in God's Eye, coauthored with Jerry Pournelle, is a memorable *first-contact story about the accidental discovery of an alien race determined to seed our solar system with their proliferating population. Niven and Pournelle have also written a sequel,* The Gripping Hand; *the disaster novel* Lucifer's Hammer; *and* Inferno, *which transports a science fiction writer to a Danteesque Hell. With Steve Barnes, Niven has written* Dream Park, The Barsoom Project, *and* The Voodoo Game, *all set in a future amusement park where imagined realities are manifested through virtual reality. Niven has also written a series of fantasies concerned with primitive magic that includes* The Magic Goes Away *and* Time of the Warlock.

*"Leviathan!" postulates a fascinating question regarding time travel: what if where a traveler ended up is not only back in time, but back in some other time stream? Moving across dimensions is a delightfully developed risk in the following story, and combines Niven's sense of humor with a practical, at least to the people in the story, application for time travel.*

# LEVIATHAN!

## LARRY NIVEN

TWO MEN STOOD on one side of a thick glass wall.

"You'll be airborne," Svetz's beefy red-faced boss was saying. "We made some improvements in the small extension cage while you were in the hospital. You can hover it, or fly it at up to fifty miles per hour, or let it fly itself; there's a constant-altitude setting. Your field of vision is total. We've made the shell of the extension cage completely transparent."

On the other side of the thick glass, something was trying to kill them. It was forty feet long from nose to tail and was equipped with vestigial batlike wings. Otherwise it was built something like a slender lizard. It screamed and scratched at the glass with murderous claws.

The sign on the glass read:

GILA MONSTER
RETRIEVED FROM THE YEAR 1230 ANTE ATOMIC, APPROXIMATELY,
FROM THE REGION OF CHINA, EARTH. EXTINCT.

"You'll be well out of his reach," said Ra Chen.

"Yes, sir." Svetz stood with his arms folded about him, as if he had a chill. He was being sent after the biggest animal that had ever lived; and Svetz was afraid of animals.

"For Science's sake! What are you worried about, Svetz? It's only a big fish!"

"Yes, sir. You said that about the Gila monster. It's just an extinct lizard, you said."

"We only had a drawing in a children's book to go by. How could we know it would be so big?"

The Gila monster drew back from the glass. It inhaled hugely, took aim—yellow and orange flame spewed from its nostrils and played across the glass. Svetz squeaked and jumped for cover.

"He can't get through," said Ra Chen.

Svetz picked himself up. He was a slender, small-boned man with pale skin, light blue eyes, and very fine ash-blond hair. "How could we know it would breathe fire?" he mimicked. "That lizard almost *cremated* me. I spent four months in the hospital as it was. And what really burns me is, he looks less like the drawing every time I see him. Sometimes I wonder if I didn't get the wrong animal."

"What's the difference, Svetz? The Secretary-General loved him. That's what counts."

"Yes, sir. Speaking of the Secretary-General, what does he want with a sperm whale? He's got a horse, he's got a Gila monster—"

"That's a little complicated." Ra Chen grimaced. "Palace politics! It's *always* complicated. Right now, Svetz, somewhere in the United Nations Palace, a hundred plots are in various stages of development. And every last one of them involves getting the attention of the Secretary-General, and *holding* it. Keeping his attention isn't easy."

Svetz nodded. Everybody knew about the Secretary-General.

The family that had ruled the United Nations for seven hundred years was somewhat inbred.

The Secretary-General was twenty-eight years old. He was a happy person; he loved animals and flowers and pictures and people. Pictures of planets and multiple star systems made him clap his hands and coo with delight; and so the Institute for Space Research was mighty in the United Nations government. But he liked extinct animals too.

"Someone managed to convince the Secretary-General that he wants the largest animal on Earth. The idea may have been to take us down a peg or two," said Ra Chen. "Someone may think we're getting too big a share of the budget.

"By the time I got onto it, the Secretary-General wanted a brontosaur. We'd never have gotten him that. No extension cage will reach that far."

"Was it your idea to get him a sperm whale, sir?"

"Yah. It wasn't easy to persuade him. Sperm whales have been extinct for so long that we don't even have pictures. All I had to show him was a crystal sculpture from Archeology—dug out of the Steuben Glass Building—and a Bible and a dictionary. I managed to convince him that Leviathan and the sperm whale were one and the same."

"That's not strictly true." Svetz had read a computer-produced condensation of the Bible. The condensation had ruined the plot, in Svetz's opinion. "Leviathan could be anything big and destructive, even a horde of locusts."

"Thank Science you weren't there to help, Svetz! The issue was confused enough. Anyway, I promised the Secretary-General the largest animal that ever lived on Earth. All the literature says that that animal was a sperm whale. There were sperm whale herds all over the oceans as recently as the first century Ante Atomic. You shouldn't have any trouble finding one."

"In twenty minutes?"

Ra Chen looked startled. "What?"

"If I try to keep the big extension cage in the past for more than twenty minutes, I'll never be able to bring it home. The—"

"I know that."

"—uncertainty factor in the energy constants—"

"Svetz—"

"—blow the Institute right off the map."

"We thought of that, Svetz. You'll go back in the small extension cage. When you find a whale, you'll signal the big extension cage."

"Signal it how?"

"We've found a way to send a simple on-off pulse through time. Let's go back to the Institute and I'll show you."

Malevolent golden eyes watched them through the glass as they walked away.

The extension cage was the part of the time machine that did the moving. Within its transparent shell, Svetz seemed to ride a flying armchair equipped with an airplane passenger's lunch tray; except that the lunch tray was covered with lights and buttons and knobs and crawling green lines. He was somewhere off the east coast of North America, in or around the year 100 Ante Atomic or 1845 Anno Domini. The inertial calendar was not particularly accurate.

Svetz skimmed low over water the color of lead, beneath a sky the color of slate. But for the rise and fall of the sea, he might almost have been suspended in an enormous sphere painted half light, half dark. He let the extension cage fly itself, twenty meters above the water, while he watched the needle on the NAI, the Nervous Activities Indicator.

Hunting Leviathan.

His stomach was uneasy. Svetz had thought he was adjusting to the peculiar gravitational side effects of time travel. But apparently not.

At least he would not be here long.

On this trip he was not looking for a mere forty-foot Gila monster. Now he hunted the largest animal that had ever lived. A most conspicuous beast. And now he had a life-seeking instrument, the NAI . . .

The needle jerked hard over, and trembled.

Was it a whale? But the needle was trembling in apparent indecision. A cluster of sources, then. Svetz looked in the direction indicated.

A clipper ship, winged with white sail, long and slender and graceful as hell. Crowded, too, Svetz guessed. Many humans, closely packed, would affect the NAI in just that manner. A sperm whale—a single center of complex nervous activity—would attract the needle as violently, without making it jerk about like that.

The ship would interfere with reception. Svetz turned east and away; but not without regret. The ship was beautiful.

The uneasiness in Svetz's belly was getting worse, not better.

Endless gray-green water, rising and falling beneath Svetz's flying armchair.

Enlightenment came like something clicking in his head. *Seasick.* On automatic, the extension cage matched its motion to the surface over which it flew; and that surface was heaving in great dark swells.

No wonder his stomach was uneasy! Svetz grinned and reached for the manual controls.

The NAI needle suddenly jerked hard over. A bite! thought Svetz, and he looked off to the right. No sign of a ship. And submarines hadn't been invented yet. Had they? No, of course they hadn't.

The needle was rock-steady.

Svetz flipped the call button.

The source of the tremendous NAI signal was off to his right, and moving. Svetz turned to follow it. It would be minutes before the call signal reached the Institute for Temporal Research and brought the big extension cage with its weaponry for hooking Leviathan.

———

Many years ago, Ra Chen had dreamed of rescuing the Library at Alexandria from Caesar's fire. For this purpose he had built the big extension cage. Its door was a gaping iris, big enough to be loaded while the Library was actually burning. Its hold, at a guess, was at least twice large enough to hold all the scrolls in that ancient Library.

The big cage had cost a fortune in government money. It had failed to go back beyond 400 A.A., or 1550 A.D. The books burned at Alexandria were still lost to history, or at least to historians.

Such a boondoggle would have broken other men. Somehow Ra Chen had survived the blow to his reputation.

He had pointed out the changes to Svetz after they returned from the Zoo. "We've fitted the cage out with heavy-duty stunners and antigravity beams. You'll operate them by remote control. Be careful not to let the stun beam touch you. It would kill even a sperm whale if you held it on him for more than a few seconds, and it'd kill a man instantly. Other than that you should have no problems."

It was at that moment that Svetz's stomach began to hurt.

"Our major change is the call button. It will actually send us a signal through time, so that we can send the big extension cage back to you. We can land it right beside you, no more than a few minutes off. That took considerable research, Svetz. The Treasury raised our budget for this year so that we could get that whale."

Svetz nodded.

"Just be sure you've got a whale before you call for the big extension cage."

Now, twelve hundred years earlier, Svetz followed an underwater source of nervous impulse. The signal was intensely powerful. It could not be anything smaller than an adult bull sperm whale.

A shadow formed in the air to his right. Svetz watched it take shape: a great gray-blue sphere floating beside him. Around the rim of the door were antigravity beamers and heavy duty stun guns. The opposite side of the sphere wasn't there; it simply faded away.

To Svetz that was the most frightening thing about any time machine: the way it seemed to turn a corner that wasn't there.

Svetz was almost over the signal. Now he used the remote controls to swing the antigravity beamers around and down.

He had them locked on the source. He switched them on, and dials surged.

Leviathan was *heavy*. More massive than Svetz had expected. Svetz upped the power, and watched the NAI needle swing as Leviathan rose invisibly through the water.

Where the surface of the water bulged upward under the attack of the antigravity beams, a shadow formed. Leviathan rising . . .

Was there something wrong with the shape?

Then a trembling spherical bubble of water rose shivering from the ocean, and Leviathan was within it.

Partly within it. He was too big to fit, though he should not have been.

He was four times as massive as a sperm whale should have been, and a dozen times as long. He looked nothing like the crystal Steuben sculpture. Leviathan was a kind of serpent armored with red-bronze scales as big as a Viking's shield, armed with teeth like ivory spears. His triangular jaws gaped wide. As he floated toward Svetz he writhed, seeking with his bulging yellow eyes for whatever strange enemy had subjected him to this indignity.

Svetz was paralyzed with fear and indecision. Neither then nor later did he doubt that what he saw was the Biblical Leviathan. This had to be the largest beast that had ever roamed the sea; a beast large enough and fierce enough to be synonymous with anything big and destructive. Yet— if the crystal sculpture was anything like representational, this was not a sperm whale at all.

In any case, he was far too big for the extension cage.

Indecision stayed his hand—and then Svetz stopped thinking entirely, as the great slitted irises found him.

The beast was floating past him. Around its waist was a sphere of weightless water, that shrank steadily as gobbets dripped away and rained back to the sea. The beast's nostrils flared—it was obviously an air-breather, though not a cetacean.

It stretched, reaching for Svetz with gaping jaws.

Teeth like scores of elephant's tusks all in a row. Polished and needle sharp. Svetz saw them close about him from above and below, while he sat frozen in fear.

At the last moment he shut his eyes tight.

When death did not come, Svetz opened his eyes.

The jaws had not entirely closed on Svetz and his armchair. Svetz heard them grinding faintly against—against the invisible surface of the extension cage, whose existence Svetz had forgotten entirely.

Svetz resumed breathing. He would return home with an empty extension cage, to face the wrath of Ra Chen . . . a fate better than death. Svetz moved his fingers to cut the antigravity beams from the big extension cage.

Metal whined against metal. Svetz whiffed hot oil, while red lights bloomed all over his lunch-tray control board. He hastily turned the beams on again.

The red lights blinked out one by reluctant one.

Through the transparent shell Svetz could hear the grinding of teeth. Leviathan was trying to chew his way into the extension cage.

His released weight had nearly torn the cage loose from the rest of the time machine. Svetz would have been stranded in the past, a hundred miles out to sea, in a broken extension cage that probably wouldn't float, with an angry sea monster waiting to snap him up. No, he couldn't turn off the antigravity beamers.

But the beamers were on the big extension cage, and he couldn't keep the big extension cage more than about fifteen minutes longer. When the big extension cage was gone, what would prevent Leviathan from pulling him to his doom?

"I'll stun him off," said Svetz.

There was dark red palate above him, and red gums and forking tongue beneath, and the long curved fangs all around. But between the two rows of teeth Svetz could see the big extension cage, and the battery of stunners around the door. By eye he rotated the stunners until they pointed straight toward Leviathan.

"I must be out of my mind," said Svetz, and he spun the stunners away from him. He couldn't fire the stunners at Leviathan without hitting himself.

And Leviathan wouldn't let go.

Trapped.

No, he thought with a burst of relief. He could escape with his life. The go-home lever would send his small extension cage out from between the jaws of Leviathan, back into the time stream, back to the Institute. His mission had failed, but that was hardly his fault. Why had Ra Chen been unable to uncover mention of a sea serpent bigger than a sperm whale?

"It's all his fault," said Svetz. And he reached for the go-home lever. But he stayed his hand.

"I can't just tell him so," he said. For Ra Chen terrified him.

The grinding of teeth came itchingly through the extension cage.

"Hate to just quit," said Svetz. "Think I'll try something . . . "

He could see the antigravity beamers by looking between the teeth. He could feel their influence, so nearly were they focused on the extension cage itself. If he focused them just on himself . . .

He felt the change; he felt both strong and lightheaded, like a drunken ballet master. And if he now narrowed the focus . . .

The monster's teeth seemed to grind harder. Svetz looked between them, as best he could.

Leviathan was no longer floating. He was hanging straight down from the extension cage, hanging by his teeth. The antigravity beamers still balanced the pull of his mass; but now they did so by pulling straight up on the extension cage.

The monster was in obvious distress. Naturally. A water beast, he was supporting his own mass for the first time in his life. And by his teeth! His yellow eyes rolled frantically. His tail twitched slightly at the very tip. And still he clung . . .

"Let go," said Svetz. "Let go, you . . . monster."

The monster's teeth slid screeching down the transparent surface, and he fell.

Svetz cut the antigravity a fraction of a second late. He smelled burnt oil, and there were tiny red lights blinking off one by one on his lunch-tray control board.

Leviathan hit the water with a sound of thunder. His long, sinuous body rolled over and floated to the surface and lay as if dead. But his tail flicked once, and Svetz knew that he was alive.

"I could kill you," said Svetz. "Hold the stunners on you until you're dead. There's time enough . . . "

But he still had ten minutes to search for a sperm whale. It wasn't time enough. It didn't begin to be time enough, but if he used it all . . .

The sea serpent flicked its tail and began to swim away. Once he rolled to look at Svetz, and his jaws opened wide in fury. He finished his roll and was fleeing again.

"Just a minute," Svetz said thickly. "Just a science-perverting minute there . . . " And he swung the stunners to focus.

———

Gravity behaved strangely inside an extension cage. While the cage was moving forward in time, *down* was all directions outward from the center of the cage. Svetz was plastered against the curved wall. He waited for the trip to end.

Seasickness was nothing compared to the motion sickness of time travel.

Free-fall, then normal gravity. Svetz moved unsteadily to the door.

Ra Chen was waiting to help him out. "Did you get it?"

"Leviathan? No sir." Svetz looked past his boss. "Where's the big extension cage?"

"We're bringing it back slowly, to minimize the gravitational side effects. But if you don't have the whale—"

"I said I don't have Leviathan."

"Well, just what *do* you have?" Ra Chen demanded.

Somewhat later he said, "It wasn't?"

Later yet he said, "You killed him? Why, Svetz? Pure spite?"

"No, sir. It was the most intelligent thing I did during the entire trip."

"But *why*? Never mind, Svetz, here's the big extension cage." A gray-blue shadow congealed in the hollow cradle of the time machine. "And there does seem to be something in it. Hi, you idiots, throw an antigravity beam inside the cage! Do you want the beast crushed?"

The cage had arrived. Ra Chen waved an arm in signal. The door opened.

Something tremendous hovered within the big extension cage. It looked like a malevolent white mountain in there, peering back at its captors with a single tiny, angry eye. It was trying to get at Ra Chen, but it couldn't swim in air.

Its other eye was only a torn socket. One of its flippers was ripped along the trailing edge. Rips and ridges and puckers of scar tissue, and a forest of broken wood and broken steel, marked its tremendous expanse of albino skin. Lines trailed from many of the broken harpoons. High up on one flank, bound to the beast by broken and tangled lines, was the corpse of a bearded man with one leg.

"Hardly in mint condition, is he?" Ra Chen observed.

"Be careful, sir. He's a killer. I saw him ram a sailing ship and sink it clean before I could focus the stunners on him."

"What amazes me is that you found him at all in the time you had left. Svetz, I do not understand your luck. Or am I missing something?"

"It wasn't luck, sir. It was the most intelligent thing I did the entire trip."

"You said that before. About killing Leviathan."

Svetz hurried to explain. "The sea serpent was just leaving the vicinity. I wanted to kill him, but I knew I didn't have the time. I was about to leave myself, when he turned back and bared his teeth.

"He was an obvious carnivore. Those teeth were built strictly for killing, sir. I should have noticed earlier. And I could think of only one animal big enough to feed a carnivore that size."

"Ah-h-h. Brilliant, Svetz."

"There was corroborative evidence. Our research never found any mention of giant sea serpents. The great geological surveys of the first century Post Atomic should have turned up something. Why didn't they?"

"Because the sea serpent quietly died out two centuries earlier, after whalers killed off his food supply."

Svetz colored. "Exactly. So I turned the stunners on Leviathan before he could swim away, and I kept the stunners on him until the NAI said he was dead. I reasoned that if Leviathan was here, there must be whales in the vicinity."

"And Leviathan's nervous output was masking the signal."

"Sure enough, it was. The moment he was dead the NAI registered another signal. I followed it to—" Svetz jerked his head. They were floating the whale out of the extension cage. "To him."

———

Days later, two men stood on one side of a thick glass wall.

"We took some clones from him, then passed him on to the Secretary-General's vivarium," said Ra Chen. "Pity you had to settle for an albino." He waved aside Svetz's protest: "I know, I know, you were pressed for time."

Beyond the glass, the one-eyed whale glared at Svetz through murky seawater. Surgeons had removed most of the harpoons, but scars remained along his flanks; and Svetz, awed, wondered how long the beast had been at war with Man. Centuries? How long did sperm whales live?

Ra Chen lowered his voice. "We'd all be in trouble if the Secretary-General found out that there was once a bigger animal than his. You understand that, don't you, Svetz?"

"Yes sir."

"Good." Ra Chen's gaze swept across another glass wall, and a fire-breathing Gila monster. Further down, a horse looked back at him along the dangerous spiral horn in its forehead.

"Always we find the unexpected," said Ra Chen. "Sometimes I wonder . . ."

*If you'd do your research better,* Svetz thought . . .

"Did you know that time travel wasn't even a concept until the first-century Ante Atomic? A writer invented it. From then until the fourth century Post Atomic, time travel was pure fantasy. It violates everything the scientists of the time thought were natural laws. Logic. Conservation of matter and energy. Momentum, reaction, any law of motion that makes time a part of the statement. Relativity."

"It strikes me," said Ra Chen, "that every time we push an extension cage past that particular four-century period, we shove it into a kind of fantasy world. That's why you keep finding giant sea serpents and fire breathing—"

"That's nonsense," said Svetz. He was afraid of his boss, yes; but there were limits.

"You're right," Ra Chen said instantly. Almost with relief. "Take a month's vacation, Svetz, then back to work. The Secretary-General wants a bird."

"A bird?" Svetz smiled. A bird sounded harmless enough. "I suppose he found it in another children's book?"

"That's right. Ever hear of a bird called a *roc?*"

# JOE HALDEMAN

---

*Praised for its authentic portrayal of the emotional detachment and psychological dislocation of soldiers in a millennium-long future war, Joe Haldeman's first science fiction novel,* The Forever War, *won the Hugo, Nebula, and Ditmar Awards when it was published in 1974 and later was adapted into a three-part graphic novel series. Since then, Haldeman has returned to the theme of future war several times, notably in his trilogy* Worlds, Worlds Apart, *and* Worlds Enough and Time, *about a future Earth facing nuclear extinction, and in* Forever Peace, *a further exploration of the dehumanizing potential of armed conflict. Haldeman's other novels include* Mindbridge, All My Sins Remembered, *and the alternate world opus* The Hemingway Hoax, *expanded from his Nebula Award–winning novella of the same name. Haldeman's stories have been collected in* Infinite Dreams *and* Dealing in Futures, *and several of his essays are mixed with fiction in* Vietnam and Other Alien Worlds. *His powerful non–science-fiction writing includes* War Year, *drawn from experiences during his tour of duty in Vietnam, and* 1968, *a portrait of America in the Vietnam era. He has also coedited the anthologies* Body Armor: 2000, Space-Fighters, *and* Supertanks. *His twenty novels, three story collections, six anthologies, and one poetry collection have appeared in eighteen languages.*

*"Anniversary Project" is one of the few stories in this collection that*

*deals with traveling forward into the future, and in the hands of Joe Halde-man, it is a dizzying ride indeed. Given when it was published (1975), the topical events of Korea, Vietnam, and the next few decades play a surpris-ing role in the events of the story, despite most of the action's taking place a million years in the future.*

# ANNIVERSARY PROJECT

## JOE HALDEMAN

HIS NAME IS Three-phasing and he is bald and wrinkled, slightly over one meter tall, large-eyed, toothless and all bones and skin, sagging pale skin shot through with traceries of delicate blue and red. He is considered very beautiful but most of his beauty is in his hands and is due to his extreme youth. He is over two hundred years old and is learning how to talk. He has become reasonably fluent in sixty-three languages, all dead ones, and has only ten to go.

The book he is reading is a facsimile of an early edition of Goethe's *Faust*. The nervous angular Fraktur letters goose-step across pages of paper-thin platinum.

The *Faust* had been printed electrolytically and, with several thousand similarly worthwhile books, sealed in an argon-filled chamber and carefully lost, in 2012 A.D.; a very wealthy man's legacy to the distant future.

In 2012 A.D., Polaris had been the pole star. Men eventually got to Polaris and built a small city on a frosty planet there. By that time, they weren't dating by prophets' births any more, but it would have been around 4900 A.D. The pole star by then, because of precession of the equinoxes, was a dim thing once called Gamma Cephei. The celestial pole kept reeling around, past Deneb and Vega and through barren patches of sky around Hercules and Draco; a patient clock but not the slowest one of use, and when it came back to the region of Polaris, then 26,000 years had passed and men had come back from the stars, to stay, and the book-filled chamber had shifted 130 meters on the floor of the Pacific, had rolled onto a shallow trench, and eventually was buried in an underwater landslide.

The thirty-seventh time this slow clock ticked, men had moved the Pacific, not because they had to, and had found the chamber, opened it up, identified the books and carefully sealed them up again. Some things by then were more important to men than the accumulation of knowledge: in half of one more circle of the poles would come the millionth anniversary of the written word. They could wait a few millennia.

As the anniversary, as nearly as they could reckon it, approached, they caused to be born two individuals: Nine-hover (nominally female) and Three-phasing (nominally male). Three-phasing was born to learn how to read and speak. He was the first human being to study these skills in more than a quarter of a million years.

Three-phasing has read the first half of *Faust* forwards and, for amusement and exercise, is reading the second half backwards. He is singing as he reads, lisping.

"Fain' Looee w'mun . . . wif all'r die-mun ringf . . . " He has not put in his teeth because they make his gums hurt.

Because he is a child of two hundred, he is polite when his father interrupts his reading and singing. His father's "voice" is an arrangement of logic and aesthetic that appears in Three-phasing's mind. The flavor is lost by translating into words:

"Three-phasing my son-ly atavism of tooth and vocal cord," sarcastically in the reverent mode, "Couldst tear thyself from objects of manifest symbol, and visit to share/help/learn, me?"

"?" He responds, meaning "with/with/of what?"

Withholding mode: "Concerning thee: past, future."

He shuts the book without marking his place. It would never occur to him to mark his place, since he remembers perfectly the page he stops on, as well as every word preceding, as well as every event, no matter how trivial, that he has observed from the precise age of one year. In this respect, at least, he is normal.

He thinks the proper coordinates as he steps over the mover-transom, through a microsecond of black, and onto his father's mover-transom, about four thousand kilometers away on a straight line through the crust and mantle of the earth.

Ritual mode: "As ever, father." The symbol he uses for "father" is purposefully wrong, chiding. Crude biological connotation.

His father looks cadaverous and has in fact been dead twice. In the infant's small-talk mode he asks, "From crude babblings of what sort have I torn your interest?"

"The tale called *Faust*, of a man so named, never satisfied with {symbol for slow but continuous accretion} of his knowledge and power; written in the language of Prussia."

"Also depended-ing on this strange word of immediacy, your Prussian language?"

"As most, yes. The word of 'to be': *sein*. Very important illusion in this and related languages/cultures; that events happen at the 'time' of perception, infinitesimal midpoint between past and future."

"Convenient illusion but retarding."

"As we discussed 129 years ago, yes." Three-phasing is impatient to get back to his reading, but adds:

"Obvious that to-be-ness $\left\{ \begin{array}{l} \text{same order of illusion as three-dimensionality of external world.} \\ \\ \text{thrust upon observer by geometric limitation of synaptic degrees of freedom.} \end{array} \right\}$"

"You always stick up for them."

"I have great regard for what they accomplished with limited faculties and so short lives." Stop beatin' around the bush, Dad. *Tempis fugit*, eight to the bar. Did Mr. Handy Moves-dat-man-around-by-her-apron-strings, 20th-century American poet, intend cultural translation of *Lysistrata*? If so, inept. African were-beast legendry, yes.

Withholding mode (coy): "Your father stood with Nine-hover all morning."

"," broadcasts Three-phasing: well?

"The machine functions, perhaps inadequately."

The young polyglot tries to radiate calm patience.

"Details I perceive you want; the idea yet excites you. You can never have satisfaction with your knowledge, either. What happened-s to the man in your Prussian book?"

"He lived-s one hundred years and died-s knowing that a man can never achieve true happiness, despite the appearance of success."

"For an infant, a reasonable perception."

Respectful chiding mode: "One hundred years makes-ed Faust a very old man, for a Dawn man."

"As I stand," same mode, less respect, "yet an infant." They trade silent symbols of laughter.

After a polite tenth-second interval, Three-phasing uses the light interrogation mode: "The machine of Nine-hover . . . ?"

"It begins to work but so far not perfectly." This is not news.

Mild impatience: "As before, then, it brings back only rocks and earth and water and plants?"

"Negative, beloved atavism." Offhand: "This morning she caught two animals that look as man may once have looked.

"!" Strong impatience, "I go?"

"." His father ends the conversation just two seconds after it began.

Three-phasing stops off to pick up his teeth, then goes directly to Nine-hover.

A quick exchange of greeting-symbols and Nine-hover presents her prizes. "Thinking I have two different species," she stands: uncertainty, query.

Three-phasing is amused. "Negative, time-caster. The male and female took very dissimilar forms in the Dawn times." He touches one of them. "The round organs, here, served-ing to feed infants, in the female."

The female screams.

"She manipulates spoken symbols now," observes Nine-hover.

Before the woman has finished her startled yelp, Three-phasing explains: "Not manipulating concrete symbols; rather, she communicates in a way called 'non-verbal,' the use of such communication predating even speech." Slipping into the pedantic mode: "My reading indicates that such a loud noise occurs either

$$\begin{cases} \text{following a stimulus} \\ \text{under conditions of} \end{cases}$$

$$\text{that produces pain} \begin{cases} \\ \end{cases} \qquad \text{since she seems not in pain, then}$$
$$\text{extreme agitation}$$

she must fear me or you or both of us."

"Or the machine," Nine-hover adds.

Symbol for continuing. "We have no symbol for it but in Dawn days most humans observed 'xenophobia,' reacting to the strange with fear instead of delight. We stand as strange to them as they do to us, thus they register fear. In their era this attitude encouraged-s survival.

"Our silence must seem strange to them, as well as our appearance and the speed with which we move. I will attempt to speak to them, so they will know they need not fear us."

————

Bob and Sarah Graham were having a desperately good time. It was September of 1951 and the papers were full of news about the brilliant landing of U.S. Marines at Inchon. Bob was a Marine private with two days left of the thirty days' leave they had given him, between boot camp and disembarkation for Korea. Sarah had been Mrs. Graham for three weeks.

Sarah poured some more bourbon into her Coke. She wiped the sand off her thumb and stoppered the Coke bottle, then shook it gently. "What if you just don't show up?" she said softly.

Bob was staring out over the ocean and part of what Sarah said was lost in the crash of breakers rolling in. "What if I what?"

"Don't show up." She took a swig and offered the bottle. "Just stay here with me. With us." Sarah was sure she was pregnant. It was too early to tell, of course; her calendar was off but there could be other reasons.

He gave the Coke back to her and sipped directly from the bourbon bottle. "I suppose they'd go on without me. And I'd still be in jail when they came back."

"Not if—"

"Honey, don't even talk like that. It's a just cause."

She picked up a small shell and threw it toward the water.

"Besides, you read the *Examiner* yesterday."

"I'm cold. Let's go up." She stood and stretched and delicately brushed sand away. Bob admired her long naked dancer's body. He shook out the blanket and draped it over her shoulders.

"It'll be over by the time I get there. We'll push those bastards—"

"Let's not talk about Korea. Let's not talk."

He put his arm around her and they started walking back toward the cabin. Halfway there, she stopped and enfolded the blanket around both of them, drawing him toward her. He always closed his eyes when they kissed, but she always kept hers open. She saw it: the air turning luminous, the seascape fading to be replaced by bare metal walls. The sand turns hard under her feet.

At her sharp intake of breath, Bob opens his eyes. He sees a grotesque dwarf, eyes and skull too large, body small and wrinkled. They stare at one another for a fraction of a second. Then the dwarf spins around and speeds across the room to what looks like a black square painted on the floor. When he gets there, he disappears.

"What the hell?" Bob says in a hoarse whisper.

Sarah turns around just a bit too late to catch a glimpse of Three-phasing's father. She does see Nine-hover before Bob does. The nominally-female time-caster is a flurry of movement, sitting at the console of her time net, clicking switches and adjusting various dials. All of the motions are unnecessary, as is the console. It was built at Three-phasing's suggestion, since humans from the era into which they could cast would feel more comfortable in the presence of a machine that looked like a machine. The actual time net was roughly the size and shape of an asparagus stalk, was controlled completely by thought, and had no moving parts. It does not exist any more, but can still be used, once understood. Nine-hover has been trained from birth for this special understanding.

Sarah nudges Bob and points to Nine-hover. She can't find her voice; Bob stares open-mouthed.

In a few seconds, Three-phasing appears. He looks at Nine-hover for a moment, then scurries over to the Dawn couple and reaches up to touch Sarah on the left nipple. His body temperature is considerably higher than hers, and the unexpected warm moistness, as much as the suddenness of the motion, makes her jump back and squeal.

Three-phasing correctly classified both Dawn people as Caucasian, and so assumes that they speak some Indo-European language.

"*GuttenTagsprechesieDeutsch?*" he says in a rapid soprano.

"Huh?" Bob says.

"*Guten-Tag-sprechen-sie-Deutsch?*' Three-phasing clears his throat and drops his voice down to the alto he uses to sing about the St. Louis woman. "*Guten Tag,*" he says, counting to a hundred between each word. "*Sprechen sie Deutsch?*"

"That's Kraut," says Bob, having grown up on jingoistic comic books. "Don't tell me you're a—"

Three-phasing analyzes the first five words and knows that Bob is an American from the period 1935–1955. "Yes, yes—and no, no—to wit, how very very clever of you to have identified this phrase as having come from the language of Prussia, Germany as you say; but I am, no, not a German person; at least, I no more belong to the German nationality than I do to any other, but I suppose that is not too clear and perhaps I should fully elucidate the particulars of your own situation at this, as you say, 'time,' and 'place.' "

The last English-language author Three-phasing studied was Henry James.

"Huh?" Bob says again.

"Ah, I should simplify." He thinks for a half-second, and drops his voice down another third. "Yeah, simple. Listen, Mac. First thing I gotta know's whatcher name. Whatcher broad's name."

"Well . . . I'm Bob Graham. This is my wife, Sarah Graham."

"Pleasta meetcha, Bob. Likewise, Sarah. Call me, uh . . ." The only twentieth-century language in which Three-phasing's name makes sense is propositional calculus. "George. George Boole.

"I 'poligize for bumpin' into ya, Sarah. That broad in the corner, she don't know what a tit is, so I was just usin' one of yours. Uh, lack of immediate cultural perspective, I shoulda knowed better."

Sarah feels a little dizzy, shakes her head slowly. "That's all right. I know you didn't mean anything by it."

"I'm dreaming," Bob says. "Shouldn't have —"

"No you aren't," says Three-phasing, adjusting his diction again. "You're in the future. Almost a million years. Pardon me." He scurries to the mover-transom, is gone for a second, reappears with a bedsheet, which he hands to Bob. "I'm sorry, we don't wear clothing. This is the best I can do, for now." The bedsheet is too small for Bob to wear the way Sarah is using the blanket. He folds it over and tucks it around his waist, in a kilt. "Why us?" he asks.

"You were taken at random. We've been time casting" — he checks with Nine-hover — "for twenty-two years, and have never before caught a human being. Let alone two. You must have been in close contact with one another when you intersected the time-caster beam. I assume you were copulating."

"What-ing?" Bob says.

"No, we weren't!" Sarah says indignantly.

"Ah, quite so." Three-phasing doesn't pursue the topic. He knows the humans of this culture were reticent about their sexual activity. But from their literature he knows they spent most of their "time" thinking about, arranging for, enjoying, and recovering from a variety of sexual contacts.

"Then that must be a time machine over there," Bob says, indicating the fake console.

"In a sense, yes." Three-phasing decides to be partly honest. "But the actual machine no longer exists. People did a lot of time-traveling about a quarter of a million years ago. Shuffled history around. Changed it back. The fact that the machine once existed, well, that enables us to use it, if you see what I mean."

"Uh, no. I don't." Not with synapses limited to three degrees of freedom.

"Well, never mind. It's not really important." He senses the next question. "You will be going back . . . I don't know exactly when. It depends on a lot of things. You see, time is like a rubber band." No, it isn't. "Or a spring." No, it isn't. "At any rate, within a few days, weeks at most, you will leave this present and return to the moment you were experiencing when the time-caster beam picked you up."

"I've read stories like that," Sarah says. "Will we remember the future, after we go back?"

"Probably not," he says charitably. Not until your brains evolve. "But you can do us a great service."

Bob shrugs. "Sure, long as we're here. Anyhow, you did us a favor." He puts his arm around Sarah. "I've gotta leave Sarah in a couple of days; don't know for how long. So you're giving us more time together."

"Whether we remember it or not," Sarah says.

"Good, fine. Come with me." They follow Three-phasing to the mover-transom, where he takes their hands and transports them to his home. It is as unadorned as the time-caster room, except for bookshelves along one wall, and a low podium upon which the volume of *Faust* rests. All of the books are bound identically, in shiny metal with flat black letters along the spines.

Bob looks around. "Don't you people ever sit down?"

"Oh," Three-phasing says. "Thoughtless of me." With his mind he shifts the room from utility mood to comfort mood. Intricate tapestries now hang on the walls; soft cushions that look like silk are strewn around in pleasant disorder. Chiming music, not quite discordant, hovers at the edge of audibility, and there is a faint odor of something like jasmine. The metal floor has become a kind of soft leather, and the room has somehow lost its corners.

"How did that happen?" Sarah asks.

"I don't know." Three-phasing tries to copy Bob's shrug, but only manages a spasmodic jerk. "Can't remember not being able to do it."

Bob drops into a cushion and experimentally pushes at the floor with a finger. "What is it you want us to do?"

Trying to move slowly, Three-phasing lowers himself into a cushion and gestures at a nearby one, for Sarah. "It's very simple, really. Your being here is most of it.

"We're celebrating the millionth anniversary of the written word." How to phrase it? "Everyone is interested in this anniversary, but . . . nobody reads any more."

Bob nods sympathetically. "Never have time for it myself."

"Yes, uh . . . you *do* know how to read, though?"

"He knows," Sarah says. "He's just lazy."

"Well, yeah." Bob shifts uncomfortably in the cushion. "Sarah's the one you want. I kind of, uh, prefer to listen to the radio."

"I read all the time," Sarah says with a little pride. "Mostly mysteries. But sometimes I read good books, too."

"Good, good." It was indeed fortunate to have found this pair, Three-phasing realizes. They had used the metal of the ancient books to "tune" the time-caster, so potential subjects were limited to those living some eighty years before and after 2012 A.D. Internal evidence in the books indicated that most of the Earth's population was illiterate during this period.

"Allow me to explain. Any one of us can learn how to read. But to us it is like a code; an unnatural way of communicating. Because we are all natural telepaths. We can reach each other's minds from the age of one year."

"Golly!" Sarah says. "Read minds?" And Three-phasing sees in her mind a fuzzy kind of longing, much of which is love for Bob and frustration that she knows him only imperfectly. He dips into Bob's mind and finds things she is better off not knowing.

"That's right. So what we want is for you to read some of these books, and allow us to go into your minds while you're doing it. This way we will be able to recapture an experience that has been lost to the race for over a half-million years."

"I don't know," Bob says slowly. "Will we have time for anything else? I mean, the world must be pretty strange. Like to see some of it."

"Of course; sure. But the rest of the world is pretty much like my place here. Nobody goes outside any more. There isn't any air." He doesn't want to tell them how the air was lost, which might disturb them, but they seem to accept that as part of the distant future.

"Uh, George." Sarah is blushing. "We'd also like, uh, some time to ourselves. Without anybody . . . inside our minds."

"Yes, I understand perfectly. You will have your own room, and plenty of time to yourselves." Three-phasing neglects to say that there is no such thing as privacy in a telepathic society.

But sex is another thing they don't have any more. They're almost as curious about that as they are about books.

———

So the kindly men of the future gave Bob and Sarah Graham plenty of time to themselves: Bob and Sarah reciprocated. Through the Dawn couple's eyes and brains, humanity shared again the visions of Fielding and Melville and Dickens and Shakespeare and almost a dozen others. And as for the 98% more, that they didn't have time to read or that were in foreign languages—Three-phasing got the hang of it and would spend several millennia entertaining those who were amused by this central illusion of literature: that there could be order, that there could be beginnings and endings and logical workings-out in between; that you could count on the third act or the last chapter to tie things up. They knew how profound an illusion this was because each of them knew every other living human with an intimacy and accuracy far superior to that which even Shakespeare could bring to the study of even himself. And as for Sarah and as for Bob:

Anxiety can throw a person's ovaries 'way off schedule. On that beach in California, Sarah was no more pregnant than Bob was. But up there in the future, some somatic tension finally built up to the breaking point, and an egg went sliding down the left Fallopian tube, to be met by a wiggling intruder approximately halfway; together they were the first manifestation of organism that nine months later, or a million years earlier, would be christened Douglas MacArthur Graham.

This made a problem for time, or Time, which is neither like a rubber band nor like a spring; nor even like a river nor a carrier wave—but which, like all of these things, can be deformed by certain stresses. For instance, two people going into the future and three coming back on the same time-casting beam.

In an earlier age, when time travel was more common, time-casters would have made sure that the baby, or at least its aborted embryo, would stay in the future when the mother returned to her present. Or they could arrange for the mother to stay in the future. But these subtleties had long been forgotten when Nine-hover relearned the dead art. So

Sarah went back to her present with a hitch-hiker, an interloper, firmly imbedded in the lining of her womb. And its dim sense of life set up a kind of eddy in the flow of time, that Sarah had to share.

The mathematical explanation is subtle, and can't be comprehended by those of us who synapse with fewer than four degrees of freedom. But the end effect is clear: Sarah had to experience all of her own life backwards, all the way back to that embrace on the beach. Some highlights were:

In 1992, slowly dying of cancer, in a mental hospital.

In 1979, seeing Bob finally succeed at suicide on the American Plan, not quite finishing his 9,527th bottle of liquor.

In 1970, having her only son returned in a sealed casket from a country she'd never heard of.

In the 1960's, helplessly watching her son become more and more neurotic because of something that no one could name.

In 1953, Bob coming home with one foot, the other having been lost to frostbite; never having fired a shot in anger.

In 1952, the agonizing breech presentation.

Like her son, Sarah would remember no details of the backward voyage through her life. But the scars of it would haunt her forever.

They were kissing on the beach.

Sarah dropped the blanket and made a little noise. She started crying and slapped Bob as hard as she could, then ran on alone, up to the cabin.

Bob watched her progress up the hill with mixed feelings. He took a healthy slug from the bourbon bottle, to give him an excuse to wipe his own eyes.

He could go sit on the beach and finish the bottle; let her get over it by herself. Or he could go comfort her.

He tossed the bottle away, the gesture immediately making him feel stupid, and followed her. Later that night she apologized, saying she didn't know what had gotten into her.

# JACK DANN

Jack Dann has written or edited over fifty books, many dealing with humanity's own consciousness and its role in comprehending the universe. His novels include the international best-seller The Memory Cathedral, about the travels of Leonardo da Vinci outside his native Italy and the changes his fertile mind brings to other countries. Other works include The Man Who Melted, in which three Nebula-nominated novellas about a future society under assault by its citizens are woven into a story of an amnesiac man searching for his wife. Dann collaborated with Jack C. Haldeman II on the novel High Steel, which took ruthless American corporations into space and pitted them against a Native American protagonist trying to hold on to his history while working out in space. His short fiction was recently collected in the anthology Jubilee, which features the title story about the reality-altering effects of an alien consciousness attempting to contact Earth. Dann's work has been compared to that of Jorge Luis Borges, Roald Dahl, Lewis Carroll, Carlos Castañeda, J. G. Ballard, Philip K. Dick, and Mark Twain. He is a recipient of the Nebula Award, the World Fantasy Award, the Australian Aurealis Award (twice), the Ditmar Award (twice), and the Premios Gilgames de Narrativa Fantastica award. He has also been honored by the Mark Twain Society (Esteemed Knight).

Dann takes a metaphysical, existential look at time travel in "Timetipping," mingling his Jewish heritage with a world where people and things slip in and out of different times every instant of the day, and *a person can find himself in a new dimension in the blink of an eye. The hero of his story, an everyday sort just trying to get by, is stuck in this world, but unlike everyone else, he watches everything around him change, while never timetipping himself, and it is this singular point of view that the story is built on.*

# TIMETIPPING

## JACK DANN

SINCE TIMETIPPING, everything moved differently. Nothing was for certain, anything could change (depending on your point of view), and almost anything could happen, especially to forgetful old men who often found themselves in the wrong century rather than on the wrong street.

Take Moishe Hodel, who was too old and fat to be climbing ladders; yet he insisted on climbing to the roof of his suburban house so that he could sit on the top of a stone-tuff church in Goreme six hundred years in the past. Instead of praying, he would sit and watch monks. He claimed that since time and space were *meshuggeneh* (what's crazy in any other language?), he would search for a quick and Godly way to travel to synagogue. Let the goyim take the trains.

Of course, Paley Litwak, who was old enough to know something, knew from nothing when the world changed and everything went blip. His wife disappeared, and a new one returned in her place. A new Golde, one with fewer lines and dimples, one with starchy white hair and missing teeth.

Upon arrival all she said was, "This is almost right. You're almost the same, Paley. Still, you always go to shul?"

"Shul?" Litwak asked, resolving not to jump and scream and ask God for help. With all the changing, Litwak would stand straight and wait for God. "What's a shul?"

"You mean you don't know from shul, and yet you wear such a yarmulke on your head?" She pulled her babushka through her fingers. "A shul. A synagogue, a temple. Do you pray?"

Litwak was not a holy man, but he could hold up his head and not be afraid to wink at God. Certainly he prayed. And in the following weeks Litwak found himself in shul more often than not—so she had an effect on him; after all, she was his wife. Where else was there to be? With God he had a one-way conversation—from Litwak's mouth to God's ears—but at home it was turned around. There, Litwak had no mouth, only ears. How can you talk with a woman who thinks fornicating with other men is holy?

But Litwak was a survivor; with the rest of the world turned over and doing flip-flops, he remained the same. Not once did he trip into a different time, not even an hour did he lose or gain; and the only places he went were those he could walk to. He was the exception to the rule. The rest of the world was adrift; everyone was swimming by, blipping out of the past or future and into the present here or who-knows-where.

It was a new world. Every street was filled with commerce, every night was carnival. Days were built out of strange faces, and nights went by so fast that Litwak remained in the synagogue just to smooth out time. But there was no time for Litwak, just services, and prayers, and holy smells.

Yet the world went on. Business almost as usual. There were still rabbis and chasids and grocers and cabalists; fat Hoffa, a congregant with a beard that would make a storybook Baal Shem jealous, even claimed that he knew a cabalist that had invented a new gemetria for foretelling everything concerning money.

"So who needs gemetria?" Litwak asked. "Go trip tomorrow and find out what's doing."

"Wrong," said Hoffa as he draped his prayer shawl over his arm, waiting for a lull in the conversation to say the holy words before putting on the talis. "It does no good to go there if you can't get back. And when you come back, everything is changed, anyway. Who do you know that's really returned? Look at you, you didn't have gray hair and earlocks yesterday."

"Then that wasn't *me* you saw. Anyway, if everybody but me is tripping and tipping back and forth, in and out of the devil's mouth, so to speak, then what time do you have to use this new gemetria?"

Hoffa paused and said, "So the world must go on. You think it stops because heaven shakes it. . . ."

"You're so sure it's heaven?"

" . . . but *you* can go see the cabalist; you're stuck in the present, you sit on one line. Go talk to him; he speaks a passable Yiddish, and his wife walks around with a bare behind."

"So how do you know he's there now?" asked Litwak. "They come and go. Perhaps a Neanderthal or a *klezmer* from the future will take his place."

"So? If he isn't there, what matter? At least you know he's some-where else. No? Everything goes on. Nothing gets lost. Everything fits, somehow. That's what's important."

It took Litwak quite some time to learn the new logic of the times, but once learned, it became an advantage—especially when his pension checks didn't arrive. Litwak became a fair second-story man, but he robbed only according to society's logic and his own ethical system: one-half for the shul and the rest for Litwak.

Litwak found himself spending more time on the streets than in the synagogue, but by standing still on one line he could not help but learn. He was putting the world together, seeing where it was, would be, might be, might not be. When he became confused, he used logic.

And the days passed faster, even with praying and sleeping nights in the shul for more time. Everything whirled around him. The city was a moving kaleidoscope of colors from every period of history, all melting into different costumes as the thieves and diplomats and princes and merchants strolled down the cobbled streets of Brooklyn.

With prisms for eyes, Litwak would make his way home through the crowds of slaves and serfs and commuters. Staking out fiefdoms in Brooklyn was difficult, so the slaves momentarily ran free, only to trip somewhere else where they would be again grabbed and raped and worked until they could trip again, and again and again until old logic fell apart. King's Highway was a bad part of town. The Boys' Club had been turned into a slave market and gallows room.

Litwak's tiny apartment was the familiar knot at the end of the rope. Golde had changed again, but it was only a slight change. Golde kept changing as her different time lines met in Litwak's kitchen, and bed-room. A few Goldes he liked, but change was gradual, and Goldes tended to run down. So for every sizzling Golde with blond-dyed hair, he suffered fifty or a thousand Goldes with missing teeth and croaking voices.

The latest Golde had somehow managed to buy a parakeet, which turned into a blue jay, a parrot with red feathers, and an ostrich, which provided supper. Litwak had discovered that smaller animals usually timetipped at a faster rate than men and larger animals; perhaps, he thought, it was a question of metabolism. Golde killed the ostrich before something else could take its place. Using logic and compassion, Litwak blessed it to make it kosher—the rabbi was not to be found, and he was a new chasid (imagine) who didn't know Talmud from soap opera; worse yet, he read Hebrew with a Brooklyn twang, not unheard of with such new rabbis. Better that Litwak bless his own meat; let the rabbi bless goyish food.

Another meal with another Golde, this one dark-skinned and pimply, overweight and sagging, but her eyes were the color of the ocean seen from an airplane on a sunny day. Litwak could not concentrate on food. There was a pitched battle going on two streets away, and he was worried about getting to shul.

"More soup?" Golde asked.

She had pretty hands, too, Litwak thought. "No, thank you," he said before she disappeared.

In her place stood a squat peasant woman, hands and ragged dress still stained with rich, black soil. She didn't scream or dash around or attack Litwak; she just wrung her hands and scratched her crotch. She spoke the same language, in the same low tones, that Litwak had listened to for several nights in shul. An Egyptian named Rhampsinitus had found his way into the synagogue, thinking it was a barbarian temple for Baiti, the clown god.

"Baiti?" she asked, her voice rising. "Baiti," she answered, convinced.

So here it ends, thought Litwak, just beginning to recognize the rancid odor in the room as sweat.

Litwak ran out of the apartment before she turned into something more terrible. Changes, he had expected. Things change and shift—that's logic. But not so fast. He had slowed down natural processes in the past (he thought), but now he was slipping, sinking like the rest of them. A bald Samson adrift on a raft.

Time isn't a river, Litwak thought as he pushed his way through larger crowds, all adrift, shouting, laughing, blipping in and out, as old men were replaced by ancient monsters and fears; but dinosaurs occupied too much space, always slipped, and could enter the present world only in torn pieces—a great ornithischian wing, a stegosaurian tail with two pairs of bony spikes, or, perhaps, a four-foot-long tyrannosaurus head.

Time is a hole, Litwak thought. He could feel its pull.

Whenever Litwak touched a stranger—someone who had come too

many miles and minutes to recognize where he was—there was a pop and a skip, and the person disappeared. Litwak had disposed of three gilded ladies, an archdeacon, a birdman, a knight with Norman casque, and several Sumerian serfs in this manner. He almost tripped over a young boy who was doggedly trying to extract a tooth from the neatly severed head of a tyrannosaurus.

The boy grabbed Litwak's leg, racing a few steps on his knees to do so, and bit him. Screaming in pain, Litwak pulled his leg away, felt an unfamiliar pop, and found the synagogue closer than he had remembered. But this wasn't his shul; it was a cathedral, a caricature of his beloved synagogue.

"Catch him," shouted the boy with an accent so thick that Litwak could barely make out what he said. "He's the thief who steals from the shul."

"*Gevalt*, this is the wrong place," Litwak said, running toward the cathedral.

A few hands reached for him, but then he was inside. There, in God's salon, everything was, would be, and had to be the same: large clerestory windows; double aisles for Thursday processions; radiating chapels modeled after Amiens 1247; and nave, choir, and towers, all styled to fit the stringent requirements of halakic law.

Over the altar, just above the holy ark, hung a bronze plate representing the egg of Khumu, who created the substance of the world on a potter's wheel. And standing on the plush pulpit, his square face buried in a prayer book, was Rabbi Rhampsinitus.

"Holy, holy, holy," he intoned. Twenty-five old men sang and wailed and prayed on cue. They all had beards and earlocks and wore conical caps and prayer garments.

"That's him," shouted the boy.

Litwak ran to the pulpit and kissed the holy book.

"Thief, robber, purloiner, depredator."

"Enough," Rhampsinitus said. "The service is concluded. God has not winked his eye. Make it good," he told the boy.

"Well, look who it is."

Rhampsinitus recognized Litwak at once. "So it is the thief. Stealer from God's coffers, you have been excommunicated as a second-story man."

"But I haven't stolen from the shul. This is not even my time or place."

"He speaks a barbarian tongue," said Rhampsinitus. "What's shul?"

"This Paley Litwak is twice, or thrice, removed," interrupted Moishe Hodel, who could timetip at will to any synagogue God chose to place around him. "He's new. Look and listen. *This* Paley Litwak probably does not steal from the synagogue. Can you blame him for what some-one else does?"

"Moishe Hodel?" asked Litwak. "Are you the same one I knew from Beth David on King's Highway?"

"Who knows?" said Hodel. "I know a Beth David, but not on King's Highway, and I know a Paley Litwak who was stuck in time and had a wife named Golde who raised hamsters."

"That's close, but—"

"So don't worry. I'll speak for you. It takes a few hours to pick up the slang, but it's like Yinglish, only drawled out and spiced with too many Egyptisms."

"Stop blaspheming," said Rhampsinitus. "Philosophy and logic are very fine indeed," he said to Hodel. "But this is a society of law, not philosophers, and law demands reparations."

"But I have money," said Litwak.

"There's your logic," said Rhampsinitus. "Money, especially such barbarian tender as yours, cannot replace the deed. Private immorality and public indecency are one and the same."

"He's right," said Hodel with a slight drawl.

"Jail the tergiversator," said the boy.

"Done," answered Rhampsinitus. He made a holy sign and gave Litwak a quick blessing. Then the boy's sheriffs dragged him away.

"Don't worry, Paley," shouted Moishe Hodel. "Things change."

Litwak tried to escape from the sheriffs, but he could not change times. It's only a question of will, he told himself. With God's help, he could initiate a change and walk, or slip, into another century, a friend-lier time.

But not yet. Nothing shifted; they walked a straight line to the jail, a large pyramid still showing traces of its original limestone casing.

"Here we are," said one of the sheriffs. "This is a humble town. We don't need ragabrash and riffraff—it's enough we have foreigners. So timetip or slip or flit somewhere else. There's no other way out of this de-pository."

They deposited him in a narrow passageway and dropped the en-trance stone behind him.

It was hard to breathe, and the damp air stank. It was completely dark. Litwak could not see his hands before his eyes.

*Gottenyu*, he thought, as he huddled on the cold stone floor. For a penny they plan to incarcerate me. He recited the *Shma Yisroel* and kept repeating it to himself, ticking off the long seconds with each syllable.

For two days he prayed; at least it seemed like two days. Perhaps it was four hours. When he was tired of praying, he cursed Moishe Hodel, wishing him hell and broken fingers. Litwak sneezed, developed a nervous cough, and his eyes became rheumy. "It's God's will," he said aloud.

Almost in reply, a thin faraway voice sang, "Oh, my goddess, oh, my goddess, oh, my goddess, Clem-en-tine!"

It was a familiar folk tune, sung in an odd Spanish dialect. But Litwak could understand it, for his mother's side of the family spoke in Ladino, the vernacular of Spanioli Jews.

So there, he thought. He felt the change. Once he had gained God's patience, he could slip, tip, and stumble away.

Litwak followed the voice. The floor began to slope upward as he walked through torchlit corridors and courtyards and rooms. In some places, not yet hewn into living quarters, stalactite and stalagmite remained. Some of the rooms were decorated with wall paintings of clouds, lightning, the sun, and masked dancers. In one room was a frieze of a great plumed serpent; in another were life-size mountain lions carved from lava. But none of the rooms were occupied.

He soon found the mouth of the cave. The bright sunlight blinded him for an instant.

"I've been waiting for you," said Castillo Moldanado in a variation of Castilian Spanish. "You're the third. A girl arrived yesterday, but she likes to keep to herself."

"Who are you?" asked Litwak.

"A visitor, like you." Moldanado picked at a black mole under his eye and smoothed his dark, thinning hair.

Litwak's eyes became accustomed to the sunlight. Before him was desert. Hills of cedar and piñon were mirages in the sunshine. In the far distance, mesa and butte overlooked red creeks and dry washes. This was a thirsty land of dust and sand and dirt and sun, broken only by a few brown fields, a ranch, or an occasional trading post and mission. But to his right and left, and hidden behind him, pueblos thrived on the faces of sheer cliffs. Cliff dwellings and cities made of smooth-hewn stone commanded valley and desert.

"It looks dead," Moldanado said. "But all around you is life. The Indians are all over the cliffs and desert. Their home is the rock itself. Behind you is Cliff Palace, which contains one hundred and fifty rooms. And they have rock cities in Cañon del Muerto and, farther south, in Walnut Canyon."

"I see no one here but us," Litwak said.

"They're hiding," said Moldanado. "They see the change and think we're gods. They're afraid of another black kachina, an evil spirit."

"Ah," Litwak said. "A dybbuk."

"You'll see natives soon enough. Ayoyewe will be here shortly to rekindle the torches, and for the occasion, he'll dress in his finest furs and turkey feathers. They call this cave Keet Seel, mouth of the gods. It was given to me. And I give it to you.

"Soon there will be more natives about, and more visitors. We'll change the face of their rocks and force them out. With greed."

"And logic," said Litwak.

Moldanado was right. More visitors came every day and settled in the desert and caves and pueblos. Romans, Serbs, Egyptians, Americans, Skymen, Mormons, Baalists, and Trackers brought culture and religion and weapons. They built better buildings, farmed, bartered, stole, prayed, invented, and fought until they were finally visited by governors and diplomats. But that changed, too, when everyone else began to timetip.

Jews also came to the pueblos and caves. They came from different places and times, bringing their conventions, babel, tragedies, and hopes. Litwak hoped for a Maimonides, a Moses ben Nachman, a Luria, even a Schwartz, but there were no great sages to be found, only Jews. And Litwak was the first. He directed, instigated, ordered, soothed, and founded a minion for prayer. When they grew into a full-time congregation, built a shul and elected a rabbi, they gave Litwak the honor of sitting on the pulpit in a plush-velvet chair.

Litwak was happy. He had prayer, friends, and authority.

Nighttime was no longer dark. It was a circus of laughter and trade. Everything sparkled with electric light and prayer. The Indians joined the others, merged, blended, were wiped out. Even a few Jews disappeared. It became faddish to wear Indian clothes and feathers.

Moldanado was always about now, teaching and leading, for he knew the land and native customs. He was a natural politico; when Litwak's shul was finished, he even attended a mairev service. It was then that he told Litwak about "forty-nine" and Clementine.

"What about that song?" Litwak had asked.

"You know the tune."

"But not the words."

"Clementine was the goddess of Los Alamos," Moldanado said. "She was the first nuclear reactor in the world to utilize fissionable material. It blew up, of course. 'Forty-nine' was the code name for the project that exploded the first atom bomb. But I haven't felt right about incorporating 'forty-nine' into the song."

"I don't think this is a proper subject to discuss in God's house," Litwak said. "This is a place of prayer, not bombs."

"But this is also Los Alamos."

"Then we must pray harder," Litwak said.

"Have you ever heard of the atom bomb?" asked Moldanado.

"No," said Litwak, turning the pages in his prayer book.

Moldanado found time to introduce Litwak to Baptista Founce, the second visitor to arrive in Los Alamos. She was dark and fragile and reminded Litwak of his first Golde. But she was also a shikseh who wore a gold cross around her neck. She teased, chased, and taunted Litwak until he had her behind the shul in daylight.

Thereafter, he did nothing but pray. He starved himself, beat his chest, tore his clothes, and waited on God's patience. The shul was being rebuilt, so Litwak took to praying in the desert. When he returned to town for food and rest, he could not even find the shul. Everything was changing.

Litwak spent most of his time in the desert, praying. He prayed for a sign and tripped over a trachodon's head that was stuck in the sand.

So it changes, he thought, as he stared at the rockscape before him. He found himself atop a ridge, looking down on an endless field of rocks, a stone tableau of waves in a gray sea. To his right was a field of cones. Each cone cast a flat black shadow. But behind him, cliffs of soft tuff rose out of the stone sea. A closer look at the rock revealed hermitages and monasteries cut into the living stone.

Litwak sighed as he watched a group of monks waiting their turn to climb a rope ladder into a monastic compound. They spoke in a strange tongue and crossed themselves before they took to the ladder.

There'll be no shul here, he said to himself. This is my punishment. A dry goyish place. But there was no thick, rich patina of sophisticated culture here. This was a simple place, a rough, real hinterland, not yet invaded by dybbuks and kachinas.

Litwak made peace with the monks and spent his time sitting on the top of a stone-tuff church in Goreme six hundred years in the past. He prayed, and sat, and watched the monks. Slowly he regained his will, and the scenery changed.

There was a monk that looked like Rhampsinitus.

Another looked like Moldanado.

At least, Litwak thought, there could be no Baptista Founce here. With that (and by an act of unconscious will), he found himself in his shul on King's Highway.

"Welcome back, Moishe," said Hoffa. "You should visit this synagogue more often."

"Moishe?" asked Litwak.

"Well, aren't you Moishe Hodel, who timetips to synagogue?"

"I'm Paley Litwak. No one else." Litwak looked at his hands. They were his own.

But he was in another synagogue. "Holy, holy, holy," Rabbi Rhampsinitus intoned. Twenty-five old men sang and wailed and prayed on cue. They all had beards and earlocks and wore conical caps and prayer garments.

"So, Moishe," said Rhampsinitus, "you still return. You really have mastered God's chariot."

Litwak stood still, decided, and then nodded his head and smiled. He thought of the shul he had built and found himself sitting in his plush chair. But Baptista Founce was sitting in the first row praying.

Before she could say, "Paley," he was sitting on a stone-tuff church six hundred years in the past.

Perhaps tomorrow he'd go to shul. Today he'd sit and watch monks.

# CONNIE WILLIS

Connie Willis burst onto the science-fiction scene in the early 1980s with her powerful short stories featuring all-too-human characters. Her work has won multiple Nebula and Hugo awards, and she edited The New Hugo Winners (Vol. III). Her first solo novel, Lincoln's Dreams, featured a woman who shares dreams about the Civil War. It showed her assured characterization and deft plotting skills, and hinted of powerful books to come. Her later novels have not disappointed; they include the powerful Doomsday Book, a time-travel novel featuring a future researcher trapped back in medieval times during the Black Plague; Uncharted Territory, about the exploration of an alien planet; and Remake, her look at retro-active censorship and a possible version of political correctness in the future. Her short fiction has been collected in Fire Watch, Distress Call, Daisy, in the Sun, and Impossible Things.

"Fire Watch" could be seen as a precursor to Doomsday Book, about a graduate student sent back to study London during the Blitz of World War II, saving St. Paul's Cathedral while he's there. The fact that things are very different in his time does not lessen the impact of the idea of a time traveler experiencing history firsthand, a concept that Willis brings out in full effect here.

# FIRE WATCH

## CONNIE WILLIS

*History hath triumphed over time, which besides it nothing but eternity hath triumphed over.*

—SIR WALTER RALEIGH

SEPTEMBER 20—Of course the first thing I looked for was the fire watch stone. And of course it wasn't there yet. It wasn't dedicated until 1951, accompanying speech by the Very Reverend Dean Walter Matthews, and this is only 1940. I knew that. I went to see the fire watch stone only yesterday, with some kind of misplaced notion that seeing the scene of the crime would somehow help. It didn't.

The only things that would have helped were a crash course in London during the Blitz and a little more time. I had not gotten either.

"Traveling in time is not like taking the tube, Mr. Bartholomew," the esteemed Dunworthy had said, blinking at me through those antique spectacles of his. "Either you report on the twentieth or you don't go at all."

"But I'm not ready," I'd said. "Look, it took me four years to get ready to travel with St. Paul. *St. Paul.* Not St. Paul's. You can't expect me to get ready for London in the Blitz in two days."

"Yes," Dunworthy had said. "We can." End of conversation.

"Two days!" I had shouted at my roommate Kivrin. "All because some computer adds an 's. And the esteemed Dunworthy doesn't even bat an eye when I tell him. 'Time travel is not like taking the tube, young man,' he says. 'I'd suggest you get ready. You're leaving day after tomorrow.' The man's a total incompetent."

"No," she said. "He isn't. He's the best there is. He wrote the book on St. Paul's. Maybe you should listen to what he says."

I had expected Kivrin to be at least a little sympathetic. She had been practically hysterical when she got her practicum changed from fifteenth- to fourteenth-century England, and how did either century qualify as a practicum? Even counting infectious diseases they couldn't have been more than a five. The Blitz is an eight, and St. Paul's itself is, with my luck, a ten.

"You think I should go see Dunworthy again?" I said.

"Yes."

"And then what? I've got two days. I don't know the money, the language, the history. Nothing."

"He's a good man," Kivrin said. "I think you'd better listen to him while you can." Good old Kivrin. Always the sympathetic ear.

The good man was responsible for my standing just inside the propped-open west doors, gawking like the country boy I was supposed to be, looking for a stone that wasn't there. Thanks to the good man, I was about as unprepared for my practicum as it was possible for him to make me.

I couldn't see more than a few feet into the church. I could see a candle gleaming feebly a long way off and a closer blur of white moving toward me. A verger, or possibly the Very Reverend Dean himself. I pulled out the letter from my clergyman uncle in Wales that was supposed to gain me access to the dean, and patted my back pocket to make sure I hadn't lost the microfiche *Oxford English Dictionary, Revised, with Historical Supplements* I'd smuggled out of the Bodleian. I couldn't pull it out in the middle of the conversation, but with luck I could muddle through the first encounter by context and look up the words I didn't know later.

"Are you from the ayarpee?" he said. He was no older than I am, a head shorter and much thinner. Almost ascetic looking. He reminded me of Kivrin. He was not wearing white, but clutching it to his chest. In other circumstances I would have thought it was a pillow. In other circumstances I would know what was being said to me, but there had been no time to unlearn sub-Mediterranean Latin and Jewish law and learn Cockney and air raid procedures. Two days, and the esteemed Dunworthy, who wanted to talk about the sacred burdens of the historian instead of telling me what the ayarpee was.

"Are you?" he demanded again.

I considered whipping out the OED after all on the grounds that Wales was a foreign country, but I didn't think they had microfilm in 1940. Ayarpee. It could be anything, including a nickname for the fire watch, in which case the impulse to say no was not safe at all. "No," I said.

He lunged suddenly toward and past me and peered out the open doors. "Damn," he said, coming back to me. "Where are they then? Bunch of lazy bourgeois tarts!" And so much for getting by on context.

He looked at me closely, suspiciously, as if he thought I was only pretending not to be with the ayarpee. "The church is closed," he said finally.

I held up the envelope and said, "My name's Bartholomew. Is Dean Matthews in?"

He looked out the door a moment longer as if he expected the lazy bourgeois tarts at any moment and intended to attack them with the white bundle; then he turned and said, as if he were guiding a tour, "This way, please," and took off into the gloom.

He led me to the right and down the south aisle of the nave. Thank God I had memorized the floor plan or at that moment, heading into total darkness, led by a raving verger, the whole bizarre metaphor of my situation would have been enough to send me out the west doors and back to St. John's Wood. It helped a little to know where I was. We should have been passing number twenty-six: Hunt's painting of *The Light of the World*—Jesus with his lantern—but it was too dark to see it. We could have used the lantern ourselves.

He stopped abruptly ahead of me, still raving. "We weren't asking for the bloody Savoy, just a few cots. Nelson's better off than we are—at least he's got a pillow provided." He brandished the white bundle like a torch in the darkness. It was a pillow after all. "We asked for them over a fortnight ago, and here we still are, sleeping on the bleeding generals from Trafalgar because those bitches want to play tea and crumpets with the Tommies at Victoria and the hell with us!"

He didn't seem to expect me to answer his outburst, which was good, because I had understood perhaps one key word in three. He stomped on ahead, moving out of sight of the one pathetic altar candle and stopping again at a black hole. Number twenty-five: stairs to the Whispering Gallery, the Dome, the library (not open to the public). Up the stairs, down a hall, stop again at a medieval door and knock. "I've got to go wait for them," he said. "If I'm not there they'll likely take them over to the Abbey. Tell the Dean to ring them up again, will you?" and he took off down the stone steps, still holding his pillow like a shield against him.

He had knocked, but the door was at least a foot of solid oak, and it was obvious the Very Reverend Dean had not heard. I was going to have to knock again. Yes, well, and the man holding the pinpoint had to let go of it, too, but even knowing it will all be over in a moment and you won't feel a thing doesn't make it any easier to say, "Now!" So I stood in front of the door, cursing the history department and the esteemed Dunworthy and the computer that had made the mistake and brought me here to this dark door with only a letter from a fictitious uncle that I trusted no more than I trusted the rest of them.

Even the old reliable Bodleian had let me down. The batch of research stuff I cross-ordered through Balliol and the main terminal is probably sitting in my room right now, a century out of reach. And Kivrin, who had already done her practicum and should have been bursting with advice, walked around as silent as a saint until I begged her to help me.

"Did you go to see Dunworthy?" she said.

"Yes. You want to know what priceless bit of information he had for me? 'Silence and humility are the sacred burdens of the historian.' He also told me I would love St. Paul's. Golden gems from the Master. Unfortunately, what I need to know are the times and places of the bombs so one doesn't fall on me." I flopped down on the bed. "Any suggestions?"

"How good are you at memory retrieval?" she said.

I sat up. "I'm pretty good. You think I should assimilate?"

"There isn't time for that," she said. "I think you should put everything you can directly into long-term."

"You mean endorphins?" I said.

The biggest problem with using memory-assistance drugs to put information into your long-term memory is that it never sits, even for a microsecond, in your short-term memory, and that makes retrieval complicated, not to mention unnerving. It gives you the most unsettling sense of déjà vu to suddenly know something you're positive you've never seen or heard before.

The main problem, though, is not eerie sensations but retrieval. Nobody knows exactly how the brain gets what it wants out of storage, but short-term is definitely involved. That brief, sometimes miscroscopic, time information spends in short-term is apparently used for something besides tip-of-the-tongue availability. The whole complex sort-and-file process of retrieval is apparently centered in short-term, and without it, and without the help of the drugs that put it there or artificial substitutes, information can be impossible to retrieve. I'd used endorphins for examinations and never had any difficulty with retrieval, and it looked like it was the only way to store all the information I needed in anything approaching the time I had left, but it also meant that I would *never* have known any of the things I needed to know, even for long enough to have forgotten them. If and when I could retrieve the information, I would know it. Till then I was as ignorant of it as if it were not stored in some cobwebbed corner of my mind at all.

"You can retrieve without artificials, can't you?" Kivrin said, looking skeptical.

"I guess I'll have to."

"Under stress? Without sleep? Low body endorphin levels?" What exactly had her practicum been? She had never said a word about it, and undergraduates are not supposed to ask. Stress factors in the Middle Ages? I thought everybody slept through them.

"I hope so," I said. "Anyway, I'm willing to try this idea if you think it will help."

She looked at me with that martyred expression and said, "Nothing will help." Thank you, St. Kivrin of Balliol.

But I tried it anyway. It was better than sitting in Dunworthy's rooms having him blink at me through his historically accurate eyeglasses and tell me I was going to love St. Paul's. When my Bodleian requests didn't come, I overloaded my credit and bought out Blackwell's. Tapes on World War II, Celtic literature, history of mass transit, tourist guidebooks, everything I could think of. Then I rented a high-speed recorder and shot up. When I came out of it, I was so panicked by the feeling of not knowing any more than I had when I started that I took the tube to London and raced up Ludgate Hill to see if the fire watch stone would trigger any memories. It didn't.

"Your endorphin levels aren't back to normal yet," I told myself and tried to relax, but that was impossible with the prospect of the practicum looming up before me. And those are real bullets, kid. Just because you're a history major doing his practicum doesn't mean you can't get killed. I read history books all the way home on the tube and right up until Dunworthy's flunkies came to take me to St. John's Wood this morning.

Then I jammed the microfiche OED in my back pocket and went off feeling as if I would have to survive by my native wit and hoping I could get hold of artificials in 1940. Surely I could get through the first day without mishap, I thought, and now here I was, stopped cold by almost the first word that was spoken to me.

Well, not quite. In spite of Kivrin's advice that I not put anything in short-term, I'd memorized the British money, a map of the tube system, a map of my own Oxford. It had gotten me this far. Surely I would be able to deal with the Dean.

Just as I had almost gotten up the courage to knock, he opened the door, and as with the pinpoint, it really was over quickly and without pain. I handed him my letter and he shook my hand and said something understandable like, "Glad to have another man, Bartholomew." He looked strained and tired and as if he might collapse if I told him the Blitz had just started. I know, I know: Keep your mouth shut. The sacred silence, etc.

He said, "We'll get Langby to show you round, shall we?" I assumed that was my Verger of the Pillow, and I was right. He met us at the foot of the stairs, puffing a little but jubilant.

"The cots came," he said to Dean Matthews. "You'd have thought they were doing us a favor. All high heels and hoity-toity. 'You made us miss our tea, luv,' one of them said to me. 'Yes, well, and a good thing, too,' I said. 'You look as if you could stand to lose a stone or two.'"

Even Dean Matthews looked as though he did not completely understand him. He said, "Did you set them up in the crypt?" and then introduced us. "Mr. Bartholomew's just got in from Wales," he said. "He's come to join our volunteers." Volunteers, not fire watch.

Langby showed me around, pointing out various dimnesses in the general gloom and then dragged me down to see the ten folding canvas cots set up among the tombs in the crypt, and also, in passing, Lord Nelson's black marble sarcophagus. He told me I don't have to stand a watch the first night and suggested I go to bed, since sleep is the most precious commodity in the raids. I could well believe it. He was clutching that silly pillow to his breast like his beloved.

"Do you hear the sirens down here?" I asked, wondering if he buried his head in it.

He looked around at the low stone ceilings. "Some do, some don't. Brinton has to have his Horlich's. Bence-Jones would sleep if the roof fell in on him. I have to have a pillow. The important thing is to get your eight in no matter what. If you don't, you turn into one of the walking dead. And then you get killed."

On that cheering note he went off to post the watches for tonight, leaving his pillow on one of the cots with orders for me to let nobody touch it. So here I sit, waiting for my first air raid siren and trying to get all this down before I turn into one of the walking or non-walking dead.

I've used the stolen OED to decipher a little Langby. Middling success. A tart is either a pastry or a prostitute (I assume the latter, although I was wrong about the pillow). Bourgeois is a catchall term for all the faults of the middle class. A Tommy's a soldier. Ayarpee I could not find under any spelling and I had nearly given up when something in long-term about the use of acronyms and abbreviations in wartime popped forward (bless you, St. Kivrin) and I realized it must be an abbreviation. ARP. Air Raid Precautions. Of course. Where else would you get the bleeding cots from?

———

*September 21*—Now that I'm past the first shock of being here, I realize that the history department neglected to tell me what I'm supposed to do in the three-odd months of this practicum. They handed me this journal, the letter from my uncle, and ten pounds in pre-war money and sent me packing into the past. The ten pounds (already depleted by train and tube fares) is supposed to last me until the end of December and get me back to St. John's Wood for pickup when the second letter calling me back to Wales to sick uncle's bedside comes. Till then I live here in the crypt with Nelson, who, Langby tells me, is pickled in alcohol inside his coffin. If we take a direct hit, will he burn like a torch or simply trickle out in a decaying stream onto the crypt floor, I wonder. Board is provided by a gas ring, over which are cooked wretched tea and inde-scribable kippers. To pay for all this luxury I am to stand on the roofs of St. Paul's and put out incendiaries.

I must also accomplish the purpose of this practicum, whatever it may be. Right now the only purpose I care about is staying alive until the second letter from uncle arrives and I can go home.

I am doing make-work until Langby has time to "show me the ropes." I've cleaned the skillet they cook the foul little fishes in, stacked wooden folding chairs at the altar end of the crypt (flat instead of standing because they tend to collapse like bombs in the middle of the night), and tried to sleep.

I am apparently not one of the lucky ones who can sleep through the raids. I spent most of the night wondering what St. Paul's risk rating is. Practica have to be at least six. Last night I was convinced this was a ten, with the crypt as ground zero, and that I might as well have applied for Denver.

The most interesting thing that's happened so far is that I've seen a cat. I am fascinated, but trying not to appear so, since they seem commonplace here.

———

*September 22*—Still in the crypt. Langby comes dashing through periodically cursing various government agencies (all abbreviated) and promising to take me up on the roofs. In the meantime I've run out of make-work and taught myself to work a stirrup pump. Kivrin was overly concerned about my memory retrieval abilities. I have not had any trouble so far. Quite the opposite. I called up fire-fighting information and got the whole manual with pictures, including instructions on the use of the stirrup pump. If the kippers set Lord Nelson on fire, I shall be a hero.

Excitement last night. The sirens went early and some of the chars who clean offices in the City sheltered in the crypt with us. One of them woke me out of a sound sleep, going like an air raid siren. Seems she'd seen a mouse. We had to go whacking at tombs and under the cots with a rubber boot to persuade her it was gone. Obviously what the history department had in mind: murdering mice.

———

*September 24*—Langby took me on rounds. Into the choir, where I had to learn the stirrup pump all over again, assigned rubber boots and a tin helmet. Langby says Commander Allen is getting us asbestos firemen's coats, but hasn't yet, so it's my own wool coat and muffler and very cold on the roofs even in September. It feels like November and looks it, too, bleak and cheerless with no sun. Up to the dome and onto the roofs, which should be flat but in fact are littered with towers, pinnacles, gutters, statues, all designed expressly to catch and hold incendiaries out of reach. Shown how to smother an incendiary with sand before it burns through the roof and sets the church on fire. Shown the ropes (literally) lying in a heap at the base of the dome in case somebody has to go up one of the west towers or over the top of the dome. Back inside and down to the Whispering Gallery.

Langby kept up a running commentary through the whole tour, part practical instruction, part church history. Before we went up into the Gallery he dragged me over to the south door to tell me how Christopher Wren stood in the smoking rubble of Old St. Paul's and asked a workman to bring him a stone from the graveyard to mark the cornerstone. On the stone was written in Latin, "I shall rise again," and Wren was so impressed by the irony that he had the words inscribed above the door. Langby looked as smug as if he had not told me a story every firstyear history student knows, but I suppose without the impact of the fire watch stone, the other is just a nice story.

Langby raced me up the steps and onto the narrow balcony circling the Whispering Gallery. He was already halfway around to the other side, shouting dimensions and acoustics at me. He stopped facing the wall opposite and said softly, "You can hear me whispering because of the shape of the dome. The sound waves are reinforced around the perimeter of the dome. It sounds like the very crack of doom up here during a raid. The dome is one hundred and seven feet across. It is eighty feet above the nave."

I looked down. The railing went out from under me and the blackand-white marble floor came up with dizzying speed. I hung on to something in front of me and dropped to my knees, staggered and sick at heart. The sun had come out, and all of St. Paul's seemed drenched in gold. Even the carved wood of the choir, the white stone pillars, the leaden pipes of the organ, all of it golden, golden.

Langby was beside me, trying to pull me free. "Bartholomew," he shouted, "what's wrong? For God's sake, man."

I knew I must tell him that if I let go, St. Paul's and all the past would fall in on me, and that I must not let that happen because I was an historian. I said something, but it was not what I intended because Langby merely tightened his grip. He hauled me violently free of the railing and back onto the stairway, then let me collapse limply on the steps and stood back from me, not speaking.

"I don't know what happened in there," I said. "I've never been afraid of heights before."

"You're shaking," he said sharply. "You'd better lie down." He led me back to the crypt.

*September 25* — Memory retrieval: ARP manual. Symptoms of bombing victims. Stage one — shock; stupefaction; unawareness of injuries; words may not make sense except to victim. Stage two — shivering; nausea; injuries, losses felt; return to reality. Stage three — talkativeness that cannot be controlled; desire to explain shock behavior to rescuers.

Langby must surely recognize the symptoms, but how does he account for the fact there was no bomb? I can hardly explain my shock behavior to him, and it isn't just the sacred silence of the historian that stops me.

He has not said anything, in fact assigned me my first watches for tomorrow night as if nothing had happened, and he seems no more preoccupied than anyone else. Everyone I've met so far is jittery (one thing I had in short-term was how calm everyone was during the raids) and the raids have not come near us since I got here. They've been mostly over the East End and the docks.

There was a reference tonight to a UXB, and I have been thinking about the Dean's manner and the church being closed when I'm almost sure I remember reading it was open through the entire Blitz. As soon as I get a chance, I'll try to retrieve the events of September. As to retrieving anything else, I don't see how I can hope to remember the right information until I know what it is I am supposed to do here, if anything.

There are no guidelines for historians, and no restrictions either. I could tell everyone I'm from the future if I thought they would believe me. I could murder Hitler if I could get to Germany. Or could I? Time paradox talk abounds in the history department, and the graduate students back from their practica don't say a word one way or the other. Is there a tough, immutable past? Or is there a new past every day and do we, the historians, make it? And what are the consequences of what we do, if there are consequences? And how do we dare do anything without knowing them? Must we interfere boldly, hoping we do not bring about all our downfalls? Or must we do nothing at all, not interfere, stand by and watch St. Paul's burn to the ground if need be so that we don't change the future?

All those are fine questions for a late-night study session. They do not matter here. I could no more let St. Paul's burn down than I could kill Hitler. No, that is not true. I found that out yesterday in the Whispering Gallery. I could kill Hitler if I caught him setting fire to St. Paul's.

———

*September 26*—I met a young woman today. Dean Matthews has opened the church, so the watch have been doing duties as chars and people have started coming in again. The young woman reminded me of Kivrin, though Kivrin is a good deal taller and would never frizz her hair like that. She looked as if she had been crying. Kivrin has looked like that since she got back from her practicum. The Middle Ages were too much for her. I wonder how she would have coped with this. By pouring out her fears to the local priest, no doubt, as I sincerely hoped her look-alike was not going to do.

"May I help you?" I said, not wanting in the least to help. "I'm a volunteer."

She looked distressed. "You're not paid?" she said, and wiped at her reddened nose with a handkerchief. "I read about St. Paul's and the fire watch and all, and I thought perhaps there's a position there for me. In the canteen, like, or something. A paying position." There were tears in her red-rimmed eyes.

"I'm afraid we don't have a canteen," I said as kindly as I could, considering how impatient Kivrin always makes me, "and it's not actually a real shelter. Some of the watch sleep in the crypt. I'm afraid we're all volunteers, though."

"That won't do, then," she said. She dabbed at her eyes with the handkerchief. "I love St. Paul's, but I can't take on volunteer work, not with my little brother Tom back from the country." I was not reading this situation properly. For all the outward signs of distress she sounded quite cheerful and no closer to tears than when she had come in. "I've got to get us a proper place to stay. With Tom back, we can't go on sleeping in the tubes."

A sudden feeling of dread, the kind of sharp pain you get sometimes from involuntary retrieval, went over me. "The tubes?" I said, trying to get at the memory.

"Marble Arch, usually," she went on. "My brother Tom saves us a place early and I go . . ." She stopped, held the handkerchief close to her nose, and exploded into it. "I'm sorry," she said, "this awful cold!"

Red nose, watering eyes, sneezing. Respiratory infection. It was a wonder I hadn't told her not to cry. It's only by luck that I haven't made some unforgivable mistake so far, and this is not because I can't get at the long-term memory. I don't have half the information I need even stored:

cats and colds and the way St. Paul's looks in full sun. It's only a matter of time before I am stopped cold by something I do not know. Nevertheless, I am going to try for retrieval tonight after I come off watch. At least I can find out whether and when something is going to fall on me.

I have seen the cat once or twice. He is coal-black with a white patch on his throat that looks as if it were painted on for the blackout.

————

*September 27*—I have just come down from the roofs. I am still shaking.

Early in the raid the bombing was mostly over the East End. The view was incredible. Searchlights everywhere, the sky pink from the fires and reflecting in the Thames, the exploding shells sparkling like fireworks. There was a constant, deafening thunder broken by the occasional droning of the planes high overhead, then the repeating stutter of the ack-ack guns.

About midnight the bombs began falling quite near with a horrible sound like a train running over me. It took every bit of will I had to keep from flinging myself flat on the roof, but Langby was watching. I didn't want to give him the satisfaction of watching a repeat performance of my behavior in the dome. I kept my head up and my sand bucket firmly in hand and felt quite proud of myself.

The bombs stopped roaring past about three, and there was a lull of about half an hour, and then a clatter like hail on the roofs. Everybody except Langby dived for shovels and stirrup pumps. He was watching me. And I was watching the incendiary.

It had fallen only a few meters from me, behind the clock tower. It was much smaller than I had imagined, only about thirty centimeters long. It was sputtering violently, throwing greenish-white fire almost to where I was standing. In a minute it would simmer down into a molten mass and begin to burn through the roof. Flames and the frantic shouts of firemen, and then the white rubble stretching for miles, and nothing, nothing left, not even the fire watch stone.

It was the Whispering Gallery all over again. I felt that I had said something, and when I looked at Langby's face he was smiling crookedly.

"St. Paul's will burn down," I said. "There won't be anything left."

"Yes," Langby said. "That's the idea, isn't it? Burn St. Paul's to the ground? Isn't that the plan?"

"Whose plan?" I said stupidly.

"Hitler's, of course," Langby said. "Who did you think I meant?" and, almost casually, picked up his stirrup pump.

The page of the ARP manual flashed suddenly before me. I poured the bucket of sand around the still-sputtering bomb, snatched up another bucket and dumped that on top of it. Black smoke billowed up in such a cloud that I could hardly find my shovel. I felt for the smothered bomb with the tip of it and scooped it into the empty bucket, then shoveled the sand in on top of it. Tears were streaming down my face from the acrid smoke. I turned to wipe them on my sleeve and saw Langby.

He had not made a move to help me. He smiled. "It's not a bad plan, actually. But of course we won't let it happen. That's what the fire watch is here for. To see that it doesn't happen. Right, Bartholomew?"

I know now what the purpose of my practicum is. I must stop Langby from burning down St. Paul's.

————

*September 28*—I try to tell myself I was mistaken about Langby last night, that I misunderstood what he said. Why would he want to burn down St. Paul's unless he is a Nazi spy? How can a Nazi spy have gotten on the fire watch? I think about my faked letter of introduction and shudder.

How can I find out? If I set him some test, some fatal thing that only a loyal Englishman in 1940 would know, I fear I am the one who would be caught out. I *must* get my retrieval working properly.

Until then, I shall watch Langby. For the time being at least that should be easy. Langby has just posted the watches for the next two weeks. We stand every one together.

————

*September 30*—I know what happened in September. Langby told me.

Last night in the choir, putting on our coats and boots, he said, "They've already tried once, you know."

I had no idea what he meant. I felt as helpless as that first day when he asked me if I was from the ayarpee.

"The plan to destroy St. Paul's. They've already tried once. The tenth of September. A high explosive bomb. But of course you didn't know about that. You were in Wales."

I was not even listening. The minute he had said "high explosive bomb" I had remembered it all. It had burrowed in under the road and lodged on the foundations. The bomb squad had tried to defuse it, but there was a leaking gas main. They decided to evacuate St. Paul's, but Dean Matthews refused to leave, and they got it out after all and exploded it in Barking Marshes. Instant and complete retrieval.

"The bomb squad saved her that time," Langby was saying. "It seems there's always somebody about."

"Yes," I said, "there is," and walked away from him.

————

*October 1* —I thought last night's retrieval of the events of September tenth meant some sort of breakthrough, but I have been lying here on my cot most of the night trying for Nazi spies in St. Paul's and getting nothing. Do I have to know exactly what I'm looking for before I can remember it? What good does that do me?

Maybe Langby is not a Nazi spy. Then what is he? An arsonist? A madman? The crypt is hardly conducive to thought, being not at all as silent as a tomb. The chars talk most of the night and the sound of the bombs is muffled, which somehow makes it worse. I find myself straining to hear them. When I did get to sleep this morning, I dreamed about one of the tube shelters being hit, broken mains, drowning people.

————

*October 4* —I tried to catch the cat today. I had some idea of persuading it to dispatch the mouse that has been terrifying the chars. I also wanted to see one up close. I took the water bucket I had used with the stirrup pump last night to put out some burning shrapnel from one of the antiaircraft guns. It still had a bit of water in it, but not enough to drown the cat, and my plan was to clamp the bucket over him, reach under, and pick him up, then carry him down to the crypt and point him at the mouse. I did not even come close to him.

I swung the bucket, and as I did so, perhaps an. inch of water splashed out. I thought I remembered that the cat was a domesticated animal, but I must have been wrong about that. The cat's wide complacent face pulled back into a skull-like mask that was absolutely terrifying, vicious claws extended from what I had thought were harmless paws, and the cat let out a sound to top the chars.

In my surprise I dropped the bucket and it rolled against one of the pillars. The cat disappeared. Behind me, Langby said, "That's no way to catch a cat."

"Obviously," I said, and bent to retrieve the bucket.

"Cats hate water," he said, still in that expressionless voice.

"Oh," I said, and started in front of him to take the bucket back to the choir. "I didn't know that."

"Everybody knows it. Even the stupid Welsh."

————

*October 8*—We have been standing double watches for a week— bomber's moon. Langby didn't show up on the roofs, so I went looking for him in the church. I found him standing by the west doors talking to an old man. The man had a newspaper tucked under his arm and he handed it to Langby, but Langby gave it back to him. When the man saw me, he ducked out. Langby said, "Tourist. Wanted to know where the Windmill Theatre is. Read in the paper the girls are starkers."

I know I looked as if I didn't believe him because he said, "You look rotten, old man. Not getting enough sleep, are you? I'll get somebody to take the first watch for you tonight."

"No," I said coldly. "I'll stand my own watch. I like being on the roofs," and added silently, where I can watch you.

He shrugged and said, "I suppose it's better than being down in the crypt. At least on the roofs you can hear the one that gets you."

————

*October 10*—I thought the double watches might be good for me, take my mind off my inability to retrieve. The watched-pot idea. Actually, it sometimes works. A few hours of thinking about something else, or a good night's sleep, and the fact pops forward without any prompting, without any artificials.

The good night's sleep is out of the question. Not only do the chars talk constantly, but the cat has moved into the crypt and sidles up to everyone, making siren noises and begging for kippers. I am moving my cot out of the transept and over by Nelson before I go on watch. He may be pickled, but he keeps his mouth shut.

————

*October 11*—I dreamed of Trafalgar, ships' guns and smoke and falling plaster and Langby shouting my name. My first waking thought was that the folding chairs had gone off. I could not see for all the smoke.

"I'm coming," I said, limping toward Langby and pulling on my boots. There was a heap of plaster and tangled folding chairs in the transept. Langby was digging in it. "Bartholomew!" he shouted, flinging a chunk of plaster aside. "Bartholomew!"

I still had the idea it was smoke. I ran back for the stirrup pump and then knelt beside him and began pulling on a splintered chair back. It resisted, and it came to me suddenly. There is a body under here. I will reach for a piece of the ceiling and find it is a hand. I leaned back on my heels, determined not to be sick, then went at the pile again.

Langby was going far too fast, jabbing with a chair leg. I grabbed his hand to stop him, and he struggled against me as if I were a piece of rubble to be thrown aside. He picked up a large flat square of plaster, and under it was the floor. I turned and looked behind me. Both chars huddled in the recess by the altar. "Who are you looking for?" I said, keeping hold of Langby's arm.

"Bartholomew," he said, and swept the rubble aside, his hands bleeding through the coating of smoky dust.

"I'm here," I said. "I'm all right." I choked on the white dust. "I moved my cot out of the transept."

He turned sharply to the chars and then said quite calmly, "What's under here?"

"Only the gas ring," one of them said timidly from the shadowed recess, "and Mrs. Galbraith's pocketbook." He dug through the mess until he had found them both. The gas ring was leaking at a merry rate, though the flame had gone out.

"You've saved St. Paul's and me after all," I said, standing there in my underwear and boots, holding the useless stirrup pump. "We might all have been asphyxiated."

He stood up. "I shouldn't have saved you," he said.

Stage one: shock, stupefaction, unawareness of injuries, words may not make sense except to victim. He would not know his hand was bleeding yet. He would not remember what he had said. He had said he shouldn't have saved my life.

"I shouldn't have saved you," he repeated. "I have my duty to think of."

"You're bleeding," I said sharply. "You'd better lie down." I sounded just like Langby in the gallery.

———

*October 13*—It was a high-explosive bomb. It blew a hole in the Choir, and some of the marble statuary is broken, but the ceiling of the crypt did not collapse, which is what I thought at first. It only jarred some plaster loose.

I do not think Langby has any idea what he said. That should give me some sort of advantage, now that I am sure where the danger lies, now that I am sure it will not come crashing down from some other direction. But what good is all this knowing, when I do not know what he will do? Or when?

Surely I have the facts of yesterday's bomb in long-term, but even falling plaster did not jar them loose this time. I am not even trying for retrieval, now. I lie in the darkness waiting for the roof to fall in on me. And remembering how Langby saved my life.

———

*October 15*—The girl came in again today. She still has the cold, but she has gotten her paying position. It was a joy to see her. She was wearing a smart uniform and open-toed shoes, and her hair was in an elaborate frizz around her face. We are still cleaning up the mess from the bomb, and Langby was out with Allen getting wood to board up the Choir, so I let the girl chatter at me while I swept. The dust made her sneeze, but at least this time I knew what she was doing.

She told me her name is Enola and that she's working for the WVS, running one of the mobile canteens that are sent to the fires. She came, of all things, to thank me for the job. She said that after she told the WVS that there was no proper shelter with a canteen for St. Paul's, they gave her a run in the City. "So I'll just pop in when I'm close and let you know how I'm making out, won't I just?"

She and her brother Tom are still sleeping in the tubes. I asked her if that was safe and she said probably not, but at least down there you couldn't hear the one that got you and that was a blessing.

———

*October 18*—I am so tired I can hardly write this. Nine incendiaries tonight and a land mine that looked as though it was going to catch on

the dome till the wind drifted its parachute away from the church. I put
out two of the incendiaries. I have done that at least twenty times since I
got here and helped with dozens of others, and still it is not enough. One
incendiary, one moment of not watching Langby, could undo it all.

I know that is partly why I feel so tired. I wear myself out every night
trying to do my job and watch Langby, making sure none of the incendiaries falls without my seeing it. Then I go back to the crypt and wear
myself out trying to retrieve something, anything, about spies, fires, St.
Paul's in the fall of 1940, anything. It haunts me that I am not doing
enough, but I do not know what else to do. Without the retrieval, I am
as helpless as these poor people here, with no idea what will happen tomorrow.

If I have to, I will go on doing this till I am called home. He cannot
burn down St. Paul's so long as I am here to put out the incendiaries. "I
have my duty," Langby said in the crypt.

And I have mine.

————

*October 21* — It's been nearly two weeks since the blast and I just now
realized we haven't seen the cat since. He wasn't in the mess in the
crypt. Even after Langby and I were sure there was no one in there, we
sifted through the stuff twice more. He could have been in the Choir,
though.

Old Bence-Jones says not to worry. "He's all right," he said. "The Jerries could bomb London right down to the ground and the cats would
waltz out to greet them. You know why? They don't love anybody. That's
what gets half of us killed. Old lady out in Stepney got killed the other
night trying to save her cat. Bloody cat was in the Anderson."

"Then where is he?"

"Someplace safe, you can bet on that. If he's not around St. Paul's, it
means we're for it. That old saw about the rats deserting a sinking ship,
that's a mistake, that is. It's cats, not rats."

————

*October 25* — Langby's tourist showed up again. He cannot still be looking for the Windmill Theatre. He had a newspaper under his arm again
today, and he asked for Langby, but Langby was across town with Allen,
trying to get the asbestos firemen's coats. I saw the name of the paper. It
was *The Worker.* A Nazi newspaper?

————

*November 2*—I've been up on the roofs for a week straight, helping some incompetent workmen patch the hole the bomb made. They're doing a terrible job. There's still a great gap on one side a man could fall into, but they insist it'll be all right because, after all, you wouldn't fall clear through but only as far as the ceiling, and "the fall can't kill you." They don't seem to understand it's a perfect hiding place for an incendiary.

And that is all Langby needs. He does not even have to set a fire to destroy St. Paul's. All he needs to do is let one burn uncaught until it is too late.

I could not get anywhere with the workmen. I went down into the church to complain to Matthews, and saw Langby and his tourist behind a pillar, close to one of the windows. Langby was holding a newspaper and talking to the man. When I came down from the library an hour later, they were still there. So is the gap. Matthews says we'll put planks across it and hope for the best.

————

*November 5*—I have given up trying to retrieve. I am so far behind on my sleep I can't even retrieve information on a newspaper whose name I already know. Double watches the permanent thing now. Our chars have abandoned us altogether (like the cat), so the crypt is quiet, but I cannot sleep.

If I do manage to doze off, I dream. Yesterday I dreamed Kivrin was on the roofs, dressed like a saint. "What was the secret of your practicum?" I said. "What were you supposed to find out?"

She wiped her nose with a handkerchief and said, "Two things. One, that silence and humility are the sacred burdens of the historian. Two"—she stopped and sneezed into the handkerchief—"don't sleep in the tubes."

My only hope is to get hold of an artificial and induce a trance. That's a problem. I'm positive it's too early for chemical endorphins and probably hallucinogens. Alcohol is definitely available, but I need something more concentrated than ale, the only alcohol I know by name. I do not dare ask the watch. Langby is suspicious enough of me already. It's back to the OED, to look up a word I don't know.

————

*November 11*—The cat's back. Langby was out with Allen again, still trying for the asbestos coats, so I thought it was safe to leave St. Paul's. I
went to the grocer's for supplies, and hopefully an artificial. It was late,
and the sirens sounded before I had even gotten to Cheapside, but the
raids do not usually start until after dark. It took a while to get all the gro-
ceries and to get up my courage to ask whether he had any alcohol—he
told me to go to a pub—and when I came out of the shop, it was as if I
had pitched suddenly into a hole.

I had no idea where St. Paul's lay, or the street, or the shop I had just
come from. I stood on what was no longer the sidewalk, clutching my
brown-paper parcel of kippers and bread with a hand I could not have
seen if I held it up before my face. I reached up to wrap my muffler
closer about my neck and prayed for my eyes to adjust, but there was no
reduced light to adjust to. I would have been glad of the moon, for all St.
Paul's watch cursed it and called it a fifth columnist. Or a bus, with its
shuttered headlights giving just enough light to orient myself by. Or a
searchlight. Or the kickback flare of an ack-ack gun. Anything.

Just then I did see a bus, two narrow yellow slits a long way off. I
started toward it and nearly pitched off the curb. Which meant the bus
was sideways in the street, which meant it was not a bus. A cat meowed,
quite near, and rubbed against my leg. I looked down into the yellow
lights I had thought belonged to the bus. His eyes were picking up light
from somewhere, though I would have sworn there was not a light for
miles, and reflecting it flatly up at me.

"A warden'll get you for those lights, old Tom," I said, and then as a
plane droned overhead, "Or a Jerry."

The word exploded suddenly into light, the searchlights and a glow
along the Thames seeming to happen almost simultaneously, lighting
my way home.

"Come to fetch me, did you, old Tom?" I said gaily. "Where've you
been? Knew we were out of kippers, didn't you? I call that loyalty." I
talked to him all the way home and gave him half a tin of the kippers for
saving my life. Bence-Jones said he smelled the milk at the grocer's.

———

*November 13*—I dreamed I was lost in the blackout. I could not see my
hands in front of my face, and Dunworthy came and shone a pocket
torch at me, but I could only see where I had come from and not where
I was going.

"What good is that to them?" I said. "They need a light to show them where they're going."

"Even the light from the Thames? Even the light from the fires and the ack-ack guns?" Dunworthy said.

"Yes. Anything is better than this awful darkness." So he came closer to give me the pocket torch. It was not a pocket torch, after all, but Christ's lantern from the Hunt picture in the south nave. I shone it on the curb before me so I could find my way home, but it shone instead on the fire watch stone and I hastily put the light out.

————

*November 20*—I tried to talk to Langby today. "I've seen you talking to the old gentleman," I said. It sounded like an accusation. I meant it to. I wanted him to think it was and stop whatever he was planning.

"Reading," he said. "Not talking." He was putting things in order in the Choir, piling up sandbags.

"I've seen you reading then," I said belligerently, and he dropped a sandbag and straightened.

"What of it?" he said. "It's a free country. I can read to an old man if I want, same as you can talk to that little WVS tart."

"What do you read?" I said.

"Whatever he wants. He's an old man. He used to come home from his job, have a bit of brandy and listen to his wife read the papers to him. She got killed in one of the raids. Now I read to him. I don't see what business it is of yours."

It sounded true. It didn't have the careful casualness of a lie, and I almost believed him, except that I had heard the tone of truth from him before. In the crypt. After the bomb.

"I thought he was a tourist looking for the Windmill," I said.

He looked blank only a second, and then he said, "Oh, yes, that. He came in with the paper and asked me to tell him where it was. I looked it up to find the address. Clever, that. I didn't guess he couldn't read it for himself." But it was enough. I knew that he was lying.

He heaved a sandbag almost at my feet. "Of course you wouldn't understand a thing like that, would you? A simple act of human kindness?"

"No," I said coldly. "I wouldn't."

None of this proves anything. He gave away nothing, except perhaps the name of an artificial, and I can hardly go to Dean Matthews and accuse Langby of reading aloud.

I waited till he had finished in the Choir and gone down to the crypt. Then I lugged one of the sandbags up to the roof and over to the chasm. The planking has held so far, but everyone walks gingerly around it, as if it were a grave. I cut the sandbag open and spilled the loose sand into the bottom. If it has occurred to Langby that this is the perfect spot for an incendiary, perhaps the sand will smother it.

———

*November 21* — I gave Enola some of "uncle's" money today and asked her to get me the brandy. She was more reluctant than I thought she'd be, so there must be societal complications I am not aware of, but she agreed.

I don't know what she came for. She started to tell me about her brother and some prank he'd pulled in the tubes that got him in trouble with the guard, but after I asked her about the brandy, she left without finishing the story.

———

*November 25* — Enola came today, but without bringing the brandy. She is going to Bath for the holidays to see her aunt. At least she will be away from the raids for a while. I will not have to worry about her. She finished the story of her brother and told me she hopes to persuade this aunt to take Tom for the duration of the Blitz but is not at all sure the aunt will be willing.

Young Tom is apparently not so much an engaging scapegrace as a near criminal. He has been caught twice picking pockets in the Bank tube shelter, and they have had to go back to Marble Arch. I comforted her as best I could, told her all boys were bad at one time or another. What I really wanted to say was that she needn't worry at all, that young Tom strikes me as a true survivor type, like my own tom, like Langby, totally unconcerned with anybody but himself, well equipped to survive the Blitz and rise to prominence in the future.

Then I asked her whether she had gotten the brandy.

She looked down at her open-toed shoes and muttered unhappily, "I thought you'd forgotten all about that."

I made up some story about the watch taking turns buying a bottle, and she seemed less unhappy, but I am not convinced she will not use this trip to Bath as an excuse to do nothing. I will have to leave St. Paul's and buy it myself, and I don't dare leave Langby alone in the church. I made her promise to bring the brandy today before she leaves. But she is still not back, and the sirens have already gone.

———

*November 26* — No Enola, and she said their train left at noon. I suppose I should be grateful that at least she is safely out of London. Maybe in Bath she will be able to get over her cold.

Tonight one of the ARP girls breezed in to borrow half our cots and tell us about a mess over in the East End where a surface shelter was hit. Four dead, twelve wounded. "At least it wasn't one of the tube shelters!" she said. "Then you'd see a real mess, wouldn't you?"

———

*November 30* — I dreamed I took the cat to St. John's Wood.

"Is this a rescue mission?" Dunworthy said.

"No, sir," I said proudly. "I know what I was supposed to find in my practicum. The perfect survivor. Tough and resourceful and selfish. This is the only one I could find. I had to kill Langby, you know, to keep him from burning down St. Paul's. Enola's brother has gone to Bath, and the others will never make it. Enola wears open-toed shoes in the winter and sleeps in the tubes and puts her hair up on metal pins so it will curl. She cannot possibly survive the Blitz."

Dunworthy said, "Perhaps you should have rescued her instead. What did you say her name was?"

"Kivrin," I said, and woke up cold and shivering.

———

*December 5* — I dreamed Langby had the pinpoint bomb. He carried it under his arm like a brown paper parcel, coming out of St. Paul's Station and around Ludgate Hill to the west doors.

"This is not fair," I said, barring his way with my arm. "There is no fire watch on duty."

He clutched the bomb to his chest like a pillow. "That is your fault," he said, and before I could get to my stirrup pump and bucket, he tossed it in the door.

The pinpoint was not even invented until the end of the twentieth century, and it was another ten years before the dispossessed communists got hold of it and turned it into something that could be carried under your arm. A parcel that could blow a quarter mile of the City into oblivion. Thank God that is one dream that cannot come true.

It was a sunlit morning in the dream, and this morning when I came off watch the sun was shining for the first time in weeks. I went down to the crypt and then came up again, making the rounds of the roofs twice more, then the steps and the grounds and all the treacherous alleyways between where an incendiary could be missed. I felt better after that, but when I got to sleep I dreamed again, this time of fire and Langby watching it, smiling.

———

*December 15*—I found the cat this morning. Heavy raids last night, but most of them over toward Canning Town and nothing on the roofs to speak of. Nevertheless the cat was quite dead. I found him lying on the steps this morning when I made my own, private rounds. Concussion. There was not a mark on him anywhere except the white blackout patch on his throat, but when I picked him up, he was all jelly under the skin.

I could not think what to do with him. I thought for one mad moment of asking Matthews if I could bury him in the crypt. Honorable death in war or something. Trafalgar, Waterloo, London, died in battle. I ended by wrapping him in my muffler and taking him down Ludgate Hill to a building that had been bombed out and burying him in the rubble. It will do no good. The rubble will be no protection from dogs or rats, and I shall never get another muffler. I have gone through nearly all of uncle's money.

I should not be sitting here. I haven't checked the alleyways or the rest of the steps, and there might be a dud or a delayed incendiary or something that I missed.

When I came here, I thought of myself as the noble rescuer, the savior of the past. I am not doing very well at the job. At least Enola is out of it. I wish there were some way I could send St. Paul's to Bath for safekeeping. There were hardly any raids last night. Bence-Jones said cats can survive anything. What if he was coming to get me, to show me the way home? All the bombs were over Canning Town.

———

*December 16*—Enola has been back a week. Seeing her, standing on the west steps where I found the cat, sleeping in Marble Arch and not safe at all, was more than I could absorb. "I thought you were in Bath," I said stupidly.

"My aunt said she'd take Tom but not me as well. She's got a houseful of evacuation children, and what a noisy lot. Where is your muffler?" she said. "It's dreadful cold up here on the hill."

"I . . ." I said, unable to answer. "I lost it."

"You'll never get another one," she said. "They're going to start rationing clothes. And wool, too. You'll never get another one like that."

"I know," I said, blinking at her.

"Good things just thrown away," she said. "It's absolutely criminal, that's what it is."

I don't think I said anything to that, just turned and walked away with my head down, looking for bombs and dead animals.

———

*December 20* — Langby isn't a Nazi. He's a communist. I can hardly write this. A communist.

One of the chars found *The Worker* wedged behind a pillar and brought it down to the crypt as we were coming off the first watch.

"Bloody communists," Bence-Jones said. "Helping Hitler, they are. Talking against the king, stirring up trouble in the shelters. Traitors, that's what they are."

"They love England same as you," the char said.

"They don't love nobody but themselves, bloody selfish lot. I wouldn't be surprised to hear they were ringing Hitler up on the telephone," Bence-Jones said. " 'Ello, Adolf, here's where to drop the bombs."

The kettle on the gas ring whistled. The char stood up and poured the hot water into a chipped teapot, then sat back down. "Just because they speak their minds don't mean they'd burn down old St. Paul's, does it now?"

"Of course not," Langby said, coming down the stairs. He sat down and pulled off his boots, stretching his feet in their wool socks. "Who wouldn't burn down St. Paul's?"

"The communists," Bence-Jones said, looking straight at him, and I wondered if he suspected Langby too.

Langby never batted an eye. "I wouldn't worry about them if I were you," he said. "It's the Jerries that are doing their bloody best to burn her down tonight. Six incendiaries so far, and one almost went into that great hole over the Choir." He held out his cup to the char, and she poured him a cup of tea.

I wanted to kill him, smashing him to dust and rubble on the floor of the crypt while Bence-Jones and the char looked on in helpless surprise, shouting warnings to them and the rest of the watch. "Do you know what the communists did?" I wanted to shout. "Do you? We have to stop him." I even stood up and started toward him as he sat with his feet stretched out before him and his asbestos coat still over his shoulders.

And then the thought of the Gallery drenched in gold, the communist coming out of the tube station with the package so casually under his arm, made me sick with the same staggering vertigo of guilt and helplessness, and I sat back down on the edge of my cot and tried to think what to do.

They do not realize the danger. Even Bence-Jones, for all his talk of traitors, thinks they are capable only of talking against the king. They do not know, cannot know, what the communists will become. Stalin is an ally. Communists mean Russia. They have never heard of Karinsky or the New Russia or any of the things that will make "communist" into a synonym for "monster." They will never know it. By the time the communists become what they became, there will be no fire watch. Only I know what it means to hear the name "communist" uttered here, so carelessly, in St. Paul's.

A communist. I should have known. I should have known.

———

*December 22*—Double watches again. I have not had any sleep and I am getting very unsteady on my feet. I nearly pitched into the chasm this morning, only saved myself by dropping to my knees. My endorphin levels are fluctuating wildly, and I know I must get some sleep soon or I will become one of Langby's walking dead, but I am afraid to leave him alone on the roofs, alone in the church with his communist party leader, alone anywhere. I have taken to watching him when he sleeps.

If I could just get hold of an artificial, I think I could induce a trance, in spite of my poor condition. But I cannot even go out to a pub. Langby is on the roofs constantly, waiting for his chance. When Enola comes again I must convince her to get the brandy for me. There are only a few days left.

*December 28*—Enola came this morning while I was on the west porch, picking up the Christmas tree. It has been knocked over three nights running by concussion. I righted the tree and was bending down to pick up the scattered tinsel when Enola appeared suddenly out of the fog like some cheerful saint. She stooped quickly and kissed me on the cheek. Then she straightened up, her nose red from her perennial cold, and handed me a box wrapped in colored paper.

"Merry Christmas," she said. "Go on then, open it. It's a gift."

My reflexes are almost totally gone. I knew the box was far too shallow for a bottle of brandy. Nevertheless, I believed she had remembered, had brought me my salvation. "You darling," I said, and tore it open.

It was a muffler. Gray wool. I stared at it for fully half a minute without realizing what it was. "Where's the brandy?" I said.

She looked shocked. Her nose got redder and her eyes started to blur. "You need this more. You haven't any clothing coupons and you have to be outside all the time. It's been so dreadful cold."

"I *needed* the brandy," I said angrily.

"I was only trying to be kind," she started, and I cut her off.

"Kind?" I said. "I asked you for brandy. I don't recall ever saying I needed a muffler." I shoved it back at her and began untangling a string of colored lights that had shattered when the tree fell.

She got that same holy martyr look Kivrin is so wonderful at. "I worry about you all the time up here," she said in a rush. "They're *trying* for St. Paul's, you know. And it's so close to the river. I didn't think you should be drinking. I—it's a crime when they're trying so hard to kill us all that you won't take care of yourself. It's like you're in it with them. I worry someday I'll come up to St. Paul's and you won't be here."

"Well, and what exactly am I supposed to do with a muffler? Hold it over my head when they drop the bombs?"

She turned and ran, disappearing into the gray fog before she had gone down two steps. I started after her, still holding the string of broken lights, tripped over it, and fell almost all the way to the bottom of the steps.

Langby picked me up. "You're off watches," he said grimly.

"You can't do that," I said.

"Oh, yes, I can. I don't want any walking dead on the roofs with me."

I let him lead me down here to the crypt, make me a cup of tea, put me to bed, all very solicitous. No indication that this is what he has been waiting for. I will lie here till the sirens go. Once I am on the roofs he will not be able to send me back without seeming suspicious. Do you know what he said before he left, asbestos coat and rubber boots, the dedicated fire watcher? "I want you to get some sleep." As if I could sleep with Langby on the roofs. I would be burned alive.

————

*December 30*—The sirens woke me, and old Bence-Jones said, "That should have done you some good. You've slept the clock round."

"What day is it?" I said, going for my boots.

"The twenty-ninth," he said, and as I dived for the door, "no need to hurry. They're late tonight. Maybe they won't come at all. That'd be a blessing, that would. The tide's out."

I stopped by the door to the stairs, holding on to the cool stone. "Is St. Paul's all right?"

"She's still standing," he said. "Have a bad dream?"

"Yes," I said, remembering the bad dreams of all the past weeks—the dead cat in my arms in St. John's Wood, Langby with his parcel and his *Worker* under his arm, the fire watch stone garishly lit by Christ's lantern. Then I remembered I had not dreamed at all. I had slept the kind of sleep I had prayed for, the kind of sleep that would help me remember.

Then I remembered. Not St. Paul's, burned to the ground by communists. A headline from the dailies. "Marble Arch hit. Eighteen killed by blast." The date was not clear except for the year. Nineteen forty. There were exactly two more days left in 1940. I grabbed my coat and muffler and ran up the stairs and across the marble floor.

"Where the hell do you think you're going?" Langby shouted to me. I couldn't see him.

"I have to save Enola," I said, and my voice echoed in the dark sanctuary. "They're going to bomb Marble Arch."

"You can't leave now," he shouted after me, standing where the fire watch stone would be. "The tide's out. You dirty—"

I didn't hear the rest of it. I had already flung myself down the steps and into a taxi. It took almost all the money I had, the money I had so carefully hoarded for the trip back to St. John's Wood. Shelling started while we were still in Oxford Street, and the driver refused to go any further. He let me out into pitch blackness, and I saw I would never make it in time.

Blast. Enola crumpled on the stairway down to the tube, her open-toed shoes still on her feet, not a mark on her. And when I try to lift her, jelly under the skin. I would have to wrap her in the muffler she gave me, because I was too late. I had gone back a hundred years to be too late to save her.

I ran the last blocks, guided by the gun emplacement that had to be in Hyde Park, and skidded down the steps into Marble Arch. The woman in the ticket booth took my last shilling for a ticket to St. Paul's Station. I stuck it in my pocket and raced toward the stairs.

"No running," she said placidly. "To your left, please." The door to the right was blocked off by wooden barricades, the metal gates beyond pulled to and chained. The board with names on it for the stations was x-ed with tape, and a new sign that read ALL TRAINS was nailed to the barricade, pointing left.

Enola was not on the stopped escalators or sitting against the wall in the hallway. I came to the first stairway and could not get through. A family had set out, just where I wanted to step, a communal tea of bread and butter, a little pot of jam sealed with waxed paper, and a kettle on a ring like the one Langby and I had rescued out of the rubble, all of it spread on a cloth embroidered at the corners with flowers. I stood staring down at the layered tea, spread like a waterfall down the steps.

"I—Marble Arch—" I said. Another twenty killed by flying tiles. "You shouldn't be here."

"We've as much right as anyone," the man said belligerently, "and who are you to tell us to move on?"

A woman lifting saucers out of a cardboard box looked up at me, frightened. The kettle began to whistle.

"It's you that should move on," the man said. "Go on then." He stood off to one side so I could pass. I edged past the embroidered cloth apologetically.

"I'm sorry," I said. "I'm looking for someone. On the platform."

"You'll never find her in there, mate, it's hell in there," the man said, thumbing in that direction. I hurried past him, nearly stepping on the tea cloth, and rounded the corner into hell.

It was not hell. Shopgirls folded coats and leaned back against them, cheerful or sullen or disagreeable, but certainly not damned. Two boys scuffled for a shilling and lost it on the tracks. They bent over the edge, debating whether to go after it, and the station guard yelled to them to back away. A train rumbled through, full of people. A mosquito landed on the guard's hand and he reached out to slap it and missed. The boys laughed. And behind and before them, stretching in all directions down the deadly tile curves of the tunnel like casualties, backed into the entranceways and onto the stairs, were people. Hundreds and hundreds of people.

I stumbled back onto the stairs, knocking over a teacup. It spilled like a flood across the cloth.

"I told you, mate," the man said cheerfully. "It's hell in there, ain't it? And worse below."

"Hell," I said. "Yes." I would never find her. I would never save her. I looked at the woman mopping up the tea, and it came to me that I could not save her either. Enola or the cat or any of them, lost here in the endless stairways and cul-de-sacs of time. They were already dead a hundred years, past saving. The past is beyond saving. Surely that was the lesson the history department sent me all this way to learn. Well, fine, I've learned it. Can I go home now?

Of course not, dear boy. You have foolishly spent all your money on taxicabs and brandy, and tonight is the night the Germans burn the City. (Now it is too late, I remember it all. Twenty-eight incendiaries on the roofs.) Langby must have his chance, and you must learn the hardest lesson of all and the one you should have known from the beginning. You cannot save St. Paul's.

I went back out onto the platform and stood behind the yellow line until a train pulled up. I took my ticket out and held it in my hand all the way to St. Paul's Station. When I got there, smoke billowed toward me like an easy spray of water. I could not see St. Paul's.

"The tide's out," a woman said in a voice devoid of hope, and I went down in a snake pit of limp cloth hoses. My hands came up covered with rank-smelling mud, and I understood finally (and too late) the significance of the tide. There was no water to fight the fires.

A policeman barred my way and I stood helplessly before him with no idea what to say. "No civilians allowed here," he said. "St. Paul's is for it." The smoke billowed like a thundercloud, alive with sparks, and the dome rose golden above it.

"I'm fire watch," I said, and his arm fell away, and then I was on the roofs.

My endorphin levels must have been going up and down like an air raid siren. I do not have any short-term from then on, just moments that do not fit together: the people in the church when we brought Langby down, huddled in a corner playing cards, the whirlwind of burning scraps of wood in the dome, the ambulance driver who wore open-toed shoes like Enola and smeared salve on my burned hands. And in the center, the one clear moment when I went after Langby on a rope and saved his life.

I stood by the dome, blinking against the smoke. The City was on fire and it seemed as if St. Paul's would ignite from the heat, would crumble from the noise alone. Bence-Jones was by the northwest tower, hitting at an incendiary with a spade. Langby was too close to the patched place where the bomb had gone through, looking toward me. An incendiary clattered behind him. I turned to grab a shovel, and when I turned back, he was gone.

"Langby!" I shouted, and could not hear my own voice. He had fallen into the chasm and nobody saw him or the incendiary. Except me. I do not remember how I got across the roof. I think I called for a rope. I got a rope. I tied it around my waist, gave the ends of it into the hands of the fire watch, and went over the side. The fires lit the walls of the hole almost all the way to the bottom. Below me I could see a pile of whitish rubble. He's under there, I thought, and jumped free of the wall. The space was so narrow there was nowhere to throw the rubble. I was afraid I would inadvertently stone him, and I tried to toss the pieces of planking and plaster over my shoulder, but there was barely room to turn. For one awful moment I thought he might not be there at all, that the pieces of splintered wood would brush away to reveal empty pavement, as they had in the crypt.

I was numbed by the indignity of crawling over him. If he was dead I did not think I could bear the shame of stepping on his helpless body. Then his hand came up like a ghost's and grabbed my ankle, and within seconds I had whirled and had his head free.

He was the ghastly white that no longer frightens me. "I put the bomb out," he said. I stared at him, so overwhelmed with relief I could not speak. For one hysterical moment I thought I would even laugh, I was so glad to see him. I finally realized what it was I was supposed to say.

"Are you all right?" I said.

"Yes," he said, and tried to raise himself on one elbow. "So much the worse for you."

He could not get up. He grunted with pain when he tried to shift his weight to his right side and lay back, the uneven rubble crunching sickeningly under him. I tried to lift him gently so I could see where he was hurt. He must have fallen on something.

"It's no use," he said, breathing hard. "I put it out."

I spared him a startled glance, afraid that he was delirious and went back to rolling him onto his side.

"I know you were counting on this one," he went on, not resisting me at all. "It was bound to happen sooner or later with all these roofs. Only I went after it. What'll you tell your friends?"

His asbestos coat was torn down the back in a long gash. Under it his back was charred and smoking. He had fallen on the incendiary. "Oh, my God," I said, trying frantically to see how badly he was burned without touching him. I had no way of knowing how deep the burns went, but they seemed to extend only in the narrow space where the coat had torn. I tried to pull the bomb out from under him, but the casing was as hot as a stove. It was not melting, though. My sand and Langby's body had smothered it. I had no idea if it would start up again when it was exposed to the air. I looked around, a little wildly, for the bucket and stirrup pump Langby must have dropped when he fell.

"Looking for a weapon?" Langby said, so clearly it was hard to believe he was hurt at all. "Why not just leave me here? A bit of overexposure and I'd be done for by morning. Or would you rather do your dirty work in private?"

I stood up and yelled to the men on the roof above us. One of them shone a pocket torch down at us, but its light didn't reach.

"Is he dead?" somebody shouted down to me.

"Send for an ambulance," I said. "He's been burned."

I helped Langby up, trying to support his back without touching the burn. He staggered a little and then leaned against the wall, watching me as I tried to bury the incendiary, using a piece of the planking as a scoop. The rope came down and I tied Langby to it. He had not spoken since I helped him up. He let me tie the rope around his waist, still looking steadily at me. "I should have let you smother in the crypt," he said.

He stood leaning easily, almost relaxed against the wooden supports, his hands holding him up. I put his hands on the slack rope and wrapped it once around them for the grip I knew he didn't have. "I've been on to you since that day in the Gallery. I knew you weren't afraid of heights. You came down here without any fear of heights when you thought I'd ruined your precious plans. What was it? An attack of conscience? Kneeling there like a baby, whining. 'What have we done? What have we done?' You made me sick. But you know what gave you away first? The cat. Everybody knows cats hate water. Everybody but a dirty Nazi spy."

There was a tug on the rope. "Come ahead," I said, and the rope tautened.

"That WVS tart? Was she a spy, too? Supposed to meet you in Marble Arch? Telling me it was going to be bombed. You're a rotten spy, Bartholomew. Your friends already blew it up in September. It's open again."

The rope jerked suddenly and began to lift Langby. He twisted his hands to get a better grip. His right shoulder scraped the wall. I put up my hands and pushed him gently so that his left side was to the wall. "You're making a big mistake, you know," he said. "You should have killed me. I'll tell."

I stood in the darkness, waiting for the rope. Langby was unconscious when he reached the roof. I walked past the fire watch to the dome and down to the crypt.

This morning the letter from my uncle came and with it a five-pound note.

———

*December 31* — Two of Dunworthy's flunkies met me in St. John's Wood to tell me I was late for my exams. I did not even protest. I shuffled obediently after them without even considering how unfair it was to give an exam to one of the walking dead. I had not slept in — how long? Since yesterday when I went to find Enola. I had not slept in a hundred years.

Dunworthy was in the Examination Buildings, blinking at me. One of the flunkies handed me a test paper and the other one called time. I turned the paper over and left an oily smudge from the ointment on my burns. I stared uncomprehendingly at them. I had grabbed at the incendiary when I turned Langby over, but these burns were on the backs of my hands. The answer came to me suddenly in Langby's unyielding voice. "They're rope burns, you fool. Don't they teach you Nazi spies the proper way to come up a rope?"

I looked down at the test. I read, "Number of incendiaries that fell on St. Paul's_____ Number of land mines_____ Number of high explosive bombs_____ Method most commonly used for extinguishing incendiaries_____ land mines_____ high explosive bombs_____ Number of volunteers on first watch_____ second watch_____ Casualties_____

Fatalities____" The questions made no sense. There was only a short space, long enough for the writing of a number, after any of the questions. Method most commonly used for extinguishing incendiaries. How would I ever fit what I knew into that narrow space? Where were the questions about Enola and Langby and the cat?

I went up to Dunworthy's desk. "St. Paul's almost burned down last night," I said. "What kind of questions are these?"

"You should be answering questions, Mr. Bartholomew, not asking them."

"There aren't any questions about the people," I said. The outer casing of my anger began to melt.

"Of course there are," Dunworthy said, flipping to the second page of the test. "Number of casualties, 1940. Blast, shrapnel, other."

"Other?" I said. At any moment the roof would collapse on me in a shower of plaster dust and fury. "Other? Langby put out a fire with his own body. Enola has a cold that keeps getting worse. The cat . . ." I snatched the paper back from him and scrawled "one cat" in the narrow space next to "blast." "Don't you care about them at all?"

"They're important from a statistical point of view," he said, "but as individuals they are hardly relevant to the course of history."

My reflexes were shot. It was amazing to me that Dunworthy's were almost as slow. I grazed the side of his jaw and knocked his glasses off. "Of course they're relevant!" I shouted. "They *are* the history, not all these bloody numbers!"

The reflexes of the flunkies were very fast. They did not let me start another swing at him before they had me by both arms and were hauling me out of the room.

"They're back there in the past with nobody to save them. They can't see their hands in front of their faces and there are bombs falling down on them and you tell me they aren't important? You call that being an historian?"

The flunkies dragged me out the door and down the hall. "Langby saved St. Paul's. How much more important can a person get? You're no historian! You're nothing but a—" I wanted to call him a terrible name, but the only curses I could summon up were Langby's. "You're nothing but a dirty Nazi spy!" I bellowed. "You're nothing but a lazy bourgeois tart!"

They dumped me on my hands and knees outside the door and

slammed it in my face. "I wouldn't be an historian if you paid me!" I shouted, and went to see the fire watch stone.

————

I am having to write this in bits and pieces. My hands are in pretty bad shape, and Dunworthy's boys didn't help matters much. Kivrin comes in periodically, wearing her St. Joan look, and smears so much salve on my hands that I can't hold a pencil.

St. Paul's Station is not there, of course, so I got out at Holborn and walked, thinking about my last meeting with Dean Matthews on the morning after the burning of the city. This morning.

"I understand you saved Langby's life," he said. "I also understand that between you, you saved St. Paul's last night."

I showed him the letter from my uncle and he stared at it as if he could not think what it was. "Nothing stays saved forever," he said, and for a terrible moment I thought he was going to tell me Langby had died. "We shall have to keep on saving St. Paul's until Hitler decides to bomb something else."

The raids on London are almost over, I wanted to tell him. He'll start bombing the countryside in a matter of weeks. Canterbury, Bath, aiming always at the cathedrals. You and St. Paul's will both outlast the war and live to dedicate the fire watch stone.

"I am hopeful, though," he said. "I think the worst is over."

"Yes, sir." I thought of the stone, its letters still readable after all this time. No, sir, the worst is not over.

I managed to keep my bearings almost to the top of Ludgate Hill. Then I lost my way completely, wandering about like a man in a grave-yard. I had not remembered that the rubble looked so much like the white plaster dust Langby had tried to dig me out of. I could not find the stone anywhere. In the end I nearly fell over it, jumping back as if I had stepped on a body.

It is all that's left. Hiroshima is supposed to have had a handful of untouched trees at ground zero. Denver the capitol steps. Neither of them says, "Remember the men and women of St. Paul's Watch who by the grace of God saved this cathedral." The grace of God.

Part of the stone is sheared off. Historians argue there was another line that said, "for all time," but I do not believe that, not if Dean Matthews had anything to do with it. And none of the watch it was dedi-cated to would have believed it for a minute. We saved St. Paul's every time we put out an incendiary, and only until the next one fell. Keeping watch on the danger spots, putting out the little fires with sand and stirrup pumps, the big ones with our bodies, in order to keep the whole vast complex structure from burning down. Which sounds to me like a course description for History Practicum 401. What a fine time to discover what historians are for when I have tossed my chance for being one out the windows as easily as they tossed the pinpoint bomb in! No, sir, the worst is not over.

There are flash burns on the stone, where legend says the Dean of St. Paul's was kneeling when the bomb went off. Totally apocryphal, of course, since the front door is hardly an appropriate place for prayers. It is more likely the shadow of a tourist who wandered in to ask the whereabouts of the Windmill Theatre, or the imprint of a girl bringing a volunteer his muffler. Or a cat.

Nothing is saved forever, Dean Matthews, and I knew that when I walked in the west doors that first day, blinking into the gloom, but it is pretty bad nevertheless. Standing here knee-deep in rubble out of which I will not be able to dig any folding chairs or friends, knowing that Langby died thinking I was a Nazi spy, knowing that Enola came one day and I wasn't there. It's pretty bad.

But it is not as bad as it could be. They are both dead, and Dean Matthews too, but they died without knowing what I knew all along, what sent me to my knees in the Whispering Gallery, sick with grief and guilt: that in the end none of us saved St. Paul's. And Langby cannot turn to me, stunned and sick at heart, and say, "Who did this? Your friends the Nazis?" And I would have to say, "No, the communists." That would be the worst.

I have come back to the room and let Kivrin smear more salve on my hands. She wants me to get some sleep. I know I should pack and get gone. It will be humiliating to have them come and throw me out, but I do not have the strength to fight her. She looks so much like Enola.

———

*January 1*—I have apparently slept not only through the night, but through the morning mail drop as well. When I woke up just now, I found Kivrin sitting on the end of the bed holding an envelope. "Your grades came," she said.

I put my arm over my eyes. "They can be marvelously efficient when they want to, can't they?"

"Yes," Kivrin said.

"Well, let's see it," I said, sitting up. "How long do I have before they come and throw me out?"

She handed the flimsy computer envelope to me. I tore it along the perforation. "Wait," she said. "Before you open it, I want to say something." She put her hand gently on my burns. "You're wrong about the history department. They're very good."

It was not exactly what I expected her to say. "Good is not the word I'd use to describe Dunworthy," I said and yanked the inside slip free.

Kivrin's look did not change, not even when I sat there with the printout on my knees where she could surely see it.

"Well," I said.

The slip was hand-signed by the esteemed Dunworthy. I have taken a first. With honors.

———

*January 2*—Two things came in the mail today. One was Kivrin's assignment. The history department thinks of everything—even to keeping her here long enough to nursemaid me, even to coming up with a prefabricated trial by fire to send their history majors through.

I think I wanted to believe that was what they had done. Enola and Langby only hired actors, the cat a clever android with its clockwork innards taken out for the final effect, not so much because I wanted to believe Dunworthy was not good at all, but because then I would not have this nagging pain at not knowing what had happened to them.

"You said your practicum was England in 1400?" I said, watching her as suspiciously as I had watched Langby.

"Thirteen forty-nine," she said, and her face went slack with memory. "The plague year."

"My God," I said. "How could they do that? The plague's a ten."

"I have a natural immunity," she said, and looked at her hands.

Because I could not think of anything to say, I opened the other piece of mail. It was a report on Enola. Computer-printed, facts and dates and statistics, all the numbers the history department so dearly loves, but it told me what I thought I would have to go without knowing: that she had gotten over her cold and survived the Blitz. Young Tom had been killed in the Baedaker raids on Bath, but Enola had lived until 2006, the year before they blew up St. Paul's.

I don't know whether I believe the report or not, but it does not matter. It is, like Langby's reading aloud to the old man, a simple act of human kindness. They think of everything.

Not quite. They did not tell me what happened to Langby. But I find as I write this that I already know: I saved his life. It does not seem to matter that he might have died in the hospital the next day, and I find, in spite of all the hard lessons the history department has tried to teach me, I do not quite believe this one: that nothing is saved forever. It seems to me that perhaps Langby is.

---

*January 3* — I went to see Dunworthy today. I don't know what I intended to say — some pompous drivel about my willingness to serve in the fire watch of history, standing guard against the falling incendiaries of the human heart, silent and saintly.

But he blinked at me nearsightedly across his desk, and it seemed to me that he was blinking at that last bright image of St. Paul's in sunlight before it was gone forever and that he knew better than anyone that the past cannot be saved, and I said instead, "I'm sorry that I broke your glasses, sir."

"How did you like St. Paul's?" he said, and like my first meeting with Enola, I felt I must be somehow reading the signals all wrong, that he was not feeling loss, but something quite different.

"I loved it, sir," I said.

"Yes," he said. "So do I."

Dean Matthews is wrong. I have fought with memory my whole practicum only to find that it is not the enemy at all, and being an historian is not some saintly burden after all. Because Dunworthy is not blinking against the fatal sunlight of the last morning, but into the gloom of that first afternoon, looking in the great west doors of St. Paul's at what is, like Langby, like all of it, every moment, in us, saved forever.

# ROBERT SILVERBERG

*Robert Silverberg won the Hugo Award for most promising new author in 1956, less than two years after his first professional sale. After an apprenticeship that lasted nearly ten years and yielded millions of words, Silverberg emerged in the 1960s as one of the most articulate and conscientious writers of the time. Works from this period of his career are memorable for their psychologically complex character studies, morally trenchant themes, and vivid depictions of oppressive and limiting environments that the individual must try to transcend. "To See the Invisible Man," "Hawksbill Station," and* Thorns *are futuristic studies of the individual alienated through a variety of means: social ostracism, penal exile, and exploitative victimization. Silverberg's crowning achievement in this vein is* Dying Inside, *the poignant tale of a telepath alienated by his uniqueness who is further isolated by the loss of his powers and thus his only means of relating to normal humanity.*

*Both* Nightwings *and* Downward to Earth *present contact with alien species as potentially rejuvenating experiences with religious overtones of resurrection and redemption. The* World Inside *chronicles the dehumanizing potential of overpopulation on a society in which privacy and intimacy are virtually impossible.*

*At the dramatic core of Silverberg's strongest stories are individuals confronted with mortality. "Born with the Dead" details the difficulties of life in a world that is shared by mortals and the revived dead. The Second* Trip *centers on the idea of the death of identity; a man discovers that he is a former criminal punished with obliteration of his true personality, a spark of which is reignited and threatens to overwhelm his new persona.*

*The quest for immortality is a sounding board for ruminations on mortality in* The Book of Skulls, *about the pursuit of an occult sect that has supposedly found the secret of eternal life, and the impact of the quest on the individuals who seek it.*

*Since the late 1970s Silverberg has concentrated on the development of his Majipoor saga, an epic science fantasy series that includes the novels* Lord Valentine's Castle, The Majipoor Chronicles, *and* Valentine Pontifex. *He has also written two fantasy novels,* Gilgamesh the King *and* To the Land of the Living, *based on Sumerian mythology. His many short fiction collections include* Next Stop the Stars, To Worlds Beyond, Dimension Thirteen, Born with the Dead, *and* The Secret Sharer. *He has written many novels and works of nonfiction for children, and edited more than seventy anthologies.*

*"Sailing to Byzantium" is another story that, like Joe Haldeman's, deals with the far, far future, and it takes place in a world that Silverberg has made at once vaguely familiar through his use of history, and utterly alien by virtue of its population. A winner of the Nebula Award in 1985, it is a look at what it means to be human, now and forever.*

# SAILING TO BYZANTIUM

## ROBERT SILVERBERG

AT DAWN HE AROSE and stepped out onto the patio for his first look at Alexandria, the one city he had not yet seen. That year the five cities were Chang-an, Asgard, New Chicago, Timbuctoo, Alexandria: the usual mix of eras, cultures, realities. He and Gioia, making the long flight from Asgard in the distant north the night before, had arrived late, well after sundown, and had gone straight to bed. Now, by the gentle apricot-hued morning light, the fierce spires and battlements of Asgard seemed merely something he had dreamed.

The rumor was that Asgard's moment was finished, anyway. In a little while he had heard they were going to tear it down and replace it, elsewhere, with Mohenjo-daro. Though there were never more than five cities, they changed constantly. He could remember a time when they had had Rome of the Caesars instead of Chang-an, and Rio de Janeiro rather than Alexandria. These people saw no point in keeping anything very long.

It was not easy for him to adjust to the sultry intensity of Alexandria after the frozen splendors of Asgard. The wind, coming off the water, was brisk and torrid both at once. Soft turquoise wavelets lapped at the jetties. Strong presences assailed his senses: the hot heavy sky, the stinging scent of red lowland sand borne on the breeze, the sullen swampy aroma of the nearby sea. Everything trembled and glimmered in the early light. Their hotel was beautifully situated, high on the northern slope of the huge artificial mound known as the Paneium that was sacred to the goat-footed god. From here they had a total view of the city: the wide noble boulevards, the soaring obelisks and monuments, the palace of Hadrian just below the hill, the stately and awesome Library, the temple of Poseidon, the teeming marketplace, the royal lodge that Mark Antony had built after his defeat at Actium. And of course the Lighthouse, the wondrous many-windowed Lighthouse, the seventh wonder of the world, that immense pile of marble and limestone and reddish-purple Aswan granite rising in majesty at the end of its mile-long causeway. Black smoke from the beacon-fire at its summit curled lazily into the sky. The city was awakening. Some temporaries in short white kilts appeared and began to trim the dense dark hedges that bordered the great public buildings. A few citizens wearing loose robes of vaguely Grecian style were strolling in the streets.

There were ghosts and chimeras and phantasies everywhere about. Two slim elegant centaurs, a male and a female, grazed on the hillside. A burly thick-thighed swordsman appeared on the porch of the temple of Poseidon holding a Gorgon's severed head; he waved it in a wide arc, grinning broadly. In the street below the hotel gate three small pink sphinxes, no bigger than housecats, stretched and yawned and began to prowl the curbside. A larger one, lion-sized, watched warily from an alleyway: their mother, surely. Even at this distance he could hear her loud purring.

Shading his eyes, he peered far out past the Lighthouse and across the water. He hoped to see the dim shores of Crete or Cyprus to the north, or perhaps the great dark curve of Anatolia. *Carry me toward that great Byzantium,* he thought. *Where all is ancient, singing at the oars.* But he beheld only the endless empty sea, sun-bright and blinding though the morning was just beginning. Nothing was ever where he expected it to be. The continents did not seem to be in their proper places any longer. Gioia, taking him aloft long ago in her little flitterflitter, had shown him that. The tip of South America was canted far out into the Pacific; Africa was weirdly foreshortened; a broad tongue of ocean separated Europe and Asia. Australia did not appear to exist at all. Perhaps they had dug it up and used it for other things. There was no trace of the world he once had known. This was the fiftieth century. "The fiftieth century after *what?*" he had asked several times, but no one seemed to know, or else they did not care to say.

"Is Alexandria very beautiful?" Gioia called from within.

"Come out and see."

Naked and sleepy-looking, she padded out onto the white-tiled patio and nestled up beside him. She fit neatly under his arm. "Oh, yes, yes!"

she said softly. "So very beautiful, isn't it? Look, there, the palaces, the Library, the Lighthouse! Where will we go first? The Lighthouse, I think. Yes? And then the marketplace—I want to see the Egyptian magicians—and the stadium, the races—will they be having races today, do you think? Oh, Charles, I want to see everything!"

"Everything? All on the first day?"

"All on the first day, yes," she said. "Everything."

"But we have plenty of time, Gioia."

"Do we?"

He smiled and drew her tight against his side.

"Time enough," he said gently.

He loved her for her impatience, for her bright bubbling eagerness. Gioia was not much like the rest in that regard, though she seemed identical in all other ways. She was short, supple, slender, dark-eyed, olive-skinned, narrow-hipped, with wide shoulders and flat muscles. They were all like that, each one indistinguishable from the rest, like a horde of millions of brothers and sisters—a world of small, lithe, child-like Mediterraneans, built for juggling, for bull-dancing, for sweet white wine at midday and rough red wine at night. They had the same slim bodies, the same broad mouths, the same great glossy eyes. He had never seen anyone who appeared to be younger than twelve or older than twenty. Gioia was somehow a little different, although he did not quite know how; but he knew that it was for that imperceptible but significant difference that he loved her. And probably that was why she loved him also.

He let his gaze drift from west to east, from the Gate of the Moon down broad Canopus Street and out to the harbor, and off to the tomb of Cleopatra at the tip of long slender Cape Lochias. Everything was here and all of it perfect, the obelisks, the statues and marble colonnades, the courtyards and shrines and groves, great Alexander himself in his coffin of crystal and gold: a splendid gleaming pagan city. But there were oddities—an unmistakable mosque near the public gardens, and what seemed to be a Christian church not far from the Library. And those ships in the harbor, with all those red sails and bristling masts—surely they were medieval, and late medieval at that. He had seen such anachronisms in other places before. Doubtless these people found them amusing. Life was a game for them. They played at it unceasingly. Rome, Alexandria, Timbuctoo—why not? Create an Asgard of translucent bridges and shimmering ice-girt palaces, then grow weary of it and take it away? Replace it with Mohenjo-daro? Why not? It seemed to him a great pity to destroy those lofty Nordic feasting-halls for the sake of building a squat, brutal, sun-baked city of brown brick; but these people did not look at things the way he did. Their cities were only temporary. Someone in Asgard had said that Timbuctoo would be the next to go, with Byzantium rising in its place. Well, why not? Why not? They could have anything they liked. This was the fiftieth century, after all. The only rule was that there could be no more than five cities at once. "Limits," Gioia had informed him solemnly when they first began to travel together, "are very important." But she did not know why, or did not care to say.

He stared out once more toward the sea.

He imagined a newborn city congealing suddenly out of mists, far across the water: shining towers, great domed palaces, golden mosaics. That would be no great effort for them. They could just summon it forth whole out of time, the Emperor on his throne and the Emperor's drunken soldiery roistering in the streets, the brazen clangor of the cathedral gong rolling through the Grand Bazaar, dolphins leaping beyond the shoreside pavilions. Why not? They had Timbuctoo. They had Alexandria. Do you crave Constantinople? Then behold Constantinople! Or Avalon, or Lyonesse, or Atlantis. They could have anything they liked. It is pure Schopenhauer here: the world as will and imagination. Yes! These slender dark-eyed people journeying tirelessly from miracle to miracle. Why not Byzantium next? Yes! Why not? *That is no country for old men,* he thought. *The young in one another's arms, the birds in the trees*—yes! Yes! Anything they liked. They even had him. Suddenly he felt frightened. Questions he had not asked for a long time burst through into his consciousness. *Who am I? Why am I here? Who is this woman beside me?*

"You're so quiet all of a sudden, Charles," said Gioia, who could not abide silence for very long. "Will you talk to me? I want you to talk to me. Tell me what you're looking for out there."

He shrugged. "Nothing."

"Nothing?"

"Nothing in particular."

"I could see you seeing something."

"Byzantium," he said. "I was imagining that I could look straight across the water to Byzantium. I was trying to get a glimpse of the walls of Constantinople."

"Oh, but you wouldn't be able to see as far as that from here. Not really."

"I know."

"And anyway Byzantium doesn't exist."

"Not yet. But it will. Its time comes later on."

"Does it?" she said. "Do you know that for a fact?"

"On good authority. I heard it in Asgard," he told her. "But even if I hadn't, Byzantium would be inevitable, don't you think? Its time would have to come. How could we not do Byzantium, Gioia? We certainly will do Byzantium, sooner or later. I know we will. It's only a matter of time. And we have all the time in the world."

A shadow crossed her face. "Do we? Do we?"

———

He knew very little about himself, but he knew that he was not one of them. That he knew. He knew that his name was Charles Phillips and that before he had come to live among these people he had lived in the year 1984, when there had been such things as computers and television sets and baseball and jet planes, and the world was full of cities, not merely five but thousands of them, New York and London and Johannesburg and Paris and Liverpool and Bangkok and San Francisco and Buenos Aires and a multitude of others, all at the same time. There had been four and a half billion people in the world then; now he doubted that there were as many as four and a half million. Nearly everything had changed beyond comprehension. The moon still seemed the same, and the sun; but at night he searched in vain for familiar constellations. He had no idea how they had brought him from then to now, or why. It did no good to ask. No one had any answers for him; no one so much as appeared to understand what it was that he was trying to learn. After a time he had stopped asking; after a time had had almost entirely ceased wanting to know.

He and Gioia were climbing the Lighthouse. She scampered ahead, in a hurry as always, and he came along behind her in his more stolid fashion. Scores of other tourists, mostly in groups of two or three, were making their way up the wide flagstone ramps, laughing, calling to one another. Some of them, seeing him, stopped a moment, stared, pointed. He was used to that. He was so much taller than any of them; he was plainly not one of them. When they pointed at him he smiled. Sometimes he nodded a little acknowledgment.

He could not find much of interest in the lowest level, a massive square structure two hundred feet high built of huge marble blocks: within its cool musty arcades were hundreds of small dark rooms, the offices of the Lighthouse's keepers and mechanics, the barracks of the garrison, the stables for the three hundred donkeys that carried the fuel to the lantern far above. None of that appeared inviting to him. He forged onward without halting until he emerged on the balcony that led to the next level. Here the Lighthouse grew narrower and became octagonal: its face, granite now and handsomely fluted, rose in a stunning sweep above him.

Gioia was waiting for him there. "This is for you," she said, holding out a nugget of meat on a wooden skewer. "Roast lamb. Absolutely delicious. I had one while I was waiting for you." She gave him a cup of some cool green sherbet also, and darted off to buy a pomegranate. Dozens of temporaries were roaming the balcony, selling refreshments of all kinds.

He nibbled at the meat. It was charred outside, nicely pink and moist within. While he ate, one of the temporaries came up to him and peered blandly into his face. It was a stocky swarthy male wearing nothing but a strip of red and yellow cloth about its waist. "I sell meat," it said. "Very fine roast lamb, only five drachmas."

Phillips indicated the piece he was eating. "I already have some," he said.

"It is excellent meat, very tender. It has been soaked for three days in the juices of—"

"Please," Phillips said. "I don't want to buy any meat. Do you mind moving along?"

The temporaries had confused and baffled him at first, and there was still much about them that was unclear to him. They were not machines—they looked like creatures of flesh and blood—but they did not seem to be human beings, either, and no one treated them as if they were. He supposed they were artificial constructs, products of a technology so consummate that it was invisible. Some appeared to be more intelligent than others, but all of them behaved as if they had no more autonomy than characters in a play, which was essentially what they were. There were untold numbers of them in each of the five cities, playing all manner of roles: shepherds and swineherds, street-sweepers, merchants, boatmen, vendors of grilled meats and cool drinks, hagglers in the marketplace, schoolchildren, charioteers, policemen, grooms, gladiators, monks, artisans, whores and cutpurses, sailors—whatever was needed to sustain the illusion of a thriving, populous urban center. The dark-eyed people, Gioia's people, never performed work. There were not enough of them to keep a city's functions going, and in any case they were strictly tourists, wandering with the wind, moving from city to city as the whim took them, Chang-an to New Chicago, New Chicago to Timbuctoo, Timbuctoo to Asgard, Asgard to Alexandria, onward, ever onward.

The temporary would not leave him alone. Phillips walked away and it followed him, cornering him against the balcony wall. When Gioia returned a few minutes later, lips prettily stained with pomegranate juice, the temporary was still hovering about him, trying with lunatic persistence to sell him a skewer of lamb. It stood much too close to him, almost nose to nose, great sad cowlike eyes peering intently into his as it extolled with mournful mooing urgency the quality of its wares. It seemed to him that he had had trouble like this with temporaries on one or two earlier occasions. Gioia touched the creature's elbow lightly and said, in a short sharp tone Phillips had never heard her use before, "He isn't interested. Get away from him." It went at once. To Phillips she said, "You have to be firm with them."

"I was trying. It wouldn't listen to me."

"You ordered it to go away, and it refused?"

"I asked it to go away. Politely. Too politely, maybe."

"Even so," she said. "It should have obeyed a human, regardless."

"Maybe it didn't think I was human," Phillips suggested. "Because of the way I look. My height, the color of my eyes. It might have thought I was some kind of temporary myself."

"No," Gioia said, frowning. "A temporary won't solicit another temporary. But it won't ever disobey a citizen, either. There's a very clear boundary. There isn't ever any confusion. I can't understand why it went on bothering you." He was surprised at how troubled she seemed: far more so, he thought, than the incident warranted. A stupid device, perhaps miscalibrated in some way, overenthusiastically pushing its wares—what of it? What of it? Gioia, after a moment, appeared to come to the same conclusion. Shrugging, she said, "It's defective, I suppose. Probably such things are more common than we suspect, don't you think?" There was something forced about her tone that bothered him. She smiled and handed him her pomegranate. "Here. Have a bite, Charles.

It's wonderfully sweet. They used to be extinct, you know. Shall we go on upward?"

———

The octagonal midsection of the Lighthouse must have been several hundred feet in height, a grim claustrophobic tube almost entirely filled by the two broad spiraling ramps that wound around the huge building's central well. The ascent was slow: a donkey team was a little way ahead of them on the ramp, plodding along laden with bundles of kindling for the lantern. But at last, just as Phillips was growing winded and dizzy, he and Gioia came out onto the second balcony, the one marking the transition between the octagonal section and the Lighthouse's uppermost storey, which was cylindrical and very slender.

She leaned far out over the balustrade. "Oh, Charles, look at the view! Look at it!"

It was amazing. From one side they could see the entire city, and swampy Lake Mareotis and the dusty Egyptian plain beyond it, and from the other they peered far out into the gray and choppy Mediterranean. He gestured toward the innumerable reefs and shallows that infested the waters leading to the harbor entrance. "No wonder they needed a lighthouse here," he said. "Without some kind of gigantic landmark they'd never have found their way in from the open sea."

A blast of sound, a ferocious snort, erupted just above him. He looked up, startled. Immense statues of trumpet-wielding Tritons jutted from the corners of the Lighthouse at this level; that great blurting sound had come from the nearest of them. A signal, he thought. A warning to the ships negotiating that troubled passage. The sound was produced by some kind of steam-powered mechanism, he realized, operated by teams of sweating temporaries clustered about bonfires at the base of each Triton.

Once again he found himself swept by admiration for the clever way these people carried out their reproductions of antiquity. Or *were* they reproductions, he wondered? He still did not understand how they brought their cities into being. For all he knew, this place was the authentic Alexandria itself, pulled forward out of its proper time just as he himself had been. Perhaps this was the true and original Lighthouse, and not a copy. He had no idea which was the case, nor which would be the greater miracle.

"How do we get to the top?" Gioia asked.

"Over there, I think. That doorway."

The spiraling donkey-ramps ended here. The loads of lantern fuel went higher via a dumb-waiter in the central shaft. Visitors continued by way of a cramped staircase, so narrow at its upper end that it was impossible to turn around while climbing. Gioia, tireless, sprinted ahead. He clung to the rail and labored up and up, keeping count of the tiny window-slits to ease the boredom of the ascent. The count was nearing a hundred when finally he stumbled into the vestibule of the beacon chamber. A dozen or so visitors were crowded into it. Gioia was at the far side, by the wall that was open to the sea.

It seemed to him he could feel the building swaying in the winds, up here. How high were they? Five hundred feet, six hundred, seven? The beacon chamber was tall and narrow, divided by a catwalk into upper and lower sections. Down below, relays of temporaries carried wood from the dumb-waiter and tossed it on the blazing fire. He felt its intense heat from where he stood, at the rim of the platform on which the giant mirror of polished metal was hung. Tongues of flame leaped upward and danced before the mirror, which hurled its dazzling beam far out to sea. Smoke rose through a vent. At the very top was a colossal statue of Poseidon, austere, ferocious, looming above the lantern.

Gioia sidled along the catwalk until she was at his side. "The guide was talking before you came," she said, pointing. "Do you see that place over there, under the mirror? Someone standing there and looking into the mirror gets a view of ships at sea that can't be seen from here by the naked eye. The mirror magnifies things."

"Do you believe that?"

She nodded toward the guide. "It said so. And it also told us that if you look in a certain way, you can see right across the water into the city of Constantinople."

She is like a child, he thought. They all are. He said, "You told me yourself this very morning that it isn't possible to see that far. Besides, Constantinople doesn't exist right now."

"It will," she replied. "*You* said that to me, this very morning. And when it does, it'll be reflected in the Lighthouse mirror. That's the truth. I'm absolutely certain of it." She swung about abruptly toward the entrance of the beacon chamber. "Oh, look, Charles! Here come Nissandra and Aramayne! And there's Hawk! There's Stengard!" Gioia laughed and waved and called out names. "Oh, everyone's here! *Everyone!*"

They came jostling into the room, so many newcomers that some of those who had been there were forced to scramble down the steps on the far side. Gioia moved among them, hugging, kissing. Phillips could scarcely tell one from another—it was hard for him even to tell which were the men and which the women, dressed as they all were in the same sort of loose robes—but he recognized some of the names. These were her special friends, her set, with whom she had journeyed from city to city on an endless round of gaiety in the old days before he had come into her life. He had met a few of them before, in Asgard, in Rio, in Rome. The beacon-chamber guide, a squat wide-shouldered old temporary wearing a laurel wreath on its bald head, reappeared and began its potted speech, but no one listened to it; they were all too busy greeting one another, embracing, giggling. Some of them edged their way over to Phillips and reached up, standing on tiptoes, to touch their fingertips to his cheek in that odd hello of theirs. "Charles," they said gravely, making two syllables out of the name, as these people often did. "So good to see you again. Such a pleasure. You and Gioia—such a handsome couple. So well suited to each other."

Was that so? He supposed it was.

The chamber hummed with chatter. The guide could not be heard at all. Stengard and Nissandra had visited New Chicago for the water-dancing—Aramayne bore tales of a feast in Chang-an that had gone on for *days*—Hawk and Hekna had been to Timbuctoo to see the arrival of the salt caravan, and were going back there soon—a final party soon to celebrate the end of Asgard that absolutely should not be missed—the plans for the new city, Mohenjo-daro—we have reservations for the opening, we wouldn't pass it up for anything—and, yes, they were definitely going to do Constantinople after that, the planners were already deep into their Byzantium research—so good to see you, you look so beautiful all the time—have you been to the Library yet? The zoo? To the temple of Serapis?—

To Phillips they said, "What do you think of our Alexandria, Charles? Of course you must have known it well in your day. Does it look the way you remember it?" They were always asking things like that. They did not seem to comprehend that the Alexandria of the Lighthouse and the Library was long lost and legendary by his time. To them, he suspected, all the places they had brought back into existence were more or less contemporary. Rome of the Caesars, Alexandria of the Ptolemies, Venice of the Doges, Chang-an of the T'angs, Asgard of the

Aesir, none any less real than the next nor any less unreal, each one simply a facet of the distant past, the fantastic immemorial past, a plum plucked from that dark backward and abysm of time. They had no contexts for separating one era from another. To them all the past was one borderless timeless realm. Why then should he not have seen the Lighthouse before, he who had leaped into this era from the New York of 1984? He had never been able to explain it to them. Julius Caesar and Hannibal, Helen of Troy and Charlemagne, Rome of the gladiators and New York of the Yankees and Mets, Gilgamesh and Tristan and Othello and Robin Hood and George Washington and Queen Victoria—to them, all equally real and unreal, none of them any more than bright figures moving about on a painted canvas. The past, the past, the elusive and fluid past—to them it was a single place of infinite accessibility and infinite connectivity. Of course they would think he had seen the Lighthouse before. He knew better than to try again to explain things. "No," he said simply. "This is my first time in Alexandria."

———

They stayed there all winter long, and possibly some of the spring. Alexandria was not a place where one was sharply aware of the change of seasons, nor did the passage of time itself make itself very evident when one was living one's entire life as a tourist.

During the day there was always something new to see. The zoological garden, for instance: a wondrous park, miraculously green and lush in this hot dry climate, where astounding animals roamed in enclosures so generous that they did not seem like enclosures at all. Here were camels, rhinoceroses, gazelles, ostriches, lions, wild asses; and here too, casually adjacent to those familiar African beasts, were hippogriffs, unicorns, basilisks, and fire-snorting dragons with rainbow scales. Had the original zoo of Alexandria had dragons and unicorns? Phillips doubted it. But this one did; evidently it was no harder for the backstage craftsmen to manufacture mythic beasts than it was for them to turn out camels and gazelles. To Gioia and her friends all of them were equally mythical, anyway. They were just as awed by the rhinoceros as by the hippogriff. One was no more strange—nor any less—than the other. So far as Phillips had been able to discover, none of the mammals or birds of his era had survived into this one except for a few cats and dogs, though many had been reconstructed.

And then the Library! All those lost treasures, reclaimed from the jaws of time! Stupendous columned marble walls, airy high-vaulted reading-rooms, dark coiling stacks stretching away to infinity. The ivory handles of seven hundred thousand papyrus scrolls bristling on the shelves. Scholars and librarians gliding quietly about, smiling faint scholarly smiles but plainly preoccupied with serious matters of the mind. They were all temporaries, Phillips realized. Mere props, part of the illusion. But were the scrolls illusions too? "Here we have the complete dramas of Sophocles," said the guide with a blithe wave of its hand, indicating shelf upon shelf of texts. Only seven of his hundred twenty-three plays had survived the successive burnings of the library in ancient times by Romans, Christians, Arabs: were the lost ones here, the *Triptolemus*, the *Nausicaa*, the *Jason*, and all the rest? And would he find here too, miraculously restored to being, the other vanished treasures of ancient literature—the memoirs of Odysseus, Cato's history of Rome, Thucydides' life of Pericles, the missing volumes of Livy? But when he asked if he might explore the stacks, the guide smiled apologetically and said that all the librarians were busy just now. Another time, perhaps? Perhaps, said the guide. It made no difference, Phillips decided. Even if these people somehow had brought back those lost masterpieces of antiquity, how would he read them? He knew no Greek.

The life of the city buzzed and throbbed about him. It was a dazzlingly beautiful place: the vast bay thick with sails, the great avenues running rigidly east-west, north-south, the sunlight rebounding almost audibly from the bright walls of the palaces of kings and gods. They have done this very well, Phillips thought: very well indeed. In the marketplace hard-eyed traders squabbled in half a dozen mysterious languages over the price of ebony, Arabian incense, jade, panther-skins. Gioia bought a dram of pale musky Egyptian perfume in a delicate tapering glass flask. Magicians and jugglers and scribes called out stridently to passersby, begging for a few moments of attention and a handful of coins for their labor. Strapping slaves, black and tawny and some that might have been Chinese, were put up for auction, made to flex their muscles, to bare their teeth, to bare their breasts and thighs to prospective buyers. In the gymnasium naked athletes hurled javelins and discuses, and wrestled with terrifying zeal. Gioia's friend Stengard came rushing up with a gift for her, a golden necklace that would not have embarrassed Cleopatra. An hour later she had lost it, or perhaps had given it away while

Phillips was looking elsewhere. She bought another, even finer, the next day. Anyone could have all the money he wanted, simply by asking: it was as easy to come by as air, for these people.

Being here was much like going to the movies, Phillips told himself. A different show every day: not much plot, but the special effects were magnificent and the detail-work could hardly have been surpassed. A megamovie, a vast entertainment that went on all the time and was being played out by the whole population of Earth. And it was all so effortless, so spontaneous: just as when he had gone to a movie he had never troubled to think about the myriad technicians behind the scenes, the cameramen and the costume designers and the set-builders and the electricians and the model-makers and the boom operators, so too here he chose not to question the means by which Alexandria had been set before him. It felt real. It *was* real. When he drank the strong red wine it gave him a pleasant buzz. If he leaped from the beacon chamber of the Lighthouse he suspected he would die, though perhaps he would not stay dead for long: doubtless they had some way of restoring him as often as was necessary. Death did not seem to be a factor in these people's lives.

By day they saw sights. By night he and Gioia went to parties, in their hotel, in seaside villas, in the palaces of the high nobility. The usual people were there all the time, Hawk and Hekna, Aramayne, Stengard and Shelimir, Nissandra, Asoka, Afonso, Protay. At the parties there were five or ten temporaries for every citizen, some as mere servants, others as entertainers or even surrogate guests, mingling freely and a little daringly. But everyone knew, all the time, who was a citizen and who just a temporary. Phillips began to think his own status lay somewhere between. Certainly they treated him with a courtesy that no one ever would give a temporary, and yet there was a condescension to their manner that told him not simply that he was not one of them but that he was someone or something of an altogether different order of existence. That he was Gioia's lover gave him some standing in their eyes, but not a great deal: obviously he was always going to be an outsider, a primitive, ancient and quaint. For that matter he noticed that Gioia herself, though unquestionably a member of the set, seemed to be regarded as something of an outsider, like a tradesman's great-granddaughter in a gathering of Plantagenets. She did not always find out about the best parties in time to attend; her friends did not always reciprocate her effusive greetings with the same degree of warmth; sometimes he noticed her straining to hear some bit of gossip that was not quite being shared with her. Was it because she had taken him for her lover? Or was it the other way around: that she had chosen to be his lover precisely because she was *not* a full member of their caste?

Being a primitive gave him, at least, something to talk about at their parties. "Tell us about war," they said. "Tell us about elections. About money. About disease." They wanted to know everything, though they did not seem to pay close attention: their eyes were quick to glaze. Still, they asked. He described traffic jams to them, and politics, and deodorants, and vitamin pills. He told them about cigarettes, newspapers, subways, telephone directories, credit cards, and basketball.

"Which was your city?" they asked. New York, he told them. "And when was it? The seventh century, did you say?" The twentieth, he told them. They exchanged glances and nodded. "We will have to do it," they said. "The World Trade Center, the Empire State Building, the Citicorp Center, the Cathedral of St. John the Divine: how fascinating! Yankee Stadium. The Verrazzano Bridge. We will do it all. But first must come Mohenjo-daro. And then, I think, Constantinople. Did your city have many people?" Seven million, he said. Just in the five boroughs alone. They nodded, smiling amiably, unfazed by the number.

Seven million, seventy million—it was all the same to them, he sensed. They would just bring forth the temporaries in whatever quantity was required. He wondered how well they would carry the job off. He was no real judge of Alexandrias and Asgards, after all. Here they could have unicorns and hippogriffs in the zoo, and live sphinxes prowling in the gutters, and it did not trouble him. Their fanciful Alexandria was as good as history's, or better. But how sad, how disillusioning it would be, if the New York that they conjured up had Greenwich Village uptown and Times Square in the Bronx, and the New Yorkers, gentle and polite, spoke with the honeyed accents of Savannah or New Orleans. Well, that was nothing he needed to brood about just now. Very likely they were only being courteous when they spoke of doing his New York. They had all the vastness of the past to choose from: Nineveh, Memphis of the Pharaohs, the London of Victoria or Shakespeare or Richard the Third, Florence of the Medici, the Paris of Abelard and Heloise or the Paris of Louis XIV, Moctezuma's Tenochtitlan and Atahuallpa's Cuzco; Damascus, St. Petersburg, Babylon, Troy. And then there were all the cities like New Chicago, out of time that was time yet unborn to him but ancient history to them. In such richness, such an infinity of choices, even mighty New York might have to wait a long while for its turn. Would he still be among them by the time they got around to it? By then, perhaps, they might have become bored with him and returned him to his own proper era. Or possibly he would simply have grown old and died. Even here, he supposed, he would eventually die, though no one else ever seemed to. He did not know. He realized that in fact he did not know anything.

————

The north wind blew all day long. Vast flocks of ibises appeared over the city, fleeing the heat of the interior, and screeched across the sky with their black necks and scrawny legs extended. The sacred birds, descending by the thousands, scuttered about in every crossroad, pouncing on spiders and beetles, on mice, on the debris of the meat-shops and the bakeries. They were beautiful but annoyingly ubiquitous, and they splashed their dung over the marble buildings; each morning squadrons of temporaries carefully washed it off. Gioia said little to him now. She seemed cool, withdrawn, depressed; and there was something almost intangible about her, as though she were gradually becoming transparent. He felt it would be an intrusion upon her privacy to ask her what was wrong. Perhaps it was only restlessness. She became religious, and presented costly offerings at the temples of Serapis, Isis, Poseidon, Pan. She went to the necropolis west of the city to lay wreaths on the tombs in the catacombs. In a single day she climbed the Lighthouse three times without any sign of fatigue. One afternoon he returned from a visit to the Library and found her naked on the patio; she had anointed herself all over with some aromatic green salve. Abruptly she said, "I think it's time to leave Alexandria, don't you?"

————

She wanted to go to Mohenjo-daro, but Mohenjo-daro was not yet ready for visitors. Instead they flew eastward to Chang-an, which they had not seen in years. It was Phillips' suggestion: he hoped that the cosmopolitan gaudiness of the old T'ang capital would lift her mood.

They were to be guests of the Emperor this time: an unusual privilege, which ordinarily had to be applied for far in advance, but Phillips had told some of Gioia's highly placed friends that she was unhappy, and they had quickly arranged everything. Three endlessly bowing functionaries in flowing yellow robes and purple sashes met them at the Gate of Brilliant Virtue in the city's south wall and conducted them to their pavilion, close by the imperial palace and the Forbidden Garden. It was a light, airy place, thin walls of plastered brick braced by graceful columns of some dark, aromatic wood. Fountains played on the roof of green and yellow tiles, creating an unending cool rainfall of recirculating water. The balustrades were of carved marble, the door-fittings were of gold.

There was a suite of private rooms for him, and another for her, though they would share the handsome damask-draped bedroom at the heart of the pavilion. As soon as they arrived Gioia announced that she must go to her rooms to bathe and dress. "There will be a formal reception for us at the palace tonight," she said. "They say the imperial receptions are splendid beyond anything you could imagine. I want to be at my best." The Emperor and all his ministers, she told him, would receive them in the Hall of the Supreme Ultimate; there would be a banquet for a thousand people; Persian dancers would perform, and the celebrated jugglers of Chung-nan. Afterward everyone would be conducted into the fantastic landscape of the Forbidden Garden to view the dragon-races and the fireworks.

He went to his own rooms. Two delicate little maid-servants undressed him and bathed him with fragrant sponges. The pavilion came equipped with eleven temporaries who were to be their servants: soft-voiced unobtrusive cat-like Chinese, done with perfect verisimilitude, straight black hair, glowing skin, epicanthic folds. Phillips often wondered what happened to a city's temporaries when the city's time was over. Were the towering Norse heroes of Asgard being recycled at this moment into wiry dark-skinned Dravidians for Mohenjo-daro? When Timbuctoo's day was done, would its brightly robed black warriors be converted into supple Byzantines to stock the arcades of Constantinople? Or did they simply discard the old temporaries like so many excess props, stash them in warehouses somewhere, and turn out the appropriate quantities of the new model? He did not know; and once when he had asked Gioia about it she had grown uncomfortable and vague. She did not like him to probe for information, and he suspected it was because she had very little to give. These people did not seem to question the workings of their own world; his curiosities were very twentieth-century of him, he was frequently told, in that gently patronizing way of theirs. As his two little maids patted him with their sponges he thought of asking them where they had served before Chang-an: Rio? Rome?

Haroun al-Raschid's Baghdad? But these fragile girls, he knew, would only giggle and retreat if he tried to question them. Interrogating temporaries was not only improper, but pointless: it was like interrogating one's luggage.

When he was bathed and robed in rich red silks he wandered the pavilion for a little while, admiring the tinkling pendants of green jade dangling on the portico, the lustrous auburn pillars, the rainbow hues of the intricately interwoven girders and brackets that supported the roof. Then, wearying of his solitude, he approached the bamboo curtain at the entrance to Gioia's suite. A porter and one of the maids stood just within. They indicated that he should not enter; but he scowled at them and they melted from him like snowflakes. A trail of incense led him through the pavilion to Gioia's innermost dressing-room. There he halted, just outside the door.

Gioia sat naked with her back to him at an ornate dressing-table of some rare flame-colored wood inlaid with bands of orange and green porcelain. She was studying herself intently in a mirror of polished bronze held by one of her maids: picking through her scalp with her fingernails, as a woman might do who was searching out her gray hairs.

But that seemed strange. Gray hair, on Gioia? On a citizen? A temporary might display some appearance of aging, perhaps, but surely not a citizen. Citizens remained forever young. Gioia looked like a girl. Her face was smooth and unlined, her flesh was firm, her hair was dark: that was true of all of them, every citizen he had ever seen. And yet there was no mistaking what Gioia was doing. She found a hair, frowned, drew it taut, nodded, plucked it. Another. Another. She pressed the tip of her finger to her cheek as if testing it for resilience. She tugged at the skin below her eyes, pulling it downward. Such familiar little gestures of vanity; but so odd here, he thought, in this world of the perpetually young. Gioia, worried about growing old? Had he simply failed to notice the signs of age on her? Or was it that she worked hard behind his back at concealing them? Perhaps that was it. Was he wrong about the citizens, then? Did they age even as the people of less blessed eras had always done, but simply have better ways of hiding it? How old was she, anyway? Thirty? Sixty? Three hundred?

Gioia appeared satisfied now. She waved the mirror away; she rose; she beckoned for her banquet robes. Phillips, still standing unnoticed by the door, studied her with admiration: the small round buttocks, almost but not quite boyish, the elegant line of her spine, the surprising breadth of her shoulders. No, he thought, she is not aging at all. Her body is still like a girl's. She looks as young as on the day they first had met, however long ago that was—he could not say; it was hard to keep track of time here; but he was sure some years had passed since they had come together. Those gray hairs, those wrinkles and sags for which she had searched just now with such desperate intensity, must all be imaginary, mere artifacts of vanity. Even in this remote future epoch, then, vanity was not extinct. He wondered why she was so concerned with the fear of aging. An affectation? Did all these timeless people take some perverse pleasure in fretting over the possibility that they might be growing old? Or was it some private fear of Gioia's, another symptom of the mysterious depression that had come over her in Alexandria?

Not wanting her to think that he had been spying on her, when all he had really intended was to pay her a visit, he slipped silently away to dress for the evening. She came to him an hour later, gorgeously robed, swaddled from chin to ankles in a brocade of brilliant colors shot through with threads of gold, face painted, hair drawn up tightly and fastened with ivory combs: very much the lady of the court. His servants had made him splendid also, a lustrous black surplice embroidered with golden dragons over a sweeping floor-length gown of shining white silk, a necklace and pendant of red coral, a five-cornered gray felt hat that rose in tower upon tower like a ziggurat. Gioia, grinning, touched her fingertips to his cheek. "You look marvelous!" she told him. "Like a grand mandarin!"

"And you like an empress," he said. "Of some distant land: Persia, India. Here to pay a ceremonial visit on the Son of Heaven." An excess of love suffused his spirit, and, catching her lightly by the wrist, he drew her toward him, as close as he could manage it considering how elaborate their costumes were. But as he bent forward and downward, meaning to brush his lips lightly and affectionately against the tip of her nose, he perceived an unexpected strangeness, an anomaly: the coating of white paint that was her makeup seemed oddly to magnify rather than mask the contours of her skin, highlighting and revealing details he had never observed before. He saw a pattern of fine lines radiating from the corners of her eyes, and the unmistakable beginning of a quirk-mark in her cheek just to the left of her mouth, and perhaps the faint indentation of frown-lines in her flawless forehead. A shiver traveled along the nape of his neck. So it was not affectation, then, that had had her studying her mirror so fiercely. Age was in truth beginning to stake its claim on her, despite all that he had come to believe about these people's agelessness. But a moment later he was not so sure. Gioia turned and slid gently half a step back from him—she must have found his stare disturbing—and the lines he had thought he had seen were gone. He searched for them and saw only girlish smoothness once again. A trick of the light? A figment of an overwrought imagination? He was baffled.

"Come," she said. "We mustn't keep the Emperor waiting."

Five mustachioed warriors in armor of white quilting and seven musicians playing cymbals and pipes escorted them to the Hall of the Supreme Ultimate. There they found the full court arrayed: princes and ministers, high officials, yellow-robed monks, a swarm of imperial concubines. In a place of honor to the right of the royal thrones, which rose like gilded scaffolds high above all else, was a little group of stern-faced men in foreign costumes, the ambassadors of Rome and Byzantium, of Arabia and Syria, of Korea, Japan, Tibet, Turkestan. Incense smouldered in enameled braziers. A poet sang a delicate twanging melody, accompanying himself on a small harp. Then the Emperor and Empress entered: two tiny aged people, like waxen images, moving with infinite slowness, taking steps no greater than a child's. There was the sound of trumpets as they ascended their thrones. When the little Emperor was seated—he looked like a doll up there, ancient, faded, shrunken, yet still somehow a figure of extraordinary power—he stretched forth both his hands, and enormous gongs began to sound. It was a scene of astonishing splendor, grand and overpowering.

These are all temporaries, Phillips realized suddenly. He saw only a handful of citizens—eight, ten, possibly as many as a dozen—scattered here and there about the vast room. He knew them by their eyes, dark, liquid, knowing. They were watching not only the imperial spectacle but also Gioia and him; and Gioia, smiling secretly, nodding almost imperceptibly to them, was acknowledging their presence and their interest. But those few were the only ones in here who were autonomous living beings. All the rest—the entire splendid court, the great mandarins and paladins, the officials, the giggling concubines, the haughty and resplendent ambassadors, the aged Emperor and Empress themselves, were simply part of the scenery. Had the world ever seen entertainment on so grand a scale before? All this pomp, all this pageantry, conjured up each night for the amusement of a dozen or so viewers?

At the banquet the little group of citizens sat together at a table apart, a round onyx slab draped with translucent green silk. There turned out to be seventeen of them in all, including Gioia; Gioia appeared to know all of them, though none, so far as he could tell, was a member of her set that he had met before. She did not attempt introductions. Nor was conversation at all possible during the meal: there was a constant astounding roaring din in the room. Three orchestras played at once and there were troupes of strolling musicians also, and a steady stream of monks and their attendants marched back and forth between the tables loudly chanting sutras and waving censers to the deafening accompaniment of drums and gongs. The Emperor did not descend from his throne to join the banquet; he seemed to be asleep, though now and then he waved his hand in time to the music. Gigantic half-naked brown slaves with broad cheekbones and mouths like gaping pockets brought forth the food, peacock tongues and breast of phoenix heaped on mounds of glowing saffron-colored rice, served on frail alabaster plates. For chopsticks they were given slender rods of dark jade. The wine, served in glistening crystal beakers, was thick and sweet, with an aftertaste of raisins, and no beaker was allowed to remain empty for more than a moment.

Phillips felt himself growing dizzy: when the Persian dancers emerged he could not tell whether there were five of them or fifty, and as they performed their intricate whirling routines it seemed to him that their slender muslin-veiled forms were blurring and merging one into another. He felt frightened by their proficiency, and wanted to look away, but he could not. The Chung-nan jugglers that followed them were equally skillful, equally alarming, filling the air with scythes, flaming torches, live animals, rare porcelain vases, pink jade hatchets, silver bells, gilded cups, wagon-wheels, bronze vessels, and never missing a catch. The citizens applauded politely but did not seem impressed. After the jugglers, the dancers returned, performing this time on stilts; the waiters brought platters of steaming meat of a pale lavender color, unfamiliar in taste and texture: filet of camel, perhaps, or haunch of hippopotamus, or possibly some choice chop from a young dragon. There was more wine. Feebly Phillips tried to wave it away, but the servitors were implacable. This was a drier sort, greenish-gold, austere, sharp on the tongue. With it came a silver dish, chilled to a polar coldness, that held shaved ice flavored with some potent smoky-flavored brandy. The jugglers were doing a second turn, he noticed. He thought he was going to be ill. He looked helplessly toward Gioia, who seemed sober but fiercely animated, almost manic, her eyes blazing like rubies. She touched his cheek fondly.

A cool draft blew through the hall: they had opened one entire wall, revealing the garden, the night, the stars. Just outside was a colossal wheel of oiled paper stretched on wooden struts. They must have erected it in the past hour: it stood a hundred fifty feet high or even more, and on it hung lanterns by the thousands, glimmering like giant fireflies. The guests began to leave the hall. Phillips let himself be swept along into the garden, where under a yellow moon strange crook-armed trees with dense black needles loomed ominously. Gioia slipped her arm through his. They went down to a lake of bubbling crimson fluid and watched scarlet flamingo-like birds ten feet tall fastidiously spearing angry-eyed turquoise eels. They stood in awe before a fat-bellied Buddha of gleaming blue tilework, seventy feet high. A horse with a golden mane came prancing by, striking showers of brilliant red sparks wherever its hooves touched the ground. In a grove of lemon trees that seemed to have the power to wave their slender limbs about, Phillips came upon the Emperor, standing by himself and rocking gently back and forth. The old man seized Phillips by the hand and pressed something into his palm, closing his fingers tight about it; when he opened his fist a few moments later he found his palm full of gray irregular pearls. Gioia took them from him and cast them into the air, and they burst like exploding firecrackers, giving off splashes of colored light. A little later, Phillips realized that he was no longer wearing his surplice or his white silken undergown. Gioia was naked too, and she drew him gently down into a carpet of moist blue moss, where they made love until dawn, fiercely at first, then slowly, languidly, dreamily. At sunrise he looked at her tenderly and saw that something was wrong.

"Gioia?" he said doubtfully.

She smiled. "Ah, no. Gioia is with Fenimon tonight. I am Belilala."

"With—Fenimon?"

"They are old friends. She had not seen him in years."

"Ah. I see. And you are—?"

"Belilala," she said again, touching her fingertips to his cheek.

———

It was not unusual, Belilala said. It happened all the time; the only unusual thing was that it had not happened to him before now. Couples formed, traveled together for a while, drifted apart, eventually reunited. It did not mean that Gioia had left him forever. It meant only that just now she chose to be with Fenimon. Gioia would return. In the meanwhile he would not be alone. "You and I met in New Chicago," Belilala told him. "And then we saw each other again in Timbuctoo. Have you forgotten? Oh, yes, I see that you have forgotten!" She laughed prettily; she did not seem at all offended.

She looked enough like Gioia to be her sister. But, then, all the citizens looked more or less alike to him. And apart from their physical resemblance, so he quickly came to realize, Belilala and Gioia were not really very similar. There was a calmness, a deep reservoir of serenity, in Belilala that Gioia, eager and volatile and ever impatient, did not seem to have. Strolling the swarming streets of Chang-an with Belilala, he did not perceive in her any of Gioia's restless feverish need always to know what lay beyond, and beyond, and beyond even that. When they toured the Hsing-ch'ing Palace, Belilala did not after five minutes begin—as Gioia surely would have done—to seek directions to the Fountain of Hsuan-tsung or the Wild Goose Pagoda. Curiosity did not consume Belilala as it did Gioia. Plainly she believed that there would always be enough time for her to see everything she cared to see. There were some days when Belilala chose not to go out at all, but was content merely to remain at their pavilion playing a solitary game with flat porcelain counters, or viewing the flowers of the garden.

He found, oddly, that he enjoyed the respite from Gioia's intense world-swallowing appetites; and yet he longed for her to return. Belilala— beautiful, gentle, tranquil, patient—was too perfect for him. She seemed unreal in her gleaming impeccability, much like one of those Sung celadon vases that appear too flawless to have been thrown and glazed by human hands. There was something a little soulless about her: an immaculate finish outside, emptiness within. Belilala might almost have been a temporary, he thought, though he knew she was not. He could explore the pavilions and palaces of Chang-an with her, he could make graceful conversation with her while they dined, he could certainly enjoy coupling with her; but he could not love her or even contemplate the possibility. It was hard to imagine Belilala worriedly studying herself in a mirror for wrinkles and gray hairs. Belilala would never be any older than she was at this moment; nor could Belilala ever have been any younger. Perfection does not move along an axis of time. But the perfection of Belilala's glossy surface made her inner being impenetrable to him. Gioia was more vulnerable, more obviously flawed—her restlessness, her moodiness, her vanity, her fears—and therefore she was more accessible to his own highly imperfect twentieth-century sensibility.

Occasionally he saw Gioia as he roamed the city, or thought he did. He had a glimpse of her among the miracle-vendors in the Persian Bazaar, and outside the Zoroastrian temple, and again by the goldfish pond in the Serpentine Park. But he was never quite sure that the woman he saw was really Gioia, and he never could get close enough to her to be certain: she had a way of vanishing as he approached, like some mysterious Lorelei luring him onward and onward in a hopeless chase. After a while he came to realize that he was not going to find her until she was ready to be found.

He lost track of time. Weeks, months, years? He had no idea. In this city of exotic luxury, mystery, and magic all was in constant flux and transition and the days had a fitful, unstable quality. Buildings and even whole streets were torn down of an afternoon and re-erected, within days, far away. Grand new pagodas sprouted like toadstools in the night. Citizens came in from Asgard, Alexandria, Timbuctoo, New Chicago, stayed for a time, disappeared, returned. There was a constant round of court receptions, banquets, theatrical events, each one much like the one before. The festivals in honor of past emperors and empresses might have given some form to the year, but they seemed to occur in a random way, the ceremony marking the death of T'ai Tsung coming around twice the same year, so it seemed to him, once in a season of snow and again in high summer, and the one honoring the ascension of the Empress Wu being held twice in a single season. Perhaps he had misunderstood something. But he knew it was no use asking anyone.

————

One day Belilala said unexpectedly, "Shall we go to Mohenjo-daro?"

"I didn't know it was ready for visitors," he replied.

"Oh, yes. For quite some time now."

He hesitated. This had caught him unprepared. Cautiously he said, "Gioia and I were going to go there together, you know."

Belilala smiled amiably, as though the topic under discussion were nothing more than the choice of that evening's restaurant.

"Were you?" she asked.

"It was all arranged while we were still in Alexandria. To go with you instead—I don't know what to tell you, Belilala." Phillips sensed that he was growing terribly flustered. "You know that I'd like to go. With you. But on the other hand I can't help feeling that I shouldn't go there until I'm back with Gioia again. If I ever am." How foolish this sounds, he thought. How clumsy, how adolescent. He found that he was having trouble looking straight at her. Uneasily he said, with a kind of desperation in his voice, "I did promise her—there was a commitment, you understand—a firm agreement that we would go to Mohenjo-daro together—"

"Oh, but Gioia's already there!" said Belilala in the most casual way.

He gaped as though she had punched him.

"*What?*"

"She was one of the first to go, after it opened. Months and months ago. You didn't know?" she asked, sounding surprised, but not very. "You really didn't know?"

That astonished him. He felt bewildered, betrayed, furious. His cheeks grew hot, his mouth gaped. He shook his head again and again, trying to clear it of confusion. It was a moment before he could speak. "Already there?" he said at last. "Without waiting for me? After we had talked about going there together—after we had agreed—"

Belilala laughed. "But how could she resist seeing the newest city? You know how impatient Gioia is!"

"Yes. Yes."

He was stunned. He could barely think.

"Just like all short-timers," Belilala said. "She rushes here, she rushes there. She must have it all, now, now, right away, at once, instantly. You ought never expect her to wait for you for anything for very long: the fit seizes her, and off she goes. Surely you must know that about her by now."

"A short-timer?" He had not heard that term before.

"Yes. You knew that. You must have known that." Belilala flashed her sweetest smile. She showed no sign of comprehending his distress. With a brisk wave of her hand she said, "Well, then, shall we go, you and I? To Mohenjo-daro?"

"Of course," Phillips said bleakly.

"When would you like to leave?"

"Tonight," he said. He paused a moment. "What's a short-timer, Belilala?"

Color came to her cheeks. "Isn't it obvious?" she asked.

Had there ever been a more hideous place on the face of the earth than the city of Mohenjo-daro? Phillips found it difficult to imagine one. Nor could he understand why, out of all the cities that had ever been, these people had chosen to restore this one to existence. More than ever they seemed alien to him, unfathomable, incomprehensible.

From the terrace atop the many-towered citadel he peered down into grim claustrophobic Mohenjo-daro and shivered. The stark, bleak city looked like nothing so much as some prehistoric prison colony. In the manner of an uneasy tortoise it huddled, squat and compact, against the gray monotonous Indus River plain: miles of dark burnt-brick walls enclosing miles of terrifyingly orderly streets, laid out in an awesome, monstrous gridiron pattern of maniacal rigidity. The houses themselves were dismal and forbidding too, clusters of brick cells gathered about small airless courtyards. There were no windows, only small doors that opened not onto the main boulevards but onto the tiny mysterious lanes that ran between the buildings. Who had designed this horrifying metropolis? What harsh, sour souls they must have had, these frightening and frightened folk, creating for themselves in the lush fertile plains of India such a Supreme Soviet of a city!

"How lovely it is," Belilala murmured. "How fascinating!"

He stared at her in amazement.

"Fascinating? Yes," he said. "I suppose so. The same way that the smile of a cobra is fascinating."

"What's a cobra?"

"Poisonous predatory serpent," Phillips told her. "Probably extinct. Or formerly extinct, more likely. It wouldn't surprise me if you people had re-created a few and turned them loose in Mohenjo to make things livelier."

"You sound angry, Charles."

"Do I? That's not how I feel."

"How do you feel, then?"

"I don't know," he said after a long moment's pause. He shrugged. "Lost, I suppose. Very far from home."

"Poor Charles."

"Standing here in this ghastly barracks of a city, listening to you tell me how beautiful it is, I've never felt more alone in my life."

"You miss Gioia very much, don't you?"

He gave her another startled look.

"Gioia has nothing to do with it. She's probably been having ecstasies over the loveliness of Mohenjo just like you. Just like all of you. I suppose I'm the only one who can't find the beauty, the charm. I'm the only one who looks out there and sees only horror, and then wonders why nobody else sees it, why in fact people would set up a place like this for *entertainment*, for *pleasure*—"

Her eyes were gleaming. "Oh, you are angry! You really are!"

"Does that fascinate you too?" he snapped. "A demonstration of genuine primitive emotion? A typical quaint twentieth-century outburst?" He paced the rampart in short quick anguished steps. "Ah. Ah. I think I understand it now, Belilala. Of course: I'm part of your circus, the star of the sideshow. I'm the first experiment in setting up the next stage of it, in fact." Her eyes were wide. The sudden harshness and violence in his voice seemed to be alarming and exciting her at the same time. That angered him even more. Fiercely he went on, "Bringing whole cities back out of time was fun for a while, but it lacks a certain authenticity, eh? For some reason you couldn't bring the inhabitants too; you couldn't just grab a few million prehistorics out of Egypt or Greece or India and dump them down in this era, I suppose because you might have too much trouble controlling them, or because you'd have the problem of disposing of them once you were bored with them. So you had to settle for creating temporaries to populate your ancient cities. But now you've got me. I'm something more real than a temporary, and that's a terrific novelty for you, and novelty is the thing you people crave more than anything else: maybe the *only* thing you crave. And here I am, complicated, unpredictable, edgy, capable of anger, fear, sadness, love, and all those other formerly extinct things. Why settle for picturesque architecture when you can observe picturesque emotion, too? What fun I must be for all of you! And if you decide that I was really interesting, maybe you'll ship me back where I came from and check out a few other ancient types—a Roman gladiator, maybe, or a Renaissance pope, or even a Neanderthal or two—"

"Charles," she said tenderly. "Oh, Charles, Charles, Charles, how lonely you must be, how lost, how troubled! Will you ever forgive me? Will you ever forgive us all?"

Once more he was astounded by her. She sounded entirely sincere, altogether sympathetic. Was she? Was she, really? He was not sure he had ever had a sign of genuine caring from any of them before, not even Gioia. Nor could he bring himself to trust Belilala now. He was afraid of her, afraid of all of them, of their brittleness, their slyness, their elegance. He wished he could go to her and have her take him in her arms; but he felt too much the shaggy prehistoric just now to be able to risk asking that comfort of her.

He turned away and began to walk around the rim of the citadel's massive wall.

"Charles?"

"Let me alone for a little while," he said.

He walked on. His forehead throbbed and there was a pounding in his chest. All stress systems going full blast, he thought: secret glands dumping gallons of inflammatory substances into his bloodstream. The heat, the inner confusion, the repellent look of this place—

Try to understand, he thought. Relax. Look about you. Try to enjoy your holiday in Mohenjo-daro.

He leaned warily outward, over the edge of the wall. He had never seen a wall like this; it must be forty feet thick at the base, he guessed, perhaps even more, and every brick perfectly shaped, meticulously set. Beyond the great rampart, marshes ran almost to the edge of the city, although close by the wall the swamps had been dammed and drained for agriculture. He saw lithe brown farmers down there, busy with their wheat and barley and peas. Cattle and buffaloes grazed a little farther out. The air was heavy, dank, humid. All was still. From somewhere close at hand came the sound of a droning, whining stringed instrument and a steady insistent chanting.

Gradually a sort of peace pervaded him. His anger subsided. He felt himself beginning to grow calm again. He looked back at the city, the rigid interlocking streets, the maze of inner lanes, the millions of courses of precise brickwork.

It is a miracle, he told himself, that this city is here in this place and at this time. And it is a miracle that I am here to see it.

Caught for a moment by the magic within the bleakness, he thought he began to understand Belilala's awe and delight, and he wished now that he had not spoken to her so sharply. The city was alive. Whether it was the actual Mohenjo-daro of thousands upon thousands of years ago, ripped from the past by some wondrous hook, or simply a cunning reproduction, did not matter at all. Real or not, this was the true Mohenjo-daro. It had been dead and now, for the moment, it was alive again. These people, these *citizens*, might be trivial, but reconstructing Mohenjo-daro was no trivial achievement. And that the city that had been reconstructed was oppressive and sinister-looking was unimportant. No one was compelled to live in Mohenjo-daro any more. Its time had come and gone, long ago; those little dark-skinned peasants and craftsmen and merchants down there were mere temporaries, mere inanimate things, conjured up like zombies to enhance the illusion. They did not need his pity. Nor did he need to pity himself. He knew that he should be grateful for the chance to behold these things. Some day, when this dream had ended and his hosts had returned him to the world of subways and computers and income tax and television networks, he would think of Mohenjo-daro as he had once beheld it, lofty walls of tightly woven dark brick under a heavy sky, and he would remember only its beauty.

Glancing back, he searched for Belilala and could not for a moment find her. Then he caught sight of her carefully descending a narrow staircase that angled down the inner face of the citadel wall.

"Belilala!" he called.

She paused and looked his way, shading her eyes from the sun with her hand. "Are you all right?"

"Where are you going?"

"To the baths," she said. "Do you want to come?"

He nodded. "Yes. Wait for me, will you? I'll be right there." He began to run toward her along the top of the wall.

————

The baths were attached to the citadel: a great open tank the size of a large swimming pool, lined with bricks set on edge in gypsum mortar and waterproofed with asphalt, and eight smaller tanks just north of it in a kind of covered arcade. He supposed that in ancient times the whole complex had had some ritual purpose, the large tank used by common folk and the small chambers set aside for the private ablutions of priests or nobles. Now the baths were maintained, it seemed, entirely for the pleasure of visiting citizens. As Phillips came up the passageway that led to the main bath he saw fifteen or twenty of them lolling in the water or padding languidly about, while temporaries of the dark-skinned Mohenjo-daro type served them drinks and pungent little morsels of spiced meat as though this were some sort of luxury resort. Which was, he realized, exactly what it was. The temporaries wore white cotton loincloths; the citizens were naked. In his former life he had encountered that sort of casual public nudity a few times on visits to California and the south of France, and it had made him mildly uneasy. But he was growing accustomed to it here.

The changing-rooms were tiny brick cubicles connected by rows of closely placed steps to the courtyard that surrounded the central tank. They entered one and Belilala swiftly slipped out of the loose cotton robe that she had worn since their arrival that morning. With arms folded she stood leaning against the wall, waiting for him. After a moment he dropped his own robe and followed her outside. He felt a little giddy, sauntering around naked in the open like this.

On the way to the main bathing area they passed the private baths. None of them seemed to be occupied. They were elegantly constructed chambers, with finely jointed brick floors and carefully designed runnels to drain excess water into the passageway that led to the primary drain. Phillips was struck with admiration for the cleverness of the prehistoric engineers. He peered into this chamber and that to see how the conduits and ventilating ducts were arranged, and when he came to the last room in the sequence he was surprised and embarrassed to discover that it was in use. A brawny grinning man, big-muscled, deep-chested, with exuberantly flowing shoulder-length red hair and a flamboyant, sharply tapering beard, was thrashing about merrily with two women in the small tank. Phillips had a quick glimpse of a lively tangle of arms, legs, breasts, buttocks.

"Sorry," he muttered. His cheeks reddened. Quickly he ducked out, blurting apologies as he went. "Didn't realize the room was occupied—no wish to intrude—"

Belilala had proceeded on down the passageway. Phillips hurried after her. From behind him came peals of cheerful raucous booming laughter and high-pitched giggling and the sound of splashing water. Probably they had not even noticed him.

He paused a moment, puzzled, playing back in his mind that one startling glimpse. Something was not right. Those women, he was fairly sure, were citizens: little slender elfin dark-haired girlish creatures, the standard model. But the man? That great curling sweep of red hair? Not a citizen. Citizens did not affect shoulder-length hair. And *red*? Nor had he ever seen a citizen so burly, so powerfully muscular. Or one with a beard. But he could hardly be a temporary, either. Phillips could conceive no reason why there would be so Anglo-Saxon-looking a temporary at Mohenjo-daro; and it was unthinkable for a temporary to be frolicking like that with citizens, anyway.

"Charles?"

He looked up ahead. Belilala stood at the end of the passageway, outlined in a nimbus of brilliant sunlight. "Charles?" she said again. "Did you lose your way?"

"I'm right here behind you," he said. "I'm coming."

"Who did you meet in there?"

"A man with a beard."

"With a what?"

"A beard," he said. "Red hair growing on his face. I wonder who he is."

"Nobody I know," said Belilala. "The only one I know with hair on his face is you. And yours is black, and you shave it off every day." She laughed. "Come along, now! I see some friends by the pool!"

He caught up with her and they went hand in hand out into the courtyard. Immediately a waiter glided up to them, an obsequious little temporary with a tray of drinks. Phillips waved it away and headed for the pool. He felt terribly exposed: he imagined that the citizens disporting themselves here were staring intently at him, studying his hairy primitive body as though he were some mythical creature, a Minotaur, a werewolf, summoned up for their amusement. Belilala drifted off to talk to someone and he slipped into the water, grateful for the concealment it offered. It was deep, warm, comforting. With swift powerful strokes he breast-stroked from one end to the other.

A citizen perched elegantly on the pool's rim smiled at him. "Ah, so you've come at last, Charles!" Char-less. Two syllables. Someone from Gioia's set: Stengard, Hawk, Aramayne? He could not remember which one. They were all so much alike.

Phillips returned the man's smile in a half-hearted, tentative way. He searched for something to say and finally asked, "Have you been here long?"

"Weeks. Perhaps months. What a splendid achievement this city is, eh, Charles? Such utter unity of mood—such a total statement of a uniquely single-minded esthetic—"

"Yes. Single-minded is the word," Phillips said drily.

"Gioia's word, actually. Gioia's phrase. I was merely quoting."

*Gioia.* He felt as if he had been stabbed.

"You've spoken to Gioia lately?" he said.

"Actually, no. It was Hekna who saw her. You do remember Hekna, eh?" He nodded toward two naked women standing on the brick platform that bordered the pool, chatting, delicately nibbling morsels of meat. They could have been twins. "There is Hekna, with your Belilala." Hekna, yes. So this must be Hawk, Phillips thought, unless there has been some recent shift of couples. "How sweet she is, your Belilala," Hawk said. "Gioia chose very wisely when she picked her for you."

Another stab: a much deeper one. "Is that how it was?" he said. "Gioia *picked* Belilala for me?"

"Why, of course!" Hawk seemed surprised. It went without saying, evidently. "What did you think? That Gioia would merely go off and leave you to fend for yourself?"

"Hardly. Not Gioia."

"She's very tender, very gentle, isn't she?"

"You mean Belilala? Yes, very," said Phillips carefully. "A dear woman, a wonderful woman. But of course I hope to get together with Gioia again soon." He paused. "They say she's been in Mohenjo-daro almost since it opened."

"She was here, yes."

"*Was?*"

"Oh, you know Gioia," Hawk said lightly. "She's moved along by now, naturally."

Phillips leaned forward. "Naturally," he said. Tension thickened his voice. "Where has she gone this time?"

"Timbuctoo, I think. Or New Chicago. I forget which one it was. She was telling us that she hoped to be in Timbuctoo for the closing-down party. But then Fenimon had some pressing reason for going to New Chicago. I can't remember what they decided to do." Hawk gestured sadly. "Either way, a pity that she left Mohenjo before the new visitor came. She had such a rewarding time with you, after all: I'm sure she'd have found much to learn from him also."

The unfamiliar term twanged an alarm deep in Phillips' consciousness. "*Visitor?*" he said, angling his head sharply toward Hawk. "What visitor do you mean?"

"You haven't met him yet? Oh, of course, you've only just arrived."

Phillips moistened his lips. "I think I may have seen him. Long red hair? Beard like this?"

"That's the one! Willoughby, he's called. He's—what?—a Viking, a pirate, something like that. Tremendous vigor and force. Remarkable person. We should have many more visitors, I think. They're far superior to temporaries, everyone agrees. Talking with a temporary is a little like talking to one's self, wouldn't you say? They give you no significant illumination. But a visitor—someone like this Willoughby—or like you, Charles—a visitor can be truly enlightening, a visitor can transform one's view of reality—"

"Excuse me," Phillips said. A throbbing began behind his forehead. "Perhaps we can continue this conversation later, yes?" He put the flats of his hands against the hot brick of the platform and hoisted himself swiftly from the pool. "At dinner, maybe—or afterward—yes? All right?" He set off at a quick half-trot back toward the passageway that led to the private baths.

———

As he entered the roofed part of the structure his throat grew dry, his breath suddenly came short. He padded quickly up the hall and peered into the little bath-chamber. The bearded man was still there, sitting up in the tank, breast-high above the water, with one arm around each of the women. His eyes gleamed with fiery intensity in the dimness. He was grinning in marvelous self-satisfaction; he seemed to brim with intensity, confidence, gusto.

Let him be what I think he is, Phillips prayed. I have been alone among these people long enough.

"May I come in?" he asked.

"Aye, fellow!" cried the man in the tub thunderously. "By my troth, come ye in, and bring your lass as well! God's teeth, I wot there's room aplenty for more folk in this tub than we!"

At that great uproarious outcry Phillips felt a powerful surge of joy. What a joyous rowdy voice! How rich, how lusty, how totally uncitizen-like!

And those oddly archaic words! *God's teeth? By my troth?* What sort of talk was that? What else but the good pure sonorous Elizabethan diction! Certainly it had something of the roll and fervor of Shakespeare about it. And spoken with—an Irish brogue, was it? No, not quite: it was English, but English spoken in no manner Phillips had ever heard.

Citizens did not speak that way. But a *visitor* might.

So it was true. Relief flooded Phillips' soul. Not alone, then! Another relict of a former age—another wanderer—a companion in chaos, a brother in adversity—a fellow voyager, tossed even farther than he had been by the tempests of time—

The bearded man grinned heartily and beckoned to Phillips with a toss of his head. "Well, join us, join us, man! 'Tis good to see an English face again, amidst all these Moors and rogue Portugals! But what have ye done with thy lass? One can never have enough wenches, d'ye not agree?"

The force and vigor of him were extraordinary, almost too much so. He roared, he bellowed, he boomed. He was so very much what he ought to be that he seemed more a character out of some old pirate movie than anything else, so blustering, so real, that he seemed unreal. A stage-Elizabethan, larger than life, a boisterous young Falstaff without the belly.

Hoarsely, Phillips said, "Who are you?"

"Why, Ned Willoughby's son Francis am I, of Plymouth. Late of the service of Her Most Protestant Majesty, but most foully abducted by the powers of darkness and cast away among these blackamoor Hindus, or whatever they be. And thyself?"

"Charles Phillips." After a moment's uncertainty he added, "I'm from New York."

"*New* York? What place is that? In faith, man, I know it not!"

"A city in America."

"A city in America, forsooth! What a fine fancy that is! In America, you say, and not on the Moon, or perchance underneath the sea?" To the women Willoughby said, "D'ye hear him? He comes from a city in America! With the face of an Englishman, though not the manner of one, and not quite the proper sort of speech. A city in America! A *city*. God's blood, what will I hear next?"

Phillips trembled. Awe was beginning to take hold of him. This man had walked the streets of Shakespeare's London, perhaps. He had clinked canisters with Marlowe or Essex or Walter Raleigh; he had watched the ships of the Armada wallowing in the Channel. It strained Phillips' spirit to think of it. This strange dream in which he found himself was compounding its strangeness now. He felt like a weary swimmer assailed by heavy surf, winded, dazed. The hot close atmosphere of the baths was driving him toward vertigo. There could be no doubt of it any longer. He was not the only primitive—the only *visitor*—who was wandering loose in this fiftieth century. They were conducting other experiments as well. He gripped the sides of the door to steady himself and said, "When you speak of Her Most Protestant Majesty, it's Elizabeth the First you mean, is that not so?"

"Elizabeth, aye! As to the First, that is true enough, but why trouble to name her thus? There is but one. First and Last, I do trow, and God save her, there is no other!"

Phillips studied the other man warily. He knew that he must proceed with care. A misstep at this point and he would forfeit any chance that Willoughby would take him seriously. How much metaphysical bewilderment, after all, could this man absorb? What did he know, what had anyone of his time known, of past and present and future and the notion that one might somehow move from one to the other as readily as one would go from Surrey to Kent? That was a twentieth-century idea, late nineteenth at best, a fantastical speculation that very likely no one had even considered before Wells had sent his time traveler off to stare at the reddened sun of the earth's last twilight. Willoughby's world was a world of Protestants and Catholics, of kings and queens, of tiny sailing vessels, of swords at the hip and ox-carts on the road: that world seemed to Phillips far more alien and distant than was this world of citizens and temporaries. The risk that Willoughby would not begin to understand him was great.

But this man and he were natural allies against a world they had never made. Phillips chose to take the risk.

"Elizabeth the First is the queen you serve," he said. "There will be another of her name in England, in due time. Has already been, in fact."

Willoughby shook his head like a puzzled lion. "Another Elizabeth, d'ye say?"

"A second one, and not much like the first. Long after your Virgin Queen, this one. She will reign in what you think of as the days to come. That I know without doubt."

The Englishman peered at him and frowned. "You see the future? Are you a soothsayer, then? A necromancer, mayhap? Or one of the very demons that brought me to this place?"

"Not at all," Phillips said gently. "Only a lost soul, like yourself." He stepped into the little room and crouched by the side of the tank. The two citizen-women were staring at him in bland fascination. He ignored them. To Willoughby he said, "Do you have any idea where you are?"

The Englishman had guessed, rightly enough, that he was in India: "I do believe these little brown Moorish folk are of the Hindu sort," he said. But that was as far as his comprehension of what had befallen him could go.

It had not occurred to him that he was no longer living in the sixteenth century. And of course he did not begin to suspect that this strange and somber brick city in which he found himself was a wanderer out of an era even more remote than his own. Was there any way, Phillips wondered, of explaining that to him?

He had been here only three days. He thought it was devils that had carried him off. "While I slept did they come for me," he said. "Mephistophilis Sathanas his henchmen seized me—God alone can say why—and swept me in a moment out to this torrid realm from England, where I had reposed among friends and family. For I was between one voyage and the next, you must understand, awaiting Drake and his ship—you know Drake, the glorious Francis? God's blood, there's a mariner for ye! We were to go to the Main again, he and I, but instead here I be in this other place—" Willoughby leaned close and said, "I ask you, soothsayer, how can it be, that a man go to sleep in Plymouth and wake up in India? It is passing strange, is it not?"

"That it is," Phillips said.

"But he that is in the dance must needs dance on, though he do but hop, eh? So do I believe." He gestured toward the two citizen-women. "And therefore to console myself in this pagan land I have found me some sport among these little Portugal women—"

"Portugal?" said Phillips.

"Why, what else can they be, but Portugals? Is it not the Portugals who control all these coasts of India? See, the people are of two sorts here, the blackamoors and the others, the fair-skinned ones, the lords and masters who lie here in these baths. If they be not Hindus, and I think they are not, then Portugals is what they must be." He laughed and pulled the women against himself and rubbed his hands over their breasts as though they were fruits on a vine. "Is that not what you are, you little naked shameless Papist wenches? A pair of Portugals, eh?"

They giggled, but did not answer.

"No," Phillips said. "This is India, but not the India you think you know. And these women are not Portuguese."

"Not Portuguese?" Willoughby said, baffled.

"No more so than you. I'm quite certain of that."

Willoughby stroked his beard. "I do admit I found them very odd, for Portugals. I have heard not a syllable of their Portugee speech on their lips. And it is strange also that they run naked as Adam and Eve in these baths, and allow me free plunder of their women, which is not the way of Portugals at home, God wot. But I thought me, this is India, they choose to live in another fashion here—"

"No," Phillips said. "I tell you, these are not Portuguese, nor any other people of Europe who are known to you."

"Prithee, who are they, then?"

Do it delicately, now, Phillips warned himself. *Delicately.*

He said, "It is not far wrong to think of them as spirits of some kind—demons, even. Or sorcerers who have magicked us out of our proper places in the world." He paused, groping for some means to share with Willoughby, in a way that Willoughby might grasp, this mystery that had enfolded them. He drew a deep breath. "They've taken us not only across the sea," he said, "but across the years as well. We have both been hauled, you and I, far into the days that are to come."

Willoughby gave him a look of blank bewilderment.

"Days that are to come? Times yet unborn, d'ye mean? Why, I comprehend none of that!"

"Try to understand. We're both castaways in the same boat, man! But there's no way we can help each other if I can't make you see—"

Shaking his head, Willoughby muttered, "In faith, good friend, I find your words the merest folly. Today is today, and tomorrow is tomorrow, and how can a man step from one to t'other until tomorrow be turned into today?"

"I have no idea," said Phillips. Struggle was apparent on Willoughby's face; but plainly he could perceive no more than the haziest outline of what Phillips was driving at, if that much. "But this I know," he went on, "that your world and all that was in it is dead and gone. And so is mine, though I was born four hundred years after you, in the time of the second Elizabeth."

Willoughby snorted scornfully. "Four hundred—"

"You must believe me!"

"Nay! Nay!"

"It's the truth. Your time is only history to me. And mine and yours are history to *them*—ancient history. They call us visitors, but what we are is captives." Phillips felt himself quivering in the intensity of his effort. He was aware how insane this must sound to Willoughby. It was beginning to sound insane to him. "They've stolen us out of our proper times—seizing us like gypsies in the night—"

"Fie, man! You rave with lunacy!"

Phillips shook his head. He reached out and seized Willoughby tightly by the wrist. "I beg you, listen to me!" The citizen-women were watching closely, whispering to one another behind their hands, laughing. "Ask them!" Phillips cried. "Make them tell you what century this is! The sixteenth, do you think? Ask them!"

"What century could it be, but the sixteenth of our Lord?"

"They will tell you it is the fiftieth."

Willoughby looked at him pityingly. "Man, man, what a sorry thing thou art! The fiftieth, indeed!" He laughed. "Fellow, listen to me, now. There is but one Elizabeth, safe upon her throne in Westminster. This is India. The year is Anno 1591. Come, let us you and I steal a ship from these Portugals, and make our way back to England, and peradventure you may get from there to your America—"

"There is no England."

"Ah, can you say that and not be mad?"

"The cities and nations we knew are gone. These people live like magicians, Francis." There was no use holding anything back now, Phillips thought leadenly. He knew that he had lost. "They conjure up places of long ago, and build them here and there to suit their fancy, and when they are bored with them they destroy them, and start anew. There is no England. Europe is empty, featureless, void. Do you know what cities there are? There are only five in all the world. There is Alexandria of Egypt. There is Timbuctoo in Africa. There is New Chicago in America. There is a great city in China—in Cathay, I suppose you would say. And there is this place, which they call Mohenjo-daro, and which is far more ancient than Greece, than Rome, than Babylon."

Quietly Willoughby said, "Nay. This is mere absurdity. You say we are in some far tomorrow, and then you tell me we are dwelling in some city of long ago."

"A conjuration, only," Phillips said in desperation. "A likeness of that city. Which these folk have fashioned somehow for their own amusement. Just as we are here, you and I: to amuse them. Only to amuse them."

"You are completely mad."

"Come with me, then. Talk with the citizens by the great pool. Ask them what year this is; ask them about England; ask them how you come to be here." Once again Phillips grasped Willoughby's wrist. "We should be allies. If we work together, perhaps we can discover some way to get ourselves out of this place, and—"

"Let me be, fellow."

"Please—"

"Let me be!" roared Willoughby, and pulled his arm free. His eyes were stark with rage. Rising in the tank, he looked about furiously as though searching for a weapon. The citizen-women shrank back away from him, though at the same time they seemed captivated by the big man's fierce outburst. "Go to, get you to Bedlam! Let me be, madman! Let me be!"

————

Dismally Phillips roamed the dusty unpaved streets of Mohenjo-daro alone for hours. His failure with Willoughby had left him bleak-spirited and somber; he had hoped to stand back to back with the Elizabethan against the citizens, but he saw now that that was not to be. He had bungled things; or, more likely, it had been impossible ever to bring Willoughby to see the truth of their predicament.

In the stifling heat he went at random through the confusing congested lanes of flat-roofed, windowless houses and blank, featureless walls until he emerged into a broad marketplace. The life of the city swirled madly around him: the pseudo-life, rather, the intricate interactions of the thousands of temporaries who were nothing more than wind-up dolls set in motion to provide the illusion that pre-Vedic India was still a going concern. Here vendors sold beautiful little carved stone seals portraying tigers and monkeys and strange humped cattle, and women bargained vociferously with craftsmen for ornaments of ivory, gold, copper, and bronze. Weary-looking women squatted behind immense mounds of newly made pottery, pinkish-red with black designs. No one paid any attention to him. He was the outsider here, neither citizen nor temporary. They belonged.

He went on, passing the huge granaries where workmen ceaselessly unloaded carts of wheat and others pounded grain on great circular brick platforms. He drifted into a public restaurant thronging with joyless silent people standing elbow to elbow at small brick counters, and was given a flat round piece of bread, a sort of tortilla or chapatti, in which was stuffed some spiced mincemeat that stung his lips like fire. Then he moved onward, down a wide, shallow, timbered staircase into the lower part of the city, where the peasantry lived in cell-like rooms packed together as though in hives.

It was an oppressive city, but not a squalid one. The intensity of the concern with sanitation amazed him: wells and fountains and public privies everywhere, and brick drains running from each building, leading to covered cesspools. There was none of the open sewage and pestilent gutters that he knew still could be found in the India of his own time. He wondered whether ancient Mohenjo-daro had in truth been so fastidious. Perhaps the citizens had redesigned the city to suit their own ideals of cleanliness. No: most likely what he saw was authentic, he decided, a function of the same obsessive discipline that had given the city its rigidity of form. If Mohenjo-daro had been a verminous filthy hole, the citizens probably would have re-created it in just that way, and loved it for its fascinating, reeking filth.

Not that he had ever noticed an excessive concern with authenticity on the part of the citizens; and Mohenjo-daro, like all the other restored cities he had visited, was full of the usual casual anachronisms. Phillips saw images of Shiva and Krishna here and there on the walls of buildings he took to be temples, and the benign face of the mother-goddess Kali loomed in the plazas. Surely those deities had arisen in India long after the collapse of the Mohenjo-daro civilization. Were the citizens indifferent to such matters of chronology? Or did they take a certain naughty pleasure in mixing the eras—a mosque and a church in Greek Alexandria, Hindu gods in prehistoric Mohenjo-daro? Perhaps their records of the past had become contaminated with errors over the thousands of years. He would not have been surprised to see banners bearing portraits of Gandhi and Nehru being carried in procession through the streets. And there were phantasms and chimeras at large here again too, as if the citizens were untroubled by the boundary between history and myth: little fat elephant-headed Ganeshas blithely plunging their trunks into water-fountains, a six-armed, three-headed woman sunning herself on a brick terrace. Why not? Surely that was the motto of these people: *Why not, why not, why not?* They could do as they pleased, and they did. Yet Gioia had said to him, long ago, "Limits are very important." In what, Phillips wondered, did they limit themselves, other than the number of their cities? Was there a quota, perhaps, on the number of "visitors" they allowed themselves to kidnap from the past? Until today he had thought he was the only one; now he knew there was at least one other; possibly there were more elsewhere, a step or two ahead or behind him, making the circuit with the citizens who traveled endlessly from New Chicago to Chang-an to Alexandria. We should join forces, he thought, and compel them to send us back to our rightful eras. *Compel?* How? File a class-action suit, maybe? Demonstrate in the streets? Sadly he thought of his failure to make common cause with Willoughby. We are natural allies, he thought. Together perhaps we might have won some compassion from these people. But to Willoughby it must be literally unthinkable that Good Queen Bess and her subjects were sealed away on the far side of a barrier hundreds of centuries thick. He would prefer to believe that England was just a few months' voyage away around the Cape of Good Hope, and that all he need do was commandeer a ship and set sail for home. Poor Willoughby: probably he would never see his home again.

The thought came to Phillips suddenly:

*Neither will you.*

And then, after it:

*If you could go home, would you really want to?*

One of the first things he had realized here was that he knew almost nothing substantial about his former existence. His mind was well stocked with details on life in twentieth-century New York, to be sure; but of himself he could say not much more than that he was Charles Phillips and had come from 1984. Profession? Age? Parents' names? Did he have a wife? Children? A cat, a dog, hobbies? No data: none. Possibly the citizens had stripped such things from him when they brought him here, to spare him from the pain of separation. They might be capable of that kindness. Knowing so little of what he had lost, could he truly say that he yearned for it? Willoughby seemed to remember much more of his former life, and longed for it all the more. He was spared that. Why not stay here, and go on and on from city to city, sightseeing all of time past as the citizens conjured it back into being? Why not? Why not? The chances were that he had no choice about it, anyway.

He made his way back up toward the citadel and to the baths once more. He felt a little like a ghost, haunting a city of ghosts.

Belilala seemed unaware that he had been gone for most of the day. She sat by herself on the terrace of the baths, placidly sipping some thick milky beverage that had been sprinkled with a dark spice. He shook his head when she offered him some.

"Do you remember I mentioned that I saw a man with red hair and a beard this morning?" Phillips said. "He's a visitor. Hawk told me that."

"Is he?" Belilala asked.

"From a time about four hundred years before mine. I talked with him. He thinks he was brought here by demons." Phillips gave her a searching look. "I'm a visitor too, isn't that so?"

"Of course, love."

"And how was *I* brought here? By demons also?"

Belilala smiled indifferently. "You'd have to ask someone else. Hawk, perhaps. I haven't looked into these things very deeply."

"I see. Are there many visitors here, do you know?"

A languid shrug. "Not many, no, not really. I've only heard of three or four besides you. There may be others by now, I suppose." She rested her hand lightly on his. "Are you having a good time in Mohenjo, Charles?"

He let her question pass as though he had not heard it.

"I asked Hawk about Gioia," he said.

"Oh?"

"He told me that she's no longer here, that she's gone on to Tim-buctoo or New Chicago, he wasn't sure which."

"That's quite likely. As everybody knows, Gioia rarely stays in the same place very long."

Phillips nodded. "You said the other day that Gioia is a short-timer. That means she's going to grow old and die, doesn't it?"

"I thought you understood that, Charles."

"Whereas you will not age? Nor Hawk, nor Stengard, nor any of the rest of your set?"

"We will live as long as we wish," she said. "But we will not age, no."

"What makes a person a short-timer?"

"They're born that way, I think. Some missing gene, some extra gene—I don't actually know. It's extremely uncommon. Nothing can be done to help them. It's very slow, the aging. But it can't be halted."

Phillips nodded. "That must be very disagreeable," he said. "To find yourself one of the few people growing old in a world where everyone stays young. No wonder Gioia is so impatient. No wonder she runs around from place to place. No wonder she attached herself so quickly to the barbaric hairy visitor from the twentieth century, who comes from a time when *everybody* was a short-timer. She and I have something in common, wouldn't you say?"

"In a manner of speaking, yes."

"We understand aging. We understand death. Tell me: is Gioia likely to die very soon, Belilala?"

"Soon? Soon?" She gave him a wide-eyed child-like stare. "What is soon? How can I say? What you think of as soon and what I think of as soon are not the same things, Charles." Then her manner changed: she seemed to be hearing what he was saying for the first time. Softly she said, "No, no, Charles. I don't think she will die very soon."

"When she left me in Chang-an, was it because she had become bored with me?"

Belilala shook her head. "She was simply restless. It had nothing to do with you. She was never bored with you."

"Then I'm going to go looking for her. Wherever she may be, Timbuctoo, New Chicago, I'll find her. Gioia and I belong together."

"Perhaps you do," said Belilala. "Yes. Yes, I think you really do." She sounded altogether unperturbed, unrejected, unbereft. "By all means, Charles. Go to her. Follow her. Find her. Wherever she may be."

———

They had already begun dismantling Timbuctoo when Phillips got there. While he was still high overhead, his flitterflitter hovering above the dusty tawny plain where the River Niger met the sands of the Sahara, a surge of keen excitement rose in him as he looked down at the square gray flat-roofed mud brick buildings of the great desert capital. But when he landed he found gleaming metal-skinned robots swarming everywhere, a horde of them scuttling about like giant shining insects, pulling the place apart.

He had not known about the robots before. So that was how all these miracles were carried out, Phillips realized: an army of obliging machines. He imagined them bustling up out of the earth whenever their services were needed, emerging from some sterile subterranean storehouse to put together Venice or Thebes or Knossos or Houston or whatever place was required, down to the finest detail, and then at some later time returning to undo everything that they had fashioned. He watched them now, diligently pulling down the adobe walls, demolishing the heavy metal-studded gates, bulldozing the amazing labyrinth of alleyways and thoroughfares, sweeping away the market. On his last visit to Timbuctoo that market had been crowded with a horde of veiled Tuaregs and swaggering Moors, black Sudanese, shrewd-faced Syrian traders, all of them busily dickering for camels, horses, donkeys, slabs of salt, huge green melons, silver bracelets, splendid vellum Korans. They were all gone now, that picturesque crowd of swarthy temporaries. Nor were there any citizens to be seen. The dust of destruction choked the air. One of the robots came up to Phillips and said in a dry crackling insect-voice, "You ought not to be here. This city is closed."

He stared at the flashing, buzzing band of scanners and sensors across the creature's glittering tapered snout. "I'm trying to find someone, a citizen who may have been here recently. Her name is—"

"This city is closed," the robot repeated inexorably.

They would not let him stay as much as an hour. There is no food here, the robot said, no water, no shelter. This is not a place any longer. You may not stay. You may not stay. You may not stay.

*This is not a place any longer.*

Perhaps he could find her in New Chicago, then. He took to the air again, soaring northward and westward over the vast emptiness. The land below him curved away into the hazy horizon, bare, sterile. What had they done with the vestiges of the world that had gone before? Had they turned their gleaming metal beetles loose to clean everything away? Were there no ruins of genuine antiquity anywhere? No scrap of Rome, no shard of Jerusalem, no stump of Fifth Avenue? It was all so barren down there: an empty stage, waiting for its next set to be built. He flew on a great arc across the jutting hump of Africa and on into what he supposed was southern Europe: the little vehicle did all the work, leaving him to doze or stare as he wished. Now and again he saw another flitter-flitter pass by, far away, a dark distant winged teardrop outlined against the hard clarity of the sky. He wished there was some way of making radio contact with them, but he had no idea how to go about it. Not that he had anything he wanted to say; he wanted only to hear a human voice. He was utterly isolated. He might just as well have been the last living man on Earth. He closed his eyes and thought of Gioia.

———

"Like this?" Phillips asked. In an ivory-paneled oval room sixty stories above the softly glowing streets of New Chicago he touched a small cool plastic canister to his upper lip and pressed the stud at its base. He heard a foaming sound; and then blue vapor rose to his nostrils.

"Yes," Cantilena said. "That's right."

He detected a faint aroma of cinnamon, cloves, and something that might almost have been broiled lobster. Then a spasm of dizziness hit him and visions rushed through his head: Gothic cathedrals, the Pyramids, Central Park under fresh snow, the harsh brick warrens of Mohenjo-daro, and fifty thousand other places all at once, a wild rollercoaster ride through space and time. It seemed to go on for centuries. But finally his head cleared and he looked about, blinking, realizing that the whole thing had taken only a moment. Cantilena still stood at his elbow. The other citizens in the room—fifteen, twenty of them—had scarcely moved. The strange little man with the celadon skin over by the far wall continued to stare at him.

"Well?" Cantilena asked. "What did you think?"

"Incredible."

"And very authentic. It's an actual New Chicagoan drug. The exact formula. Would you like another?"

"Not just yet," Phillips said uneasily. He swayed and had to struggle for his balance. Sniffing that stuff might not have been such a wise idea, he thought.

He had been in New Chicago a week, or perhaps it was two, and he was still suffering from the peculiar disorientation that that city always aroused in him. This was the fourth time that he had come here, and it had been the same every time. New Chicago was the only one of the re-constructed cities of this world that in its original incarnation had existed *after* his own era. To him it was an outpost of the incomprehensible future; to the citizens it was a quaint simulacrum of the archaeological past. That paradox left him aswirl with impossible confusions and tensions.

What had happened to *old* Chicago was of course impossible for him to discover. Vanished without a trace, that was clear: no Water Tower, no Marina City, no Hancock Center, no Tribune building, not a fragment, not an atom. But it was hopeless to ask any of the million-plus inhabitants of New Chicago about their city's predecessor. They were only temporaries; they knew no more than they had to know, and all that they had to know was how to go through the motions of whatever it was that they did by way of creating the illusion that this was a real city. They had no need of knowing ancient history.

Nor was he likely to find out anything from a citizen, of course. Citizens did not seem to bother much about scholarly matters. Phillips had no reason to think that the world was anything other than an amusement park to them. Somewhere, certainly, there had to be those who specialized in the serious study of the lost civilizations of the past—for how, otherwise, would these uncanny reconstructed cities be brought into being? "The planners," he had once heard Nissandra or Aramayne say, "are already deep into their Byzantium research." But who were the planners? He had no idea. For all he knew, they were the robots. Perhaps the robots were the real masters of this whole era, who created the cities not primarily for the sake of amusing the citizens but in their own diligent attempt to comprehend the life of the world that had passed away. A wild speculation, yes; but not without some plausibility, he thought.

He felt oppressed by the party gaiety all about him. "I need some air," he said to Cantilena, and headed toward the window. It was the merest crescent, but a breeze came through. He looked out at the strange city below.

New Chicago had nothing in common with the old one but its name. They had built it, at least, along the western shore of a large inland lake that might even be Lake Michigan, although when he had flown over it had seemed broader and less elongated than the lake he remembered. The city itself was a lacy fantasy of slender pastel-hued buildings rising at odd angles and linked by a webwork of gently undulating aerial bridges. The streets were long parentheses that touched the lake at their northern and southern ends and arched gracefully westward in the middle. Between each of the great boulevards ran a track for public transportation—sleek aquamarine bubble-vehicles gliding on soundless wheels—and flanking each of the tracks were lush strips of park. It was beautiful, astonishingly so, but insubstantial. The whole thing seemed to have been contrived from sunbeams and silk.

A soft voice beside him said, "Are you becoming ill?"

Phillips glanced around. The celadon man stood beside him: a compact, precise person, vaguely Oriental in appearance. His skin was of a curious gray-green hue like no skin Phillips had ever seen, and it was extraordinarily smooth in texture, as though he were made of fine porcelain.

He shook his head. "Just a little queasy," he said. "This city always scrambles me."

"I suppose it can be disconcerting," the little man replied. His tone was furry and veiled, the inflection strange. There was something feline about him. He seemed sinewy, unyielding, almost menacing. "Visitor, are you?"

Phillips studied him a moment. "Yes," he said.

"So am I, of course."

"Are you?"

"Indeed." The little man smiled. "What's your locus? Twentieth century? Twenty-first at the latest, I'd say."

"I'm from 1984. 1984 A.D."

Another smile, a self-satisfied one. "Not a bad guess, then." A brisk tilt of the head. "Y'ang-Yeovil."

"Pardon me?" Phillips said.

"Y'ang-Yeovil. It is my name. Formerly Colonel Y'ang-Yeovil of the Third Septentriad."

"Is that on some other planet?" asked Phillips, feeling a bit dazed.

"Oh, no, not at all," Y'ang-Yeovil said pleasantly. "This very world, I assure you. I am quite of human origin. Citizen of the Republic of Upper Han, native of the city of Port Ssu. And you—forgive me—your name—?"

"I'm sorry. Phillips. Charles Phillips. From New York City, once upon a time."

"Ah, New York!" Y'ang-Yeovil's face lit with a glimmer of recognition that quickly faded. "New York—New York—it was very famous, that I know—"

This is very strange, Phillips thought. He felt greater compassion for poor bewildered Francis Willoughby now. This man comes from a time so far beyond my own that he barely knows of New York—he must be a contemporary of the real New Chicago, in fact; I wonder whether he finds this version authentic—and yet to the citizens this Y'ang-Yeovil too is just a primitive, a curio out of antiquity—

"New York was the largest city of the United States of America," Phillips said.

"Of course. Yes. Very famous."

"But virtually forgotten by the time the Republic of Upper Han came into existence, I gather."

Y'ang-Yeovil said, looking uncomfortable, "There were disturbances between your time and mine. But by no means should you take from my words the impression that your city was—"

Sudden laughter resounded across the room. Five or six newcomers had arrived at the party. Phillips stared, gasped, gaped. Surely that was Stengard—and Aramayne beside him—and that other woman, half-hidden behind them—

"If you'll pardon me a moment—" Phillips said, turning abruptly away from Y'ang-Yeovil. "Please excuse me. Someone just coming in—a person I've been trying to find ever since—"

He hurried toward her.

————

"Gioia?" he called. "Gioia, it's me! Wait! Wait!"

Stengard was in the way. Aramayne, turning to take a handful of the little vapor-sniffers from Cantilena, blocked him also. Phillips pushed through them as though they were not there. Gioia, halfway out the door, halted and looked toward him like a frightened deer.

"Don't go," he said. He took her hand in his.

He was startled by her appearance. How long had it been since their strange parting on that night of mysteries in Chang-an? A year? A year and a half? So he believed. Or had he lost all track of time? Were his perceptions of the passing of the months in this world that unreliable? She seemed at least ten or fifteen years older. Maybe she really was; maybe the years had been passing for him here as in a dream, and he had never known it. She looked strained, faded, worn. Out of a thinner and strangely altered face her eyes blazed at him almost defiantly, as though saying, *See? See how ugly I have become?*

He said, "I've been hunting for you for—I don't know how long it's been, Gioia. In Mohenjo, in Timbuctoo, now here. I want to be with you again."

"It isn't possible."

"Belilala explained everything to me in Mohenjo. I know that you're a short-timer—I know what that means, Gioia. But what of it? So you're beginning to age a little. So what? So you'll only have three or four hundred years, instead of forever. Don't you think I know what it means to be a short-timer? I'm just a simple ancient man of the twentieth century, remember? Sixty, seventy, eighty years is all we would get. You and I suffer from the same malady, Gioia. That's what drew you to me in the first place. I'm certain of that. That's why we belong with each other now. However much time we have, we can spend the rest of it together, don't you see?"

"You're the one who doesn't see, Charles," she said softly.

"Maybe. Maybe I still don't understand a damned thing about this place. Except that you and I—that I love you—that I think you love me—"

"I love you, yes. But you don't understand. It's precisely because I love you that you and I—you and I can't—"

With a despairing sigh she slid her hand free of his grasp. He reached for her again, but she shook him off and backed up quickly into the corridor.

"Gioia?"

"Please," she said. "No. I would never have come here if I knew you were here. Don't come after me. Please. Please."

She turned and fled.

He stood looking after her for a long moment. Cantilena and Aramayne appeared, and smiled at him as if nothing at all had happened. Cantilena offered him a vial of some sparkling amber fluid. He refused with a brusque gesture. Where do I go now, he wondered? What do I do? He wandered back into the party.

Y'ang-Yeovil glided to his side. "You are in great distress," the little man murmured.

Phillips glared. "Let me be."

"Perhaps I could be of some help."

"There's no help possible," said Phillips. He swung about and plucked one of the vials from a tray and gulped its contents. It made him feel as if there were two of him, standing on either side of Y'ang-Yeovil. He gulped another. Now there were four of him. "I'm in love with a citizen," he blurted. It seemed to him that he was speaking in chorus.

"Love. Ah. And does she love you?"

"So I thought. So I think. But she's a short-timer. Do you know what that means? She's not immortal like the others. She ages. She's beginning to look old. And so she's been running away from me. She doesn't want me to see her changing. She thinks it'll disgust me, I suppose. I tried to remind her just now that I'm not immortal either, that she and I could grow old together, but she—"

"Oh, no," Y'ang-Yeovil said quietly. "Why do you think you will age? Have you grown any older in all the time you have been here?"

Phillips was nonplussed. "Of course I have. I—I—"

"Have you? Y'ang-Yeovil smiled. "Here. Look at yourself." He did something intricate with his fingers and a shimmering zone of mirror-like light appeared between them. Phillips stared at his reflection. A youthful face stared back at him. It was true, then. He had simply not thought about it. How many years had he spent in this world? The time had simply slipped by: a great deal of time, though he could not calculate how much. They did not seem to keep close count of it here, nor had he. But it must have been many years, he thought. All that endless travel up and down the globe—so many cities had come and gone—Rio, Rome, Asgard, those were the first three that came to mind—and there were others; he could hardly remember every one. Years. His face had not changed at all. Time had worked its harshness on Gioia, yes, but not on him.

"I don't understand," he said. "Why am I not aging?"

"Because you are not real," said Y'ang-Yeovil. "Are you unaware of that?"

Phillips blinked. "Not—real?"

"Did you think you were lifted bodily out of your own time?" the little man asked. "Ah, no, no, there is no way for them to do such a thing. We are not actual time travelers: not you, not I, not any of the visitors. I thought you were aware of that. But perhaps your era is too early for a proper understanding of these things. We are very cleverly done, my friend. We are ingenious constructs, marvelously stuffed with the thoughts and attitudes and events of our own times. We are their finest achievement, you know: far more complex even than one of these cities. We are a step beyond the temporaries—more than a step, a great deal more. They do only what they are instructed to do, and their range is very narrow. They are nothing but machines, really. Whereas we are autonomous. We move about by our own will; we think, we talk, we even, so it seems, fall in love. But we will not age. How could we age? We are not real. We are mere artificial webworks of mental responses. We are mere illusions, done so well that we deceive even ourselves. You did not know that? Indeed, you did not know?"

————

He was airborne, touching destination buttons at random. Somehow he found himself heading back toward Timbuctoo. *This city is closed. This is not a place any longer.* It did not matter to him. Why should anything matter?

Fury and a choking sense of despair rose within him. I am software, Phillips thought. I am nothing but software.

*Not real. Very cleverly done. An ingenious construct. A mere illusion.*

No trace of Timbuctoo was visible from the air. He landed anyway.

The gray sandy earth was smooth, unturned, as though there had never been anything there. A few robots were still about, handling whatever final chores were required in the shutting-down of a city. Two of them scuttled up to him. Huge bland gleaming silver-skinned insects, not friendly.

"There is no city here," they said. "This is not a permissible place."

"Permissible by whom?"

"There is no reason for you to be here."

"There's no reason for me to be anywhere," Phillips said. The robots stirred, made uneasy humming sounds and ominous clicks, waved their antennae about. They seem troubled, he thought. They seem to dislike my attitude. Perhaps I run some risk of being taken off to the home for unruly software for debugging. "I'm leaving now," he told them. "Thank you. Thank you very much." He backed away from them and climbed into his flitterflitter. He touched more destination buttons.

*We move about by our own will. We think, we talk, we even fall in love.*

He landed in Chang-an. This time there was no reception committee waiting for him at the Gate of Brilliant Virtue. The city seemed larger and more resplendent: new pagodas, new palaces. It felt like winter: a chilly cutting wind was blowing. The sky was cloudless and dazzlingly bright. At the steps of the Silver Terrace he encountered Francis Willoughby, a great hulking figure in magnificent brocaded robes, with two dainty little temporaries, pretty as jade statuettes, engulfed in his arms. "Miracles and wonders! The silly lunatic fellow is here too!" Willoughby roared. "Look, look, we are come to far Cathay, you and I!"

*We are nowhere,* Phillips thought. *We are mere illusions, done so well that we deceive even ourselves.*

To Willoughby he said, "You look like an emperor in those robes, Francis."

"Aye, like Prester John!" Willoughby cried. "Like Tamburlaine himself. Aye, am I not majestic?" He slapped Phillips gaily on the shoulder, a rough playful poke that spun him halfway about, coughing and wheezing. "We flew in the air, as the eagles do, as the demons do, as the angels do! Soared like angels! Like angels!" He came close, looming over Phillips. "I would have gone to England, but the wench Belilala said there was an enchantment on me that would keep me from England just now; and so we voyaged to Cathay. Tell me this, fellow, will you go witness for me when we see England again? Swear that all that has befallen us did in truth befall? For I fear they will say I am as mad as Marco Polo, when I tell them of flying to Cathay."

"One madman backing another?" Phillips asked. "What can I tell you? You still think you'll reach England, do you?" Rage rose to the surface in him, bubbling hot. "Ah, Francis, Francis, do you know your Shakespeare? Did you go to the plays? We aren't real. *We aren't real.* We are such stuff as dreams are made on, the two of us. That's all we are. O brave new world! What England? Where? There's no England. There's no Francis Willoughby. There's no Charles Phillips. What we are is—"

"Let him be, Charles," a cool voice cut in.

He turned. Belilala, in the robes of an empress, coming down the steps of the Silver Terrace.

"I know the truth," he said bitterly. "Y'ang-Yeovil told me. The visitor from the twenty-fifth century. I saw him in New Chicago."

"Did you see Gioia there too?" Belilala asked.

"Briefly. She looks much older."

"Yes. I know. She was here recently."

"And has gone on, I suppose?"

"To Mohenjo again, yes. Go after her, Charles. Leave poor Francis alone. I told her to wait for you. I told her that she needs you, and you need her."

"Very kind of you. But what good is it, Belilala? I don't even exist. And she's going to die."

"You exist. How can you doubt that you exist? You feel, don't you? You suffer. You love. You love Gioia: is that not so? And you are loved by Gioia. Would Gioia love what is not real?"

"You think she loves me?"

"I know she does. Go to her, Charles. Go. I told her to wait for you in Mohenjo."

Phillips nodded numbly. What was there to lose?

"Go to her," said Belilala again. "Now."

"Yes," Phillips said. "I'll go now." He turned to Willoughby. "If ever we meet in London, friend, I'll testify for you. Fear nothing. All will be well, Francis."

He left them and set his course for Mohenjo-daro, half expecting to find the robots already tearing it down. Mohenjo-daro was still there, no lovelier than before. He went to the baths, thinking he might find Gioia there. She was not; but he came upon Nissandra, Stengard, Fenimon.

"She has gone to Alexandria," Fenimon told him. "She wants to see it one last time, before they close it."

"They're almost ready to open Constantinople," Stengard explained. "The capital of Byzantium, you know, the great city by the Golden Horn. They'll take Alexandria away, you understand, when Byzantium opens. They say it's going to be marvelous. We'll see you there for the opening, naturally?"

"Naturally," Phillips said.

He flew to Alexandria. He felt lost and weary. All this is hopeless folly; he told himself. I am nothing but a puppet jerking about on its strings. But somewhere above the shining breast of the Arabian Sea the deeper implications of something that Belilala had said to him started to sink in, and he felt his bitterness, his rage, his despair, all suddenly beginning to leave him. *You exist. How can you doubt that you exist? Would Gioia love what is not real?* Of course. Of course. Y'ang-Yeovil had been wrong: visitors were something more than mere illusions. Indeed Y'ang-Yeovil had voiced the truth of their condition without understanding what he was really saying: *We think, we talk, we fall in love.* Yes. That was the heart of the situation. The visitors might be artificial, but they were not unreal. Belilala had been trying to tell him that just the other night. *You suffer. You love. You love Gioia. Would Gioia love what is not real?* Surely he was real, or at any rate real enough. What he was was something strange, something that would probably have been all but incomprehensible to the twentieth-century people whom he had been designed to simulate. But that did not mean that he was unreal. Did one have to be of woman born to be real? No. No. No. His kind of reality was a sufficient reality. He had no need to be ashamed of it. And, understanding that, he understood that Gioia did not need to grow old and die. There was a way by which she could be saved, if only she would embrace it. If only she would.

When he landed in Alexandria he went immediately to the hotel on the slopes of the Paneium where they had stayed on their first visit, so very long ago; and there she was, sitting quietly on a patio with a view of the harbor and the Lighthouse. There was something calm and resigned about the way she sat. She had given up. She did not even have the strength to flee from him any longer.

"Gioia," he said gently.

She looked older than she had in New Chicago. Her face was drawn and sallow and her eyes seemed sunken; and she was not even bothering these days to deal with the white strands that stood out in stark contrast against the darkness of her hair. He sat down beside her and put his hand over hers, and looked out toward the obelisks, the palaces, the temples, the Lighthouse. At length he said, "I know what I really am, now."

"Do you, Charles?" She sounded very far away.

"In my era we called it software. All I am is a set of commands, responses, cross-references, operating some sort of artificial body. It's infinitely better software than we could have imagined. But we were only just beginning to learn how, after all. They pumped me full of twentieth-century reflexes. The right moods, the right appetites, the right irrationalities, the right sort of combativeness. Somebody knows a lot about what it was like to be a twentieth-century man. They did a good job with Willoughby, too, all that Elizabethan rhetoric and swagger. And I suppose they got Y'ang-Yeovil right. *He* seems to think so: who better to judge? The twenty-fifth century, the Republic of Upper Han, people with gray-green skin, half Chinese and half Martian for all I know. *Somebody* knows. Somebody here is very good at programming, Gioia."

She was not looking at him.

"I feel frightened, Charles," she said in that same distant way.

"Of me? Of the things I'm saying?"

"No, not of you. Don't you see what has happened to me?"

"I see you. There are changes."

"I lived a long time wondering when the changes would begin. I thought maybe they wouldn't, not really. Who wants to believe they'll get old? But it started when we were in Alexandria that first time. In Chang-an it got much worse. And now—now—"

He said abruptly, "Stengard tells me they'll be opening Constantinople very soon."

"So?"

"Don't you want to be there when it opens?"

"I'm becoming old and ugly, Charles."

"We'll go to Constantinople together. We'll leave tomorrow, eh? What do you say? We'll charter a boat. It's a quick little hop, right across the Mediterranean. Sailing to Byzantium! There was a poem, you know, in my time. Not forgotten, I guess, because they've programmed it into me. All these thousands of years, and someone still remembers old Yeats.

*The young in one another's arms, birds in the trees.* Come with me to Byzantium, Gioia."

She shrugged. "Looking like this? Getting more hideous every hour? While *they* stay young forever? While *you*—" She faltered; her voice cracked; she fell silent.

"Finish the sentence, Gioia."

"Please. Let me alone."

"You were going to say, 'While *you* stay young forever too, Charles,' isn't that it? You knew all along that I was never going to change. I didn't know that, but you did."

"Yes. I knew. I pretended that it wasn't true—that as I aged, you'd age too. It was very foolish of me. In Chang-an, when I first began to see the real signs of it—that was when I realized I couldn't stay with you any longer. Because I'd look at you, always young, always remaining the same age, and I'd look at myself, and—" She gestured, palms upward. "So I gave you to Belilala and ran away."

"All so unnecessary, Gioia."

"I didn't think it was."

"But you don't have to grow old. Not if you don't want to!"

"Don't be cruel, Charles," she said tonelessly. "There's no way of escaping what I have."

"But there is," he said.

"You know nothing about these things."

"Not very much, no," he said. "But I see how it can be done. Maybe it's a primitive simple-minded twentieth-century sort of solution, but I think it ought to work. I've been playing with the idea ever since I left Mohenjo. Tell me this, Gioia: Why can't you go to them, to the programmers, to the artificers, the planners, whoever they are, the ones who create the cities and the temporaries and the visitors. And have yourself made into something like me!"

She looked up, startled. "What are you saying?"

"They can cobble up a twentieth-century man out of nothing more than fragmentary records and make him plausible, can't they? Or an Elizabethan, or anyone else of any era at all, and he's authentic, he's convincing. So why couldn't they do an even better job with you? Produce a Gioia so real that even Gioia can't tell the difference? But a Gioia that will never age—a Gioia-construct, a Gioia-program, a visitor-Gioia! Why not? Tell me why not, Gioia."

She was trembling. "I've never heard of doing any such thing!"

"But don't you think it's possible?"

"How would I know?"

"Of course it's possible. If they can create visitors, they can take a citizen and duplicate her in such a way that—"

"It's never been done. I'm sure of it. I can't imagine any citizen agreeing to any such thing. To give up the body—to let yourself be turned into—into—"

She shook her head, but it seemed to be a gesture of astonishment as much as of negation.

He said, "Sure. To give up the body. Your natural body, your aging, shrinking, deteriorating short-timer body. What's so awful about that?"

She was very pale. "This is craziness, Charles. I don't want to talk about it any more."

"It doesn't sound crazy to me."

"You can't possibly understand."

"Can't I? I can certainly understand being afraid to die. I don't have a lot of trouble understanding what it's like to be one of the few aging people in a world where nobody grows old. What I can't understand is why you aren't even willing to consider the possibility that—"

"No," she said. "I tell you, it's crazy. They'd laugh at me."

"Who?"

"All of my friends. Hawk, Stengard, Aramayne—" Once again she would not look at him. "They can be very cruel, without even realizing it. They despise anything that seems ungraceful to them, anything sweaty and desperate and cowardly. Citizens don't do sweaty things, Charles. And that's how this will seem. Assuming it can be done at all. They'll be terribly patronizing. Oh, they'll be sweet to me, yes, dear Gioia, how wonderful for you, Gioia, but when I turn my back they'll laugh. They'll say the most wicked things about me. I couldn't bear that."

"They can afford to laugh," Phillips said. "It's easy to be brave and cool about dying when you know you're going to live forever. How very fine for them; but why should you be the only one to grow old and die? And they won't laugh, anyway. They're not as cruel as you think. Shallow, maybe, but not cruel. They'll be glad that you've found a way to save yourself. At the very least, they won't have to feel guilty about you any longer, and that's bound to please them. You can—"

"Stop it," she said.

She rose, walked to the railing of the patio, stared out toward the sea. He came up behind her. Red sails in the harbor, sunlight glittering along the sides of the Lighthouse, the palaces of the Ptolemies stark white against the sky. Lightly he rested his hand on her shoulder. She twitched as if to pull away from him, but remained where she was.

"Then I have another idea," he said quietly. "If you won't go to the planners, I will. Reprogram me, I'll say. Fix things so that I start to age at the same rate you do. It'll be more authentic, anyway, if I'm supposed to be playing the part of a twentieth-century man. Over the years I'll very gradually get some lines in my face, my hair will turn gray, I'll walk a little more slowly—we'll grow old together, Gioia. To hell with your lovely immortal friends. We'll have each other. We won't need them."

She swung around. Her eyes were wide with horror.

"Are you serious, Charles?"

"Of course."

"No," she murmured. "No. Everything you've said to me today is monstrous nonsense. Don't you realize that?"

He reached for her hand and enclosed her fingertips in his. "All I'm trying to do is find some way for you and me to—"

"Don't say any more," she said. "Please." Quickly, as though drawing back from a suddenly flaring flame, she tugged her fingers free of his and put her hand behind her. Though his face was just inches from hers he felt an immense chasm opening between them. They stared at one another for a moment; then she moved deftly to his left, darted around him, and ran from the patio.

Stunned, he watched her go, down the long marble corridor and out of sight. It was folly to give pursuit, he thought. She was lost to him: that was clear, that was beyond any question. She was terrified of him. Why cause her even more anguish? But somehow he found himself running through the halls of the hotel, along the winding garden path, into the cool green groves of the Paneium. He thought he saw her on the portico of Hadrian's palace, but when he got there the echoing stone halls were empty. To a temporary that was sweeping the steps he said, "Did you see a woman come this way?" A blank sullen stare was his only answer.

Phillips cursed and turned away.

"Gioia?" he called. "Wait! Come back!"

Was that her, going into the Library? He rushed past the startled mumbling librarians and sped through the stacks, peering beyond the mounds of double-handled scrolls into the shadowy corridors. "Gioia?

Gioia!" It was a descration, bellowing like that in this quiet place. He scarcely cared.

Emerging by a side door, he loped down to the harbor. The Lighthouse! Terror enfolded him. She might already be a hundred steps up that ramp, heading for the parapet from which she meant to fling herself into the sea. Scattering citizens and temporaries as if they were straws, he ran within. Up he went, never pausing for breath, though his synthetic lungs were screaming for respite, his ingeniously designed heart was desperately pounding. On the first balcony he imagined he caught a glimpse of her, but he circled it without finding her. Onward, upward. He went to the top, to the beacon chamber itself: no Gioia. Had she jumped? Had she gone down one ramp while he was ascending the other? He clung to the rim and looked out, down, searching the base of the Lighthouse, the rocks offshore, the causeway. No Gioia. I will find her somewhere, he thought. I will keep going until I find her. He went running down the ramp, calling her name. He reached ground level and sprinted back toward the center of town. Where next? The temple of Poseidon? The tomb of Cleopatra?

He paused in the middle of Canopus Street, groggy and dazed.

"Charles?" she said.

"Where are you?"

"Right here. Beside you." She seemed to materialize from the air. Her face was unflushed, her robe bore no trace of perspiration. Had he been chasing a phantom through the city? She came to him and took his hand, and said, softly, tenderly, "Were you really serious, about having them make you age?"

"If there's no other way, yes."

"The other way is so frightening, Charles."

"Is it?"

"You can't understand how much."

"More frightening than growing old? Than dying?"

"I don't know," she said. "I suppose not. The only thing I'm sure of is that I don't want you to get old, Charles."

"But I won't have to. Will I?" He stared at her.

"No," she said. "You won't have to. Neither of us will."

Phillips smiled. "We should get away from here," he said after a while. "Let's go across to Byzantium, yes, Gioia? We'll show up in Constantinople for the opening. Your friends will be there. We'll tell them what you've decided to do. They'll know how to arrange it. Someone will."

"It sounds so strange," said Gioia. "To turn myself into — into a visitor? A visitor in my own world?"

"That's what you've always been, though."

"I suppose. In a way. But at least I've been *real* up to now."

"Whereas I'm not?"

"Are you, Charles?"

"Yes. Just as real as you. I was angry at first, when I found out the truth about myself. But I came to accept it: Somewhere between Mohenjo and here, I came to see that it was all right to be what I am: that I perceive things, I form ideas, I draw conclusions. I am very well designed, Gioia. I can't tell the difference between being what I am and being completely alive, and to me that's being real enough. I think, I feel, I experience joy and pain. I'm as real as I need to be. And you will be too. You'll never stop being Gioia, you know. It's only your body that you'll cast away, the body that played such a terrible joke on you anyway." He brushed her cheek with his hand. "It was all said for us before, long ago:

> *Once out of nature I shall never take*
> *My bodily form from any natural thing,*
> *But such a form as Grecian goldsmiths make*
> *Of hammered gold and gold enamelling*
> *To keep a drowsy Emperor awake;*"

"Is that the same poem?" she asked.

"The same poem, yes. The ancient poem that isn't quite forgotten yet."

"Finish it, Charles."

> "*Or set upon a golden bough to sing*
> *To lords and ladies of Byzantium*
> *Of what is past, or passing, or to come.*"

"How beautiful. What does it mean?"

"That it isn't necessary to be mortal. That we can allow ourselves to be gathered into the artifice of eternity, that we can be transformed, that we can move on beyond the flesh. Yeats didn't mean it in quite the way I do—he wouldn't have begun to comprehend what we're talking about, not a word of it—and yet, and yet—the underlying truth is the same. Live, Gioia! With me!" He turned to her and saw color coming into her pallid cheeks. "It does make sense, what I'm suggesting, doesn't it? You'll attempt it, won't you? Whoever makes the visitors can be induced to re-make you. Right? What do you think: can they, Gioia?"

She nodded in a barely perceptible way. "I think so," she said faintly. "It's very strange. But I think it ought to be possible. Why not, Charles? Why not?"

"Yes," he said. "Why not?"

———

In the morning they hired a vessel in the harbor, a low sleek pirogue with a blood-red sail, skippered by a rascally-looking temporary whose smile was irresistible. Phillips shaded his eyes and peered northward across the sea. He thought he could almost make out the shape of the great city sprawling on its seven hills, Constantine's New Rome beside the Golden Horn, the mighty dome of Hagia Sophia, the somber walls of the citadel, the palaces and churches, the Hippodrome, Christ in glory rising above all else in brilliant mosaic streaming with light.

"Byzantium," Phillips said. "Take us there the shortest and quickest way."

"It is my pleasure," said the boatman with unexpected grace.

Gioia smiled. He had not seen her looking so vibrantly alive since the night of the imperial feast in Chang-an. He reached for her hand—her slender fingers were quivering lightly—and helped her into the boat.

# JOHN KESSEL

*John Kessel's reputation as a writer of sophisticated literary fantasy and science fiction is predicated on a handful of stories that frequently invade the territory of classic writers and use the lessons in their literature as sounding boards for contemporary values and social mores. The mock essay "Herman Melville: Space Opera Virtuoso," and the Nebula Award–winning riff on Moby Dick, "Another Orphan," both chart incongruous intersections of period Melville and modern times. "The Big Dream" tells of a private detective on the trail of Raymond Chandler slowly evolving into a character in a typical Chandler crime story. "The Pure Product" (which appears here) and "Every Angel Is Terrifying" both extend ideas in the southern Gothic fiction of Flannery O'Connor. H. G. Wells is himself a character in the Wellsian tale "Buffalo." These stories, and Kessel's alternate-history tales "Some Like It Cold," "The Franchise," and "Uncle John and the Saviour," have been collected in his short fiction compilations* Meetings in Infinity *and* The Pure Product.

*The creative playfulness implicit in the "what-if" speculations of these stories extends to Kessel's work as a novelist.* Good News from Outer Space *sketches a satirical portrait of a dysfunctional America on the eve of the twenty-first century, obsessed with alien invasion and millennial irrationality.* Corrupting Dr. Nice *is a screwball time-travel story involving a father-daughter team of flim-flam artists who traverse timelines and alternate histories in search of victims. Kessel has also written the novel* Freedom Beach *in collaboration with James Patrick Kelly. In 2003 he was awarded the James Tiptree Award for his short story "Stories of Men."*

*If there were time travelers from the future, how would they see the*

*America of today? Would they look at it like the main character in Kessel's story, as an entire world to toy with, to manipulate as they choose? Would they be disinterested observers, alighting five hundred years ago, then flitting through time as they choose, interacting with whomever they happen to meet?*

# THE PURE PRODUCT

## JOHN KESSEL

I ARRIVED IN Kansas City at one o'clock on the afternoon of the thirteenth of August. A Tuesday. I was driving the beige 1983 Chevrolet Citation that I had stolen two days earlier in Pocatello, Idaho. The Kansas plates on the car I'd taken from a different car in a parking lot in Salt Lake City. Salt Lake City was founded by the Mormons, whose god tells them that in the future Jesus Christ will come again.

I drove through Kansas City with the windows open and the sun beating down through the windshield. The car had no air conditioning, and my shirt was stuck to my back from seven hours behind the wheel. Finally I found a hardware store, "Hector's" on Wornall. I pulled into the lot. The Citation's engine dieseled after I turned off the ignition; I pumped the accelerator once and it coughed and died. The heat was like syrup. The sun drove shadows deep into corners, left them flattened at the feet of the people on the sidewalk. It made the plate glass of the store window into a dark negative of the positive print that was Wornall Road. August.

The man behind the counter in the hardware store I took to be Hector himself. He looked like Hector, slain in vengeance beneath the walls of paintbrushes—the kind of semifriendly, publicly optimistic man who would tell you about his crazy wife and his ten-penny nails. I bought a gallon of kerosene and a plastic paint funnel, put them into the trunk of the Citation, then walked down the block to the Mark Twain Bank. Mark Twain died at the age of seventy-five with a heart full of bitter accusations against the Calvinist god and no hope for the future of humanity. Inside the bank I went to one of the desks, at which sat a Nice

Young Lady. I asked about starting a business checking account. She gave me a form to fill out, then sent me to the office of Mr. Graves.

Mr. Graves wielded a formidable handshake. "What can I do for you, Mr. . . . ?"

"Tillotsen, Gerald Tillotsen," I said. Gerald Tillotsen, of Tacoma, Washington, died of diphtheria at the age of four weeks—on September 24, 1938. I have a copy of his birth certificate.

"I'm new to Kansas City. I'd like to open a business account here, and perhaps take out a loan. I trust this is a reputable bank? What's your exposure in Brazil?" I looked around the office as if Graves were hiding a woman behind the hatstand, then flashed him my most ingratiating smile.

Mr. Graves did his best. He tried smiling back, then looked as if he had decided to ignore my little joke. "We're very sound, Mr. Tillotsen."

I continued smiling.

"What kind of business do you own?"

"I'm in insurance. Mutual Assurance of Hartford. Our regional office is in Oklahoma City, and I'm setting up an agency here, at 103rd and State Line." Just off the interstate.

He examined the form. His absorption was too tempting.

"Maybe I can fix you up with a policy? You look like dead meat."

Graves's head snapped up, his mouth half-open. He closed it and watched me guardedly. The dullness of it all! How I tire. He was like some cow, like most of the rest of you in this silly age, unwilling to break the rules in order to take offense. "Did he really say that?" he was thinking. "Was that his idea of a joke? He looks normal enough." I did look normal, exactly like an insurance agent. I was the right kind of person, and I could do anything. If at times I grate, if at times I fall a little short of or go a little beyond convention, there is not one of you who can call me to account.

Graves was coming around. All business.

"Ah—yes, Mr. Tillotsen. If you'll wait a moment, I'm sure we can take care of this checking account. As for the loan—"

"Forget it."

That should have stopped him. He should have asked after my credentials, he should have done a dozen things. He looked at me, and I stared calmly back at him. And I knew that, looking into my honest blue eyes, he could not think of a thing.

"I'll just start the checking account with this money order," I said, reaching into my pocket. "That will be acceptable, won't it?"

"It will be fine," he said. He took the form and the order over to one of the secretaries while I sat at the desk. I lit a cigar and blew some smoke rings. I'd purchased the money order the day before in a post office in Denver. Thirty dollars. I didn't intend to use the account very long. Graves returned with my sample checks, shook hands earnestly, and wished me a good day. Have a *good* day, he said. I *will*, I said.

Outside, the heat was still stifling. I took off my sports coat. I was sweating so much I had to check my hair in the sideview mirror of my car. I walked down the street to a liquor store and bought a bottle of chardonnay and a bottle of Chivas Regal. I got some paper cups from a nearby grocery. One final errand, then I could relax for a few hours.

In the shopping center that I had told Graves would be the location for my nonexistent insurance office, I had noticed a sporting goods store. It was about three o'clock when I parked in the lot and ambled into the shop. I looked at various golf clubs: irons, woods, even one set with fiber-glass shafts. Finally I selected a set of eight Spalding irons with matching woods, a large bag, and several boxes of Top-Flites. The salesman, who had been occupied with another customer at the rear of the store, hustled up, his eyes full of commission money. I gave him little time to think. The total cost was $612.32. I paid with a check drawn on my new account, cordially thanked the man, and had him carry all the equipment out to the trunk of the car.

I drove to a park near the bank; Loose Park, they called it. I felt loose. Cut loose, drifting free, like one of the kites people were flying that had broken its string and was ascending into the sun. Beneath the trees it was still hot, though the sunlight was reduced to a shuffling of light and shadow on the brown grass. Kids ran, jumped, swung on playground equipment. I uncorked my bottle of wine, filled one of the paper cups, and lay down beneath a tree, enjoying the children, watching young men and women walking along the footpaths.

A girl approached. She didn't look any older than seventeen. Short, slender, with clean blond hair cut to her shoulders. Her shorts were very tight. I watched her unabashedly; she saw me watching and left the path to come over to me. She stopped a few feet away, hands on her hips. "What are you looking at?" she asked.

"Your legs," I said. "Would you like some wine?"

"No thanks. My mother told me never to accept wine from strangers." She looked right through me.

"I take what I can get from strangers," I said. "Because I'm a stranger, too."

I guess she liked that. She was different. She sat down and we chatted for a while. There was something wrong about her imitation of a seventeen-year-old; I began to wonder whether hookers worked the park. She crossed her legs and her shorts got tighter. "Where are you from?" she asked.

"San Francisco. But I've just moved here to stay. I have a part interest in the sporting goods store at the Eastridge Plaza."

"You live near here?"

"On West Eighty-ninth." I had driven down Eighty-ninth on my way to the bank.

"I live on Eighty-ninth! We're neighbors."

It was exactly what one of my own might have said to test me. I took a drink of wine and changed the subject. "Would you like to visit San Francisco someday?"

She brushed her hair back behind one ear. She pursed her lips, showing off her fine cheekbones. "Have you got something going?" she asked, in queerly accented English.

"Excuse me?"

"I said, have you got something going," she repeated, still with the accent—the accent of my own time.

I took another sip. "A bottle of wine," I replied in good midwestern 1980s.

She wasn't having any of it. "No artwork, please. I don't like artwork."

I had to laugh: my life was devoted to artwork. I had not met anyone real in a long time. At the beginning I hadn't wanted to, and in the ensuing years I had given up expecting it. If there's anything more boring than you people it's us people. But that was an old attitude. When she came to me in K.C. I was lonely and she was something new.

"Okay," I said. "It's not much, but you can come for the ride. Do you want to?"

She smiled and said yes.

As we walked to my car, she brushed her hip against my leg. I switched the bottle to my left hand and put my arm around her shoulders in a fatherly way. We got into the front seat, beneath the trees on a street at the edge of the park. It was quiet. I reached over, grabbed her hair at the nape of her neck, and jerked her face toward me, covering her little mouth with mine. Surprise: she threw her arms around my neck and slid across the seat into my lap. We did not talk. I yanked at the shorts; she thrust her hand into my pants. St. Augustine asked the Lord for chastity, but not right away.

At the end she slipped off me, calmly buttoned her blouse, brushed her hair back from her forehead. "How about a push?" she asked. She had a nail file out and was filing her index fingernail to a point.

I shook my head and looked at her. She resembled my grandmother. I had never run into my grandmother, but she had a hellish reputation. "No thanks. What's your name?"

"Call me Ruth." She scratched the inside of her left elbow with her nail. She leaned back in her seat, sighed deeply. Her eyes became a very bright, very hard blue.

While she was aloft I got out, opened the trunk, emptied the rest of the chardonnay into the gutter, and used the funnel to fill the bottle with kerosene. I plugged it with a kerosene-soaked rag. Afternoon was sliding into evening as I started the car and cruised down one of the residential streets. The houses were like those of any city or town of that era of the Midwest USA: white frame, forty or fifty years old, with large porches and small front yards. Dying elms hung over the street. Shadows stretched across the sidewalks. Ruth's nose wrinkled; she turned her face lazily toward me, saw the kerosene bottle, and smiled.

Ahead on the left-hand sidewalk I saw a man walking leisurely. He was an average sort of man, middle-aged, probably just returning from work, enjoying the quiet pause dusk was bringing to the hot day. It might have been Hector; it might have been Graves. It might have been any one of you. I punched the cigarette lighter, readied the bottle in my right hand, steering with my leg as the car moved slowly forward.

"Let me help," Ruth said. She reached out and steadied the wheel with her slender fingertips. The lighter popped out. I touched it to the rag; it smoldered and caught. Greasy smoke stung my eyes. By now the man had noticed us. I hung my arm, holding the bottle, out the window. As we passed him, I tossed the bottle at the sidewalk like a newsboy tossing a rolled-up newspaper. The rag flamed brighter as it whipped through the air; the bottle landed at his feet and exploded, dousing him with burning kerosene. I floored the accelerator; the motor coughed, then roared, the tires and Ruth both squealing in delight. I could see the flaming man in the rearview mirror as we sped away.

————

On the Great American Plains, the summer nights are not silent. The fields sing the summer songs of insects—not individual sounds, but a high-pitched drone of locusts, crickets, cicadas, small chirping things for which I have no names. You drive along the superhighway and that sound blends with the sound of wind rushing through your opened windows, hiding the thrum of the automobile, conveying the impression of incredible velocity. Wheels vibrate, tires beat against the pavement, the steering wheel shudders, alive in your hands, droning insects alive in your ears. Reflecting posts at the roadside leap from the darkness with metronomic regularity, glowing amber in the headlights, only to vanish abruptly into the ready night when you pass. You lose track of time, how long you have been on the road, where you are going. The fields scream in your ears like a thousand lost, mechanical souls, and you press your foot to the accelerator, hurrying away.

When we left Kansas City that evening we were indeed hurrying. Our direction was in one sense precise: Interstate 70, more or less due east, through Missouri in a dream. They might remember me in Kansas City, at the same time wondering who and why. Mr. Graves scans the morning paper over his grapefruit: MAN BURNED BY GASOLINE BOMB. The clerk wonders why he ever accepted an unverified counter check, without a name or address printed on it, for six hundred dollars. The check bounces. They discover it was a bottle of chardonnay. The story is pieced together. They would eventually figure out how—I wouldn't lie to myself about that (I never lie to myself)—but the why would always escape them. Organized crime, they would say. A plot that misfired.

Of course, they still might have caught me. The car became more of a liability the longer I held on to it. But Ruth, humming to herself, did not seem to care, and neither did I. You have to improvise those things; that's what gives them whatever interest they have.

Just shy of Columbia, Missouri, Ruth stopped humming and asked me, "Do you know why Helen Keller can't have any children?"

"No."

"Because she's dead."

I rolled up the window so I could hear her better. "That's pretty funny," I said.

"Yes. I overheard it in a restaurant." After a minute she asked, "Who's Helen Keller?"

"A dead woman." An insect splattered itself against the windshield. The lights of the oncoming cars glinted against the smear it left.

"She must be famous," said Ruth. "I like famous people. Have you met any? Was that man you burned famous?"

"Probably not. I don't care about famous people anymore." The last time I had anything to do, even peripherally, with anyone famous was when I changed the direction of the tape over the lock in the Watergate so Frank Wills would see it. Ruth did not look like the kind who would know about that. "I was there for the Kennedy assassination," I said, "but I had nothing to do with it."

"Who was Kennedy?"

That made me smile. "How long have you been here?" I pointed at her tiny purse. "That's all you've got with you?"

She slid across the seat and leaned her head against my shoulder. "I don't need anything else."

"No clothes?"

"I left them in Kansas City. We can get more."

"Sure," I said.

She opened the purse and took out a plastic Bayer aspirin case. From it she selected two blue-and-yellow caps. She shoved her palm up under my nose. "Serometh?"

"No thanks."

She put one of the caps back into the box and popped the other under her nose. She sighed and snuggled tighter against me. We had reached Columbia and I was hungry. When I pulled in at a McDonald's she ran across the lot into the shopping mall before I could stop her. I was a little nervous about the car and sat watching it as I ate (Big Mac, small Dr Pepper). She did not come back. I crossed the lot to the mall, found a drugstore, and bought some cigars. When I strolled back to the car she was waiting for me, hopping from one foot to another and tugging at the door handle. Serometh makes you impatient. She was wearing a pair of shiny black pants, pink- and white-checked sneakers, and a hot pink blouse. " 's go!" she hissed.

I moved even slower. She looked like she was about to wet herself, biting her soft lower lip with a line of perfect white teeth. I dawdled over my keys. A security guard and a young man in a shirt and tie hurried out of the mall entrance and scanned the lot. "Nice outfit," I said. "Must have cost you something."

She looked over her shoulder, saw the security guard, who saw her. "Hey!" he called, running toward us. I slid into the car, opened the passenger door. Ruth had snapped open her purse and pulled out a small gun. I grabbed her arm and yanked her into the car; she squawked and her shot went wide. The guard fell down anyway, scared shitless. For the second time that day I tested the Citation's acceleration; Ruth's door slammed shut and we were gone.

"You scut," she said as we hit the entrance ramp of the interstate. "You're a scut-pumping Conservative. You made me miss." But she was smiling, running her hand up the inside of my thigh. I could tell she hadn't ever had so much fun in the twentieth century.

For some reason I was shaking. "Give me one of those seromeths," I said.

―――――――

Around midnight we stopped in St. Louis at a Holiday Inn. We registered as Mr. and Mrs. Gerald Bruno (an old acquaintance) and paid in advance. No one remarked on the apparent difference in our ages. So discreet. I bought a copy of the *Post Dispatch*, and we went to the room. Ruth flopped down on the bed, looking bored, but thanks to her gunplay I had a few more things to take care of. I poured myself a glass of Chivas, went into the bathroom, removed the toupee and flushed it down the toilet, showered, put a new blade in my old razor, and shaved the rest of the hair from my head. The Lex Luthor look. I cut my scalp. That got me laughing, and I could not stop. Ruth peeked through the doorway to find me dabbing the crown of my head with a bloody Kleenex.

"You're a wreck," she said.

I almost fell off the toilet laughing. She was absolutely right. Between giggles I managed to say, "You must not stay anywhere too long, if you're as careless as you were tonight."

She shrugged. "I bet I've been at it longer than you." She stripped and got into the shower. I got into bed.

The room enfolded me in its gold-carpet green-bedspread mediocrity. Sometimes it's hard to remember that things were ever different. In 1596 I rode to court with Essex; I slept in a chamber of supreme garishness (gilt escutcheons in the corners of the ceiling, pink cupids romping on the walls), in a bed warmed by any of the trollops of the city I might want. And there in the Holiday Inn I sat with my drink, in my pastel blue pajama bottoms, reading a late-twentieth-century newspaper, smoking a cigar. An earthquake in Peru estimated to have killed eight thousand in Lima alone. Nope. A steel worker in Gary, Indiana, discovered to be the murderer of six prepubescent children, bodies found buried in his basement. Perhaps. The president refuses to enforce the ruling of his Supreme Court because it "subverts the will of the American people." Probably not.

We are everywhere. But not everywhere.

Ruth came out of the bathroom, saw me, did a double take. "You look—perfect!" she said. She slid in the bed beside me, naked, and sniffed at my glass of Chivas. Her lip curled. She looked over my shoulder at the paper. "You can understand that stuff?"

"Don't kid me. Reading is a survival skill. You couldn't last here without it."

"Wrong."

I drained the scotch. Took a puff on the cigar. Dropped the paper to the floor beside the bed. I looked her over. Even relaxed, the muscles in her arms and along the tops of her thighs were well defined.

"You even smell like one of them," she said.

"How did you get the clothes past their store security? They have those beeper tags clipped to them."

"Easy. I tried on the shoes and walked out when they weren't looking. In the second store I took the pants into a dressing room, cut the alarm tag out of the waistband, and put them on. I held the alarm tag that was clipped to the blouse in my armpit and walked out of that store, too. I put the blouse on in the mall women's room."

"If you can't read, how did you know which was the women's room?"

"There's a picture on the door."

I felt tired and old. Ruth moved close. She rubbed her foot up my leg, drawing the pajama leg up with it. Her thigh slid across my groin. I started to get hard. "Cut it out," I said. She licked my nipple.

I could not stand it. I got off the bed. "I don't like you."

She looked at me with true innocence. "I don't like you, either."

Although he was repulsed by the human body, Jonathan Swift was passionately in love with a woman named Esther Johnson. "What you did at the mall was stupid," I said. "You would have killed that guard."

"Which would have made us even for the day."

"Kansas City was different."

"We should ask the cops there what they think."

"You don't understand. That had some grace to it. But what you did was inelegant. Worst of all it was not gratuitous. You stole those clothes for yourself, and I hate that." I was shaking.

"Who made all these laws?"

"I did."

She looked at me with amazement. "You're not just a Conservative. You're gone native!"

I wanted her so much I ached. "No I haven't," I said, but even to me my voice sounded frightened.

Ruth got out of the bed. She glided over, reached one hand around to the small of my back, pulled herself close. She looked up at me with a face that held nothing but avidity. "You can do whatever you want," she whispered. With a feeling that I was losing everything, I kissed her. You don't need to know what happened then.

I woke when she displaced herself: there was a sound like the sweep of an arm across fabric, a stirring of air to fill the place where she had been. I looked around the still brightly lit room. It was not yet morning. The chain was across the door; her clothes lay on the dresser. She had left the aspirin box beside my bottle of scotch.

She was gone. Good, I thought, now I can go on. But I found that I couldn't sleep, could not keep from thinking. Ruth must be very good at that, or perhaps her thought is a different kind of thought from mine. I got out of the bed, resolved to try again but still fearing the inevitable. I filled the tub with hot water. I got in, breathing heavily. I took the blade from my razor. Holding my arm just beneath the surface of the water, hesitating only a moment, I cut deeply one, two, three times along the veins in my left wrist. The shock was still there, as great as ever. With blood streaming from me I cut the right wrist. Quickly, smoothly. My heart beat fast and light, the blood flowed frighteningly; already the water was stained. I felt faint—yes—it was going to work this time, yes. My vision began to fade—but in the last moments before consciousness fell away I saw, with sick despair, the futile wounds closing themselves once again, as they had so many times before. For in the future the practice of medicine may progress to the point where men need have little fear of death.

The dawn's rosy fingers found me still unconscious. I came to myself about eleven, my head throbbing, so weak I could hardly rise from the cold bloody water. There were no scars. I stumbled into the other room and washed down one of Ruth's megamphetamines with two fingers of scotch. I felt better immediately. It's funny how that works sometimes, isn't it? The maid knocked as I was cleaning the bathroom. I shouted for her to come back later, finished as quickly as possible, and left the hotel immediately. I ate Shredded Wheat with milk and strawberries for breakfast. I was full of ideas. A phone book gave me the location of a likely country club.

The Oak Hill Country Club of Florissant, Missouri, is not a spectacularly wealthy institution, or at least it does not give that impression. I'll bet you that the membership is not as purely white as the stucco clubhouse. That was all right with me. I parked the Citation in the mostly empty parking lot, hauled my new equipment from the trunk, and set off for the locker room, trying hard to look like a dentist. I successfully ran the gauntlet of the pro shop, where the proprietor was telling a bored caddy why the Cardinals would fade in the stretch. I could hear running water from the showers as I shuffled into the locker room and slung the bag into a corner. Someone was singing the "Ode to Joy," abominably.

I began to rifle through the lockers, hoping to find an open one with someone's clothes in it. I would take the keys from my benefactor's pocket and proceed along my merry way. Ruth would have accused me of self-interest; there was a moment in which I accused myself. Such hesitation is the seed of failure: as I paused before a locker containing a likely set of clothes, another golfer entered the room along with the locker-room attendant. I immediately began undressing, lowering my head so that the locker door hid my face. The golfer was soon gone, but the attendant sat down and began to leaf through a worn copy of *Penthouse*. I could come up with no better plan than to strip and enter the showers. Amphetamine daze. Perhaps the kid would develop a hard-on and go to the john to take care of it.

There was only one other man in the shower, the symphonic soloist, a somewhat portly gentleman who mercifully shut up as soon as I entered. He worked hard at ignoring me. I ignored him in return: *alle Menschen werden Brüder*. I waited a long five minutes after he left; two more men came into the showers, and I walked out with what composure I could muster. The locker-room boy was stacking towels on a table. I fished a five from my jacket in the locker and walked up behind him. Casually I took a towel.

"Son, get me a pack of Marlboros, will you?"

He took the money and left.

In the second locker I found a pair of pants that contained the keys to some sort of Audi. I was not choosy. Dressed in record time, I left the new clubs beside the rifled locker. My note read, "The pure products of America go crazy." There were three eligible cars in the lot, two 4000s and a Fox. The key would not open the door of the Fox. I was jumpy, but almost home free, coming around the front of a big Chrysler. . . .

"Hey!"

My knee gave way and I ran into the fender of the car. The keys slipped out of my hand and skittered across the hood to the ground, jingling. Grimacing, I hopped toward them, plucked them up, glancing over my shoulder at my pursuer as I stooped. It was the locker-room attendant.

"Your cigarettes." He looked at me the way a sixteen-year-old looks at his father; that is, with bored skepticism. All our gods in the end become pitiful. It was time for me to be abruptly courteous. As it was, he would remember me too well.

"Thanks," I said. I limped over, put the pack into my shirt pocket. He started to go, but I couldn't help myself. "What about my change?"

Oh, such an insolent silence! I wonder what you told them when they asked you about me, boy. He handed over the money. I tipped him a quarter, gave him a piece of Mr. Graves's professional smile. He studied me. I turned and inserted the key into the lock of the Audi. A fifty percent chance. Had I been the praying kind I might have prayed to one of those pitiful gods. They key turned without resistance; the door opened. The kid slouched back toward the clubhouse, pissed at me and his lackey's job. Or perhaps he found it in his heart to smile. Laughter— the Best Medicine.

A bit of a racing shift, then back to Interstate 70. My hip twinged all the way across Illinois.

———

I had originally intended to work my way east to Buffalo, New York, but after the Oak Hill business I wanted to cut it short. If I stayed on the interstate I was sure to get caught; I had been lucky to get as far as I had. Just outside of Indianapolis I turned onto Route 37 north to Fort Wayne and Detroit.

I was not, however, entirely cowed. Twenty-five years in one time had given me the right instincts, and with the coming of the evening and the friendly insects to sing me along, the boredom of the road became a new recklessness. Hadn't I already been seen by too many people in those twenty-five years? Thousands had looked into my honest face — and where were they? Ruth had reminded me that I was not stuck here. I would soon make an end to this latest adventure one way or another, and once I had done so, there would be no reason in God's green world to suspect me.

And so: north of Fort Wayne, on Highway 6 east, a deserted country road (what was he doing there?), I pulled over to pick up a young hitch-hiker. He wore a battered black leather jacket. His hair was short on the sides, stuck up in spikes on top, hung over his collar in back; one side was carrot-orange, the other brown with a white streak. His sign, pinned to a knapsack, said "?" He threw the pack into the backseat and climbed into the front.

"Thanks for picking me up." He did not sound like he meant it. "Where you going?"

"Flint. How about you?"

"Flint's as good as anywhere."

"Suit yourself." We got up to speed. I was completely calm. "You should fasten your seat belt," I said.

"Why?"

The surly type. "It's not just a good idea. It's the law."

He ignored me. He pulled a crossword puzzle book and a pencil from his jacket pocket. "How about turning on the light."

I flicked on the dome light for him. "I like to see a young man improve himself," I said.

His look was an almost audible sigh. "What's a five-letter word for 'the lowest point'?"

"Nadir," I replied.

"That's right. How about 'widespread'; four letters."

"Rife."

"You're pretty good." He stared at the crossword for a minute, then rolled down his window and threw the book, and the pencil, out of the car. He rolled up the window and stared at his reflection in it. I couldn't let him get off that easily. I turned off the interior light, and the darkness leapt inside.

"What's your name, son? What are you so mad about?"

"Milo. Look, are you queer? If you are, it doesn't matter to me but it will cost you . . . if you want to do anything about it."

I smiled and adjusted the rearview mirror so I could watch him—and he could watch me. "No, I'm not queer. The name's Loki." I extended my right hand, keeping my eyes on the road.

He looked at the hand. "Loki?"

As good a name as any. "Yes. Same as the Norse god."

He laughed. "Sure, Loki. Anything you like. Fuck you."

Such a musical voice. "Now there you go. Seems to me, Milo—if you don't mind my giving you my unsolicited opinion—that you have something of an attitude problem." I punched the cigarette lighter, reached back and pulled a cigar from my jacket on the backseat, in the process weaving the car all over Highway 6. I bit the end off the cigar and spat it out the window, stoked it up. My insects wailed. I cannot explain to you how good I felt.

"Take for instance this crossword puzzle book. Why did you throw it out the window?"

I could see Milo watching me in the mirror, wondering whether he should take me seriously. The headlights fanned out ahead of us, the white lines at the center of the road pulsing by like a rapid heartbeat. Take a chance, Milo. What have you got to lose?

"I was pissed," he said. "It's a waste of time. I don't care about stupid games."

"Exactly. It's just a game, a way to pass the time. Nobody ever really learns anything from a crossword puzzle. Corporation lawyers don't get their Porsches by building their word power with crosswords, right?"

"I don't care about Porsches."

"Neither do I, Milo. I drive an Audi."

Milo sighed.

"I know, Milo. That's not the point. The point is that it's all a game, crosswords or corporate law. Some people devote their lives to Jesus; some devote their lives to artwork. It all comes to pretty much the same thing. You get old. You die."

"Tell me something I don't already know."

"Why do you think I picked you up, Milo? I saw your question mark and it spoke to me. You probably think I'm some pervert out to take advantage of you. I have a funny name. I don't talk like your average middle-aged businessman. Forget about that." The old excitement was upon me; I was talking louder and louder, leaning on the accelerator. The car sped along. "I think you're as troubled by the materialism and cant of life in America as I am. Young people like you, with orange hair, are trying to find some values in a world that offers them nothing but crap for ideas. But too many of you are turning to extremes in response. Drugs, violence, religious fanaticism, hedonism. Some, like you I suspect, to suicide. Don't do it, Milo. Your life is too valuable." The speedometer touched eighty, eighty-five. Milo fumbled for his seat belt but couldn't find it.

I waved my hand, holding the cigar, at him. "What's the matter, Milo? Can't find the belt?" Ninety now. A pickup went by us going the other way, the wind of its passing beating at my head and shoulder. Ninety-five.

"Think, Milo! If you're upset with the present, with your parents and the schools, think about the future. What will the future be like if this trend toward valuelessness continues in the next hundred years? Think of the impact of the new technologies! Gene splicing, gerontology, artificial intelligence, space exploration, biological weapons, nuclear proliferation! All accelerating this process! Think of the violent reactionary movements that could arise—are arising already, Milo, as we speak—from people's desire to find something to hold on to. Paint yourself a picture, *Milo*, of the kind of man or woman another hundred years of this process might produce!"

"What are you talking about?" He was terrified.

"I'm talking about the survival of values in America! Simply that." Cigar smoke swirled in front of the dashboard lights, and my voice had reached a shout. Milo was gripping the sides of his seat. The speedometer read 105. "And you, *Milo*, are at the heart of this process! If people continue to think the way you do, *Milo*, throwing their crossword puzzle books out the windows of their Audis all across America, the future will be full of absolutely valueless people! Right, MILO?" I leaned over, taking my eyes off the road, and blew smoke into his face, screaming, "ARE YOU LISTENING, MILO? MARK MY WORDS!"

"Y-yes."

"GOO, GOO, GA-GA-GAA!"

I put my foot all the way to the floor. The wind howled through the window, the gray highway flew beneath us.

"Mark my words, Milo," I whispered. He never heard me. "Twenty-five across. Eight letters. N-i-h-i-l—"

My pulse roared in my ears, there joining the drowned choir of the fields and the roar of the engine. Body slimy with sweat, fingers clenched through the cigar, fists clamped on the wheel, smoke stinging my eyes. I slammed on the brakes, downshifting immediately, sending the transmission into a painful whine as the car slewed and skidded off the pavement, clipping a reflecting marker and throwing Milo against the windshield. The car stopped with a jerk in the gravel at the side of the road, just shy of a sign announcing, WELCOME TO OHIO.

There were no other lights on the road, I shut off my own and sat behind the wheel, trembling, the night air cool on my skin. The insects wailed. The boy was slumped against the dashboard. There was a star fracture in the glass above his head, and warm blood came away on my fingers when I touched his hair. I got out of the car, circled around to the passenger's side, and dragged him from the seat into the field adjoining the road. He was surprisingly light. I left him there, in a field of Ohio soybeans on the evening of a summer's day.

———

The city of Detroit was founded by the French adventurer Antoine de la Mothe, sieur de Cadillac, a supporter of Comte de Pontchartrain, minister of state to the Sun King, Louis XIV. All of these men worshiped the Roman Catholic god, protected their political positions, and let the future go hang. Cadillac, after whom an American automobile was named, was seeking a favorable location to advance his own economic interests. He came ashore on July 24, 1701, with fifty soldiers, an equal number of settlers, and about one hundred friendly Indians near the present site of the Veterans Memorial Building, within easy walking distance of the Greyhound Bus Terminal.

The car did not run well after the accident, developing a reluctance to go into fourth, but I didn't care. The encounter with Milo had gone exactly as such things should go, and was especially pleasing because it had been totally unplanned. An accident—no order, one would guess—but exactly as if I had laid it all out beforehand. I came into Detroit late at night via Route 12, which eventually turned into Michigan Avenue.

The air was hot and sticky. I remember driving past the Cadillac plant; multitudes of red, yellow, and green lights glinting off dull masonry and the smell of auto exhaust along the city streets. I found the sort of neighborhood I wanted not far from Tiger Stadium: pawnshops, an all-night deli, laundromats, dimly lit bars with red Stroh's signs in the windows. Men on street corners walked casually from noplace to noplace.

I parked on a side street just around the corner from a 7-Eleven. I left the motor running. In the store I dawdled over a magazine rack until at last I heard the racing of an engine and saw the Audi flash by the window. I bought a copy of *Time* and caught a downtown bus at the corner. At the Greyhound station I purchased a ticket for the next bus to Toronto and sat reading my magazine until departure time.

We got onto the bus. Across the river we stopped at customs and got off again. "Name?" they asked me.

"Gerald Spotsworth."

"Place of birth?"

"Calgary." I gave them my credentials. The passport photo showed me with hair. They looked me over. They let me go.

I work in the library of the University of Toronto. I am well read, a student of history, a solid Canadian citizen. There I lead a sedentary life. The subways are clean, the people are friendly, the restaurants are excellent. The sky is blue. The cat is on the mat.

We got back on the bus. There were few other passengers, and most of them were soon asleep; the only light in the darkened interior was that which shone above my head. I was very tired, but I did not want to sleep. Then I remembered that I had Ruth's pills in my jacket pocket. I smiled, thinking of the customs people. All that was left in the box were a couple of tiny pink tabs. I did not know what they were, but I broke one down the middle with my fingernail and took it anyway. It perked me up immediately. Everything I could see seemed sharply defined. The dark green plastic of the seats. The rubber mat in the aisle. My fingernails. All details were separate and distinct, all interdependent. I must have been focused on the threads in the weave of my pants leg for ten minutes when I was surprised by someone sitting down next to me. It was Ruth. "You're back!" I exclaimed.

"We're all back," she said. I looked around and it was true: on the opposite side of the aisle, two seats ahead, Milo sat watching me over his shoulder, a trickle of blood running down his forehead. One corner of his mouth pulled tighter in a rueful smile. Mr. Graves came back from the front seat and shook my hand. I saw the fat singer from the country club, still naked. The locker-room boy. A flickering light from the back of the bus: when I turned around there stood the burning man, his eye sockets two dark hollows behind the wavering flames. The shopping-mall guard. Hector from the hardware store. They all looked at me.

"What are you doing here?" I asked Ruth.

"We couldn't let you go on thinking like you do. You act like I'm some monster. I'm just a person."

"A rather nice-looking young lady," Graves added.

"People are monsters," I said.

"Like you, huh?" Ruth said. "But they can be saints, too."

That made me laugh. "Don't feed me platitudes. You can't even read."

"You make such a big deal out of reading. Yeah, well, times change. I get along fine, don't I?"

The mall guard broke in. "Actually, miss, the reason we caught on to you is that someone saw you walk into the men's room." He looked embarrassed.

"But you didn't catch me, did you?" Ruth snapped back. She turned to me. "You're afraid of change. No wonder you live back here."

"This is all in my imagination," I said. "It's because of your drugs."

"It is all in your imagination," the burning man repeated. His voice was a whisper. "What you see in the future is what you are able to see. You have no faith in God or your fellow man."

"He's right," said Ruth.

"Bull. Psychobabble."

"Speaking of babble," Milo said, "I figured out where you got that goo-goo-goo stuff. Talk—"

"Never mind that," Ruth broke in. "Here's the truth. The future is just a place. The people there are just people. They live differently. So what? People make what they want of the world. You can't escape human failings by running into the past." She rested her hand on my leg. "I'll tell you what you'll find when you get to Toronto," she said. "Another city full of human beings."

This was crazy. I knew it was crazy. I knew it was all unreal, but somehow I was getting more and more afraid. "So the future is just the present writ large," I said bitterly. "More bull."

"You tell her, pal," the locker-room boy said.

Hector, who had been listening quietly, broke in. "For a man from the future, you talk a lot like a native."

"You're the king of bullshit, man," Milo said. " 'Some people devote themselves to artwork'! Jesus!"

I felt dizzy. "Scut down, Milo. That means 'Fuck you too.' " I shook my head to try to make them go away. That was a mistake: the bus began to pitch like a sailboat. I grabbed for Ruth's arm but missed. "Who's driving this thing?" I asked, trying to get out of the seat.

"Don't worry," said Graves. "He knows what he's doing."

"He's brain-dead," Milo said.

"You couldn't do any better," said Ruth, pulling me back down.

"No one is driving," said the burning man.

"We'll crash!" I was so dizzy now that I could hardly keep from being sick. I closed my eyes and swallowed. That seemed to help. A long time passed; eventually I must have fallen asleep.

When I woke it was late morning and we were entering the city, cruising down Eglinton Avenue. The bus had a driver after all—a slender black man with neatly trimmed sideburns who wore his uniform hat at a rakish angle. A sign above the windshield said, YOUR DRIVER—SAFE, COURTEOUS, and below that, on the slide-in nameplate, WILBERT CAUL. I felt like I was coming out of a nightmare. I felt happy. I stretched some of the knots out of my back. A young soldier seated across the aisle from me looked my way; I smiled, and he returned it briefly.

"You were mumbling to yourself in your sleep last night," he said.

"Sorry. Sometimes I have bad dreams."

"It's okay. I do too, sometimes." He had a round open face, an apologetic grin. He was twenty, maybe. Who knew where his dreams came from? We chatted until the bus reached the station; he shook my hand and said he was pleased to meet me. He called me "sir."

I was not due back at the library until Monday, so I walked over to Yonge Street. The stores were busy, the tourists were out in droves, the adult theaters were doing a brisk business. Policemen in sharply creased trousers, white gloves, sauntered along among the pedestrians. It was a bright, cloudless day, but the breeze coming up the street from the lake was cool. I stood on the sidewalk outside one of the strip joints and watched the videotaped come-on over the closed circuit. The Princess Laya. Sondra Nieve, the Human Operator. Technology replaces the traditional barker, but the bodies are more or less the same. The persistence of your faith in sex and machines is evidence of your capacity to hope.

Francis Bacon, in his masterwork *The New Atlantis*, foresaw the utopian world that would arise through the application of experimental science to social problems. Bacon, however, could not solve the problems of his own time and was eventually accused of accepting bribes, fined £40,000, and imprisoned in the Tower of London. He made no appeal to God, but instead applied himself to the development of the virtues of patience and acceptance. Eventually he was freed. Soon after, on a freezing day in late March, we were driving near Highgate when I suggested to him that cold might delay the process of decay. He was excited by the idea. On impulse he stopped the carriage, purchased a hen, wrung its neck, and stuffed it with snow. He eagerly looked forward to the results of his experiment. Unfortunately, in haggling with the street vendor he had exposed himself thoroughly to the cold and was seized by a chill that rapidly led to pneumonia, of which he died on April 9, 1626.

There's no way to predict these things.

When the videotape started repeating itself I got bored, crossed the street, and lost myself in the crowd.

# CHARLES SHEFFIELD

*Charles Sheffield (1935–2002) was born in England and educated at St. John's College, Cambridge. He was president and fellow of the American Astronautical Society, a fellow of the American Association for the Advancement of Science, a past president of the Science Fiction Writers of America, a fellow of the British Interplanetary Society, a distinguished lecturer for the American Institute of Aeronautics and Astronautics, and a member of the International Astronomical Union. His forty-one published books include best-sellers of both fact and fiction. He wrote more than a hundred technical papers on subjects ranging from astronomy to large-scale computer systems, and served as a reviewer of science texts for the* New Scientist, The World and I, *and the* Washington Post. *His writing awards include the Hugo, the Nebula, the Japanese Sei-un Award, the John W. Campbell Memorial Award, and the Isaac Asimov Memorial Award for writing that contributes significantly to the public knowledge and understanding of science. He was the creator of the Jupiter line of science fiction for young adults, and authored or coauthored the first four books of that series. His 1999 book,* Borderlands of Science, *explored the boundaries of current science for the benefit of would-be writers. He was married to fellow author Nancy Kress, who also appears in this volume.*

*"Trapalanda" embodies several pervasive human myths—the quest, the search for lost lands, and the undeniable human urge to solve any mystery that is placed before us. Sheffield's novella brings together a group who go out looking for one thing and find quite another, to the utter detriment of the narrator, illustrating the old truth that some searches cause more questions than answers.*

# TRAPALANDA

## CHARLES SHEFFIELD

JOHN KENYON MARTINDALE seldom did things the usual way. Until a first-class return air ticket and a check for $10,000 arrived at my home in Lausanne I did not know he existed. The enclosed note said only: "For consulting services of Klaus Jacobi in New York, June 6th–7th." It was typed on his letterhead and initialed, JKM. The check was drawn on the Riggs Bank of Washington, D.C. The tickets were for Geneva–New York on June 5th, with an open return.

I did not need work. I did not need money. I had no particular interest in New York, and a transatlantic telephone call to John Kenyon Martindale revealed only that he was out of town until June 5th. Why would I bother with him? It is easy to forget what killed the cat.

The limousine that met me at Kennedy Airport drove to a stone mansion on the East River, with a garden that went right down to the water's edge. An old woman with the nose, chin, and hairy moles of a storybook witch opened the door. She took me upstairs to the fourth floor, while my baggage disappeared under the house with the limousine. The mansion was amazingly quiet. The elevator made no noise at all, and when we stepped out of it the deeply carpeted floors of the corridor were matched by walls thick with oriental tapestries. I was not used to so much silence. When I was ushered into a long, shadowed conservatory filled with flowering plants and found myself in the presence of a man and woman, I wanted to shout. Instead I stared.

Shirley Martindale was a brunette, with black hair, thick eyebrows, and a flawless, creamy skin. She was no more than five feet three, but full-figured and strongly built. In normal company she would have been a center of attention; with John Kenyon Martindale present, she was ignored.

He was of medium height and slender build, with a wide, smiling mouth. His hair was thin and wheat-colored, combed straight back from his face. Any other expression he might have had was invisible. From an inch below his eyes to two inches above them, a flat, black shield extended across his whole face. Within that curved strip of darkness colored shadows moved, little darting points and glints of light that flared red and green and electric blue. They were hypnotic, moving in patterns that could be followed but never quite predicted, and they drew and held the attention. They were so striking that it took me a few moments to realize that John Kenyon Martindale must be blind.

He did not act like a person without sight. When I came into the room he at once came forward and confidently shook my hand. His grip was firm, and surprisingly strong for so slight a man.

"A long trip," he said, when the introductions were complete. "May I offer a little refreshment?"

Although the witch was still standing in the room, waiting, he mixed the drinks himself, cracking ice, selecting bottles, and pouring the correct measures slowly but without error. When he handed a glass to me and smilingly said "There! How's that?" I glanced at Shirley Martindale and replied, "It's fine; but before we start the toasts I'd like to learn what we are toasting. Why am I here?"

"No messing about, eh? You are very direct. Very Swiss—even though you are not one." He turned his head to his wife, and the little lights twinkled behind the black mask. "What did I tell you, Shirley? This is the man." And then to me. "You are here to make a million dollars. Is that enough reason?"

"No. Mr. Martindale, it is not. It was not money that brought me here. I have enough money."

"Then perhaps you are here to become a Swiss citizen. Is that a better offer?"

"Yes. If you can pay in advance." Already I had an idea what John Martindale wanted of me. I am not psychic, but I can read and see. The inner wall of the conservatory was papered with maps of South America.

"Let us say, I will pay half in advance. You will receive five hundred thousand dollars in your account before we leave. The remainder, and the Swiss citizenship papers, will be waiting when we return from Patagonia."

"We? Who are 'we'?"

"You and I. Other guides if you need them. We will be going through difficult country, though I understand that you know it better than anyone."

I looked at Shirley Martindale, and she shook her head decisively. "Not me, Klaus. Not for one million dollars, not for ten million dollars. This is all John's baby."

"Then my answer must be no." I sipped the best pisco sour I had tasted since I was last in Peru, and wondered where he had learned the technique. "Mr. Martindale, I retired four years ago to Switzerland. Since then I have not set foot in Argentina, even though I still carry those citizenship papers. If you want someone to lead you through the *echter Rand* of Patagonia, there must now be a dozen others more qualified than I. But that is beside the point. Even when I was in my best condition, even when I was so young and cocky that I thought nothing could kill me or touch me—even then I would have refused to lead a blind man to the high places that you display on your walls. With your wife's presence and her assistance to you for personal matters, it might barely be possible. Without her—have you any idea at all what conditions are like there?"

"Better than most people." He leaned forward. "Mr. Jacobi, let us perform a little test. Take something from your pocket, and hold it up in front of you. Something that should be completely unfamiliar to me."

I hate games, and this smacked of one; but there was something infinitely persuasive about that thin, smiling man. What did I have in my pocket? I reached in, felt my wallet, and slipped out a photograph. I did not look at it, and I was not sure myself what I had selected. I held it between thumb and forefinger, a few feet away from Martindale's intent face.

"Hold it very steady," he said. Then, while the points of light twinkled and shivered, "It is a picture, a photograph of a woman. It is your assistant, Helga Korein. Correct?"

I turned it to me. It was a portrait of Helga, smiling into the camera. "You apparently know far more about me than I know of you. However, you are not quite correct. It is a picture of my wife, Helga Jacobi. I married her four years ago, when I retired. You are not blind?"

"Legally, I am completely blind and have been since my twenty-second year, when I was foolish enough to drive a racing car into a retaining wall." Martindale tapped the black shield. "Without this, I can see nothing. With it, I am neither blind nor seeing. I receive charge-coupled diode inputs directly to my optic nerves, and I interpret them. I see neither at the wavelengths nor with the resolution provided by the human eye, nor is what I reconstruct anything like the images that I remember from the time before I became blind; but I see. On another occasion I will be happy to tell you all that I know about the technology. What you need to know tonight is that I will be able to pull my own weight on any journey. I can give you that assurance. And now I ask again: will you do it?"

It was, of course, curiosity that killed the cat. Martindale had given me almost no information as to where he wanted to go, or when, or why. But something was driving John Martindale, and I wanted to hear what it was.

I nodded my head, convinced now that he would see my movement. "We certainly need to talk in detail; but for the moment let us use that fine old legal phrase, and say there is agreement in principle."

*There is agreement in principle.* With that sentence, I destroyed my life.

———

Shirley Martindale came to my room that night. I was not surprised. John Martindale's surrogate vision was a miracle of technology, but it had certain limitations. The device could not resolve the fleeting look in a woman's eye, or the millimeter jut to a lower lip. I had caught the signal in the first minute.

We did not speak until it was done and we were lying side by side in my bed. I knew it was not finished. She had not relaxed against me. I waited. "There is more than he told you," she said at last.

I nodded. "There is always more. But he was quite right about that place. I have felt it myself, many times."

As South America narrows from the great equatorial swell of the Amazon Basin, the land becomes colder and more broken. The great spine of the Andean cordillera loses height as one travels south. Ranges that tower to twenty-three thousand feet in the tropics dwindle to a modest twelve thousand. The land is shared between Argentina and Chile, and along their border, beginning with the chill depths of Lago Buenos Aires (sixty miles long, ten miles wide; bigger than anything in Switzerland), a great chain of mountain lakes straddles the frontier, all the way south to Tierra del Fuego and the flowering Chilean city of Punta Arenas.

For fourteen years, the Argentina–Chile borderland between latitude 46 and 50 South had been my home, roughly from Lago Buenos Aires to Lago Argentina. It had become closer to me than any human, closer even than Helga. The east side of the Andes in this region is a bitter, parched desert, where gale-force winds blow incessantly three hundred and sixty days of the year. They come from the snowbound slopes of the mountains, freezing whatever they touch. I knew the country and I loved it, but Helga had persuaded me that it was not a land to which a man could retire. The buffeting wind was an endless drain, too much for old blood. Better, she said, to leave in early middle age, when a life elsewhere could still be shaped.

When the time came for us to board the aircraft that would take me away to Buenos Aires and then to Europe, I wanted to throw away my ticket. I am not a sentimental man, but only Helga's presence allowed me to leave the Kingdom of the Winds.

Now John Martindale was tempting me to return there, with more than money. At one end of his conservatory-study stood a massive globe, about six feet across. Presumably it dated from the time before he had acquired his artificial eyes, because it differed from all other globes I had ever seen in one important respect; namely, it was a relief globe. Oceans were all smooth surface, while mountain ranges of the world stood out from the surface of the flattened sphere. The degree of relief had been exaggerated, but everything was in proportion. Himalayan and Karakoram ranges projected a few tenths of an inch more than the Rockies and the Andes, and they in turn were a little higher than the Alps or the volcanic ranges of Indonesia.

When my drink was finished Martindale had walked me across to that globe. He ran his finger down the backbone of the Americas, following the continuous mountain chains from their beginning in Alaska, through the American Rockies, through Central America, and on to the rising Andes and northern Chile. When he finally came to Patagonia his fingers slowed and stopped.

"Here," he said. "It begins here."

His fingertip was resting on an area very familiar to me. It was right on the Argentina–Chile border, with another of the cold mountain lakes at the center of it. I knew the lake as Lago Pueyrredon, but as usual with

bodies of water that straddle the border there was a different name—
Lago Cochrane—in use on the Chilean side. The little town of Paso
Roballo, where I had spent a dozen nights in a dozen years, lay just to
the northeast.

If I closed my eyes I could see the whole landscape that lay beneath
his finger. To the east it was dry and dusty, sustaining only thornbush and
tough grasses on the dark surface of old volcanic flows; westward were
the tall flowering grasses and the thicketed forests of redwood, cypress,
and Antarctic beech. Even in the springtime of late November there
would be snow on the higher ground, with snow-fed lake waters lying
black as jet under a Prussian-blue sky.

I could see all this, but it seemed impossible that John Martindale
could do so. His blind skull must hold a different vision.

"*What* begins here?" I asked, and wondered again how much he
could receive through those arrays of inorganic crystal.

"The anomalies. This region has weather patterns that defy all logic
and all models."

"I agree with that, from personal experience. That area has the most
curious pattern of winds of any place in the world." It had been a long
flight and a long day, and by this time I was feeling a little weary. I was
ready to defer discussion of the weather until tomorrow, and I wanted
time to reflect on our "agreement in principle." I continued, "However,
I do not see why those winds should interest you."

"I am a meteorologist. Now wait a moment." His sensor array must
have caught something of my expression. "Do not jump to a wrong conclusion. Mine is a perfect profession for a blind man. Who can see the
weather? I was ten times as sensitive as a sighted person to winds, to
warmth, to changes in humidity and barometric pressure. What I could
not see was cloud formations, and those are consequences rather than
causes. I could deduce their appearance from other variables. Eight
years ago I began to develop my own computer models of weather patterns, analyzing the interaction of snow, winds, and topography. Five
years ago I believed that my method was completely general, and completely accurate. Then I studied the Andean system; and in one area—
only one—it failed." He tapped the globe. "Here. Here there are winds
with no sustaining source of energy. I can define a circulation pattern
and locate a vortex, but I cannot account for its existence."

"The area you show is known locally as the Kingdom of the Winds."

"I know. I want to go there."

And so did I.

When he spoke I felt a great longing to return, to see again the *altiplano* of the eastern Andean slopes and hear the banshee music of the western wind. It was all behind me. I had sworn to myself that Argentina existed only in my past, that the Patagonian spell was broken forever. John Martindale was giving me a million dollars and Swiss citizenship, but more than that he was giving me an *excuse*. For four years I had been unconsciously searching for one.

I held out my glass. "I think, Mr. Martindale, that I would like another drink."

Or two. Or three.

Shirley Martindale was moving by my side now, running her hand restlessly along my arm. "There is more. He wants to understand the winds, but there is more. He hopes to find Trapalanda."

She did not ask me if I had heard of it. No one who spends more than a week in central Patagonia can be ignorant of Trapalanda. For three hundred years, explorers have searched for the "City of the Caesars," *Trapalanda*, the Patagonian version of El Dorado. Rumor and speculation said that Trapalanda would be found at about 47 degrees South, at the same latitude as Paso Roballo. Its fabled treasure-houses of gold and gemstones had drawn hundreds of men to their death in the high Andes. People did not come back, and say, "I sought Trapalanda, and I failed to find it." They did not come back at all. I was an exception.

"I am disappointed," I said. "I had thought your husband to be a wiser man."

"What do you mean?"

"Everyone wants to find Trapalanda. Four years of my life went into the search for it, and I had the best equipment and the best knowledge. I told your husband that there were a dozen better guides, but I was lying. I know that country better than any man alive. He is certain to fail."

"He believes that he has special knowledge. And you are going to do it. You are going to take him there. For Trapalanda."

She knew better than I. Until she spoke, I did not know what I would do. But she was right. Forget the "agreement in principle." I would go.

"You want me to do it, don't you?" I said. "But I do not understand *your* reasons. You are married to a very wealthy man. He seems to have as much money as he can ever spend."

"John is curious, always curious. He is like a little boy. He is not doing this for money. He does not care about money."

She had not answered my implied question. I had never asked for John Kenyon Martindale's motives, I had been looking for *her* reasons why he should go. Then it occurred to me that her presence, here in my bed, told me all I needed to know. He would go to the Kingdom of the Winds. If he found what he was looking for, it would bring enormous wealth. Should he fail to return, Shirley Martindale would be a free and very wealthy widow.

"Sex with your husband is not good?" I asked.

"What do you think? I am here, am I not?" Then she relented. "It is worse than not good, it is terrible. It is as bad with him as it is exciting with you. John is a gentle, thoughtful man, but I need someone who takes me and does not ask or explain. You are a strong man, and I suspect that you are a cold, selfish man. Since we have been together, you have not once spoken my name, or said a single word of affection. You do not feel it is necessary to pretend to commitments. And you are sexist. I noticed John's reaction when you said, 'I married Helga.' He would always say it differently, perhaps 'Shirley and I got married.'" Her hands moved from my arm, and were touching me more intimately. She sighed. "I do not mind your attitude. What John finds hard to stand, I *need*. You saw what you did to me here, without one word. You make me shiver."

I turned to bring our bodies into full contact. "And John?" I said. "Why did he marry you?" There was no need to ask why she had married him.

"What do you think," she said. "Was it my wit, my looks, my charm? Give me your hand." She gently moved my fingers along her face and breasts. "It was five years ago. John was still blind. We met, and when we said good night he felt my cheek." Her voice was bitter. "He married me for my pelt."

The texture was astonishing. I could feel no roughness, no blemish, not even the most delicate of hairs. Shirley Martindale had the warm, flawless skin of a six-month-old baby. It was growing warm under my touch.

Before we began she raised herself high above me, propping herself on straight arms. "Helga. What is she like? I cannot imagine her."

"You will see," I said. "Tomorrow I will telephone Lausanne and tell her to come to New York. She will go with us to Trapalanda."

*Trapalanda.* Had I said that? I was very tired, I had meant to say Patagonia.

I reached up to touch her breasts. "No talk now," I said. "No more talk." Her eyes were as black as jet, as dark as mountain lakes. I dived into their depths.

———

Shirley Martindale did not meet Helga; not in New York, not anywhere, not ever. John Kenyon Martindale made his position clear to me the next morning as we walked together around the seventh floor library. "I won't allow her to stay in this house," he said. "It's not for my sake or yours, and certainly not for Shirley's. It is for her sake. I know how Shirley would treat her."

He did not seem at all annoyed, but I stared at the blind black mask and revised my ideas about how much he could see with his CCDs and fiber optic bundles.

"Did she tell you last night why I am going to Patagonia?" he asked, as he picked out a book and placed it in the hopper of an iron potbellied stove with electronic aspirations.

I hesitated, and told the truth. "She said you were seeking Trapalanda."

He laughed. "I wanted to go to Patagonia. The easiest way to do it without an argument from Shirley was to hold out a fifty billion dollar bait. The odd thing, though, is that she is quite right. I am seeking Trapalanda." And he laughed again, more heartily than anything he had said would justify.

The black machine in front of us made a little purr of contentment, and a pleasant woman's voice began to read aloud. It was a mathematics text on the foundations of geometry. I had noticed that although Martindale described himself as a meteorologist, four-fifths of the books in the library were mathematics and theoretical physics. There were too many things about John Martindale that were not what they seemed.

"Shirley's voice," he said, while we stood by the machine and listened to a mystifying definition of the intrinsic curvature of a surface. "And a very pleasant voice, don't you think, to have whispering sweet epsilons in your ear? I borrowed it for use with this optical character recognition equipment, before I got my eyes."

"I didn't think there was a machine in the world that could do that."

"Oh, yes." He switched it off, and Shirley halted in midword. "This isn't even state-of-the-art anymore. It was, when it was made, and it cost the earth. Next year it will be an antique, and they'll give this much capability out in cereal packets. Come on, let's go and join Shirley for a prelunch aperitif."

If John Martindale were angry with me or with his wife, he concealed it well. I realized that the mask extended well beyond the black casing.

Five days later we flew to Argentina. When Martindale mentioned his idea of being in the Kingdom of the Winds in time for the winter solstice, season of the anomaly's strongest showing, I dropped any thoughts of a trip back to Lausanne. I arranged for Helga to pack what I needed and meet us in Buenos Aires. She would wait at Ezeiza Airport without going into the city proper, and we would fly farther south at once. Even if our travels went well, we would need luck as well as efficiency to have a week near Paso Roballo before solstice.

It amused me to see Martindale searching for Helga in the airport arrival lounge as we walked off the plane. He had seen her photograph, and I had assured him that she would be there. He could not find her. Within seconds, long before it was possible to see her features, I had picked her out. She was staring down at a book on her lap. Every fifteen seconds her head lifted for a rapid radarlike scan of the passenger lounge, and returned to the page. Martindale did not notice her until we were at her side.

I introduced them. Helga nodded but did not speak. She stood up and led the way. She had rented a four-seater plane on open charter, and in her usual efficient way she had arranged for our luggage to be transferred to it.

Customs clearance, you ask? Let us be realistic. The Customs Office in Argentina is no more corrupt than that of, say, Bolivia or Ecuador; that is quite sufficient. Should John Martindale be successful in divining the legendary treasures of Trapalanda, plenty of hands would help to remove them illegally from the country.

Helga led the way through the airport. She was apparently not what he had expected of my wife, and I could see him studying her closely. Helga stood no more than five feet two, to my six-two, and her thin body was not quite straight. Her left shoulder dipped a bit, and she favored her left leg a trifle as she walked.

Since I was the only one with a pilot's license I sat forward in the copilot's chair, next to Owen Davies. I had used Owen before as a by-

the-day hired pilot. He knew the Kingdom of the Winds, and he respected it. He would not take risks. In spite of his name he was Argentina
born—one of the many Welshmen who found almost any job preferable
to their parents' Argentinean sheep-farming. Martindale and Helga sat
behind us, side-by-side in the back, as we flew to Comodoro Rivadavia
on the Atlantic coast. It was the last real airfield we would see for a while
unless we dipped across the Chilean border to Cochrane. I preferred not
to try that. In the old days, you risked a few machine-gun bullets from
frontier posts. Today it is likely to be a surface-to-air missile.

We would complete our supplies in Comodoro Rivadavia, then use
dry dirt airstrips the rest of the way. The provisions were supposed to be
waiting for us. While Helga and Owen were checking to make sure that
the delivery included everything we had ordered, Martindale came up
to my side.

"Does she never talk?" he said. "Or is it just my lack of charm?" He
did not sound annoyed, merely puzzled.

"Give her time." I looked to see what Owen and Helga were doing.
They were pointing at three open chests of supplies, and Owen was becoming rather loud.

"You noticed how Helga walks, and how she holds her left arm?"

The black shield dipped down and up, making me suddenly curious
as to what lay behind it. "I even tried to hint at a question in that direction," he said. "Quite properly she ignored it."

"She was not born that way. When Helga walked into my office nine
years ago, I assumed that I was looking at some congenital condition.
She said nothing, nor did I. I was looking for an assistant, someone who
was as interested in the high border country as I was, and Helga fitted.
She was only twenty-one years old and still green, but I could tell she was
intelligent and trainable."

"Biddable," said Martindale. "Sorry, go on."

"You have to be fit to wander around in freezing temperatures at ten
thousand feet," I said. "As part of Helga's condition of employment, she
had to take a full physical. She didn't want to. She agreed only when she
saw that the job depended on it. She was in excellent shape and passed
easily; but the doctor—quite improperly—allowed me to look at her
X rays."

Were the eyebrows raised, behind that obsidian visor? Martindale
cocked his head to the right, a small gesture of inquiry. Helga and Owen
Davies were walking our way.

"She was put together like a jigsaw puzzle. Almost every bone in her arms and legs showed marks of fracture and healing. Her ribs, too. When she was small she had been what these enlightened times call 'abused.' Tortured. As a very small child, Helga learned to keep quiet. The best thing she could hope for was to be ignored. You saw already how invisible she can be."

"I have never heard you angry before," he said. "You sound like her father, not her husband." His tone was calm, but something new hid behind that mask. "And is that," he continued, "why in New York—"

He was interrupted. "Tomorrow," said Owen from behind him. "He says he'll have the rest then. I believe him. I told him he's a fat idle bastard, and if we weren't on our way by noon I'd personally kick the shit out of him."

Martindale nodded at me. Conversation closed. We headed into town for Alberto McShane's bar and the uncertain pleasures of nightlife in Comodoro Rivadavia. Martindale didn't give up. All the way there he talked quietly to Helga. He may have received ten words in return.

It had been five years. Alberto McShane didn't blink when we walked in. He took my order without comment, but when Helga walked past him he reached out his good arm and gave her a big hug. She smiled like the sun. She was home. She had hung around the *Guanaco* bar since she was twelve years old, an oil brat brought here in the boom years. When her parents left, she stayed. She hid among the beer barrels in McShane's cellar until the plane took off. Then she could relax for the first time in her life. Poverty and hard work were luxuries after what she had been through.

The decor of the bar hadn't changed since last time. The bottle of dirty black oil (the first one pumped at Comodoro Rivadavia, if you believe McShane) hung over the bar, and the same stuffed guanaco and rhea stood beside it. McShane's pet armadillo, or its grandson, ambled among the tables looking for beer heeltaps.

I knew our search plans, but Helga and Owen Davies needed briefing. Martindale took Owen's 1:1,000,000 scale ONC's, with their emendations and local detail in Owen's careful hand, added to them the 1:250,000 color photomaps that had been made for him in the United States, and spread the collection out to cover the whole table.

"From here, to here," he said. His fingers tapped the map near Laguna del Sello, then moved south and west until they reached Lago Belgrano.

Owen studied them for a few moments. "All on this side of the border," he said. "That's good. What do you want to do there?"

"I want to land. Here, and here, and here." Martindale indicated seven points, on a roughly north-south line.

Owen Davies squinted down, assessing each location. "Lago Gio, Paso Roballo, Lago Posadas. Know 'em all. Tough landing at two, and that last point is in the middle of the Perito Moreno National Park; but we can find a place." He looked up, not at Martindale but at me. "You're not in the true high country, though. You're twenty miles too far east. What do you want to do when you get there?"

"I want to get out, and look west," said Martindale. "After that, I'll tell you where we have to go."

Owen Davies said nothing more, but when we were at the bar picking up more drinks he gave me a shrug. *Too far east,* it said. *You're not in the high country. You won't find Trapalanda there, where he's proposing to land. What's the story?*

Owen was an honest man and a great pilot who had made his own failed attempt at Trapalanda (sometimes I thought that was true of everyone who lived below 46 degrees South). He found it hard to believe that anyone could succeed where he had not, but he couldn't resist the lure.

"He knows something he's not telling us," I said. "He's keeping information to himself. Wouldn't you?"

Owen nodded. Barrels of star rubies and tons of platinum and gold bars shone in his dark Welsh eyes.

When we returned to the table John Martindale had made his breakthrough. Helga was talking and bubbling with laughter. "How did you *do* that," she was saying. "He's untouchable. What did you *do* to him?" McShane's armadillo was sitting on top of the table, chewing happily at a piece of apple. Martindale was rubbing the ruffle of horny plates behind its neck, and the armadillo was pushing itself against his hand.

"He thinks I'm one of them." Martindale touched the black screen across his eyes. "See? We've both got plates. I'm just one of the family." His face turned up to me. I read the satisfaction behind the mask. *And should I do to your wife, Klaus, what you did to mine?* it said. *It would be no more than justice.*

Those were not Martindale's thoughts. I realized that. They were mine. And that was the moment when my liking for John Kenyon Martindale began to tilt toward resentment.

———

At ground level, the western winds skim off the Andean slopes at seventy knots or more. At nine thousand feet, they blow at less then thirty. Owen was an economy-minded pilot. He flew west at ten thousand until we were at the preferred landing point, then dropped us to the ground in three sickening sideslips.

He had his landing already planned. Most of Patagonia is built of great level slabs, rising like terraces from the high coastal cliffs on the Atlantic Ocean to the Andean heights in the west. The exception was in the area we were exploring. Volcanic eruptions there have pushed great layers of basalt out onto the surface. The ground is cracked and irregular, and scarred by the scouring of endless winds. It takes special skill to land a plane when the wind speed exceeds the landing airspeed, and Owen Davies had it. We showed an airspeed of over a hundred knots when we touched down, light as a dust mote, and rolled to a perfect landing. "Good enough," said Owen.

He had brought us down on a flat strip of dark lava, at three o'clock in the afternoon. The sun hung low on the northwest horizon, and we stepped out into the teeth of a cold and dust-filled gale. The wind beat and tugged and pushed our bodies, trying to blow us back to the Atlantic. Owen, Helga, and I wore goggles and helmets against the driving clouds of grit and sand.

Martindale was bareheaded. He planted a GPS transponder on the ground to confirm our exact position, and faced west. With his head tilted upward and his straw-colored hair blowing wild, he made an adjustment to the side of his visor, then nodded. "It is there," he said. "I knew it must be."

We looked, and saw nothing. "What is there?" said Helga.

"I'll tell you in a moment. Note these down. I'm going to read off heights and headings." Martindale looked at the sun and the compass. He began to turn slowly from north to south. Every fifteen degrees he stopped, stared at the featureless sky, and read off a list of numbers. When he was finished he nodded to Owen. "All right. We can do the next one now."

"You mean that's *it*? *The whole thing*? All you're going to do is stand there?" Owen is many good things, but he is not diplomatic.

"That's it—for the moment." Martindale led the way back to the aircraft.

I could not follow. Not at once. I had lifted my goggles and was peering with wind-teared eyes to the west. The land there fell upward to the dark-blue twilight sky. It was the surge of the Andes, less than twenty miles away, rolling up in long, snowcapped breakers. I walked across the tufts of bunchgrass and reached out a hand to steady myself on an isolated ten-foot beech tree. Wind-shaped and stunted it stood, trunk and branches curved to the east, hiding its head from the deadly western wind. It was the only one within sight.

This was my Patagonia, the true, the terrible.

I felt a gentle touch on my arm. Helga stood there, waiting. I patted her hand in reply, and she instinctively recoiled. Together we followed Martindale and Davies back to the aircraft.

"I found what I was looking for," Martindale said, when we were all safely inside. The gale buffeted and rocked the craft, resenting our presence. "It's no secret now. When the winds approach the Andes from the Chilean side, they shed all the moisture they have picked up over the Pacific; and they accelerate. The energy balance equation is the same everywhere in the world. It depends on terrain, moisture, heating, and atmospheric layers. The same equation everywhere—except that *here*, in the Kingdom of the Winds, something goes wrong. The winds pick up so much speed that they are thermodynamically impossible. There is a mechanism at work, pumping energy into the moving air. I knew it before I left New York City; and I knew what it must be. There had to be a long, horizontal line-vortex, running north to south and transmitting energy to the western wind. But that too was impossible. First, then, I had to confirm that the vortex existed." He nodded vigorously. "It does. With my vision sensors I can see the patterns of compression and rarefaction. In other words, I can see direct evidence of the vortex. With half a dozen more readings, I will pinpoint the exact origin of its energy source."

"But what's all that got to do with finding . . . " Owen trailed off and looked at me guiltily. I had told him what Martindale was after, but I had also cautioned him never to mention it.

"With finding Trapalanda?" finished Martindale. "Why, it has everything to do with it. There must be one site, a specific place where the generator exists to power the vortex line. Find that, and we will have found Trapalanda."

Like God, Duty, or Paradise, Trapalanda means different things to different people. I could see from the expression on Owen's face that a line-vortex power generator was not *his* Trapalanda, no matter what it meant to Martindale.

———

I had allowed six days; it took three. On the evening of June 17th, we sat around the tiny table in the aircraft's rear cabin. There would be no flying tomorrow, and Owen had produced a bottle of *usquebaugh australis*; "southern whiskey," the worst drink in the world.

"On foot," John Martindale was saying. "Now it has to be on foot — and just in case, one of us will stay at the camp in radio contact."

"Helga," I said. She and Martindale shook heads in unison. "Suppose you have to carry somebody out?" she said. "I can't do that. It must be you or Owen."

At least she was taking this seriously, which Owen Davies was not. He had watched with increasing disgust while Martindale made atmospheric observations at seven sites. Afterward he came to me secretly. "We're working for a madman," he said. "We'll find no treasure. I'd almost rather work for Diego."

Diego Luria — "Mad Diego" — believed that the location of Trapalanda could be found by a correct interpretation of the Gospel According to Saint John. He had made five expeditions to the *altiplano*, four of them with Owen as pilot. It was harder on Owen than you might think, since Diego sometimes said that human sacrifice would be needed before Trapalanda could be discovered. They had found nothing; but they had come back, and that in itself was no mean feat.

Martindale had done his own exact triangulation, and pinpointed a place on the map. He had calculated UTM coordinates accurate to within twenty meters. They were not promising. When we flew as close as possible to his chosen location we found that we were looking at a point halfway up a steep rock face, where a set of broken waterfalls cascaded down a near-vertical cliff.

"I am sure," he said, in reply to my implied question. "The data-fit residuals are too small to leave any doubt." He tapped the map, and looked out of the aircraft window at the distant rock face. "Tomorrow. You, and Helga, and I will go. You, Owen, you stay here and monitor our transmission frequency. If we are off the air for more than twelve hours, come and get us."

He was taking this *too* seriously. Before the light faded I went outside again and trained my binoculars on the rock face. According to Martindale, at that location was a power generator that could modify the flow of winds along two hundred and fifty miles of mountain range. I saw nothing but the blown white spray of falls and cataracts, and a gray highland fox picking its way easily up the vertical rock face.

"Trust me." Martindale had appeared suddenly at my side. "I can *see* those wind patterns when I set my sensors to function at the right wavelengths. What's your problem?"

"Size." I turned to him. "Can you make your sensors provide telescopic images?"

"Up to three inch effective aperture."

"Then take a look up there. You're predicting that we'll find a machine which produces tremendous power—"

"Many gigawatts."

"—more power than a whole power station. And there is nothing there, nothing to see. That's impossible."

"Not at all." The sun was crawling along the northern horizon. The thin daylight lasted for only eight hours, and already it was fading. John Kenyon Martindale peered off westward and shook his head. He tapped his black visor. "You've had a good look at this," he said. "Suppose I had wanted to buy something that could do what this does, say, five years ago. Do you know what it would have weighed?"

"*Weighed?*" I shook my head.

"At least a ton. And ten years ago, it would have been impossible to build, no matter how big you allowed it to be. In another ten years, this assembly will fit easily inside a prosthetic eye. The way is toward miniaturization, higher energy densities, more compact design. I expect the generator to be small." He suddenly turned again to look right into my face. "I have a question for you, and it is an unforgivably personal one. Have you ever consummated your marriage with Helga?"

He had anticipated my lunge at him, and he backed away rapidly. "Do not misunderstand me," he said. "Helga's extreme aversion to physical contact is obvious. If it is total, there are New York specialists who can probably help her. I have influence there."

I looked down at my hands as they held the binoculars. They were trembling. "It is—total," I said.

"You knew that—and yet you married her. Why?"

"Why did you marry *your* wife, knowing you would be cuckolded?" I was lashing out, not expecting an answer.

"Did she tell you it was for her skin?" His voice was weary, and he was turning away as he spoke. "I'm sure she did. Well, I will tell you. I married Shirley—because she wanted me to."

Then I was standing alone in the deepening darkness. Shirley Martindale had warned me, back in New York. He was like a child, curious about everything. Including me, including Helga, including me and Helga.

*Damn you, John Martindale.* I looked at the bare hillside, and prayed that Trapalanda would somehow swallow him whole. Then I would never again have to endure that insidious, probing voice, asking the unanswerable.

————

The plane had landed on the only level piece of ground in miles. Our destination was a mile and a half away, but it was across some formidable territory. We would have to descend a steep scree, cross a quarter mile of boulders until we came to a fast-moving stream, and follow that watercourse upward, until we were in the middle of the waterfalls themselves.

The plain of boulders showed the translucent sheen of a thin ice coating. The journey could not be done in poor light. We would wait until morning, and leave promptly at ten.

Helga and I went to bed early, leaving Martindale with his calculations and Owen Davies with his *usquebaugh australis.* At a pinch the aircraft would sleep four, but Helga and I slept outside in a small reinforced tent brought along for the purpose. The floor area was five feet by seven. We had pitched the tent in the lee of the aircraft, where the howl of the wind was muted. I listened to Helga's breathing, and knew after half an hour that she was still awake.

"Think we'll find anything?" I said softly.

"I don't know." And then, after maybe one minute. "It's not that. It's you, Klaus."

"I've never been better."

"That's the problem. I've seen you, these last few days. You love it here. I should never have taken you away."

"I'm not complaining."

"That's part of the problem, too. You never complain. I wish you would." I heard her turn to face me in the dark, and for one second I imagined a hand was reaching out toward me. It was an illusion. She went on, "When I said I wanted to leave Patagonia and live in Europe, you agreed without an argument. But your heart has always been here."

"Oh, well, I don't know . . ." The lie stuck in my throat.

"And there's something else. I wasn't going to tell you, because I was afraid that you would misunderstand. But I will tell you. John Martindale tried to touch me."

I stirred, began to sit up, and felt the rough canvas against my forehead. Outside, the wind gave a sudden scream around the tent. "You mean he tried to—to—"

"No. He reached out, and tried to touch the back of my hand. That was all. I don't know why he did it, but I think it was just curiosity. He watches everything, and he has been watching us. I pulled my hand away before he got near. But it made me think of you. I have not been a wife to you, Klaus. You've done your best, and I've tried my hardest but it hasn't improved at all. Be honest with yourself, you know it hasn't. So if you want to stay here when this work is finished . . ."

I hated to hear her sound so confused and lost. "Let's not discuss it now," I said.

*In other words, I can't bear to talk about it.*

We had tried so hard at first, with Helga gritting her teeth at every gentle touch. When I finally realized that the sweat on her forehead and the quiver in her thin limbs was a hundred percent fear and zero percent arousal, I stopped trying. After that we had been happy—or at least, I had. I had not been faithful physically, but I could explain that well enough. And then, with this trip and the arrival on the scene of John Kenyon Martindale, the whole relationship between Helga and me felt threatened. And I did not know why.

"We ought to get as much sleep as we can tonight," I said, after another twenty seconds or so. "Tomorrow will be a tough day."

She said nothing, but she remained awake for a long, long time.

And so, of course, did I.

————

The first quarter mile was easy, a walk down a gently sloping incline of weathered basalt. Owen Davies had watched us leave with an odd mixture of disdain and greed on his face. We were not going to find anything, he was quite sure of that—but on the other hand, if by some miracle we *did*, and he was not there to see it . . .

We carried minimal packs. I thought it would be no more than a two-hour trek to our target point, and we had no intention of being away overnight.

When we came to the field of boulders I revised my estimate. Every square millimeter of surface was coated with the thinnest and most treacherous layer of clear ice. In principle its presence was impossible. With an atmosphere of this temperature and dryness, that ice should have sublimed away.

We picked our way carefully across, concentrating on balance far more than progress. The wind buffeted us, always at the worst moments. It took another hour and a half before we were at the bottom of the waterfalls and could see how to tackle the rock face. It didn't look too bad. There were enough cracks and ledges to make the climb fairly easy.

"That's the spot," said Martindale. "Right in there."

We followed his pointing finger. About seventy feet above our heads one of the bigger waterfalls came cascading its way out from the cliff for a thirty-foot vertical drop.

"The waterfall?" said Helga. Her tone of voice said more than her words. *That's supposed to be a generator of two hundred and fifty miles of gale-force winds?* she was saying. *Tell me another one.*

"Behind it." Martindale was walking along the base of the cliff, looking for a likely point where he could begin the climb. "The coordinates are actually *inside* the cliff. Which means we have to look *behind* the waterfall. And that means we have to come at it from the side."

We had brought rock-climbing gear with us. We did not need it. Martindale found a diagonal groove that ran at an angle of thirty degrees up the side of the cliff, and after following it to a vertical chimney, we found another slanting ledge running the other way. Two more changes of route, neither difficult, and we were on a ledge about two feet wide that ran up to and right behind our waterfall.

Two feet is a lot less when you are seventy feet up and walking a rock ledge slippery with water. Even here, the winds plucked restlessly at our clothes. We roped ourselves together, Martindale leading, and inched our way forward. When we were a few feet from the waterfall Martindale lengthened the rope between him and me, and went on alone behind the cascading water.

"It's all right." He had to shout to be heard above the crash of water. "It gets easier. The ledge gets wider. It runs into a cave in the face of the cliff. Come on."

We were carrying powerful electric flashlights, and we needed them. Once we were in behind the screen of water, the light paled and dwindled. We shone the lights toward the back of the cave. We were standing on a flat area, maybe ten feet wide and twelve feet deep. So much for Owen's dream of endless caverns of treasure; so much for my dreams, too, though they had been a lot less grandiose than his.

Standing about nine feet in from the edge of the ledge stood a dark blue cylinder, maybe four feet long and as thick as a man's thigh. It was smooth-surfaced and uniform, with no sign of controls or markings on its surface. I heard Martindale grunt in satisfaction.

"Bingo," he said. "That's it."

"The whole thing?"

"Certainly. Remember what I said last night, about advanced technology making this smaller? There's the source of the line-vortex—the power unit for the whole Kingdom of the Winds." He took two steps toward it, and as he did so Helga cried out, "Look out!"

The blank wall at the back of the cave had suddenly changed. Instead of damp gray stone, a rectangle of striated darkness had formed, maybe seven feet high and five feet wide.

Martindale laughed in triumph, and turned back to us. "Don't move for the moment. But don't worry, this is exactly what I hoped we might find. I suspected something like this when I first saw that anomaly. The winds are just an accidental by-product—like an eddy. The equipment here must be a little bit off in its tuning. But it's still working, no doubt about that. Feel the inertial dragging?"

I could feel something, a weak but persistent force drawing me toward the dark rectangle. I leaned backward to counteract it and looked more closely at the opening. As my eyes adjusted I realized that it was not true darkness there. Faint blue lines of luminescence started in from the edges of the aperture and flew rapidly toward a vanishing point at the center. There they disappeared, while new blue threads came into being at the outside.

"Where did the opening come from?" said Helga. "It wasn't there when we came in."

"No. It's a portal. I'm sure it only switches on when it senses the right object within range." Martindale took another couple of steps forward. Now he was standing at the very edge of the aperture, staring through at something invisible to me.

"What is it?" I said. In spite of Martindale's words I too had taken a couple of steps closer, and so had Helga.

"A portal—a gate to some other part of the universe, built around a gravitational line singularity." He laughed, and his voice sounded half an octave lower in pitch. "Somebody left it here for us humans, and it leads to the stars. You wanted Trapalanda? This is it—the most priceless discovery in the history of the human race."

He took one more step forward. His moving leg stretched out forever in front of him, lengthening and lengthening. When his foot came down, the leg looked fifty yards long and it dwindled away to the tiny, distant speck of his foot. He lifted his back foot from the ground, and as he leaned forward his whole body rippled and distorted, stretching away from me. Now he looked his usual self—but he was a hundred yards away, carried with one stride along a tunnel that ran as far as the eye could follow.

Martindale turned, and reached out his hand. A long arm zoomed back toward us, still attached to that distant body, and a normal-sized right hand appeared out of the aperture.

"Come on." The voice was lower again in tone, and strangely slowed. "Both of you. Don't you want to see the rest of the universe? Here's the best chance that you will ever have."

Helga and I took another step forward, staring in to the very edge of the opening. Martindale reached out his left hand too, and it hurtled toward us, growing rapidly, until it was there to be taken and held. I took another step, and I was within the portal itself. I felt normal, but I was aware of that force again, tugging us harder toward the tunnel. Suddenly I was gripped by an irrational and irresistible fear. I had to get away. I turned to move back from the aperture, and found myself looking at Helga. She was thirty yards away, drastically diminished, standing in front of a tiny wall of falling water.

One more step would have taken me outside again to safety, clear of the aperture and its persistent, tugging field. But as I was poised to take that step, Helga acted. She closed her eyes and took a long, trembling step forward. I could see her mouth moving, almost as though in prayer. And then the action I could not believe: she leaned forward to grasp convulsively at John Martindale's outstretched hand.

I heard her gasp, and saw her shiver. Then she was taking another step forward. And another.

"Helga!" I changed my direction and blundered after her along that endless tunnel. "This way. I'll get us out."

"No." She had taken another shivering step, and she was still clutching Martindale's hand. "No, Klaus." Her voice was breathless. "He's right. This is the biggest adventure ever. It's worth everything."

"Don't be afraid," said a hollow, booming voice. It was Martindale, and now all I could see of him was a shimmering silhouette. The man had been replaced by a sparkling outline. "Come on, Klaus. It's almost here."

The tugging force was stronger, pulling on every cell of my body. I looked at Helga, a shining outline now like John Martindale. They were dwindling, vanishing. They were gone. I wearily turned around and tried to walk back the way we had come. Tons of weight hung on me, wreathed themselves around every limb. I was trying to drag the whole world up an endless hill. I forced my legs to take one small step, then another. It was impossible to see if I was making progress. I was surrounded by that roaring silent pattern of rushing blue lines, all going in the opposite direction from me, every one doing its best to drag me back.

I inched along. Finally I could see the white of the waterfall ahead. It was growing in size, but at the same time it was losing definition. My eyes ached. By the time I took the final step and fell on my face on the stone floor of the cave, the waterfall was no more than a milky haze and a sound of rushing water.

––––––

Owen Davies saved my life, what there is of it. I did my part to help him. I wanted to live when I woke up, and weak as I was, and half-blind, I managed to crawl down that steep rock face. I was dragging myself over the icy boulders when he found me. My clothes were shredding, falling off my body, and I was shivering and weeping from cold and fear. He wrapped me in his own jacket and helped me back to the aircraft.

Then he went off to look for John Martindale and Helga. He never came back. I do not know to this day if he found and entered the portal, or if he came to grief somewhere on the way.

I spent two days in the aircraft, knowing that I was too sick and my eyes were too bad to dream of flying anywhere. My front teeth had all gone, and I ate porridge or biscuits soaked in tea. Three more days, and I began to realize that if I did not fly myself, I was not going anywhere. On the seventh day I managed a faltering, incompetent takeoff and flew northeast, peering at the instruments with my newly purblind eyes. I made a crash landing at Comodoro Rivadavia, was dragged from the wreckage, and flown to a hospital in Bahía Blanca. They did what they could for me, which was not too much. By that time I was beginning to have some faint idea what had happened to my body, and as soon as the hospital was willing to release me I took a flight to Buenos Aires, and went on at once to Geneva's Lakeside Hospital. They removed the cataracts from my eyes. Three weeks later I could see again without that filmy mist over everything.

Before I left the hospital I insisted on a complete physical. Thanks to John Martindale's half-million dollar deposit, money was not going to be a problem. The doctor who went over the results with me was about thirty years old, a Viennese Jew who had been practicing for only a couple of years. He looked oddly similar to one of my cousins at that age. "Well, Mr. Jacobi," he said (after a quick look at his dossier to make sure of my name), "there are no organic abnormalities, no cardiovascular problems, only slight circulation problems. You have some osteoarthritis in your hips and your knees. I'm delighted to be able to tell you that you are in excellent overall health for your age."

"If you didn't know," I said, "how old would you think I am?"

He looked again at his crib sheet, but found no help there. I had deliberately left out my age at the place where the hospital entry form required it. "Well," he said. He was going to humor me. "Seventy-six?"

"Spot on," I said.

I had the feeling that he had knocked a couple of years off his estimate, just to make me feel good. So let's say my biological age was seventy-eight or seventy-nine. When I flew with John Martindale to Buenos Aires, I had been one month short of my forty-fourth birthday.

At that point I flew to New York, and went to John Kenyon Martindale's house. I met with Shirley—briefly. She did not recognize me, and I did not try to identify myself. I gave my name as Owen Davies. In John's absence, I said, I was interested in contacting some of the mathematician friends that he had told me I would like to meet. Could she remember the names of any of them, so I could call them even before John came back? She looked bored, but she came back with a telephone book and produced three names. One was in San Francisco, one was in Boston, and the third was here in New York, at the Courant Institute.

He was in his middle twenties, a fit-looking curly-haired man with bright blue eyes and a big smile. The thing that astonished him about my visit, I think, was not the subject matter. It was the fact that I made the visit. He found it astonishing that a spavined antique like me would come to his office to ask about this sort of topic in theoretical physics.

"What you are suggesting is not just *permitted* in today's view of space and time, Mr. Davies," he said. "It's absolutely *required*. You can't do something to *space*—such as making an instantaneous link between two places, as you have been suggesting—without at the same time having profound effects on *time*. Space and time are really a single entity. Distances and elapsed times are intimately related, like two sides of the same coin."

"And the line-vortex generator?" I said. I had told him far less about this, mainly because all I knew of it had been told to us by John Martindale.

"Well, if the generator in some sense approximated an infinitely long, rapidly rotating cylinder, then yes. General relativity insists that very peculiar things would happen there. There could be global causality violations—'before' and 'after' getting confused, cause and effect becoming mixed up, that sort of thing. God knows what time and space look like near the line singularity itself. But don't misunderstand me. Before any of these things could happen, you would have to be dealing with a huge system, something many times as massive as the sun."

I resisted the urge to tell him he was wrong. Apparently he did not accept John Martindale's unshakable confidence in the idea that with better technology came increase in capability *and* decrease in size. I stood up and leaned on my cane. My left hip was a little dodgy and became tired if I walked too far. "You've been very helpful."

"Not at all." He stood up, too, and said, "Actually, I'm going to be giving a lecture at the institute on these subjects in a couple of weeks. If you'd like to come . . ."

I noted down the time and place, but I knew I would not be there. It was three months to the day since John Martindale, Helga, and I had climbed the rock face and walked behind the waterfall. Time—my time—was short. I had to head south again.

The flight to Argentina was uneventful. Comodoro Rivadavia was the same as always. Now I am sitting in Alberto McShane's bar, drinking one last beer (all that my digestion today will permit) and waiting for the pilot. McShane did not recognize me, but the armadillo did. It trundled to my table, and sat looking up at me. *Where's my friend John Martindale*, it was saying.

Where indeed? I will tell you soon. The plane is ready. We are going to Trapalanda.

It will take all my strength, but I think I can do it. I have added equipment that will help me to cross that icy field of boulders and ascend the rock face. It is September. The weather will be warmer, and the going easier. If I close my eyes I can see the portal now, behind the waterfall, its black depths and shimmering blue streaks rushing away toward the vanishing point.

Thirty-five years. That is what the portal owes me. It sucked them out of my body as I struggled back against the gravity gradient. Maybe it is impossible to get them back. I don't know. My young mathematician friend insisted that time is infinitely fluid, with no more constraints on movement through it than there are on travel through space. I don't know, but I want my thirty-five years. If I die in the attempt, I will be losing little.

I am terrified of that open gate, with its alien twisting of the world's geometry. I am more afraid of it than I have ever been of anything. Last time I failed, and I could not go through it. But I will go through it now.

This time I have something more than Martindale's scientific curiosity to drive me on. It is not thoughts of danger or death that fill my mind as I sit here. I have that final image of Helga, reaching out and taking John Martindale's hand in hers. Reaching out, to grasp his hand, voluntarily. I love Helga, I am sure of that, but I cannot make sense of my other emotions; fear, jealousy, resentment, hope, excitement. She was *touching* him. Did she do it because she wanted to go through the portal, wanted it so much that every fear was insignificant? Or had she, after thirty years, finally found someone whom she could touch without cringing and loathing?

The pilot has arrived. My glass is empty. Tomorrow I will know.

# NANCY KRESS

Nancy Kress is the author of twenty-one books: thirteen novels of science fiction or fantasy, one young-adult novel, two thrillers, three story collections, and two books on writing. Her books include Probability Space—the conclusion of a trilogy that began with Probability Moon and Probability Sun—and Crossfire. The trilogy concerns quantum physics, a space war, and the nature of reality. Crossfire, set in a different universe, explores various ways humanity might coexist with aliens, even though mankind never understands either them or itself very well. Her latest novel, Nothing Human, is set on a bleak future earth, where children have to be genetically engineered and the arrival of an alien race brings with it the frightening thought that humanity's next generation may not be human at all.

Her short fiction has won three Nebulas: in 1985 for "Out of All Them Bright Stars," in 1991 for the novella version of "Beggars in Spain" (which also won a Hugo), and in 1998 for "The Flowers of Aulit Prison." Her work has been translated into Swedish, French, Italian, German, Spanish, Portuguese, Polish, Croatian, Lithuanian, Romanian, Japanese, and Russian. She is also the monthly Fiction columnist for Writer's Digest magazine, and is a regular teacher at the Science Fiction and Fantasy Clarion Writers' Workshop.

In "The Price of Oranges," the epitome of a humanist science-fiction story, time travel isn't through hundreds or thousands of years—it begins and ends in the twentieth century. And yet it is easy to understand the poor traveler's bewilderment at the events that have happened in the time that is skipped during his travels, events that are yet to come in his own time, which may be the most fearful idea of all.

# THE PRICE OF ORANGES

## NANCY KRESS

"I'M WORRIED ABOUT my granddaughter," Harry Kramer said, passing half of his sandwich to Manny Feldman. Manny took it eagerly. The sandwich was huge, thick slices of beef and horseradish between fresh slabs of crusty bread. Pigeons watched the park bench hopefully.

"Jackie. The granddaughter who writes books," Manny said. Harry watched to see that Manny ate. You couldn't trust Manny to eat enough; he stayed too skinny. At least in Harry's opinion. Manny, Jackie—the world, Harry sometimes thought, had all grown too skinny when he somehow hadn't been looking. Skimpy. Stretch-feeling. Harry nodded to see horseradish spurt in a satisfying stream down Manny's scraggly beard.

"Jackie. Yes," Harry said.

"So what's wrong with her? She's sick?" Manny eyed Harry's strudel, cherry with real yeast bread. Harry passed it to him. "Harry, the whole thing? I couldn't."

"Take it, take it, I don't want it. You should eat. No, she's not sick. She's miserable." When Manny, his mouth full of strudel, didn't answer, Harry put a hand on Manny's arm. "*Miserable.*"

Manny swallowed hastily. "How do you know? You saw her this week?"

"No. Next Tuesday. She's bringing me a book by a friend of hers. I know from this." He drew a magazine from an inner pocket of his coat. The coat was thick tweed, almost new, with wooden buttons. On the cover of the glossy magazine a woman smiled contemptuously. A woman with hollow, starved-looking cheeks who obviously didn't get enough to eat either.

"That's not a book," Manny pointed out.

"So she writes stories, too. Listen to this. Just listen. 'I stood in my backyard, surrounded by the false bright toxin-fed green, and realized that the earth was dead. What else could it be, since we humans swarmed upon it like maggots on carrion, growing our hectic gleaming molds, leaving our slime trails across the senseless surface?' Does that sound like a happy woman?"

"Hoo boy," Manny said.

"It's all like that. 'Don't read my things, Popsy,' she says. 'You're not in the audience for my things.' Then she smiles without ever once showing her teeth." Harry flung both arms wide. "Who else should be in the audience but her own grandfather?"

Manny swallowed the last of the strudel. Pigeons fluttered angrily. "She never shows her teeth when she smiles? Never?"

"Never."

"Hoo boy," Manny said. "Did you want all of that orange?"

"No, I brought it for you, to take home. But did you finish that whole half a sandwich already?"

"I thought I'd take it home," Manny said humbly. He showed Harry the tip of the sandwich, wrapped in the thick brown butcher paper, protruding from the pocket of his old coat.

Harry nodded approvingly. "Good, good. Take the orange, too. I brought it for you."

Manny took the orange. Three teenagers carrying huge shrieking radios sauntered past. Manny started to put his hands over his ears, received a look of dangerous contempt from the teenager with green hair, and put his hands on his lap. The kid tossed an empty beer bottle onto the pavement before their feet. It shattered. Harry scowled fiercely but Manny stared straight ahead. When the cacophony had passed, Manny said, "Thank you for the orange. Fruit, it costs so much this time of year."

Harry still scowled. "Not in 1937."

"Don't start that again, Harry."

Harry said sadly, "Why won't you ever believe me? Could I afford to bring all this food if I got it at 1988 prices? Could I afford this coat? Have you seen buttons like this in 1988, on a new coat? Have you seen sandwiches wrapped in that kind of paper since we were young? Have you? Why won't you believe me?"

Manny slowly peeled his orange. The rind was pale, and the orange had seeds. "Harry. Don't start."

"But why won't you just come to my room and *see?*"

Manny sectioned the orange. "Your room. A cheap furnished room in a Social Security hotel. Why should I go? I know what will be there. What will be there is the same thing in my room. A bed, a chair, a table, a hot plate, some cans of food. Better I should meet you here in the park, get at least a little fresh air." He looked at Harry meekly, the orange clutched in one hand. "Don't misunderstand. It's not from a lack of friendship I say this. You're good to me, you're the best friend I have. You bring me things from a great deli, you talk to me, you share with me the family I don't have. It's enough, Harry. It's *more* than enough. I don't need to see where you live like I live."

Harry gave it up. There were moods, times, when it was just impossible to budge Manny. He dug in, and in he stayed. "Eat your orange."

"It's a good orange. So tell me more about Jackie."

"Jackie." Harry shook his head. Two kids on bikes tore along the path. One of them swerved towards Manny and snatched the orange from his hand. "Aw riggghhhtttt!"

Harry scowled after the child. It had been a girl. Manny just wiped the orange juice off his fingers onto the knee of his pants. "Is everything she writes so depressing?"

"Everything," Harry said. "Listen to this one." He drew out another magazine, smaller, bound in rough paper with a stylized linen drawing of a woman's private parts on the cover. On the cover! Harry held the magazine with one palm spread wide over the drawing, which made it difficult to keep the pages open while he read. " 'She looked at her mother in the only way possible: with contempt, contempt for all the betrayals and compromises that had been her mother's life, for the sad soft lines of defeat around her mother's mouth, for the bright artificial dress too young for her wasted years, for even the leather handbag, Gucci of course, filled with blood money for having sold her life to a man who had long since ceased to want it.' "

"Hoo boy," Manny said. "About a *mother* she wrote that?"

"About everybody. All the time."

"And where *is* Barbara?"

"Reno again. Another divorce." How many had that been? After two, did anybody count? Harry didn't count. He imagined Barbara's life as a large roulette wheel like the ones on TV, little silver men bouncing in and out of red and black pockets. Why didn't she get dizzy?

Manny said slowly, "I always thought there was a lot of love in her."

"A lot of that she's got," Harry said dryly.

"Not Barbara—Jackie. A lot of . . . I don't know. Sweetness. Under the way she is."

"The way she is," Harry said gloomily. "Prickly. A cactus. But you're right, Manny, I know what you mean. She just needs someone to soften her up. Love her back, maybe. Although *I* love her."

The two old men looked at each other. Manny said, "Harry. . . ."

"I know, I know. I'm only a grandfather, my love doesn't count, I'm just there. Like air. 'You're wonderful, Popsy,' she says, and still no teeth when she smiles. But you know, Manny—you are right!" Harry jumped up from the bench. "You are! What she needs is a young man to love her!"

Manny looked alarmed. "I didn't say—"

"I don't know why I didn't think of it before!"

"Harry—"

"And her stories, too! Full of ugly murders, ugly places, unhappy endings. What she needs is something to show her that writing could be about sweetness, too."

Manny was staring at him hard. Harry felt a rush of affection. That Manny should have the answer! Skinny wonderful Manny!

Manny said slowly, "Jackie said to me, 'I write about reality.' That's what she said, Harry."

"So there's no sweetness in reality? Put sweetness in her life, her writing will go sweet. She *needs* this, Manny. A really nice fellow!"

Two men in jogging suits ran past. One of their Reeboks came down on a shard of beer bottle. "Every fucking time!" he screamed, bending over to inspect his shoe. "Fucking park!"

"Well, what do you expect?" the other drawled, looking at Manny and Harry. "Although you'd think that if we could clean up Lake Erie. . . ."

"Fucking derelicts!" the other snarled. They jogged away.

"Of course," Harry said, "it might not be easy to find the sort of guy to convince Jackie."

"Harry, I think you should maybe think—"

"Not here," Harry said suddenly. "Not here. *There.* In 1937."

"*Harry. . . .*"

"Yeah," Harry said, nodding several times. Excitement filled him like light, like electricity. What an idea! "It was different then."

Manny said nothing. When he stood up, the sleeve of his coat exposed the number tattooed on his wrist. He said quietly, "It was no paradise in 1937 either, Harry."

Harry seized Manny's hand. "I'm going to do it, Manny. Find someone for her there. Bring him here."

Manny sighed. "Tomorrow at the chess club, Harry? At one o'clock? It's Tuesday."

"I'll tell you then how I'm coming with this."

"Fine, Harry. Fine. All my wishes go with you. You know that."

Harry stood up too, still holding Manny's hand. A middle-aged man staggered to the bench and slumped onto it. The smell of whiskey rose from him in waves. He eyed Manny and Harry with scorn. "Fucking fags."

"Good night, Harry."

"Manny—if you'd only come . . . money goes so much farther there. . . ."

"Tomorrow at one. At the chess club."

Harry watched his friend walk away. Manny's foot dragged a little; the knee must be bothering him again. Harry wished Manny would see a doctor. Maybe a doctor would know why Manny stayed so skinny.

———

Harry walked back to his hotel. In the lobby, old men slumped in upholstery thin from wear, burned from cigarettes, shiny in the seat from long sitting. Sitting and sitting, Harry thought—life measured by the seat of the pants. And now it was getting dark. No one would go out from here until the next daylight. Harry shook his head.

The elevator wasn't working again. He climbed the stairs to the third floor. Halfway there, he stopped, felt in his pocket, counted five quarters, six dimes, two nickels, and eight pennies. He returned to the lobby. "Could I have two dollar bills for this change, please? Maybe old bills?"

The clerk looked at him suspiciously. "Your rent paid up?"

"Certainly," Harry said. The woman grudgingly gave him the money.

"Thank you. You look very lovely today, Mrs. Raduski." Mrs. Raduski snorted.

In his room, Harry looked for his hat. He finally found it under his bed—how had it gotten under his bed? He dusted it off and put it on. It had cost him $3.25. He opened the closet door, parted the clothes hanging from their metal pole—like Moses parting the sea, he always thought, a Moses come again—and stepped to the back of the closet, remembering with his body rather than his mind the sharp little twist to the right just past the far gray sleeve of his good wool suit.

He stepped out into the bare corner of a warehouse. Cobwebs brushed his hat; he had stepped a little too far right. Harry crossed the empty concrete space to where the lumber stacks started, and threaded his way through them. The lumber, too, was covered with cobwebs; not much building going on. On his way out the warehouse door, Harry passed the night watchman coming on duty.

"Quiet all day, Harry?"

"As a church, Rudy," Harry said. Rudy laughed. He laughed a lot. He was also indisposed to question very much. The first time he had seen Harry coming out of the warehouse in a bemused daze, he must have assumed that Harry had been hired to work there. Peering at Rudy's round, vacant face, Harry realized that he must hold this job because he was someone's uncle, someone's cousin, someone's something. Harry had felt a small glow of approval; families should take care of their own. He had told Rudy that he had lost his key and asked him for another.

Outside it was late afternoon. Harry began walking. Eventually there were people walking past him, beside him, across the street from him. Everybody wore hats. The women wore bits of velvet or wool with dotted veils across their noses and long, graceful dresses in small prints. The men wore fedoras with suits as baggy as Harry's. When he reached the park there were children, girls in long black tights and hard shoes, boys in buttoned shirts. Everyone looked like it was Sunday morning.

Pushcarts and shops lined the sidewalks. Harry bought a pair of socks, thick gray wool, for 89 cents. When the man took his dollar, Harry held his breath: each first time made a little pip in his stomach. But no one ever looked at the dates of old bills. He bought two oranges for five cents each, and then, thinking of Manny, bought a third. At a candystore he bought *G-8 And His Battle Aces* for fifteen cents. At The Collector's Cozy in the other time they would gladly give him thirty dollars for it. Finally, he bought a cherry Coke for a nickel and headed towards the park.

"Oh, excuse me," said a young man who bumped into Harry on the sidewalk. "I'm so sorry!" Harry looked at him hard: but, no. Too young. Jackie was twenty-eight.

Some children ran past, making for the movie theater. Spencer Tracy in *Captains Courageous*. Harry sat down on a green-painted wooden bench under a pair of magnificent Dutch elms. On the bench lay a news-magazine. Harry glanced at it to see when in September this was: the 28th. The cover pictured a young blond Nazi soldier standing at stiff salute. Harry thought again of Manny, frowned, and turned the magazine cover down.

For the next hour, people walked past. Harry studied them carefully. When it got too dark to see, he walked back to the warehouse, on the way buying an apple kuchen at a bakery with a curtain behind the counter looped back to reveal a man in his shirt sleeves eating a plate of stew at a table bathed in soft yellow lamplight. The kuchen cost thirty-two cents.

At the warehouse, Harry let himself in with his key, slipped past Rudy nodding over *Paris Nights*, and walked to his cobwebby corner. He emerged from his third-floor closet into his room. Beyond the window, sirens wailed and would not stop.

———

"So how's it going?" Manny asked. He dripped kuchen crumbs on the chessboard; Harry brushed them away. Manny had him down a knight.

"It's going to take time to find somebody that's right," Harry said. "I'd like to have someone by next Tuesday when I meet Jackie for dinner, but I don't know. It's not easy. There are requirements. He has to be young enough to be attractive, but old enough to understand Jackie. He has to be sweet-natured enough to do her some good, but strong enough not to panic at jumping over fifty-two years. Somebody educated. An educated man—he might be more curious than upset by my closet. Don't you think?"

"Better watch your queen," Manny said, moving his rook. "So how are you going to find him?"

"It takes time," Harry said. "I'm working on it."

Manny shook his head. "You have to get somebody here, you have to convince him he *is* here, you have to keep him from turning right around and running back in time through your shirts. . . . I don't know, Harry. I don't know. I've been thinking. This thing is not simple. What if you did something wrong? Took somebody important out of 1937?"

"I won't pick anybody important."

"What if you made a mistake and brought your own grandfather? And something happened to him here?"

"My grandfather was already dead in 1937."

"What if you brought me? I'm already here."

"You didn't live here in 1937."

"What if you brought *you*?"

"I didn't live here either."

"What if you. . . ."

"Manny," Harry said, "I'm not bringing somebody important. I'm not bringing somebody we know. I'm not bringing somebody for permanent. I'm just bringing a nice guy for Jackie to meet, go dancing, see a different kind of nature. A different view of what's possible. An innocence. I'm sure there are fellows here that would do it, but I don't know any, and I don't know how to bring any to her. From there I know. Is this so complicated? Is this so unpredictable?"

"Yes," Manny said. He had on his stubborn look again. How could somebody so skimpy look so stubborn? Harry sighed and moved his lone knight.

"I brought you some whole socks."

"Thank you. That knight, it's not going to help you much."

"Lectures. That's what there was there that there isn't here. Everybody went to lectures. No TV, movies cost money, they went to free lectures."

"I remember," Manny said. "I was a young man myself. Harry, this thing is not simple."

"Yes, it is," Harry said stubbornly.

"1937 was not simple."

"It will work, Manny."

"Check," Manny said.

That evening, Harry went back. This time it was the afternoon of September 16. On newsstands the New York *Times* announced that President Roosevelt and John L. Lewis had talked pleasantly at the White House. Cigarettes cost thirteen cents a pack. Women wore cotton stockings and clunky, high-heeled shoes. Schrafft's best chocolates were sixty cents a pound. Small boys addressed Harry as "sir."

He attended six lectures in two days. A Madame Trefania lectured on theosophy to a hall full of badly-dressed women with thin, pursed lips. A union organizer roused an audience to a pitch that made Harry leave after the first thirty minutes. A skinny, nervous missionary showed slides of religious outposts in China. An archeologist back from a Mexican dig gave a dry, impatient talk about temples to an audience of three people. A New Deal Democrat spoke passionately about aiding the poor, but afterwards addressed all the women present as "Sister." Finally, just when Harry was starting to feel discouraged, he found it.

A museum offered a series of lectures on "Science of Today—and Tomorrow." Harry heard a slim young man with a reddish beard speak with idealistic passion about travel to the moon, the planets, the stars. It seemed to Harry that compared to stars, 1989 might seem reasonably close. The young man had warm hazel eyes and a sense of humor. When he spoke about life in a space ship, he mentioned in passing that women would be freed from much domestic drudgery they now endured. Throughout the lecture, he smoked, lighting cigarettes with a masculine squinting of eye and cupping of hands. He said that imagination was the human quality that would most help people adjust to the future. His shoes were polished.

But most of all, Harry thought, he had a *glow*. A fine golden Boy Scout glow that made Harry think of old covers for the *Saturday Evening Post*. Which here cost five cents.

After the lecture, Harry stayed in his chair in the front row, outwaiting even the girl with bright red lipstick who lingered around the lecturer, this Robert Gernshon. From time to time, Gernshon glanced over at Harry with quizzical interest. Finally the girl, red lips pouting, sashayed out of the hall.

"Hello," Harry said. "I'm Harry Kramer. I enjoyed your talk. I have something to show you that you would be very interested in."

The hazel eyes turned wary. "Oh, no, no," Harry said. "Something *scientific*. Here, look at this." He handed Gernshon a filtered Vantage Light.

"How long it is," Gernshon said. "What's this made of?"

"The filter? It's made of . . . a new filter material. Tastes milder and cuts down on the nicotine. Much better for you. Look at this." He gave Gernshon a styrofoam cup from MacDonald's. "It's made of a new material, too. Very cheap. Disposable."

Gernshon fingered the cup. "Who are you?" he said quietly.

"A scientist. I'm interested in the science of tomorrow, too. Like you. I'd like to invite you to see my laboratory, which is in my home."

"In your home?"

"Yes. In a small way. Just dabbling, you know." Harry could feel himself getting rattled; the young hazel eyes stared at him so steadily. *Jackie*, he thought. Dead earths. Maggots and carrion. Contempt for mothers. What would Gernshon say? When would Gernshon say *anything*?

"Thank you," Gernshon finally said. "When would be convenient?"

"Now?" Harry said. He tried to remember what time of day it was now. All he could picture was lecture halls.

Gernshon came. It was nine-thirty in the evening of Friday, September 17. Harry walked Gernshon through the streets, trying to talk animatedly, trying to distract. He said that he himself was very interested in travel to the stars. He said it had always been his dream to stand on another planet and take in great gulps of completely unpolluted air. He said his great heroes were those biologists who made that twisty model of DNA. He said science had been his life. Gernshon walked more and more silently.

"Of course," Harry said hastily, "like most scientists, I'm mostly familiar with my own field. You know how it is."

"What is your field, Dr. Kramer?" Gernshon asked quietly.

"Electricity," Harry said, and hit him on the back of the head with a solid brass candlestick from the pocket of his coat. The candlestick had cost him three dollars at a pawn shop.

They had walked past the stores and pushcarts to a point where the locked business offices and warehouses began. There were no passersby, no muggers, no street dealers, no Guardian Angels, no punk gangs. Only him, hitting an unarmed man with a candlestick. He was no better than the punks. But what else could he do? What else could he *do*? Nothing but hit him softly, so softly that Gernshon was struggling again almost before Harry got his hands and feet tied, well before he got on the blindfold and gag. "I'm sorry, I'm sorry," he kept saying to Gernshon. Gernshon did not look as if the apology made any difference. Harry dragged him into the warehouse.

Rudy was asleep over *Spicy Stories*. Breathing very hard, Harry pulled the young man—not more than 150 pounds, it was good Harry had looked for slim—to the far corner, through the gate, and into his closet.

"Listen," he said urgently to Gernshon after removing the gag. "Listen. I can call the Medicare Emergency Hotline. If your head feels broken. Are you feeling faint? Do you think you maybe might go into shock?"

Gernshon lay on Harry's rug, glaring at him, saying nothing.

"Listen, I know this is maybe a little startling to you. But I'm not a pervert, not a cop, not anything but a grandfather with a problem. My granddaughter. I need your help to solve it, but I won't take much of your time. You're now somewhere besides where you gave your lecture. A pretty long ways away. But you don't have to stay here long, I promise. Just two weeks, tops, and I'll send you back. I promise, on my mother's grave. And I'll make it worth your while. I promise."

"Untie me."

"Yes. Of course. Right away. Only you have to not attack me, because I'm the only one who can get you back from here." He had a sudden inspiration. "I'm like a foreign consul. You've maybe traveled abroad?"

Gernshon looked around the dingy room. "Untie me."

"I will. In two minutes. Five, tops. I just want to explain a little first."

"Where am I?"

"1989."

Gernshon said nothing. Harry explained brokenly, talking as fast as he could, saying he could move from 1989 to September 1937 when he wanted to, but he could take Gernshon back too, no problem. He said he made the trip often, it was perfectly safe. He pointed out how much farther a small Social Security check, no pension, could go at 1937 prices. He mentioned Manny's strudel. Only lightly did he touch on the problem of Jackie, figuring there would be a better time to share domestic difficulties, and his closet he didn't mention at all. It was hard to keep his eyes averted from the closet door. He did mention how bitter people could be in 1989, how lost, how weary from expecting so much that nothing was a delight, nothing a sweet surprise. He was just working up to a tirade on innocence when Gernshon said again, in a different tone, "Untie me."

"Of course," Harry said quickly, "I don't expect you to believe me. Why should you think you're in 1989? Go, see for yourself. Look at that light, it's still early morning. Just be careful out there, is all." He untied Gernshon and stood with his eyes squeezed shut, waiting.

When nothing hit him, Harry opened his eyes. Gernshon was at the door. "Wait!" Harry cried. "You'll need more money!" He dug into his pocket and pulled out a twenty-dollar bill, carefully saved for this, and all the change he had.

Gernshon examined the coins carefully, then looked up at Harry.

He said nothing. He opened the door and Harry, still trembling, sat down in his chair to wait.

Gershon came back three hours later, pale and sweating. "My God!"

"I know just what you mean," Harry said. "A zoo out there. Have a drink."

Gershon took the mixture Harry had ready in his toothbrush glass and gulped it down. He caught sight of the bottle, which Harry had left on the dresser: Seagram's V.O., with the cluttered, tiny-print label. He threw the glass across the room and covered his face with his hands.

"I'm sorry," Harry said apologetically. "But then it cost only $3.37 the fifth."

Gershon didn't move.

"I'm really sorry," Harry said. He raised both hands, palms up, and dropped them helplessly. "Would you . . . would you maybe like an orange?"

———

Gershon recovered faster than Harry had dared hope. Within an hour he was sitting in Harry's worn chair, asking questions about the space shuttle; within two hours taking notes; within three become again the intelligent and captivating young man of the lecture hall. Harry, answering as much as he could as patiently as he could, was impressed by the boy's resilience. It couldn't have been easy. What if he, Harry, suddenly had to skip fifty-two more years? What if he found himself in 2041? Harry shuddered.

"Do you know that a movie now costs six dollars?"

Gershon blinked. "We were talking about the moon landing."

"Not any more, we're not. I want to ask *you* some questions, Robert. Do you think the earth is dead, with people sliming all over it like on carrion? Is this a thought that crosses your mind?"

"I . . . no."

Harry nodded. "Good, good. Do you look at your mother with contempt?"

"Of course not. Harry—"

"No, it's my turn. Do you think a woman who marries a man, and maybe the marriage doesn't work out perfect, whose does, but they raise at least one healthy child—say a daughter—that that woman's life has been a defeat and a failure?"

"No. I—"

"What would you think if you saw a drawing of a woman's private parts on the cover of a magazine?"

Gernshon blushed. He looked as if the blush annoyed him, but also as if he couldn't help it.

"Better and better," Harry said. "Now, think carefully on this next one—take your time—no hurry. Does reality seem to you to have sweetness in it as well as ugliness? Take your time."

Gernshon peered at him. Harry realized they had talked right through lunch. "But not all the time in the world, Robert."

"Yes," Gernshon said. "I think reality has more sweetness than ugliness. And more strangeness than anything else. Very much more." He looked suddenly dazed. "I'm sorry, I just—all this has happened so—"

"Put your head between your knees," Harry suggested. "There—better now? Good. There's someone I want you to meet."

Manny sat in the park, on their late-afternoon bench. When he saw them coming, his face settled into long sorrowful ridges. "Harry. Where have you been for two days? I was worried, I went to your hotel—"

"Manny," Harry said, "this is Robert."

"So I see," Manny said. He didn't hold out his hand.

"*Him*," Harry said.

"Harry. Oh, Harry."

"How do you do, sir," Gernshon said. He held out his hand. "I'm afraid I didn't get your full name. I'm Robert Gernshon."

Manny looked at him—at the outstretched hand, the baggy suit with wide tie, the deferential smile, the golden Baden-Powell glow. Manny's lips mouthed a silent word: *sir*?

"I have a lot to tell you," Harry said.

"You can tell all of us, then," Manny said. "Here comes Jackie now."

Harry looked up. Across the park a woman in jeans strode purposefully towards them. "Manny! It's only Monday!"

"I called her to come," Manny said. "You've been gone from your room two days, Harry, nobody at your hotel could say where—"

"But *Manny*," Harry said, while Gernshon looked, frowning, from one to the other and Jackie spotted them and waved.

She had lost more weight, Harry saw. Only two weeks, yet her cheeks had hollowed out and new, tiny lines touched her eyes. Skinny lines. They filled him with sadness. Jackie wore a blue tee-shirt that said LIFE

IS A BITCH—THEN YOU DIE. She carried a magazine and a small can of mace disguised as hair spray.

"Popsy! You're here! Manny said—"

"Manny was wrong," Harry said. "Jackie, sweetheart, you look—it's good to see you. Jackie, I'd like you to meet somebody, darling. This is Robert. My friend. My friend Robert. Jackie Snyder."

"Hi," Jackie said. She gave Harry a hug, and then Manny one. Harry saw Gernshon gazing at her very tight jeans.

"Robert's a . . . a scientist," Harry said.

It was the wrong thing to say; Harry knew the moment he said it that it was the wrong thing. Science—all science—was, for some reason not completely clear to him, a touchy subject with Jackie. She tossed her long hair back from her eyes. "Oh, yeah? Not *chemical*, I hope?"

"I'm not actually a scientist," Gernshon said winningly. "Just a dabbler. I popularize new scientific concepts, write about them to make them intelligible."

"Like what?" Jackie said.

Gernshon opened his mouth, closed it again. A boy suddenly flashed past on a skateboard, holding a boom box. Metallica blasted the air. Overhead, a jet droned. Gernshon smiled weakly. "It's hard to explain."

"I'm capable of understanding," Jackie said coldly. "Women *can* understand science, you know."

"Jackie, sweetheart," Harry said, "what have you got there? Is that your new book?"

"No," Jackie said, "this is the one I said I'd bring you, by my friend. It's brilliant. It's about a man whose business partner betrays him by selling out to organized crime and framing the man. In jail he meets a guy who has founded his own religion, the House of Divine Despair, and when they both get out they start a new business, Suicide Incorporated, that helps people kill themselves for a fee. The whole thing is just a brilliant denunciation of contemporary America."

Gernshon made a small sound.

"It's a comedy," Jackie added.

"It sounds . . . it sounds a little depressing," Gernshon said.

Jackie looked at him. Very distinctly, she said, "It's reality."

Harry saw Gernshon glance around the park. A man nodded on a bench, his hands slack on his knees. Newspapers and MacDonald's wrappers stirred fitfully in the dirt. A trash container had been knocked over. From beside a scrawny tree enclosed shoulder-height by black wrought iron, a child watched them with old eyes.

"I brought you something else, too, Popsy," Jackie said. Harry hoped that Gernshon noticed how much gentler her voice was when she spoke to her grandfather. "A scarf. See, it's llama wool. Very warm."

Gernshon said, "My mother has a scarf like that. No, I guess hers is some kind of fur."

Jackie's face changed. "What kind?"

"I—I'm not sure."

"Not an endangered species, I hope."

"No. Not that. I'm sure not . . . that."

Jackie stared at him a moment longer. The child who had been watching strolled towards them. Harry saw Gernshon look at the boy with relief. About eleven years old, he wore a perfectly tailored suit and Italian shoes. Manny shifted to put himself between the boy and Gernshon. "Jackie, darling, it's so good to see you. . . ."

The boy brushed by Gernshon on the other side. He never looked up, and his voice stayed boyish and low, almost a whisper. "Crack. . . ."

"Step on one and you break your mother's back," Gernshon said brightly. He smiled at Harry, a special conspiratorial smile to suggest that children, at least, didn't change in fifty years. The boy's head jerked up to look at Gernshon.

"You talking about my mama?"

Jackie groaned. "No," she said to the kid. "He doesn't mean anything. Beat it."

"I don't forget," the boy said. He backed away slowly.

Gernshon said, frowning, "I'm sorry. I'm not sure exactly what all that was, but I'm sorry."

"Are you for real?" Jackie said angrily. "What the fucking hell *was* all that? Don't you realize this park is the only place Manny and my grandfather can get some fresh air?"

"I didn't—"

"That punk runner meant it when he said he won't forget!"

"I don't like your tone," Gernshon said. "Or your language."

"My language!" The corners of Jackie's mouth tightened. Manny looked at Harry and put his hands over his face. The boy, twenty feet away, suddenly let out a noise like a strangled animal, so piercing all four of them spun around. Two burly teenagers were running towards him. The child's face crumpled; he looked suddenly much younger. He sprang away, stumbled, made the noise again, and hurled himself, all animal terror, towards the street behind the park bench.

"No!" Gernshon shouted. Harry turned towards the shout but Gernshon already wasn't there. Harry saw the twelve-wheeler bearing down, heard Jackie's scream, saw Gernshon's wiry body barrel into the boy's. The truck shrieked past, its air brakes deafening.

Gernshon and the boy rose in the street on the other side.

Car horns blared. The boy bawled, "Leggo my suit! You tore my suit!" A red light flashed and a squad car pulled up. The two burly teenagers melted away, and then the boy somehow vanished as well.

"Never find him," the disgruntled cop told them over the clipboard on which he had written nothing. "Probably just as well." He went away.

"Are you hurt?" Manny said. It was the first time he had spoken. His face was ashen. Harry put a hand across his shoulders.

"No," Gernshon said. He gave Manny his sweet smile. "Just a little dirty."

"That took *guts*," Jackie said. She was staring at Gernshon with a frown between her eyebrows. "Why did you do it?"

"Pardon?"

"Why? I mean, given what that kid is, given—oh, all of it—" she gestured around the park, a helpless little wave of her strong young hands that tore at Harry's heart. "Why bother?"

Gernshon said gently, "What that kid is, is a kid."

Manny looked skeptical. Harry moved to stand in front of Manny's expression before anyone wanted to discuss it. "Listen, I've got a wonderful idea, you two seem to have so much to talk about, about . . . bothering, and . . . everything. Why don't you have dinner together, on me? My treat." He pulled another twenty dollar bill from his pocket. Behind him he could feel Manny start.

"Oh, I couldn't," Gernshon said, at the same moment that Jackie said warningly, "Popsy. . . ."

Harry put his palms on both sides of her face. "Please. Do this for me, Jackie. Without the questions, without the female protests. Just this once. For me."

Jackie was silent a long moment before she grimaced, nodded, and turned with half-humorous appeal to Gernshon.

Gernshon cleared his throat. "Well, actually, it would probably be better if all four of us came. I'm embarrassed to say that prices are higher in this city than in . . . that is, I'm not able to . . . but if we went somewhere less expensive, the Automat maybe, I'm sure all four of us could eat together."

"No, no," Harry said. "We already ate." Manny looked at him.

Jackie began, offended, "I certainly don't want—just what do you think is going on here, buddy? This is just to please my grandfather. Are you afraid I might try to jump your bones?"

Harry saw Gernshon's quick, involuntary glance at Jackie's tight jeans. He saw, too, that Gernshon fiercely regretted the glance the instant he had made it. He saw that Manny saw, and that Jackie saw, and that Gernshon saw that they saw. Manny made a small noise. Jackie's face began to turn so black that Harry was astounded when Gernshon cut her off with a dignity no one had expected.

"No, of course not," he said quietly. "But I would prefer all of us to have dinner together for quite another reason. My wife is very dear to me, Miss Snyder, and I wouldn't do anything that might make her feel uncomfortable. That's probably irrational, but that's the way it is."

Harry stood arrested, his mouth open. Manny started to shake with what Harry thought savagely had better not be laughter. And Jackie, after staring at Gernshon a long while, broke into the most spontaneous smile Harry had seen from her in months.

"Hey," she said softly. "That's nice. That's really, genuinely, fucking nice."

———

The weather turned abruptly colder. Snow threatened but didn't fall. Each afternoon Harry and Manny took a quick walk in the park and then went inside, to the chess club or a coffee shop or the bus station or the library, where there was a table deep in the stacks on which they could eat lunch without detection. Harry brought Manny a poor boy with mayo, sixty-three cents, and a pair of imported wool gloves, one dollar on pre-season sale.

"So where are they today?" Manny asked on Saturday, removing the gloves to peek at the inside of the poor boy. He sniffed appreciatively. "Horseradish. You remembered, Harry."

"The museum, I think," Harry said miserably.

"What museum?"

"How should I know? He says, 'The museum today, Harry,' and he's gone by eight o'clock in the morning, no more details than that."

Manny stopped chewing. "What museum opens at eight o'clock in the morning?"

Harry put down his sandwich, pastrami on rye, thirty-nine cents. He had lost weight the past week.

"Probably," Manny said hastily, "they just talk. You know, like young people do, just talk. . . ."

Harry eyed him balefully. "You mean like you and Leah did when you were young and left completely alone."

"You better talk to him soon, Harry. No, to her." He seemed to reconsider Jackie. "No, to *him*."

"Talk isn't going to do it," Harry said. He looked pale and determined. "Gernshon has to be sent back."

"Be sent?"

"He's *married*, Manny! I wanted to help Jackie, show her life can hold some sweetness, not be all struggle. What kind of sweetness is she going to find if she falls in love with a married man? You know how that goes! Jackie—" Harry groaned. How had all this happened? He had intended only the best for Jackie. Why didn't that count more? "He has to go back, Manny."

"How?" Manny said practically. "You can't hit him again, Harry. You were just lucky last time that you didn't hurt him. You don't want that on your conscience. And if you show him your, uh . . . your—"

"My closet. Manny, if you'd only come see, for a dollar you could get—"

"—then he could just come back any time he wants. So how?"

A sudden noise startled them both. Someone was coming through the stacks. "Librarians!" Manny hissed. Both of them frantically swept the sandwiches, beer (fifteen cents), and strudel into shopping bags. Manny, panicking, threw in the wool gloves. Harry swept the table free of crumbs. When the intruder rounded the nearest bookshelf, Harry was bent over *Making Paper Flowers* and Manny over *Porcelain of the Yung Cheng Dynasty*. It was Robert Gernshon.

The young man dropped into a chair. His face was ashen. In one hand he clutched a sheaf of paper, the handwriting on the last one trailing off into shaky squiggles.

After a moment of silence, Manny said diplomatically, "So where are you coming from, Robert?"

"Where's Jackie?" Harry demanded.

"Jackie?" Gernshon said. His voice was thick; Harry realized with a sudden shock that he had been crying. "I haven't seen her for a few days."

"A few *days?*" Harry said.

"No. I've been . . . I've been. . . ."

Manny sat up straighter. He looked intently at Gernshon over *Porcelain of the Yung Cheng Dynasty* and then put the book down. He moved to the chair next to Gernshon's and gently took the papers from his hand. Gernshon leaned over the table and buried his head in his arms.

"I'm so awfully sorry, I'm being such a baby. . . ." His shoulders trembled. Manny separated the papers and spread them out on the library table. Among the hand-copied notes were two slim books, one bound between black covers and the other a pamphlet. *A Memoir of Auschwitz. Countdown to Hiroshima.*

For a long moment nobody spoke. Then Harry said, to no one in particular, "I thought he was going to science museums."

Manny laid his arm, almost casually, across Gernshon's shoulders. "So now you'll know not to be at either place. More people should have only known." Harry didn't recognize the expression on his friend's face, nor the voice with which Manny said to Harry, "You're right. He has to go back."

"But Jackie. . . ."

"Can do without this 'sweetness,' " Manny said harshly. "So what's so terrible in her life anyway that she needs so much help? Is she dying? Is she poor? Is she ugly? Is anyone knocking on her door in the middle of the night? Let Jackie find her own sweetness. She'll survive."

Harry made a helpless gesture. Manny's stubborn face, carved wood under the harsh fluorescent light, did not change. "Even *him* . . . Manny, the things he knows now—"

"You should have thought of that earlier."

Gernshon looked up. "Don't, I—I'm sorry. It's just coming across it, I never thought human beings—"

"No," Manny said. "But they can. You been here, every day, at the library, reading it all?"

"Yes. That and museums. I saw you two come in earlier. I've been reading, I wanted to *know*—"

"So now you know," Manny said in that same surprisingly casual, tough voice. "You'll survive, too."

Harry said, "Does Jackie know what's going on? Why you've been doing all this . . . learning?"

"No."

"And you—what will you do with what you now know?"

Harry held his breath. What if Gernshon just refused to go back? Gernshon said slowly, "At first, I wanted to not return. At all. How can I watch it, World War II and the camps—I have *relatives* in Poland. And then later the bomb and Korea and the gulags and Vietnam and Cambodia and the terrorists and AIDS—"

"Didn't miss anything," Harry muttered.

"—and not be able to *do* anything, not be able to even hope, knowing that everything to come is already set into history—how could I watch all that without any hope that it isn't really as bad as it seems to be at the moment?"

"It all depends what you look at," Manny said, but Gernshon didn't seem to hear him.

"But neither can I stay, there's Susan and we're hoping for a baby . . . I need to think."

"No, you don't," Harry said. "You need to go *back*. This is all my mistake. I'm sorry. You need to go back, Gernshon."

"Lebanon," Gernshon said. "D.D.T. The Cultural Revolution. Nicaragua. Deforestation. Iran—"

"Penicillin," Manny said suddenly. His beard quivered. "Civil rights. Mahatma Gandhi. Polio vaccines. Washing machines." Harry stared at him, shocked. Could Manny once have worked in a hand laundry?

"Or," Manny said, more quietly, "Hitler. Auschwitz. Hoovervilles. The Dust Bowl. What you *look* at, Robert."

"I don't know," Gernshon said. "I need to think. There's so much . . . and then there's that girl."

Harry stiffened. "Jackie?"

"No, no. Someone she and I met a few days ago, at a coffee shop. She just walked in. I couldn't believe it. I looked at her and just went into shock—and maybe she did too, for all I know. The girl looked exactly like me. And she *felt* like—I don't know. It's hard to explain. She felt like *me*. I said hello but I didn't tell her my name; I didn't dare." His voice fell to a whisper. "I think she's my granddaughter."

"Hoo boy," Manny said.

Gernshon stood. He made a move to gather up his papers and booklets, stopped, left them there. Harry stood, too, so abruptly that Gernshon shot him a sudden, hard look across the library table. "Going to hit me again, Harry? Going to kill me?"

"Us?" Manny said. "Us, Robert?" His tone was gentle.

"In a way, you already have. I'm not who I was, certainly."

Manny shrugged. "So be somebody better."

"Damn it, I don't think you understand—"

"I don't think *you* do, Reuven, boychik. This is the way it *is*. That's all. Whatever you had back there, you have still. Tell me, in all that reading, did you find anything about yourself, anything personal? Are you in the history books, in the library papers?"

"The Office of Public Documents takes two weeks to do a search for birth and death certificates," Gernshon said, a little sulkily.

"So you lost nothing, because you really *know* nothing," Manny said. "Only history. History is cheap. Everybody gets some. You can have all the history you want. It's what you make of it that costs."

Gernshon didn't nod agreement. He looked a long time at Manny, and something moved behind the unhappy hazel eyes, something that made Harry finally let out a breath he didn't know he'd been holding. It suddenly seemed that Gernshon was the one that was old. And he *was*— with the fifty-two years he'd gained since last week, he was older than Harry had been in the 1937 of *Captains Courageous* and wide-brimmed fedoras and clean city parks. But that was the good time, the one that Gernshon was going back to, the one Harry himself would choose, if it weren't for Jackie and Manny . . . still, he couldn't watch as Gernshon walked out of the book stacks, parting the musty air as heavily as if it were water.

Gernshon paused. Over his shoulder he said, "I'll go back. Tonight. I will."

After he had left, Harry said, "This is my fault."

"Yes," Manny agreed.

"Will you come to my room when he goes? To . . . to help?"

"Yes, Harry."

Somehow, that only made it worse.

———

Gernshon agreed to a blindfold. Harry led him through the closet, the warehouse, the street. Neither of them seemed very good at this; they stumbled into each other, hesitated, tripped over nothing. In the warehouse Gernshon nearly walked into a pile of lumber, and in the sharp jerk Harry gave Gernshon's arm to deflect him, something twisted and gave way in Harry's back. He waited, bent over, behind a corner of a building while Gernshon removed his blindfold, blinked in the morning light, and walked slowly away.

Despite his back, Harry found that he couldn't return right away. Why not? He just couldn't. He waited until Gernshon had a large head start and then hobbled towards the park. A carousel turned, playing bright organ music: September 24. Two children he had never noticed before stood just beyond the carousel, watching it with hungry, hopeless eyes. Flowers grew in immaculate flower beds. A black man walked by, his eyes fixed on the sidewalk, his head bent. Two small girls jumping rope were watched by a smiling woman in a blue-and-white uniform. On the sidewalk, just beyond the carousel, someone had chalked a swastika. The black man shuffled over it. A Lincoln Zephyr V-12 drove by, $1090. There was no way it would fit through a closet.

When Harry returned, Manny was curled up on the white chenille bedspread that Harry had bought for $3.28, fast asleep.

---

"What did I accomplish, Manny? What?" Harry said bitterly. The day had dawned glorious and warm, unexpected Indian summer. Trees in the park showed bare branches against a bright blue sky. Manny wore an old red sweater, Harry a flannel workshirt. Harry shifted gingerly, grimacing, on his bench. Sunday strollers dropped ice cream wrappers, cigarettes, newspapers, Diet Pepsi cans, used tissues, popcorn. Pigeons quarreled and children shrieked.

"Jackie's going to be just as hard as ever—and why not?" Harry continued. "She finally meets a nice fellow, he never calls her again. Me, I leave a young man miserable on a sidewalk. Before I leave him, I ruin his life. While I leave him, I ruin my back. *After* I leave him, I sit here guilty. There's no answer, Manny."

Manny didn't answer. He squinted down the curving path.

"I don't know, Manny. I just don't know."

Manny said suddenly, "Here comes Jackie."

Harry looked up. He squinted, blinked, tried to jump up. His back made sharp protest. He stayed where he was, and his eyes grew wide.

"Popsy!" Jackie cried. "I've been looking for you!"

She looked radiant. All the lines were gone from around her eyes, all the sharpness from her face. Her very collar bones, Harry thought dazedly, looked softer. Happiness haloed her like light. She held the hand of a slim, red-haired woman with strong features and direct hazel eyes.

"This is Ann," Jackie said. "I've been looking for you, Popsy, because . . . well, because I need to tell you something." She slid onto the bench next to Harry, on the other side from Manny, and put one arm around Harry's shoulders. The other hand kept a close grip on Ann, who smiled encouragement. Manny stared at Ann as at a ghost.

"You see, Popsy, for a while now I've been struggling with something, something really important. I know I've been snappy and difficult, but it hasn't been—everybody needs somebody to love, you've often told me that, and I know how happy you and Grammy were all those years. And I thought there would never be anything like that for me, and certain people were making everything all so hard. But now . . . well, now there's Ann. And I wanted you to know that."

Jackie's arm tightened. Her eyes pleaded. Ann watched Harry closely. He felt as if he were drowning.

"I know this must come as a shock to you," Jackie went on, "but I also know you've always wanted me to be happy. So I hope you'll come to love her the way I do."

Harry stared at the red-haired woman. He knew what was being asked of him, but he didn't believe in it, it wasn't real, in the same way weather going on in other countries wasn't really real. Hurricanes. Drought. Sunshine. When what you were looking at was a cold drizzle.

"I think that of all the people I've ever known, Ann is the most together. The most compassionate. And the most moral."

"Ummm," Harry said.

"Popsy?"

Jackie was looking right at him. The longer he was silent, the more her smile faded. It occurred to him that the smile had showed her teeth. They were very white, very even. Also very sharp.

"I . . . I . . . hello, Ann."

"Hello," Ann said.

"See, I told you he'd be great!" Jackie said to Ann. She let go of Harry and jumped up from the bench, all energy and lightness. "You're wonderful, Popsy! You, too, Manny! Oh, Ann, this is Popsy's best friend, Manny Feldman. Manny, Ann Davies."

"Happy to meet you," Ann said. She had a low, rough voice and a sweet smile. Harry felt hurricanes, drought, sunshine.

Jackie said, "I know this is probably a little unexpected—"

*Unexpected.* "Well—" Harry said, and could say no more.

"It's just that it was time for me to come out of the closet."

Harry made a small noise. Manny managed to say, "So you live here, Ann?"

"Oh, yes. All my life. And my family, too, since forever."

"Has Jackie . . . has Jackie met any of them yet?"

"Not yet," Jackie said. "It might be a little . . . tricky, in the case of her parents." She smiled at Ann. "But we'll manage."

"I wish," Ann said to her, "that you could have met *my* grandfather. He would have been just as great as your Popsy here. He always was."

"Was?" Harry said faintly.

"He died a year ago. But he was just a wonderful man. Compassionate *and* intelligent."

"What . . . what did he do?"

"He taught history at the university. He was also active in lots of organizations—Amnesty International, the ACLU, things like that. During World War II he worked for the Jewish rescue leagues, getting people out of Germany."

Manny nodded. Harry watched Jackie's teeth.

"We'd like you both to come to dinner soon," Ann said. She smiled. "I'm a good cook."

Manny's eyes gleamed.

Jackie said, "I know this must be hard for you—" but Harry saw that she didn't really mean it. She didn't think it was hard. For her it was so real that it was natural weather, unexpected maybe, but not strange, not out of place, not out of time. In front of the bench, sunlight striped the pavement like bars.

Suddenly Jackie said, "Oh, Popsy, did I tell you that it was your friend Robert who introduced us? Did I tell you that already?"

"Yes, sweetheart," Harry said. "You did."

"He's kind of a nerd, but actually all right."

After Jackie and Ann left, the two old men sat silent a long time. Finally Manny said diplomatically, "You want to get a snack, Harry?"

"She's happy, Manny."

"Yes. You want to get a snack, Harry?"

"She didn't even recognize him."

"No. You want to get a snack?"

"Here, have this. I got it for you this morning." Harry held out an orange, a deep-colored navel with flawless rind: seedless, huge, guaranteed juicy, nurtured for flavor, perfect.

"Enjoy," Harry said. "It cost me ninety-two cents."

# URSULA K. LE GUIN

The term "visionary" is applicable to very few writers, but Ursula K. Le Guin's intellectually provocative fiction has earned her the accolade in general literary circles as well as the fields of fantasy and science fiction. Though she has taken a variety of approaches to a wide range of ideas, the cornerstone of her distinguished body of fiction is her series of Hainish novels, set on different planets in a pangalactic empire. The alien cultures on these planets share a common origin, but have developed differently over time, in ways both striking and subtle. Le Guin juxtaposes alien and earthly viewpoints in these stories with an eye toward showing the plurality of possible perspectives on the themes they address. Her Hugo- and Nebula Award–winning novel The Left Hand of Darkness is set on a planet whose androgynous humanoids unpredictably shift sexual identities, a process that undermines all preconceptions of identity based on gender differences. In other Hainish novels, which include Rocannon's World, Planet of Exile, City of Illusions, The Word for World Is Forest, and The Telling, Le Guin has used contrasting civilizations to measure the impact of a variety of science-fictional devices, including telepathy, instantaneous communication, and space travel.

Le Guin's other major story cycle is the Earthsea saga, which includes A Wizard of Earthsea, The Tombs of Atuan, The Farthest Shore, Tehanu: The Last Book of Earthsea, and Tales from Earthsea. These novels, which break the boundaries between adult and young-adult fiction, comprise a coming-of-age story featuring Ged, an apprentice magician who grows to maturity and faces many challenges as both man and mage over the course of the saga.

Le Guin has been praised for her understanding of the importance of rituals and myths that shape individuals and societies, and for the meticulous detail with which she brings her alien cultures to life. She has written other novels, including The Lathe of Heaven, The Dispossessed, Malafrena, and Always Coming Home. Her short fiction has been collected in The Wind's Twelve Quarters, Orsinian Tales, Buffalo Gals, Won't You Come Out Tonight, and Four Ways to Forgiveness. Le Guin has also written many celebrated essays on the craft of fantasy and science fiction, some of which have been gathered in The Language of the Night and Dancing at the Edge of the World.

Set in the world of her Hainish stories, "Another Story" is an appropriate way to close this book, with the idea of time travel viewed through a common theme of Le Guin's, that of local folklore, and combining elements of the past, present, and the future into a seamless vision that also, as many of these stories have done, explores a closely cherished dream of humanity: the ability to go back and correct mistakes in our past.

# ANOTHER STORY
## OR A FISHERMAN
## OF THE INLAND SEA

### URSULA K. LE GUIN

*To the Stabiles of the Ekumen on Hain, and to Gvonesh,*
*Director of the Churten Field Laboratories at Ve Port:*
*from Tiokunan'n Hideo, Farmholder of the Second*
*Sedoretu of Udan, Derdan'nad, Oket, on O.*

I shall make my report as if I told a story, this having been the tradition for some time now. You may, however, wonder why a farmer on the planet O is reporting to you as if he were a Mobile of the Ekumen. My story will explain that. But it does not explain itself. Story is our only boat for sailing on the river of time, but in the great rapids and the winding shallows, no boat is safe.

So: once upon a time when I was twenty-one years old I left my home and came on the NAFAL ship *Terraces of Darranda* to study at the Ekumenical Schools on Hain.

The distance between Hain and my home world is just over four light-years, and there has been traffic between O and the Hainish system for twenty centuries. Even before the Nearly As Fast As Light drive, when ships spent a hundred years of planetary time instead of four to make the crossing, there were people who would give up their old life to come to a new world. Sometimes they returned; not often. There were tales of such sad returns to a world that had forgotten the voyager. I knew also from my mother a very old story called "The Fisherman of the In-land Sea," which came from her home world, Terra. The life of a ki'O child is full of stories, but of all I heard told by her and my othermother and my fathers and grandparents and uncles and aunts and teachers, that one was my favorite. Perhaps I liked it so well because my mother told it with deep feeling, though very plainly, and always in the same words (and I would not let her change the words if she ever tried to).

The story tells of a poor fisherman, Urashima, who went out daily in his boat alone on the quiet sea that lay between his home island and the mainland. He was a beautiful young man with long, black hair, and the daughter of the king of the sea saw him as he leaned over the side of the boat and she gazed up to see the floating shadow cross the wide circle of the sky.

Rising from the waves, she begged him to come to her palace under the sea with him. At first he refused, saying, "My children wait for me at home." But how could he resist the sea king's daughter? "One night," he said. She drew him down with her under the water, and they spent a night of love in her green palace, served by strange undersea beings. Urashima came to love her dearly, and maybe he stayed more than one night only. But at last he said, "My dear, I must go. My children wait for me at home."

"If you go, you go forever," she said.

"I will come back," he promised.

She shook her head. She grieved, but did not plead with him. "Take this with you," she said, giving him a little box, wonderfully carved, and sealed shut. "Do not open it, Urashima."

So he went up onto the land, and ran up the shore to his village, to his house: but the garden was a wilderness, the windows were blank, the roof had fallen in. People came and went among the familiar houses of the village, but he did not know a single face. "Where are my children?" he cried. An old woman stopped and spoke to him: "What is your trouble, young stranger?"

"I am Urashima, of this village, but I see no one here I know!"

"Urashima!" the woman said—and my mother would look far away, and her voice as she said the name made me shiver, tears starting to my eyes—"Urashima! My grandfather told me a fisherman named Urashima was lost at sea, in the time of his grandfather's grandfather. There has been no one of that family alive for a hundred years."

So Urashima went back down to the shore; and there he opened the box, the gift of the sea king's daughter. A little white smoke came out of it and drifted away on the sea wind. In that moment Urashima's black hair turned white, and he grew old, old, old; and he lay down on the sand and died.

Once, I remember, a traveling teacher asked my mother about the fable, as he called it. She smiled and said, "In the Annals of the Emperors of my nation of Terra it is recorded that a young man named Urashima, of the Yosa district, went away in the year 477, and came back to his village in the year 825, but soon departed again. And I have heard that the box was kept in a shrine for many centuries." Then they talked about something else.

My mother, Isako, would not tell the story as often as I demanded it. "That one is so sad," she would say, and tell instead about Grandmother and the rice dumpling that rolled away, or the painted cat who came alive and killed the demon rats, or the peach boy who floated down the river. My sister and my germanes, and older people, too, listened to her tales as closely as I did. They were new stories on O, and a new story is always a treasure. The painted cat story was the general favorite, especially when my mother would take out her brush and the block of strange, black, dry ink from Terra, and sketch the animals—cat, rat— that none of us had ever seen: the wonderful cat with arched back and brave round eyes, the fanged and skulking rats, "pointed at both ends" as my sister said. But I waited always, through all other stories, for her to catch my eye, look away, smile a little and sigh, and begin, "Long, long ago, on the shore of the Inland Sea there lived a fisherman . . ."

Did I know then what that story meant to her? that it was her story? that if she were to return to her village, her world, all the people she had known would have been dead for centuries?

Certainly I knew that she "came from another world," but what that meant to me as a five-, or seven-, or ten-year-old, is hard for me now to imagine, impossible to remember. I knew that she was a Terran and had lived on Hain; that was something to be proud of. I knew that she had come to O as a Mobile of the Ekumen (more pride, vague and grandiose) and that "your father and I fell in love at the Festival of Plays in Sudiran." I knew also that arranging the marriage had been a tricky business. Getting permission to resign her duties had not been difficult— the Ekumen is used to Mobiles going native. But as a foreigner, Isako did not belong to a ki'O moiety, and that was only the first problem. I heard all about it from my othermother, Tubdu, an endless source of family history, anecdote, and scandal. "You know," Tubdu told me when I was

eleven or twelve, her eyes shining and her irrepressible, slightly wheezing, almost silent laugh beginning to shake her from the inside out—
"you know, she didn't even know women got married? Where she came
from, she said, women don't marry."

I could and did correct Tubdu: "Only in her part of it. She told me
there's lots of parts of it where they do." I felt obscurely defensive of my
mother, though Tubdu spoke without a shadow of malice or contempt;
she adored Isako. She had fallen in love with her "the moment I saw
her—that black hair! that mouth!"—and simply found it endearingly
funny that such a woman could have expected to marry only a man.

"I understand," Tubdu hastened to assure me. "I know—on Terra
it's different, their fertility was damaged, they have to think about marry-
ing for children. And they marry in twos, too. Oh, poor Isako! How
strange it must have seemed to her! I remember how she looked at
me—" And off she went again into what we children called The Great
Giggle, her joyous, silent, seismic laughter.

To those unfamiliar with our customs I should explain that on O, a
world with a low, stable human population and an ancient climax technology, certain social arrangements are almost universal. The dispersed
village, an association of farms, rather than the city or state, is the basic
social unit. The population consists of two halves or moieties. A child is
born into its mother's moiety, so that all ki'O (except the mountain folk
of Ennik) belong either to the Morning People, whose time is from midnight to noon, or the Evening People, whose time is from noon to midnight. The sacred origins and functions of the moieties are recalled in
the Discussions and the Plays and in the services at every farm shrine.
The original social function of the moiety was probably to structure ex-
ogamy into marriage and so discourage inbreeding in isolated farmholds, since one can have sex with or marry only a person of the other
moiety. The rule is severely reinforced. Transgressions, which of course
occur, are met with shame, contempt, and ostracism. One's identity as a
Morning or an Evening Person is as deeply and intimately part of oneself
as one's gender, and has quite as much to do with one's sexual life.

A ki'O marriage, called a sedoretu, consists of a Morning woman
and man and an Evening woman and man; the heterosexual pairs are
called Morning and Evening according to the woman's moiety; the
homosexual pairs are called Day—the two women—and Night—the
two men.

So rigidly structured a marriage, where each of four people must be sexually compatible with two of the others while never having sex with the fourth—clearly this takes some arranging. Making sedoretu is a major occupation of my people. Experimenting is encouraged; foursomes form and dissolve, couples "try on" other couples, mixing and matching. Brokers, traditionally elderly widowers, go about among the farmholds of the dispersed villages, arranging meetings, setting up field dances, serving as universal confidants. Many marriages begin as a love match of one couple, either homosexual or heterosexual, to which another pair or two separate people become attached. Many marriages are brokered or arranged by the village elders from beginning to end. To listen to the old people under the village great tree making a sedoretu is like watching a master game of chess or tidhe. "If that Evening boy at Erdup were to meet young Tobo during the flour-processing at Gad'd . . ." "Isn't Hodin'n of the Oto Morning a programmer? They could use a programmer at Erdup. . . ." The dowry a prospective bride or groom can offer is their skill, or their home farm. Otherwise undesired people may be chosen and honored for the knowledge or the property they bring to a marriage. The farmhold, in turn, wants its new members to be agreeable and useful. There is no end to the making of marriages on O. I should say that all in all they give as much satisfaction as any other arrangement to the participants, and a good deal more to the marriage-makers.

Of course many people never marry. Scholars, wandering Discussers, itinerant artists and experts, and specialists in the Centers seldom want to fit themselves into the massive permanence of a farmhold sedoretu. Many people attach themselves to a brother's or sister's marriage as aunt or uncle, a position with limited, clearly defined responsibilities; they can have sex with either or both spouses of the other moiety, thus sometimes increasing the sedoretu from four to seven or eight. Children of that relationship are called cousins. The children of one mother are brothers or sisters to one another; the children of the Morning and the children of the Evening are germanes. Brothers, sisters, and first cousins may not marry, but germanes may. In some less conservative parts of O germane marriages are looked at askance, but they are common and respected in my region.

My father was a Morning man of Udan Farmhold of Derdan'nad Village in the hill region of the Northwest Watershed of the Saduun River, on Oket, the smallest of the six continents of O. The village comprises seventy-seven farmholds, in a deeply rolling, stream-cut region of fields and forests on the watershed of the Oro, a tributary of the wide

Saduun. It is fertile, pleasant country, with views west to the Coast
Range and south to the great floodplains of the Saduun and the gleam of
the sea beyond. The Oro is a wide, lively, noisy river full of fish and children. I spent my childhood in or on or by the Oro, which runs through
Udan so near the house that you can hear its voice all night, the rush and
hiss of the water and the deep drumbeats of rocks rolled in its current. It
is shallow and quite dangerous. We all learned to swim very young in a
quiet bay dug out as a swimming pool, and later to handle rowboats and
kayaks in the swift current full of rocks and rapids. Fishing was one of the
children's responsibilities. I liked to spear the fat, beady-eyed, blue
ochid; I would stand heroic on a slippery boulder in midstream, the long
spear poised to strike. I was good at it. But my germane Isidri, while I was
prancing about with my spear, would slip into the water and catch six or
seven ochid with her bare hands. She could catch eels and even the darting ei. I never could do it. "You just sort of move with the water and get
transparent," she said. She could stay underwater longer than any of us,
so long you were sure she had drowned. "She's too bad to drown," her
mother, Tubdu, proclaimed. "You can't drown really bad people. They
always bob up again."

Tubdu, the Morning wife, had two children with her husband Kap:
Isidri, a year older than me, and Suudi, three years younger. Children of
the Morning, they were my germanes, as was Cousin Had'd, Tubdu's
son with Kap's brother Uncle Tobo. On the Evening side there were two
children, myself and my younger sister. She was named Koneko, an old
name in Oket, which has also a meaning in my mother's Terran language: "kitten," the young of the wonderful animal "cat" with the round
back and the round eyes. Koneko, four years younger than me, was indeed round and silky like a baby animal, but her eyes were like my
mother's, long, with lids that went up towards the temple, like the soft
sheaths of flowers before they open. She staggered around after me, calling, "Deo! Deo! Wait!"—while I ran after fleet, fearless, ever-vanishing
Isidri, calling, "Sidi! Sidi! Wait!"

When we were older, Isidri and I were inseparable companions,
while Suudi, Koneko, and Cousin Had'd made a trinity, usually coated
with mud, splotched with scabs, and in some kind of trouble—gates left
open so the yamas got into the crops, hay spoiled by being jumped on,
fruit stolen, battles with the children from Drehe Farmhold. "Bad, bad,"
Tubdu would say. "None of 'em will ever drown!" And she would shake
with her silent laughter.

My father Dohedri was a hardworking man, handsome, silent, and aloof. I think his insistence on bringing a foreigner into the tight-woven fabric of village and farm life, conservative and suspicious and full of old knots and tangles of passions and jealousies, had added anxiety to a temperament already serious. Other ki'O had married foreigners, of course, but almost always in a "foreign marriage," a pairing; and such couples usually lived in one of the Centers, where all kinds of untraditional arrangements were common, even (so the village gossips hissed under the great tree) incestuous couplings between two Morning people! two Evening people!—Or such pairs would leave O to live on Hain, or would cut all ties to all homes and become Mobiles on the NAFAL ships, only touching different worlds at different moments and then off again into an endless future with no past.

None of this would do for my father, a man rooted to the knees in the dirt of Udan Farmhold. He brought his beloved to his home, and persuaded the Evening People of Derdan'nad to take her into their moiety, in a ceremony so rare and ancient that a Caretaker had to come by ship and train from Noratan to perform it. Then he had persuaded Tubdu to join the sedoretu. As regards her Day marriage, this was no trouble at all, as soon as Tubdu met my mother; but it presented some difficulty as regards her Morning marriage. Kap and my father had been lovers for years; Kap was the obvious and willing candidate to complete the sedoretu; but Tubdu did not like him. Kap's long love for my father led him to woo Tubdu earnestly and well, and she was far too good-natured to hold out against the interlocking wishes of three people, plus her own lively desire for Isako. She always found Kap a boring husband, I think; but his younger brother, Uncle Tobo, was a bonus. And Tubdu's relation to my mother was infinitely tender, full of honor, of delicacy, of restraint. Once my mother spoke of it. "She knew how strange it all was to me," she said. "She knows how strange it all is."

"This world? Our ways?" I asked.

My mother shook her head very slightly. "Not so much that," she said in her quiet voice with the faint foreign accent. "But men and women, women and women, together—love—It is always very strange. Nothing you know ever prepares you. Ever."

The saying is, "a marriage is made by Day," that is, the relationship of the two women makes or breaks it. Though my mother and father loved each other deeply, it was a love always on the edge of pain, never easy. I have no doubt that the radiant childhood we had in that household was founded on the unshakable joy and strength Isako and Tubdu found in each other.

So, then: twelve-year-old Isidri went off on the suntrain to school at Herhot, our district educational Center, and I wept aloud, standing in the morning sunlight in the dust of Derdan'nad Station. My friend, my playmate, my life was gone. I was bereft, deserted, alone forever. Seeing her mighty eleven-year-old elder brother weeping, Koneko set up a howl too, tears rolling down her cheeks in dusty balls like raindrops on a dirt road. She threw her arms about me, roaring, "Hideo! She'll come back! She'll come back!"

I have never forgotten that. I can hear her hoarse little voice, and feel her arms round me and the hot morning sunlight on my neck.

By afternoon we were all swimming in the Oro, Koneko and I and Suudi and Had'd. As their elder, I resolved on a course of duty and stern virtue, and led the troop off to help Second-Cousin Topi at the irrigation control station, until she drove us away like a swarm of flies, saying, "Go help somebody else and let me get some work done!" We went and built a mud palace.

So, then: a year later, twelve-year-old Hideo and thirteen-year-old Isidri went off on the suntrain to school, leaving Koneko on the dusty siding, not in tears, but silent, the way our mother was silent when she grieved.

I loved school. I know that the first days I was achingly homesick, but I cannot recall that misery, buried under my memories of the full, rich years at Herhot, and later at Ran'n, the Advanced Education Center, where I studied temporal physics and engineering.

Isidri finished the First Courses at Herhot, took a year of Second in literature, hydrology, and oenology, and went home to Udan Farmhold of Derdan'nad Village in the hill region of the Northwest Watershed of the Saduun.

The three younger ones all came to school, took a year or two of Second, and carried their learning home to Udan. When she was fifteen or sixteen, Koneko talked of following me to Ran'n; but she was wanted at home because of her excellence in the discipline we call "thick planning"—farm management is the usual translation, but the words have no hint of the complexity of factors involved in thick planning, ecology politics profit tradition aesthetics honor and spirit all functioning in an intensely practical and practically invisible balance of preservation and renewal, like the homeostasis of a vigorous organism.

Our "kitten" had the knack for it, and the Planners of Udan and Derdan'nad took her into their councils before she was twenty. But by then, I was gone.

Every winter of my school years I came back to the farm for the long holidays. The moment I was home I dropped school like a book bag and became pure farm boy overnight—working, swimming, fishing, hiking, putting on Plays and farces in the barn, going to field dances and house dances all over the village, falling in and out of love with lovely boys and girls of the Morning from Derdan'nad and other villages.

In my last couple of years at Ran'n, my visits home changed mood. Instead of hiking off all over the country by day and going to a different dance every night, I often stayed home. Careful not to fall in love, I pulled away from my old, dear relationship with Sota of Drehe Farmhold, gradually letting it lapse, trying not to hurt him. I sat whole hours by the Oro, a fishing line in my hand, memorizing the run of the water in a certain place just outside the entrance to our old swimming bay. There, as the water rises in clear strands racing towards two mossy, almost-submerged boulders, it surges and whirls in spirals, and while some of these spin away, grow faint, and disappear, one knots itself on a deep center, becoming a little whirlpool, which spins slowly downstream until, reaching the quick, bright race between the boulders, it loosens and unties itself, released into the body of the river, as another spiral is forming and knotting itself round a deep center upstream where the water rises in clear strands above the boulders. . . . Sometimes that winter the river rose right over the rocks and poured smooth, swollen with rain; but always it would drop, and the whirlpools would appear again.

In the winter evenings I talked with my sister and Suudi, serious, long talks by the fire. I watched my mother's beautiful hands work on the embroidery of new curtains for the wide windows of the dining room, which my father had sewn on the four-hundred-year-old sewing machine of Udan. I worked with him on reprogramming the fertilizer systems for the east fields and the yama rotations, according to our thick-planning council's directives. Now and then he and I talked a little, never very much. In the evenings we had music; Cousin Had'd was a drummer, much in demand for dances, who could always gather a group. Or I would play Word-Thief with Tubdu, a game she adored and always lost at because she was so intent to steal my words that she forgot to protect her own. "Got you, got you!" she would cry, and melt into The Great Giggle, seizing my letterblocks with her fat, tapering, brown fingers; and next move I would take all my letters back along with most of hers. "How did you see that?" she would ask, amazed, studying the scattered words. Sometimes my otherfather Kap played with us, methodical, a bit mechanical, with a small smile for both triumph and defeat.

Then I would go up to my room under the eaves, my room of dark wood walls and dark red curtains, the smell of rain coming in the window, the sound of rain on the tiles of the roof. I would lie there in the mild darkness and luxuriate in sorrow, in great, aching, sweet, youthful sorrow for this ancient home that I was going to leave, to lose forever, to sail away from on the dark river of time. For I knew, from my eighteenth birthday on, that I would leave Udan, leave O, and go out to the other worlds. It was my ambition. It was my destiny.

I have not said anything about Isidri, as I described those winter holidays. She was there. She played in the Plays, worked on the farm, went to the dances, sang the choruses, joined the hiking parties, swam in the river in the warm rain with the rest of us. My first winter home from Ran'n, as I swung off the train at Derdan'nad Station, she greeted me with a cry of delight and a great embrace, then broke away with a strange, startled laugh and stood back, a tall, dark, thin girl with an intent, watchful face. She was quite awkward with me that evening. I felt that it was because she had always seen me as a little boy, a child, and now, eighteen and a student at Ran'n, I was a man. I was complacent with Isidri, putting her at her ease, patronizing her. In the days that followed, she remained awkward, laughing inappropriately, never opening her heart to me in the kind of long talks we used to have, and even, I thought, avoiding me. My whole last tenday at home that year, Isidri spent visiting her father's relatives in Sabtodiu Village. I was offended that she had not put off her visit till I was gone.

The next year she was not awkward, but not intimate. She had become interested in religion, attending the shrine daily, studying the Discussions with the elders. She was kind, friendly, busy. I do not remember that she and I ever touched that winter until she kissed me good-bye. Among my people a kiss is not with the mouth; we lay our cheeks together for a moment, or for longer. Her kiss was as light as the touch of a leaf, lingering yet barely perceptible.

My third and last winter home, I told them I was leaving: going to Hain, and that from Hain I wanted to go on farther and forever.

How cruel we are to our parents! All I needed to say was that I was going to Hain. After her half-anguished, half-exultant cry of "I knew it!"

my mother said in her usual soft voice, suggesting not stating, "After that, you might come back, for a while." I could have said, "Yes." That was all she asked. Yes, I might come back, for a while. With the impenetrable self-centeredness of youth, which mistakes itself for honesty, I refused to give her what she asked. I took from her the modest hope of seeing me after ten years, and gave her the desolation of believing that when I left she would never see me again. "If I qualify, I want to be a Mobile," I said. I had steeled myself to speak without palliations. I prided myself on my truthfulness. And all the time, though I didn't know it, nor did they, it was not the truth at all. The truth is rarely so simple, though not many truths are as complicated as mine turned out to be.

She took my brutality without the least complaint. She had left her own people, after all. She said that evening, "We can talk by ansible, sometimes, as long as you're on Hain." She said it as if reassuring me, not herself. I think she was remembering how she had said good-bye to her people and boarded the ship on Terra, and when she landed a few seeming hours later on Hain, her mother had been dead for fifty years. She could have talked to Terra on the ansible; but who was there for her to talk to? I did not know that pain, but she did. She took comfort in knowing I would be spared it, for a while.

Everything now was "for a while." Oh, the bitter sweetness of those days! How I enjoyed myself—standing, again, poised on the slick boulder amidst the roaring water, spear raised, the hero! How ready, how willing I was to crush all that long, slow, deep, rich life of Udan in my hand and toss it away!

Only for one moment was I told what I was doing, and then so briefly that I could deny it.

I was down in the boathouse workshop, on the rainy, warm afternoon of a day late in the last month of winter. The constant, hissing thunder of the swollen river was the matrix of my thoughts as I set a new thwart in the little red rowboat we used to fish from, taking pleasure in the task, indulging my anticipatory nostalgia to the full by imagining myself on another planet a hundred years away remembering this hour in the boathouse, the smell of wood and water, the river's incessant roar. A knock at the workshop door. Isidri looked in. The thin, dark, watchful face, the long braid of dark hair, not as black as mine, the intent, clear eyes. "Hideo," she said, "I want to talk to you for a minute."

"Come on in!" I said, pretending ease and gladness, though half-aware that in fact I shrank from talking with Isidri, that I was afraid of her—why?

She perched on the vise bench and watched me work in silence for a little while. I began to say something commonplace, but she spoke: "Do you know why I've been staying away from you?"

Liar, self-protective liar, I said, "Staying away from me?"

At that she sighed. She had hoped I would say I understood, and spare her the rest. But I couldn't. I was lying only in pretending that I hadn't noticed that she had kept away from me. I truly had never, never until she told me, imagined why.

"I found out I was in love with you, winter before last," she said. "I wasn't going to say anything about it because—well, you know. If you'd felt anything like that for me, you'd have known I did. But it wasn't both of us. So there was no good in it. But then, when you told us you're leaving . . . At first I thought, all the more reason to say nothing. But then I thought, that wouldn't be fair. To me, partly. Love has a right to be spoken. And you have a right to know that somebody loves you. That somebody has loved you, could love you. We all need to know that. Maybe it's what we need most. So I wanted to tell you. And because I was afraid you thought I'd kept away from you because I didn't love you, or care about you, you know. It might have looked like that. But it wasn't that." She had slipped down off the table and was at the door.

"Sidi!" I said, her name breaking from me in a strange, hoarse cry, the name only, no words—I had no words. I had no feelings, no compassion, no more nostalgia, no more luxurious suffering. Shocked out of emotion, bewildered, blank, I stood there. Our eyes met. For four or five breaths we stood staring into each other's soul. Then Isidri looked away with a wincing, desolate smile, and slipped out.

I did not follow her. I had nothing to say to her: literally. I felt that it would take me a month, a year, years, to find the words I needed to say to her. I had been so rich, so comfortably complete in myself and my ambition and my destiny, five minutes ago; and now I stood empty, silent, poor, looking at the world I had thrown away.

That ability to look at the truth lasted an hour or so. All my life since I have thought of it as "the hour in the boathouse." I sat on the high bench where Isidri had sat. The rain fell and the river roared and the early night came on. When at last I moved, I turned on a light, and began to try to defend my purpose, my planned future, from the terrible plain reality. I began to build up a screen of emotions and evasions and versions; to look away from what Isidri had shown me; to look away from Isidri's eyes.

By the time I went up to the house for dinner I was in control of myself. By the time I went to bed I was master of my destiny again, sure of my decision, almost able to indulge myself in feeling sorry for Isidri—but not quite. Never did I dishonor her with that. I will say that much for myself. I had had the pity that is self-pity knocked out of me in the hour in the boathouse. When I parted from my family at the muddy little station in the village, a few days after, I wept, not luxuriously for them, but for myself, in honest, hopeless pain. It was too much for me to bear. I had had so little practice in pain! I said to my mother, "I will come back. When I finish the course—six years, maybe seven—I'll come back, I'll stay a while."

"If your way brings you," she whispered. She held me close to her, and then released me.

So, then: I have come to the time I chose to begin my story, when I was twenty-one and left my home on the ship *Terraces of Darranda* to study at the Schools on Hain.

Of the journey itself I have no memory whatever. I think I remember entering the ship, yet no details come to mind, visual or kinetic; I cannot recollect being on the ship. My memory of leaving it is only of an overwhelming physical sensation, dizziness. I staggered and felt sick, and was so unsteady on my feet I had to be supported until I had taken several steps on the soil of Hain.

Troubled by this lapse of consciousness, I asked about it at the Ekumenical School. I was told that it is one of the many different ways in which travel at near-lightspeed affects the mind. To most people it seems merely that a few hours pass in a kind of perceptual limbo; others have curious perceptions of space and time and event, which can be seriously disturbing; a few simply feel they have been asleep when they "wake up" on arrival. I did not even have that experience. I had no experience at all. I felt cheated. I wanted to have felt the voyage, to have known, in some way, the great interval of space: but as far as I was concerned, there was no interval. I was at the spaceport on O, and then I was at Ve Port, dizzy, bewildered, and at last, when I was able to believe that I was there, excited.

My studies and work during those years are of no interest now. I will mention only one event, which may or may not be on record in the ansible reception file at Fourth Beck Tower, EY 21-11-93/1645. (The last time I checked, it was on record in the ansible transmission file at Ran'n, ET date 30-11-93/1645. Urashima's coming and going was on record, too, in the Annals of the Emperors.) 1645 was my first year on Hain. Early in the term I was asked to come to the ansible center, where they explained that they had received a garbled screen transmission, apparently from O, and hoped I could help them reconstitute it. After a date nine days later than the date of reception, it read:

*les oku n hide problem netru emit it hurt di it may not be salv devir*

The words were gapped and fragmented. Some were standard Hainish, but *oku* and *netru* mean "north" and "symmetrical" in Sio, my native language. The ansible centers on O had reported no record of the transmission, but the Receivers thought the message might be from O because of these two words and because the Hainish phrase "it may not be salvageable" occurred in a transmission received almost simultaneously from one of the Stabiles on O, concerning a wave-damaged desalinization plant. "We call this a creased message," the Receiver told me, when I confessed I could make nothing of it and asked how often ansible messages came through so garbled. "Not often, fortunately. We can't be certain where or when they originated, or will originate. They may be effects of a double field—interference phenomena, perhaps. One of my colleagues here calls them ghost messages."

Instantaneous transmission had always fascinated me, and though I was then only a beginner in ansible principle, I developed this fortuitous acquaintance with the Receivers into a friendship with several of them. And I took all the courses in ansible theory that were offered.

When I was in my final year in the school of temporal physics, and considering going on to the Cetian Worlds for further study—after my promised visit home, which seemed sometimes a remote, irrelevant daydream and sometimes a yearning and yet fearful need—the first reports came over the ansible from Anarres of the new theory of transilience. Not only information, but matter, bodies, people might be transported from place to place without lapse of time. "Churten technology" was suddenly a reality, although a very strange reality, an implausible fact.

I was crazy to work on it. I was about to go promise my soul and body to the School if they would let me work on churten theory when they came and asked me if I'd consider postponing my training as a Mobile for a year or so to work on churten theory. Judiciously and graciously, I consented. I celebrated all over town that night. I remember showing all my friends how to dance the fen'n, and I remember setting off fireworks in the Great Plaza of the Schools, and I think I remember singing under the Director's windows, a little before dawn. I remember what I felt like next day, too; but it didn't keep me from dragging myself over to the Ti-Phy building to see where they were installing the Churten Field Laboratory.

Ansible transmission is, of course, enormously expensive, and I had only been able to talk to my family twice during my years on Hain; but my friends in the ansible center would occasionally "ride" a screen message for me on a transmission to O. I sent a message thus to Ran'n to be posted on to the First Sedoretu of Udan Farmhold of Derdan'nad Village of the hill district of the Northwest Watershed of the Saduun, Oket, on O, telling them that "although this research will delay my visit home, it may save me four years' travel." The flippant message revealed my guilty feeling; but we did really think then that we would have the technology within a few months.

The Field Laboratories were soon moved out to Ve Port, and I went with them. The joint work of the Cetian and Hainish churten research teams in those first three years was a succession of triumphs, postponements, promises, defeats, breakthroughs, setbacks, all happening so fast that anybody who took a week off was out-of-date. "Clarity hiding mystery," Gvonesh called it. Every time it all came clear it all grew more mysterious. The theory was beautiful and maddening. The experiments were exciting and inscrutable. The technology worked best when it was most preposterous. Four years went by in that laboratory like no time at all, as they say.

I had now spent ten years on Hain and Ve, and was thirty-one. On O, four years had passed while my NAFAL ship passed a few minutes of dilated time going to Hain, and four more would pass while I returned: so when I returned I would have been gone eighteen of their years. My parents were all still alive. It was high time for my promised visit home.

But though churten research had hit a frustrating setback in the Spring Snow Paradox, a problem the Cetians thought might be insoluble, I couldn't stand the thought of being eight years out-of-date when I got back to Hain. What if they broke the paradox? It was bad enough knowing I must lose four years going to O. Tentatively, not too hopefully, I proposed to the Director that I carry some experimental materials with me to O and set up a fixed double-field auxiliary to the ansible link between Ve Port and Ran'n. Thus I could stay in touch with Ve, as Ve stayed in touch with Urras and Anarres; and the fixed ansible link might be preparatory to a churten link. I remember I said, "If you break the paradox, we might eventually send some mice."

To my surprise my idea caught on; the temporal engineers wanted a receiving field. Even our Director, who could be as brilliantly inscrutable as churten theory itself, said it was a good idea. "Mouses, bugs, gholes, who knows what we send you?" she said.

So, then: when I was thirty-one years old I left Ve Port on the NAFAL transport *Lady of Sorra* and returned to O. This time I experienced the near-lightspeed flight the way most people do, as an unnerving interlude in which one cannot think consecutively, read a clockface, or follow a story. Speech and movement become difficult or impossible. Other people appear as unreal half presences, inexplicably there or not there. I did not hallucinate, but everything seemed hallucination. It is like a high fever—confusing, miserably boring, seeming endless, yet very difficult to recall once it is over, as if it were an episode outside one's life, encapsulated. I wonder now if its resemblance to the "churten experience" has yet been seriously investigated.

I went straight to Ran'n, where I was given rooms in the New Quadrangle, fancier than my old student room in the Shrine Quadrangle, and some nice lab space in Tower Hall to set up an experimental transilience field station. I got in touch with my family right away and talked to all my parents; my mother had been ill, but was fine now, she said. I told them I would be home as soon as I had got things going at Ran'n. Every tenday I called again and talked to them and said I'd be along very soon now. I was genuinely very busy, having to catch up the lost four years and to learn Gvonesh's solution to the Spring Snow Paradox. It was, fortunately, the only major advance in theory. Technology had advanced a good deal. I had to retrain myself, and to train my assistants almost from scratch. I had had an idea about an aspect of double-field theory that I wanted to work out before I left. Five months went by before I called them up and said at last, "I'll be there tomorrow." And when I did so, I realized that all along I had been afraid.

I don't know if I was afraid of seeing them after eighteen years, of the changes, the strangeness, or if it was myself I feared.

Eighteen years had made no difference at all to the hills beside the wide Saduun, the farmlands, the dusty little station in Derdan'nad, the old, old houses on the quiet streets. The village great tree was gone, but its replacement had a pretty wide spread of shade already. The aviary at Udan had been enlarged. The yama stared haughtily, timidly at me across the fence. A road gate that I had hung on my last visit home was decrepit, needing its post reset and new hinges, but the weeds that grew beside it were the same dusty, sweet-smelling summer weeds. The tiny dams of the irrigation runnels made their multiple, soft click and thump as they closed and opened. Everything was the same, itself. Timeless, Udan in its dream of work stood over the river that ran timeless in its dream of movement.

But the faces and bodies of the people waiting for me at the station in the hot sunlight were not the same. My mother, forty-seven when I left, was sixty-five, a beautiful and fragile elderly woman. Tubdu had lost weight; she looked shrunken and wistful. My father was still handsome and bore himself proudly, but his movements were slow and he scarcely spoke at all. My otherfather Kap, seventy now, was a precise, fidgety, little old man. They were still the First Sedoretu of Udan, but the vigor of the farmhold now lay in the Second and Third Sedoretu.

I knew of all the changes, of course, but being there among them was a different matter from hearing about them in letters and transmissions. The old house was much fuller than it had been when I lived there. The south wing had been reopened, and children ran in and out of its doors and across courtyards that in my childhood had been silent and ivied and mysterious.

My sister Koneko was now four years older than I instead of four years younger. She looked very like my early memory of my mother. As the train drew in to Derdan'nad Station, she had been the first of them I recognized, holding up a child of three or four and saying, "Look, look, it's your Uncle Hideo!"

The Second Sedoretu had been married for eleven years: Koneko and Isidri, sister-germanes, were the partners of the Day. Koneko's husband was my old friend Sota, a Morning man of Drehe Farmhold. Sota and I had loved each other dearly when we were adolescents, and I had been grieved to grieve him when I left. When I heard that he and Koneko were in love I had been very surprised, so self-centered am I, but at least I am not jealous: it pleased me very deeply. Isidri's husband, a man nearly twenty years older than herself, named Hedran, had been a traveling scholar of the Discussions. Udan had given him hospitality, and his visits had led to the marriage. He and Isidri had no children.

Sota and Koneko had two Evening children, a boy of ten called Murmi, and Lasako, Little Isako, who was four.

The Third Sedoretu had been brought to Udan by Suudi, my brother-germane, who had married a woman from Aster Village; their Morning pair also came from farmholds of Aster. There were six children in that sedoretu. A cousin whose sedoretu at Ekke had broken had also come to live at Udan with her two children; so the coming and going and dressing and undressing and washing and slamming and running and shouting and weeping and laughing and eating was prodigious. Tubdu would sit at work in the sunny kitchen courtyard and watch a wave of children pass. "Bad!" she would cry. "They'll never drown, not a one of 'em!" And she would shake with silent laughter that became a wheezing cough.

My mother, who had after all been a Mobile of the Ekumen, and had traveled from Terra to Hain and from Hain to O, was impatient to hear about my research. "What is it, this churtening? How does it work, what does it do? Is it an ansible for matter?"

"That's the idea," I said. "Transilience: instantaneous transference of being from one s-tc point to another."

"No interval?"

"No interval."

Isako frowned. "It sounds wrong," she said. "Explain."

I had forgotten how direct my soft-spoken mother could be; I had forgotten that she was an intellectual. I did my best to explain the incomprehensible.

"So," she said at last, "you don't really understand how it works."

"No. Nor even what it does. Except that—as a rule—when the field is in operation, the mice in Building One are instantaneously in Building Two, perfectly cheerful and unharmed. Inside their cage, if we remembered to keep their cage inside the initiating churten field. We used to forget. Loose mice everywhere."

"What's *mice?*" said a little Morning boy of the Third Sedoretu, who had stopped to listen to what sounded like a story.

"Ah," I said in a laugh, surprised. I had forgotten that at Udan mice were unknown, and rats were fanged, demon enemies of the painted cat. "Tiny, pretty, furry animals," I said, "that come from Grandmother Isako's world. They are friends of scientists. They have traveled all over the Known Worlds."

"In tiny little spaceships?" the child said hopefully.

"In large ones, mostly," I said. He was satisfied, and went away.

"Hideo," said my mother, in the terrifying way women have of passing without interval from one subject to another because they have them all present in their mind at once, "you haven't found any kind of relationship?"

I shook my head, smiling.

"None at all?"

"A man from Alterra and I lived together for a couple of years," I said. "It was a good friendship; but he's a Mobile now. And . . . oh, you know . . . people here and there. Just recently, at Ran'n, I've been with a very nice woman from East Oket."

"I hoped, if you intend to be a Mobile, that you might make a couple-marriage with another Mobile. It's easier, I think," she said. Easier than what? I thought, and knew the answer before I asked.

"Mother, I doubt now that I'll travel farther than Hain. This churten business is too interesting; I want to be in on it. And if we do learn to control the technology, you know, then travel will be nothing. There'll be no need for the kind of sacrifice you made. Things will be different. Unimaginably different! You could go to Terra for an hour and come back here: and only an hour would have passed."

She thought about that. "If you do it, then," she said, speaking slowly, almost shaking with the intensity of comprehension, "you will . . . you will shrink the galaxy—the universe?—to . . ." and she held up her left hand, thumb and fingers all drawn together to a point.

I nodded. "A mile or a light-year will be the same. There will be no distance."

"It can't be right," she said after a while. "To have event without interval . . . Where is the dancing? Where is the way? I don't think you'll be able to control it, Hideo." She smiled. "But of course you must try."

And after that we talked about who was coming to the field dance at Drehe tomorrow.

I did not tell my mother that I had invited Tasi, the nice woman from East Oket, to come to Udan with me and that she had refused, had, in fact, gently informed me that she thought this was a good time for us to part. Tasi was tall, with a braid of dark hair, not coarse bright black like mine but soft, fine, dark, like the shadows in a forest. A typical ki'O woman, I thought. She had deflated my protestations of love skillfully and without shaming me. "I think you're in love with somebody, though," she said. "Somebody on Hain, maybe. Maybe the man from Alterra you told me about?" No, I said. No, I'd never been in love. I wasn't capable of an intense relationship, that was clear by now. I'd dreamed too long of traveling the galaxy with no attachments anywhere, and then worked too long in the churten lab, married to a damned theory that couldn't find its technology. No room for love, no time.

But why had I wanted to bring Tasi home with me?

Tall but no longer thin, a woman of forty, not a girl, not typical, not comparable, not like anyone anywhere, Isidri had greeted me quietly at the door of the house. Some farm emergency had kept her from coming to the village station to meet me. She was wearing an old smock and leggings like any field worker, and her hair, dark beginning to grey, was in a rough braid. As she stood in that wide doorway of polished wood she was Udan itself, the body and soul of that thirty-century-old farmhold, its continuity, its life. All my childhood was in her hands, and she held them out to me.

"Welcome home, Hideo," she said, with a smile as radiant as the summer light on the river. As she brought me in, she said, "I cleared the kids out of your old room. I thought you'd like to be there—would you?" Again she smiled, and I felt her warmth, the solar generosity of a woman in the prime of life, married, settled, rich in her work and being. I had not needed Tasi as a defense. I had nothing to fear from Isidri. She felt no rancor, no embarrassment. She had loved me when she was young, another person. It would be altogether inappropriate for me to feel embarrassment, or shame, or anything but the old affectionate loyalty of the years when we played and worked and fished and dreamed together, children of Udan.

So, then: I settled down in my old room under the tiles. There were new curtains, rust and brown. I found a stray toy under the chair, in the closet, as if I as a child had left my playthings there and found them now. At fourteen, after my entry ceremony in the shrine, I had carved my name on the deep window jamb among the tangled patterns of names and symbols that had been cut into it for centuries. I looked for it now. There had been some additions. Beside my careful, clear *Hideo*, surrounded by my ideogram, the cloudflower, a younger child had hacked a straggling *Dohedri*, and nearby was carved a delicate three-roofs ideogram. The sense of being a bubble in Udan's river, a moment in the permanence of life in this house on this land on this quiet world, was almost crushing, denying my identity, and profoundly reassuring, confirming my identity. Those nights of my visit home I slept as I had not slept for years, lost, drowned in the waters of sleep and darkness, and woke to the summer mornings as if reborn, very hungry.

The children were still all under twelve, going to school at home. Isidri, who taught them literature and religion and was the school planner, invited me to tell them about Hain, about NAFAL travel, about temporal physics, whatever I pleased. Visitors to ki'O farmholds are always put to use. Evening-Uncle Hideo became rather a favorite among the children, always good for hitching up the yama-cart or taking them fishing in the big boat, which they couldn't yet handle, or telling a story about his magic mice who could be in two places at the same time. I asked them if Evening-Grandmother Isako had told them about the painted cat who came alive and killed the demon rats—"And his mouf was all BLUGGY in the morning!" shouted Lasako, her eyes shining. But they didn't know the tale of Urashima.

"Why haven't you told them 'The Fisherman of the Inland Sea'?" I asked my mother.

She smiled and said, "Oh, that was your story. You always wanted it."

I saw Isidri's eyes on us, clear and tranquil, yet watchful still.

I knew my mother had had repair and healing to her heart a year before, and I asked Isidri later, as we supervised some work the older children were doing, "Has Isako recovered, do you think?"

"She seems wonderfully well since you came. I don't know. It's damage from her childhood, from the poisons in the Terran biosphere; they say her immune system is easily depressed. She was very patient about being ill. Almost too patient."

"And Tubdu—does she need new lungs?"

"Probably. All four of them are getting older, and stubborner. . . . But you look at Isako for me. See if you see what I mean."

I tried to observe my mother. After a few days I reported back that she seemed energetic and decisive, even imperative, and that I hadn't seen much of the patient endurance that worried Isidri. She laughed.

"Isako told me once," she said, "that a mother is connected to her child by a very fine, thin cord, like the umbilical cord, that can stretch light-years without any difficulty. I asked her if it was painful, and she said, 'Oh, no, it's just there, you know, it stretches and stretches and never breaks.' It seems to me it must be painful. But I don't know. I have no child, and I've never been more than two days' travel from my mothers." She smiled and said in her soft, deep voice, "I think I love

Isako more than anyone, more even than my mother, more even than Koneko. . . ."

Then she had to show one of Suudi's children how to reprogram the timer on the irrigation control. She was the hydrologist for the village and the oenologist for the farm. Her life was thick-planned, very rich in necessary work and wide relationships, a serene and steady succession of days, seasons, years. She swam in life as she had swum in the river, like a fish, at home. She had borne no child, but all the children of the farmhold were hers. She and Koneko were as deeply attached as their mothers had been. Her relation with her rather fragile, scholarly husband seemed peaceful and respectful. I thought his Night marriage with my old friend Sota might be the stronger sexual link, but Isidri clearly admired and depended on his intellectual and spiritual guidance. I thought his teaching a bit dry and disputatious; but what did I know about religion? I had not given worship for years, and felt strange, out of place, even in the home shrine. I felt strange, out of place, in my home. I did not acknowledge it to myself.

I was conscious of the month as pleasant, uneventful, even a little boring. My emotions were mild and dull. The wild nostalgia, the romantic sense of standing on the brink of my destiny, all that was gone with the Hideo of twenty-one. Though now the youngest of my generation, I was a grown man, knowing his way, content with his work, past emotional self-indulgence. I wrote a little poem for the house album about the peacefulness of following a chosen course. When I had to go, I embraced and kissed everyone, dozens of soft or harsh cheek-touches. I told them that if I stayed on O, as it seemed I might be asked to do for a year or so, I would come back next winter for another visit. On the train going back through the hills to Ran'n, I thought with a complacent gravity how I might return to the farm next winter, finding them all just the same; and how, if I came back after another eighteen years or even longer, some of them would be gone and some would be new to me and yet it would be always my home, Udan with its wide dark roofs riding time like a dark-sailed ship. I always grow poetic when I am lying to myself.

I got back to Ran'n, checked in with my people at the lab in Tower Hall, and had dinner with colleagues, good food and drink—I brought them a bottle of wine from Udan, for Isidri was making splendid wines, and had given me a case of the fifteen-year-old Kedun. We talked about the latest breakthrough in churten technology, "continuous-field send-ing," reported from Anarres just yesterday on the ansible. I went to my rooms in the New Quadrangle through the summer night, my head full of physics, read a little, and went to bed. I turned out the light and dark-ness filled me as it filled the room. Where was I? Alone in a room among strangers. As I had been for ten years and would always be. On one planet or another, what did it matter? Alone, part of nothing, part of no one. Udan was not my home. I had no home, no people. I had no future, no destiny, any more than a bubble of foam or a whirlpool in a current has a destiny. It is and it isn't. Nothing more.

I turned the light on because I could not bear the darkness, but the light was worse. I sat huddled up in the bed and began to cry. I could not stop crying. I became frightened at how the sobs racked and shook me till I was sick and weak and still could not stop sobbing. After a long time I calmed myself gradually by clinging to an imagination, a childish idea: in the morning I would call Isidri and talk to her, telling her that I needed instruction in religion, that I wanted to give worship at the shrines again, but it had been so long, and I had never listened to the Discussions, but now I needed to, and I would ask her, Isidri, to help me. So, holding fast to that, I could at last stop the terrible sobbing and lie spent, exhausted, until the day came.

I did not call Isidri. In daylight the thought which had saved me from the dark seemed foolish; and I thought if I called her she would ask advice of her husband, the religious scholar. But I knew I needed help. I went to the shrine in the Old School and gave worship. I asked for a copy of the First Discussions, and read it. I joined a Discussion group, and we read and talked together. My religion is godless, argumenta-tive, and mystical. The name of our world is the first word of its first prayer. For human beings its vehicle is the human voice and mind. As I began to rediscover it, I found it quite as strange as churten theory and in some respects complementary to it. I knew, but had never under-stood, that Cetian physics and religion are aspects of one knowledge. I wondered if all physics and religion are aspects of one knowledge.

At night I never slept well and often could not sleep at all. After the bountiful tables of Udan, college food seemed poor stuff; I had no ap-petite. But our work, my work went well—wonderfully well.

"No more mouses," said Gvonesh on the voice ansible from Hain. "Peoples."

"What people?" I demanded.

"Me," said Gvonesh.

So our Director of Research churtened from one corner of Laboratory One to another, and then from Building One to Building Two—vanishing in one laboratory and appearing in the other, smiling, in the same instant, in no time.

"What did it feel like?" they asked, of course, and Gvonesh answered, of course, "Like nothing."

Many experiments followed; mice and gholes churtened halfway around Ve and back; robot crews churtened from Anarres to Urras, from Hain to Ve, and then from Anarres to Ve, twenty-two light-years. So, then, eventually the *Shoby* and her crew of ten human beings churtened into orbit around a miserable planet seventeen light-years from Ve and returned (but words that imply coming and going, that imply distance traveled, are not appropriate) thanks only to their intelligent use of entrainment, rescuing themselves from a kind of chaos of dissolution, a death by unreality, that horrified us all. Experiments with high-intelligence lifeforms came to a halt.

"The rhythm is wrong," Gvonesh said on the ansible (she said it "rithkhom.") For a moment I thought of my mother saying, "It can't be right to have event without interval." What else had Isako said? Something about dancing. But I did not want to think about Udan. I did not think about Udan. When I did I felt, far down deeper inside me than my bones, the knowledge of being no one, no where, and a shaking like a frightened animal.

My religion reassured me that I was part of the Way, and my physics absorbed my despair in work. Experiments, cautiously resumed, succeeded beyond hope. The Terran Dalzul and his psychophysics took everyone at the research station on Ve by storm; I am sorry I never met him. As he predicted, using the continuity field he churtened without a hint of trouble, alone, first locally, then from Ve to Hain, then the great jump to Tadkla and back. From the second journey to Tadkla, his three companions returned without him. He died on that far world. It did not seem to us in the laboratories that his death was in any way caused by the churten field or by what had come to be known as "the churten experience," though his three companions were not so sure.

"Maybe Dalzul was right. One people at a time," said Gvonesh; and she made herself again the subject, the "ritual animal," as the Hainish say, of the next experiment. Using continuity technology she churtened right round Ve in four skips, which took thirty-two seconds because of the time needed to set up the coordinates. We had taken to calling the non-interval in time/real interval in space a "skip." It sounded light, trivial. Scientists like to trivialize.

I wanted to try the improvement to double-field stability that I had been working on ever since I came to Ran'n. It was time to give it a test; my patience was short, life was too short to fiddle with figures forever. Talking to Gvonesh on the ansible I said, "I'll skip over to Ve Port. And then back here to Ran'n. I promised a visit to my home farm this winter." Scientists like to trivialize.

"You still got that wrinkle in your field?" Gvonesh asked. "Some kind, you know, like a fold?"

"It's ironed out, ammar," I assured her.

"Good, fine," said Gvonesh, who never questioned what one said. "Come."

So, then: we set up the fields in a constant stable churten link with ansible connection; and I was standing inside a chalked circle in the Churten Field Laboratory of Ran'n Center on a late autumn afternoon and standing inside a chalked circle in the Churten Research Station Field Laboratory in Ve Port on a late summer day at a distance of 4.2 light-years and no interval of time.

"Feel nothing?" Gvonesh inquired, shaking my hand heartily. "Good fellow, good fellow, welcome, ammar, Hideo. Good to see. No wrinkle, hah?"

I laughed with the shock and queerness of it, and gave Gvonesh the bottle of Udan Kedun '49 that I had picked up a moment ago from the laboratory table on O.

I had expected, if I arrived at all, to churten promptly back again, but Gvonesh and others wanted me on Ve for a while for discussions and tests of the field. I think now that the Director's extraordinary intuition was at work; the "wrinkle," the "fold" in the Tiokunan'n Field still bothered her. "Is unaesthetical," she said.

"But it works," I said.

"It worked," said Gvonesh.

Except to retest my field, to prove its reliability, I had no desire to return to O. I was sleeping somewhat better here on Ve, although food was still unpalatable to me, and when I was not working I felt shaky and drained, a disagreeable reminder of my exhaustion after the night which I tried not to remember when for some reason or other I had cried so much. But the work went very well.

"You got no sex, Hideo?" Gvonesh asked me when we were alone in the Lab one day, I playing with a new set of calculations and she finishing her box lunch.

The question took me utterly aback. I knew it was not as impertinent as Gvonesh's peculiar usage of the language made it sound. But Gvonesh never asked questions like that. Her own sex life was as much a mystery as the rest of her existence. No one had ever heard her mention the word, let alone suggest the act.

When I sat with my mouth open, stumped, she said, "You used to, hah," as she chewed on a cold varvet.

I stammered something. I knew she was not proposing that she and I have sex, but inquiring after my well-being. But I did not know what to say.

"You got some kind of wrinkle in your life, hah," Gvonesh said. "Sorry. Not my business."

Wanting to assure her I had taken no offense I said, as we say on O, "I honor your intent."

She looked directly at me, something she rarely did. Her eyes were clear as water in her long, bony face softened by a fine, thick, colorless down. "Maybe is time you go back to O?" she asked.

"I don't know. The facilities here —"

She nodded. She always accepted what one said. "You read Harraven's report?" she asked, changing one subject for another as quickly and definitively as my mother.

All right, I thought, the challenge was issued. She was ready for me to test my field again. Why not? After all, I could churten to Ran'n and churten right back again to Ve within a minute, if I chose, and if the Lab could afford it. Like ansible transmission, churtening draws essentially on inertial mass, but setting up the field, disinfecting it, and holding it stable in size uses a good deal of local energy. But it was Gvonesh's suggestion, which meant we had the money. I said, "How about a skip over and back?"

"Fine," Gvonesh said. "Tomorrow."

So the next day, on a morning of late autumn, I stood inside a chalked circle in the Field Laboratory on Ve and stood —

A shimmer, a shivering of everything — a missed beat — skipped —

in darkness. A darkness. A dark room. The lab? A lab — I found the light panel. In the darkness I was sure it was the laboratory on Ve. In the light I saw it was not. I didn't know where it was. I didn't know where

I was. It seemed familiar yet I could not place it. What was it? A biology lab? There were specimens, an old subparticle microscope, the maker's ideogram on the battered brass casing, the lyre ideogram. . . . I was on O. In some laboratory in some building of the Center at Ran'n? It smelled like the old buildings of Ran'n, it smelled like a rainy night on O. But how could I have not arrived in the receiving field, the circle carefully chalked on the wood floor of the lab in Tower Hall? The field itself must have moved. An appalling, an impossible thought.

I was alarmed and felt rather dizzy, as if my body had skipped that beat, but I was not yet frightened. I was all right, all here, all the pieces in the right places, and the mind working. A slight spatial displacement? said the mind.

I went out into the corridor. Perhaps I had myself been disoriented and left the Churten Field Laboratory and come to full consciousness somewhere else. But my crew would have been there; where were they? And that would have been hours ago; it should have been just past noon on O when I arrived. A slight temporal displacement? said the mind, working away. I went down the corridor looking for my lab, and that is when it became like one of those dreams in which you cannot find the room which you must find. It was that dream. The building was perfectly familiar: it was Tower Hall, the second floor of Tower, but there was no Churten Lab. All the labs were biology and biophysics, and all were deserted. It was evidently late at night. Nobody around. At last I saw a light under a door and knocked and opened it on a student reading at a library terminal.

"I'm sorry," I said. "I'm looking for the Churten Field Lab—"

"The what lab?"

She had never heard of it, and apologized. "I'm not in Ti Phy, just Bi Phy," she said humbly.

I apologized too. Something was making me shakier, increasing my sense of dizziness and disorientation. Was this the "chaos effect" the crew of the *Shoby* and perhaps the crew of the *Galba* had experienced? Would I begin to see the stars through the walls, or turn around and see Gvonesh here on O?

I asked her what time it was. "I should have got here at noon," I said, though that of course meant nothing to her.

"It's about one," she said, glancing at the clock on the terminal. I looked at it too. It gave the time, the ten-day, the month, the year.

"That's wrong," I said.

She looked worried.

"That's not right," I said. "The date. It's not right." But I knew from the steady glow of the numbers on the clock, from the girl's round, worried face, from the beat of my heart, from the smell of the rain, that it was right, that it was an hour after midnight eighteen years ago, that I was here, now, on the day after the day I called "once upon a time" when I began to tell this story.

A major temporal displacement, said the mind, working, laboring.

"I don't belong here," I said, and turned to hurry back to what seemed a refuge, Biology Lab 6, which would be the Churten Field Lab eighteen years from now, as if I could re-enter the field, which had existed or would exist for .004 second.

The girl saw that something was wrong, made me sit down, and gave me a cup of hot tea from her insulated bottle.

"Where are you from?" I asked her, the kind, serious student.

"Herdud Farmhold of Deada Village on the South Watershed of the Saduun," she said.

"I'm from downriver," I said. "Udan of Derdan'nad." I suddenly broke into tears. I managed to control myself, apologized again, drank my tea, and set the cup down. She was not overly troubled by my fit of weeping. Students are intense people, they laugh and cry, they break down and rebuild. She asked if I had a place to spend the night: a perceptive question. I said I did, thanked her, and left.

I did not go back to the biology laboratory, but went downstairs and started to cut through the gardens to my rooms in the New Quadrangle. As I walked the mind kept working; it worked out that somebody else had been/would be in those rooms then/now.

I turned back towards the Shrine Quadrangle, where I had lived my last two years as a student before I left for Hain. If this was in fact, as the clock had indicated, the night after I had left, my room might still be empty and unlocked. It proved to be so, to be as I had left it, the mattress bare, the cyclebasket unemptied.

That was the most frightening moment. I stared at that cyclebasket for a long time before I took a crumpled bit of outprint from it and carefully smoothed it on the desk. It was a set of temporal equations scribbled on my old pocketscreen in my own handwriting, notes from Sedharad's class in Interval, from my last term at Ran'n, day before yesterday, eighteen years ago.

I was now very shaky indeed. You are caught in a chaos field, said the mind, and I believed it. Fear and stress, and nothing to do about it, not till the long night was past. I lay down on the bare bunk-mattress, ready for the stars to burn through the walls and my eyelids if I shut them. I meant to try and plan what I should do in the morning, if there was a morning. I fell asleep instantly and slept like a stone till broad daylight, when I woke up on the bare bed in the familiar room, alert, hungry, and without a moment of doubt as to who or where or when I was.

I went down into the village for breakfast. I didn't want to meet any colleagues—no, fellow students—who might know me and say, "Hideo! What are you doing here? You left on the *Terraces of Darranda* yesterday!"

I had little hope they would not recognize me. I was thirty-one now, not twenty-one, much thinner and not as fit as I had been; but my half-Terran features were unmistakable. I did not want to be recognized, to have to try to explain. I wanted to get out of Ran'n. I wanted to go home.

O is a good world to time-travel in. Things don't change. Our trains run on the same schedule to the same places for centuries. We sign for payment and pay in contracted barter or cash monthly, so I did not have to produce mysterious coins from the future. I signed at the station and took the morning train to Saduun Delta.

The little suntrain glided through the plains and hills of the South Watershed and then the Northwest Watershed, following the ever-widening river, stopping at each village. I got off in the late afternoon at the station in Derdan'nad. Since it was very early spring, the station was muddy, not dusty.

I walked out the road to Udan. I opened the road gate that I had re-hung a few days/eighteen years ago; it moved easily on its new hinges. That gave me a little gleam of pleasure. The she-yamas were all in the nursery pasture. Birthing would start any day; their woolly sides stuck out, and they moved like sailboats in a slow breeze, turning their elegant, scornful heads to look distrustfully at me as I passed. Rain clouds hung over the hills. I crossed the Oro on the humpbacked wooden bridge. Four or five great blue ochid hung in a backwater by the bridgefoot; I stopped to watch them; if I'd had a spear . . . The clouds drifted overhead trailing a fine, faint drizzle. I strode on. My face felt hot and stiff as the cool rain touched it. I followed the river road and saw the house come into view, the dark, wide roofs low on the tree-crowned hill. I came past the aviary and the collectors, past the irrigation center, under the avenue of tall bare trees, up the steps of the deep porch, to the door, the wide door of Udan. I went in.

Tubdu was crossing the hall—not the woman I had last seen, in her sixties, grey-haired and tired and fragile, but Tubdu of The Great Giggle, Tubdu at forty-five, fat and rosy-brown and brisk, crossing the hall with short, quick steps, stopping, looking at me at first with mere recognition, there's Hideo, then with puzzlement, is that Hideo? and then with shock—that can't be Hideo!

"Ombu," I said, the baby word for othermother, "Ombu, it's me, Hideo, don't worry, it's all right, I came back." I embraced her, pressed my cheek to hers.

"But, but—" She held me off, looked up at my face. "But what has happened to you, darling boy?" she cried, and then, turning, called out in a high voice, "Isako! Isako!"

When my mother saw me she thought, of course, that I had not left on the ship to Hain, that my courage or my intent had failed me; and in her first embrace there was an involuntary reserve, a withholding. Had I thrown away the destiny for which I had been so ready to throw away everything else? I knew what was in her mind. I laid my cheek to hers and whispered, "I did go, mother, and I came back. I'm thirty-one years old. I came back—"

She held me away a little just as Tubdu had done, and saw my face. "Oh Hideo!" she said, and held me to her with all her strength. "My dear, my dear!"

We held each other in silence, till I said at last, "I need to see Isidri."

My mother looked up at me intently but asked no questions. "She's in the shrine, I think."

"I'll be right back."

I left her and Tubdu side by side and hurried through the halls to the central room, in the oldest part of the house, rebuilt seven centuries ago on the foundations that go back three thousand years. The walls are stone and clay, the roof is thick glass, curved. It is always cool and still there. Books line the walls, the Discussions, the discussions of the Discussions, poetry, texts and versions of the Plays; there are drums and whispersticks for meditation and ceremony; the small, round pool which is the shrine itself wells up from clay pipes and brims its blue-green basin, reflecting the rainy sky above the skylight. Isidri was there. She had brought in fresh boughs for the vase beside the shrine, and was kneeling to arrange them.

I went straight to her and said, "Isidri, I came back. Listen—"

Her face was utterly open, startled, scared, defenseless, the soft, thin face of a woman of twenty-two, the dark eyes gazing into me.

"Listen, Isidri: I went to Hain, I studied there, I worked on a new kind of temporal physics, a new theory—transilience—I spent ten years there. Then we began experiments, I was in Ran'n and crossed over to the Hainish system in no time, using that technology, in no time, you understand me, literally, like the ansible—not at lightspeed, not faster than light, but in no time. In one place and in another place instantaneously, you understand? And it went fine, it worked, but coming back there was . . . there was a fold, a crease, in my field. I was in the same place in a different time. I came back eighteen of your years, ten of mine. I came back to the day I left, but I didn't leave, I came back, I came back to you."

I was holding her hands, kneeling to face her as she knelt by the silent pool. She searched my face with her watchful eyes, silent. On her cheekbone there was a fresh scratch and a little bruise; a branch had lashed her as she gathered the evergreen boughs.

"Let me come back to you," I said in a whisper.

She touched my face with her hand. "You look so tired," she said. "Hideo . . . Are you all right?"

"Yes," I said. "Oh, yes. I'm all right."

And there my story, so far as it has any interest to the Ekumen or to research in transilience, comes to an end. I have lived now for eighteen years as a farmholder of Udan Farm of Derdan'nad Village of the hill region of the Northwest Watershed of the Saduun on Oket, on O. I am fifty years old. I am the Morning husband of the Second Sedoretu of Udan; my wife is Isidri; my Night marriage is to Sota of Drehe, whose Evening wife is my sister Koneko. My children of the Morning with Isidri are Latubdu and Tadri; the Evening children are Murmi and Lasako. But none of this is of much interest to the Stabiles of the Ekumen.

My mother, who had had some training in temporal engineering, asked for my story, listened to it carefully, and accepted it without question; so did Isidri. Most of the people of my farmhold chose a simpler and far more plausible story, which explained everything fairly well, even my severe loss of weight and ten-year age gain overnight. At the very last moment, just before the space ship left, they said, Hideo decided not to go to the Ekumenical School on Hain after all. He came back to

Udan, because he was in love with Isidri. But it had made him quite ill, because it was a very hard decision and he was very much in love.

Maybe that is indeed the true story. But Isidri and Isako chose a stranger truth.

Later, when we were forming our sedoretu, Sota asked me for that truth. "You aren't the same man, Hideo, though you are the man I always loved," he said. I told him why, as best I could. He was sure that Koneko would understand it better than he could, and indeed she listened gravely, and asked several keen questions which I could not answer.

I did attempt to send a message to the temporal physics department of the Ekumenical Schools on Hain. I had not been home long before my mother, with her strong sense of duty and her obligation to the Ekumen, became insistent that I do so.

"Mother," I said, "what can I tell them? They haven't invented churten theory yet!"

"Apologize for not coming to study, as you said you would. And explain it to the Director, the Anarresti woman. Maybe she would understand."

"Even Gvonesh doesn't know about churten yet. They'll begin telling her about it on the ansible from Urras and Anarres about three years from now. Anyhow, Gvonesh didn't know me the first couple of years I was there." The past tense was inevitable but ridiculous; it would have been more accurate to say, "She won't know me the first couple of years I won't be there."

Or *was* I there on Hain, now? That paradoxical idea of two simultaneous existences on two different worlds disturbed me exceedingly. It was one of the points Koneko had asked about. No matter how I discounted it as impossible under every law of temporality, I could not keep from imagining that it was possible, that another I was living on Hain, and would come to Udan in eighteen years and meet myself. After all, my present existence was also and equally impossible.

When such notions haunted and troubled me I learned to replace them with a different image: the little whorls of water that slid down between the two big rocks, where the current ran strong, just above the swimming bay in the Oro. I would imagine, those whirlpools forming and dissolving, or I would go down to the river and sit and watch them. And they seemed to hold a solution to my question, to dissolve it as they endlessly dissolved and formed.

But my mother's sense of duty and obligation was unmoved by such trifles as a life impossibly lived twice.

"You should try to tell them," she said.

She was right. If my double transilience field had established itself permanently, it was a matter of real importance to temporal science, not only to myself. So I tried. I borrowed a staggering sum in cash from the farm reserves, went up to Ran'n, bought a five-thousand-word ansible screen transmission, and sent a message to my director of studies at the Ekumenical School, trying to explain why, after being accepted at the School, I had not arrived—if in fact I had not arrived.

I take it that this was the "creased message" or "ghost" they asked me to try to interpret, my first year there. Some of it is gibberish, and some words probably came from the other, nearly simultaneous transmission, but parts of my name are in it, and other words may be fragments or re-versals from my long message—problem, churten, return, arrived, time.

It is interesting, I think, that at the ansible center the Receivers used the word "creased" for a temporally disturbed transilient, as Gvonesh would use it for the anomaly, the "wrinkle" in my churten field. In fact, the ansible field was meeting a resonance resistance, caused by the ten-year anomaly in the churten field, which did fold the message back into itself, crumple it up, inverting and erasing. At that point, within the im-plication of the Tiokunan'n Double Field, my existence on O as I sent the message was simultaneous with my existence on Hain when the message was received. There was an I who sent and an I who received. Yet, so long as the encapsulated field anomaly existed, the simultaneity was literally a point, an instant, a crossing without further implication in either the ansible or the churten field.

An image for the churten field in this case might be a river winding in its floodplain, winding in deep, redoubling curves, folding back upon itself so closely that at last the current breaks through the double banks of the S and runs straight, leaving a whole reach of the water aside as a curving lake, cut off from the current, unconnected. In this analogy, my ansible message would have been the one link, other than my memory, between the current and the lake.

But I think a truer image is the whirlpools of the current itself, oc-curring and recurring, the same? or not the same?

I worked at the mathematics of an explanation in the early years of my marriage, while my physics was still in good working order. See the

"Notes toward a Theory of Resonance Interference in Doubled Ansible and Churten Fields," appended to this document. I realize that the explanation is probably irrelevant, since, on this stretch of the river, there is no Tiokunan'n Field. But independent research from an odd direction can be useful. And I am attached to it, since it is the last temporal physics I did. I have followed churten research with intense interest, but my life's work has been concerned with vineyards, drainage, the care of yamas, the care and education of children, the Discussions, and trying to learn how to catch fish with my bare hands.

Working on that paper, I satisfied myself in terms of mathematics and physics that the existence in which I went to Hain and became a temporal physicist specializing in transilience was in fact encapsulated (enfolded, erased) by the churten effect. But no amount of theory or proof could quite allay my anxiety, my fear—which increased after my marriage and with the birth of each of my children—that there was a crossing point yet to come. For all my images of rivers and whirlpools, I could not prove that the encapsulation might not reverse at the instant of transilience. It was possible that on the day I churtened from Ve to Ran'n I might undo, lose, erase my marriage, our children, all my life at Udan, crumple it up like a bit of paper tossed into a basket. I could not endure that thought.

I spoke of it at last to Isidri, from whom I have only ever kept one secret.

"No," she said, after thinking a long time, "I don't think that can be. There was a reason, wasn't there, that you came back—here."

"You," I said.

She smiled wonderfully. "Yes," she said. She added after a while, "And Sota, and Koneko, and the farmhold . . . But there'd be no reason for you to go back there, would there?"

She was holding our sleeping baby as she spoke; she laid her cheek against the small silky head.

"Except maybe your work there," she said. She looked at me with a little yearning in her eyes. Her honesty required equal honesty of me.

"I miss it sometimes," I said. "I know that. I didn't know that I was missing you. But I was dying of it. I would have died and never known why, Isidri. And anyhow, it was all wrong—my work was wrong."

"How could it have been wrong, if it brought you back?" she said, and to that I had no answer at all.

When information on churten theory began to be published I subscribed to whatever the Center Library of O received, particularly the work done at the Ekumenical Schools and on Ve. The general progress of research was just as I remembered, racing along for three years, then hitting the hard places. But there was no reference to a Tiokunan'n Hideo doing research in the field. Nobody worked on a theory of a stabilized double field. No churten field research station was set up at Ran'n.

At last it was the winter of my visit home, and then the very day; and I will admit that, all reason to the contrary, it was a bad day. I felt waves of guilt, of nausea. I grew very shaky, thinking of the Udan of that visit, when Isidri had been married to Hedran, and I a mere visitor.

Hedran, a respected traveling scholar of the Discussions, had in fact come to teach several times in the village. Isidri had suggested inviting him to stay at Udan. I had vetoed the suggestion, saying that though he was a brilliant teacher there was something I disliked about him. I got a sidelong flash from Sidi's clear dark eyes: *Is he jealous?* She suppressed a smile. When I told her and my mother about my "other life," the one thing I had left out, the one secret I kept, was my visit to Udan. I did not want to tell my mother that in that "other life" she had been very ill. I did not want to tell Isidri that in that "other life" Hedran had been her Evening husband and she had had no children of her body. Perhaps I was wrong, but it seemed to me that I had no right to tell these things, that they were not mine to tell.

So Isidri could not know that what I felt was less jealousy than guilt. I had kept knowledge from her. And I had deprived Hedran of a life with Isidri, the dear joy, the center, the life of my own life.

Or had I shared it with him? I didn't know. I don't know.

That day passed like any other, except that one of Suudi's children broke her elbow falling out of a tree. "At least we know she won't drown," said Tubdu, wheezing.

Next came the date of the night in my rooms in the New Quadrangle, when I had wept and not known why I wept. And a while after that, the day of my return, transilient, to Ve, carrying a bottle of Isidri's wine for Gvonesh. And finally, yesterday, I entered the churten field on Ve, and left it eighteen years ago on O. I spent the night, as I sometimes do, in the shrine. The hours went by quietly; I wrote, gave worship, meditated, and slept. And I woke beside the pool of silent water.

So, now: I hope the Stabiles will accept this report from a farmer they never heard of, and that the engineers of transilience may see it as at least a footnote to their experiments. Certainly it is difficult to verify, the only evidence for it being my word, and my otherwise almost inexplicable knowledge of churten theory. To Gvonesh, who does not know me, I send my respect, my gratitude, and my hope that she will honor my intent.

# PERMISSIONS

## ABOUT THE EDITORS

HARRY TURTLEDOVE was born in Los Angeles in 1949. After flunking out of CalTech, he earned a Ph.D. in Byzantine history from UCLA. He has taught ancient and medieval history at UCLA, Cal State Fullerton, and Cal State L.A., and he has published a translation of a ninth-century Byzantine chronicle, as well as several scholarly articles. His alternate history works have included many short stories, the Civil War Classic *The Guns of the South*, the epic World War I series The Great War, and the Worldwar tetralogy that began with *Worldwar: In the Balance*. He is a winner of the Sidewise Award for Best Alternate History for his novels *How Few Remain* and *Ruled Britannia*, and of the Hugo for his novella "Down in the Bottomlands."

MARTIN H. GREENBERG is a veteran anthologist and book packager with over 1,500 books to his credit. He lives in Green Bay, Wisconsin, with his wife, daughter, and four cats.

Printed in the United States
by Baker & Taylor Publisher Services